COURT OF EVIL

COURTS AND KINGS BOOK FIVE

K.A. KNIGHT

READER CONSIDERATIONS

This book contains explicit violence, explicit sexual violence, dubious consent, murder, gore, torture, kidnapping, monster relations, blood play, knife play and more.

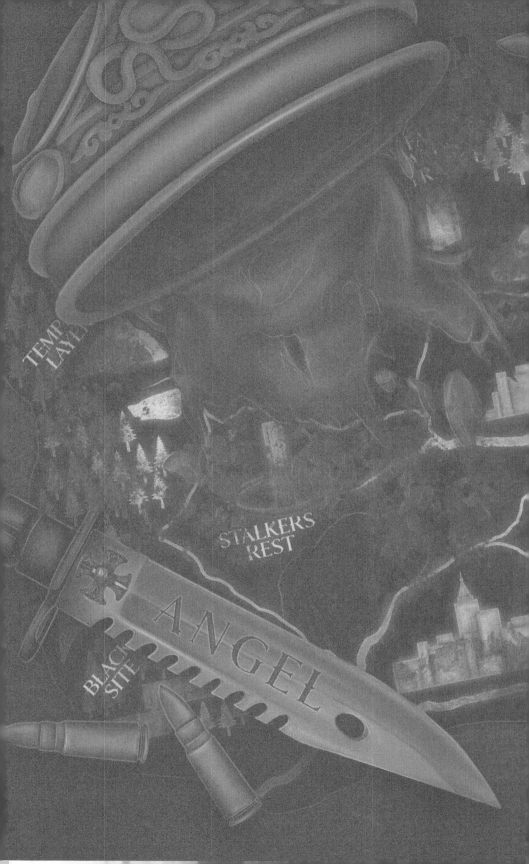

PROLOGUE

Tate

I lift my head groggily, blood dripping from my parted lips. At least two ribs are definitely broken, maybe more. Betrayal lies thick on my tongue as I stare at the men I trusted with my life.

We are family. We have been together for years. I might not have always agreed with their methods, but I agreed with the end result—until now.

As the elite of our kind, we have survived things no others have by trusting one another and fighting side by side, but as I stare at them now, all I see are strangers—strangers willing to hurt innocents and torture and imprison me, one of their own, to get what they want.

They are corrupt. It has taken me too long to see it, and now I am left without any options or freedom. Everything we have built lies in tatters, and my dreams and hopes are broken, along with my body.

"I am sorry, Tate," Eric, one of our youngest and newest recruits, calls as he heads to the cell door.

"You will be," I snarl.

"You won't make it out of here alive," Major Black replies as he wipes his blade clean of my blood and grins at me. I knew the first time I met him that he was capable of evil, but it was aimed in the right direction, until it wasn't anymore.

1

"We'll see about that." I smirk, even as it causes agony to ripple through me.

He simply spares me a disgusted look. "We could have been great together, Tate, an unstoppable unit. Such a waste. Now, if you'll excuse us, we have some hunting to do." I watch him walk away, feeling such intense hatred, I'm surprised he cannot feel it.

The outer door slams shut, followed by Black's mocking laughter, and I let fury fill me.

They won't get away with this.

I won't let them.

I will hunt down every inch of evil within our house and destroy them.

It's time I become a monster rather than just hunting them.

Sometimes, it takes evil to fight evil, and before this ends, my soul will be as black as theirs.

CHAPTER 1

Four years ago . . .

I hoist my duffle higher, and the material catches on the worn shoulder of my trusty leather duster. The other shoulder houses my patch, which identifies me as a hunter. Some of them aren't smart, so it's better to make them aware of who I am right off the bat so they don't shoot first.

It's cooler up here, which is nice because my leather gloves aren't filled with sweat.

My waist-length ginger hair is held back by two braids interwoven with my trusty wire—easy to conceal and even easier to use. I prefer my guns and blades, but in a pinch, the wire is useful in cutting off heads or choking people. You can never have too many weapons.

My bright eyes zone in on the base. It looks like any other skyscraper, apart from the fact that it's in the middle of butt fuck nowhere, not on any maps, and surrounded by trees and grass. It's the hub of the northeast sector. All new recruits pass through here for training. This land is covered in traps, cages of monsters to hunt, and everything a new hunter could need—all owned by a shell company that is listed as some form of resort to keep prying eyes out.

It's been two years since I passed basic, but watching the newbies run drills brings back memories. It isn't easy being a female in the hunters' guild. Nearly all members are males, but I never had a choice. My father was a hunter, and even though he wanted a son, he got me and he trained me just like he would have taught a son, so when it came time to apply when I turned eighteen, I didn't hesitate. He is gone now, but his training remains with me, as does the need to carry on our legacy and honour him and our beliefs.

Blowing out a breath, I quit stalling and set off towards the sixty-floor glass skyscraper. The building is heavily fortified for both ground and air attacks. We have bases scattered across the country, but only four main hubs—north, south, east, and west. They've been attacked in the past, and they always fail, but this base is the longest standing tower of the four.

It's where the best of the best come.

My dad wasn't top brass, just an everyday hunter, and that's how he liked it—not because he was no good, but to keep me and my mother safe.

I keep walking until I reach the entrance, a concrete wall stretching as far as the eye can see, making this the only exit and entrance. Turrets and outposts with guards are positioned on the sides, and I sense the current of electricity in the air that alerts me to alarms and cameras.

It isn't normal for humans to be able to sense that, so I keep my ability hidden. Some of us are just . . . sensitive, as my dad liked to call it. Either way, it's a trick I use often. I'll use everything in my power to keep myself and my team alive, even the things they don't know about.

Stepping under the arched concrete gate, I feel magic flow over me —stolen or traded magic. We look the other way if they help, a necessary evil when you are fighting monsters.

The sign above makes me grin.

STALKERS' REST
Here, death rejoices and life is given.

Poetic, but very true. Hunters do not tend to live long, and the ones that do . . . Well, there is a reason why, and it tends to leave them a little less than sane.

I wonder what that says about me.

A whistle cuts through the air, and the unit training to my left stills as all eyes turn to me.

"Well, look at this, boys, we got a new recruit, and a girl at that," one remarks as he steps forward. I almost sigh at the predictability of his comment. Men love to measure dicks, especially against girls. His head is shaved, showcasing new nicks and scars on his skull. His eyebrows are thick and arched as he surveys me, his cool gaze running over me from head to toe. His tongue is caught between his lips as he flips a knife back and forth in his hand, trying to show off.

Only fools show their hand like that.

I could gut him before he even knew I moved.

He's muscular, a few inches over my six-one frame, and he obviously cannot read body language because he doesn't stop until he stands before me. His unit follows, sensing an impending commotion.

Hunters are gossips, and they love a good fight.

"Did you come to play with the big boys and be a hunter?" one teases.

"I don't think we have a female recruit," another adds.

"She sure is hot though," Baldie comments, his eyes locked on my legs encased in my combat trousers. "If you want in, newbie, then you have to fuck me first."

Laughter breaks out, and more of them move closer, everything else forgotten as they focus on me. Like I said, there aren't many women in our ranks, and this right here is one of the reasons. Men who like to kill monsters aren't always good men.

Dropping my bag, I push my duster back as I smirk at them. "Yeah? I'd rather fight you than fuck you. Let's make this quick, shall we? I have places to be."

"I don't fight girls," he sneers. "At least not pretty ones."

"Too bad because this one fights men bigger than you every day," I retort, and before he can respond or react, I lunge at him. I knock his blade from his hand, sinking it into the bullseye of a target, then I sweep my leg out. He goes down hard, and I step back, grinning.

"Still don't fight girls?" I ask. "Because right now, you look like a fool."

His lips thin as he leaps to his feet, shaking his hands out as he walks towards me. "Fine. If you want to fight, let's fight. After I break you, I'll fuck you and then let my entire unit do the same."

"Not if I fuck you first. Don't worry, I brought my strap-on." I dodge under his meaty fists. He's fast and well trained, but I'm faster.

He doesn't stand a chance. I leap over his next leg sweep, predictable as it was, wrap my legs around his throat, and spin us. He flips, and I kick his back so he falls to his knees, and then my boot meets the side of his head, knocking him on his side. Pressing my boot to his neck, I reach down, wrench one arm up and around, and press on it until it almost breaks as he cries out.

"Still want to fuck me?" I grin down at him, digging my boot into his neck until he taps out. Dropping him, I step back and look at the gathered hunters. "Does anyone else have a problem and want to work that out with me?"

"Lieutenant Tate?" a voice calls, and we all turn to see a brown-haired hunter. He's young, maybe even younger than me, with glasses pushed up his nose as he looks at me and then the crowd. "You are Lieutenant Tate?"

"That's me." Grabbing my bag, I wink at Baldie and his unit. "It's been fun. Thanks for playing with me." I step towards Glasses. "Is my new major waiting for me?"

"And the commander."

I raise my eyebrows at that. Commanders do not meet with hunters, not unless you are high, like a major. It took me two years to reach lieutenant, so to meet the commander?

Well, colour me fucking curious.

A path forms between the recruits, and I follow after the young man as we head towards the glass doors of the building. Once there, I have to put my bag in a scanner, and their eyebrows rise at the number of weapons in it as I spread my arms and let them search me.

"All weapons must be surrendered. You only need them outside," Glasses says. He nods at another box. "Put them there. You can collect them when you leave."

Even though I knew it was coming, I'm not thrilled. I take off my duster and fold it, holding it out to him. "Hold this for me?" He takes it, his nose wrinkling as he holds it as far from his torso as possible.

Ah, this must be an intelligence officer, not a ground hunter. Makes sense. Both are important. Hunters wouldn't get anywhere without our information, and their job is to keep all hunter colonies in contact, gather reports, and map them.

Pulling my pistols from each hip, I carefully unload them and pop the bullets from the chambers, then I put them all in the open box. Whistling to myself, I reach down and tug my mini gun from my boot and add that before slowly pulling each blade from my leg sheaths— eight on each—then the two up my sleeves.

"Is that everything?" the hunter behind the box asks, wide-eyed.

"Oh, I almost forgot." Reaching back, I pull the sword from the sheath down my spine and hold it out. "Where do you want this? I don't think it will fit in your little box."

He blinks, reaches out, and takes it. "Um, I'll put it in another one."

"Thanks. Take good care of it. It was my dad's," I warn him, and he gulps, nodding seriously.

"The ones in your bag?" Glasses comments, passing my coat back. I slide it on.

"Those too? Seriously?" I mutter before walking over, my boots squeaking on the shiny floor. Ripping open my zip, I pull out my sawed-off shotguns and put them in, adding my blades, my homemade UV grenades, and my holy water. "What about poisons and herbs?" I query. The man just blinks again and nods. Pulling out my vials, I add them along with my electric arc I won from a pixie and my blessed blade from the fae. "Okay, that's all."

They scan my bag again and hand it over.

I watch the man struggle to shut the box, and I point at him. "If you lose any of those, you're the one I'm coming for. Consider that a friendly warning." I turn away and face Glasses, who sighs.

"Come with me. I will explain the base as I lead you to the meeting."

I have to shorten my strides as I walk with him towards a bank of elevators. I scan everything. The armouries are locked with only a hatch to look inside, and to the right are the emergency stairs and exit, as well as a security room.

"Here at Stalkers' Rest, we have state-of-the-art equipment. All of the glass is bulletproof, with shutters that will come down over the building in an emergency. Newbies sleep on the lowest floor." That's typical. In case of an attack, they are fodder. "The higher rank you are, the higher you go," he explains, eyeing me curiously. "The shooting range is outside to the left, and the gym and training grounds are to the right. The armoury is on the ground floor—well, you passed it. You must have an ID and security checks to receive any equipment."

"And if you lose or break it, it comes from your pay." I arch a brow. "I know the drill. I heard the commander here is a real hard ass."

He snorts as he scans his card at the elevators. Another scanner comes down, taking his fingerprint and a retinal scan before an elevator opens to the left. I follow him inside, watching him through the reflection of the shiny doors as it shuts and we rise.

"Commander Vilaran is the youngest commander ever. He moved through the ranks from a newbie in under five years and was given control due to his exceptional skills and intelligence. He is the best."

"He's not a legacy?" I ask. Not much is known about him, especially if you aren't under his control, but I've heard enough rumours. He's young, brutal, and can be a real prick. You would have to be to reach his position, especially if he joined and wasn't born into this like most.

"No, he joined with his friends before serving in the military, then he came back," Glasses snaps, and my eyebrows rise.

"Defensive much?" I scoff. "Are his friends here with him? Are they still a unit?" Commanders don't hunt. They hold down the base, but once a hunter, always a hunter.

"They are all dead," he answers darkly as the doors open. He stomps out, throwing me a dirty look. "If you want to live, don't mention it."

Well, damn, I guess not everyone is feeling friendly. Keeping my comments to myself, I follow him down the carpeted hallway to a double door at the end. He knocks and waits.

"Come in," someone calls, and I follow Glasses inside before freezing when I see the two men waiting for me.

I'm so fucked.

CHAPTER 2

Shamus

I watch her in the courtyard, hiding my smirk behind my mug as I sip my coffee.

She's exactly what we need, and she'll need to keep that spirit to survive what I have planned.

"I handpick my team. I have always done that," the annoying voice whines from behind me. Okay, more like argues, but to me it sounds like whining.

Sighing, I turn my attention back to him. This is a delicate game, keeping him outside while also earning his trust enough to discover the truth. "And you have. I picked this one because she will be a good fit."

"A female will not fit my unit—"

"This is final," I state, my voice deadly, and he swallows. I know he hates having to answer to a man half his age, but he has no choice. He respects the chain of command, and he respects this organisation and what we stand for. I arch my eyebrow. "Are we clear?"

"Yes, sir," he grates out. "And if she cannot cut it?"

"Then we let her go, same as always. All I'm asking is that you try her first. I think you'll get along well. They say she's a beast that even other hunters fear. She has out tested every other candidate in the last two years. She will fit your unit well."

He nods, grinding his teeth, and we lapse into silence as we wait for her to arrive. She's here within ten minutes, a knock sounding on the door.

Major Black stands, his new title grating on my nerves, another thing that was not my choice, and I turn, eyeing the door, wondering how she will react. "Come in," I command.

An officer steps inside, and she follows. Everything I thought I knew about her pales in comparison. I have seen footage and photos, but she is so much better in person. I can see the muscles on her body and the strength in her bright green gaze as she shrewdly scans the office before looking at us. Her lips curve down ever so slightly, giving her away.

She's good and very beautiful. That wasn't something I was expecting.

She has scars, most hunters do, but she is truly beautiful in a way most humans aren't.

"Tate Havelock, I presume?" I ask as I sit and indicate the two seats opposite my desk.

She nods, eyeing Black. Her eyes tell me she knows who he is.

"Sit," I order her.

"With all due respect, not until he does. Only a fool would give their back to a hunter like Major Black."

Clever girl.

"We are all on the same side here," I tell her, steepling my fingers as I watch her. "Black, sit."

His jaw grinds once more, but he heads over and sinks into the chair opposite mine. She finally heads our way and sits as well, eyeing us both.

She knows Black's reputation. Her gaze darts to me, challenging me. I bet she's wondering if I brought her here to die or if this is a test. It's neither—not that I will tell her or Black that.

"Tate Havelock, this is Major Black. He will be your new commanding officer. You will be joining his elite unit of hunters. That is why you were brought here, for this honour. Black, you will have time to test and train her to fit, but please explain what you need from her." I gesture for him to speak, leaning back in my chair.

She keeps her eyes on me, knowing I'm the biggest threat in this room.

Oh yes, she's good. Black might be a rabid dog, but I'm a silent stalker.

That is why it is called Stalkers' Rest.

"My unit is the top performing unit. We take missions no one else can. We work together and have each other's backs. I will push you harder than anyone else ever has. I expect results—"

I watch her as Black speaks. She slides her hand over my desk discreetly. One of her gloves is off, and her gaze becomes unfocused for a moment. It makes me wonder what she is doing.

Are the rumours true?

Her eyes rise to mine, and she pulls her hand back, sliding her leather glove back into place.

Interesting.

"Is that understood, lieutenant?" Black demands sharply.

She looks at him. "Understood, major. I am honoured to join a unit such as yours, and I look forward to killing monsters with you," she replies sweetly, but her eyes are piercing as she watches him.

He smirks and looks at me. "Maybe you're right." He stands. "I will meet you on level forty, which is our level. You will bunk there with us." He leaves, and she turns her attention back to me, waiting to be dismissed.

"Major Black's unit is one of the best here. You will do well to learn from them—"

"Why me?" she interrupts. "Thousands of hunters apply for that unit every day." Her eyes run over my face. "So why me? Why now?"

"Because you have something I need," I admit.

"What's that?"

"The strength to survive." I nod at the door. "You can leave now. Come to me with any issues in your unit. Welcome to Stalkers' Rest."

She purses her lips, knowing she is being dismissed, even if she wants answers. She stands, offering me a respectful incline of her head before turning and heading to the door.

"Oh, angel?" I call. "See anything interesting?" I nod at my desk, and she blanches.

"My name is Tate or lieutenant."

I smirk. "I prefer angel. Your hair makes you look like you have a halo."

"Then I'll tell everyone I hate to be called that," she snaps, "and only my friends can call me Tate." She turns and stomps from my office.

She is perfect.

"Are you sure she can do this?" Ronan asks from the corner he's hanging out in—not that they would see that. "It could be a death sentence."

"You and I both know death isn't the end." I eye him meaningfully. "No, she's exactly what we need. Follow her, all of you, and report back to me. I cannot interfere, but I am curious how it will play out."

"You've got it, brother." He heads out the door, a habit he cannot break, and then he's gone. I'm alone again, something I'm not used to.

One of them is always here, ever since my birth, but it is a necessary evil for this to work.

CHAPTER 3

Tate

The elevator opens on the fortieth floor, and Glasses hands me a card. "For the building and essentials. Do not lose it. I will not get you another one no matter how much you threaten or bribe me." He steps back into the elevator as he looks me over. "Good luck. You're going to need it." The door shuts, and I turn back to the level.

He's not wrong.

I'll need all the luck I can get while serving under Major Black and his elite soldiers. They are the best, but they also have the highest mortality rate due to what they hunt—not to mention I hear he can be a picky, cruel bastard.

He's my leader now, though, and I plan on doing as I'm told. I will make myself indispensable. Besides, this is what I wanted—a path to the top to become the best I can be. This is where I'll do it.

"Watch out!" a voice barks.

I duck as a blade whizzes over my head, then I stand and look at the blond-haired Adonis who's grinning as he hurries my way. "Sorry, drop, didn't know anyone was coming."

"Drop?" I ask as I glance over my shoulder to see the blade embedded in the wall next to the elevator.

"Yeah, anyone who comes to us always drops dead or out." He chuckles, flashing straight white teeth. He has dazzling blue eyes and messy, short blond hair. He's taller than me, stacked with muscles, and dotted with scars, and he has the hunter brand across his shoulder.

"I thought we couldn't have weapons inside," I say, refusing to acknowledge what he said. I won't be doing either.

He grins, pressing his finger to his lips. "Oops. I won't tell if you don't." He sticks out his hand. "Name's Mav, and you're the new kid."

"Not a kid." I take his proffered hand, adding pressure, and he groans as I let go.

"Got it." He shakes out his hand. "Shit, you're strong. What's your name?"

"Tate."

"Well, come on, Tate. Let me introduce you to the team." Sticking his hands in his pockets, he waits for me.

I follow him down the hall. It's pretty short, with a thin grey carpet. The walls are the same grey, and it has blade marks adorning parts of it. Once we walk through the door at the end, the utilitarian ambiance changes.

Talk about luxury digs. I'm used to sleeping in my car, motels, or even the shared bunks at outposts. This is a fucking penthouse. There are sofas in a pit facing a huge TV and a bar to the right before the windows. A basketball hoop hangs before me and a hallway leading away.

It looks like two floors were converted into one, with stairs heading up the middle and the walkway lined with doors.

"Those are our bunks," Mav tells me. "Down here is the rec room. We have a private gym too—elite perks. Come on, they will probably be in the kitchen."

Nodding, I drop my bag on the wood floor before I follow him to the hallway and down to the first open door. Music pours from inside. There are three guys sitting at the table, and Mav nods at a skinny one. "That's Goose, as in duck, duck, goose," he says. "The bigger one next to him is Santos, and the one on his other side is Wick."

I turn to the man at the countertop, happily chopping away.

"That's Ara. Yo, guys, meet the newbie."

They turn, with Ara throwing his knife as if we are coming to attack him, not just entering the room. It makes me wonder what kind of situations he's faced if he throws first and asks questions after, but Mav ducks like he's used to it.

I don't.

Catching the knife midair, I raise my eyebrow. "How many times will I have knives thrown at me today?" I remark with a smirk before tossing it back. It embeds into the cupboard.

"Thanks." Ara nods, plucks it free, and returns to carving carrots.

"Newbie, huh?" Santos glances at the others. "I give her three days."

"A week." Wick throws some cash on the table.

Goose eyes me, and something in those big orbs unnerves me. "I give her a year. She looks like a killer."

"Nah, I think she's in it for the long run," Mav says as he jumps into a chair and grins at me. "So, Tate, what do you think?"

"I'm not going anywhere. I'll take that bet." I throw some bills on the table. "Is this it?"

"Yup, this is it, plus Black. Welcome to the elites. Let's see if you can hack it."

Four Years Later

"Come out, come out, wherever you are," Mav sings, making me smirk behind my mask as his voice fills my ears. Goose and I share a look, and I nod to the left, gesturing with two fingers. He nods, his gun held out, and quickly but silently moves down the corridor branching off this hellhole of a maze.

Mav and Wick are on the next level up, Santos and Ara on the bottom level, and Black is on the top. I drew the lucky straw and got the newbie, Eric. I suppose he technically isn't new anymore, but we all treat him as such. Hell, it took me almost two years to stop being the newbie and for them to accept that I wasn't going to drop out or die. It's hard to believe I've been with them four years, but our team just keeps growing, as does Black's control. He's in charge of nearly the entire northwest now, his name more famous than any other hunter's, and we are right there with him.

"This way, kid," I murmur, keeping my back to the hallway wall of the abandoned hotel that was marked as a vamp hotspot. Two teams were sent in, and none made it back, which is why they called us.

We get the job done when no one else can. It's one of the reasons I hung in there through all the shit I experienced. It was rough at the beginning. They weren't open to accepting a new hunter, never mind a woman, but I proved myself time and time again, and even Major Black has come to respect and trust me. It's made us into an unstoppable unit, a family—something I didn't even know I needed after my father passed, but I'll admit it's nice having someone to watch my back.

They have become my brothers, my friends, and the people I trust most in this world. I might have had my reservations because of the rumours about this unit, but I know now that most are unfounded. They might have different ways of dealing with shit sometimes, but they always get the job done and, more often than not, the stuff they do is to keep this world and our unit safe. Others wouldn't understand, especially that commanding prick Vilaran who tries to mess with our every hunt—always calling meetings and wanting to talk.

Always calling me an angel.

Shaking my head, I focus on the hunt. A distracted hunter is a dead hunter, and I don't plan on dying tonight nor any night after this.

"T, you good?" Santos checks in. "Anyone got anything?"

"Nah, this is too quiet," Wick comments dryly. "Maybe they are hiding in the walls."

"Or the floor like the rats they are," Ara hisses. He really hates vamps, but no one hates them as much as our commander.

"Silence," Black barks. "Move silently and clear your floors. No more chatter unless it's to count the fangs you pulled."

"Yes, sir," we answer in unison. We might give each other shit and joke, even sometimes with Black, but we all accept his power. It's probably why he's such an asshole. Trying to control six wild, opinionated hunters? Yeah, can't be fucking easy.

I do not envy him his job, though they are right—it's too quiet. We need more information before we end up like the other teams.

"What are you doing?" Eric whispers to me.

"Watch my back," I respond softly as I lower my gun, my torch hitting the mouldy carpet as I tug off my glove. I glance over to see him turning, scanning the hallway, the back of his hunting uniform blending into the shadows. Turning to the wall, I find a spot where the plaster isn't caved in, eaten, or broken.

Closing my eyes for a moment, I lay my ungloved hand on the peeling wall and focus on the images that flood my brain—images and flashes from those who have recently touched it.

One touch is all it takes and I see it all, which is why I always wear gloves. I don't want to know the last time my friend wanked off to the thought of me, so they stay on unless necessary.

Like now.

"T, report," Black commands, no doubt knowing I have grown bored of this game. He doesn't question how I know things, just uses it like a skill. It's something they all accept.

I open my eyes and smirk as I step back, lifting my gun. "They heard us coming and ran. Most are hiding in a false ceiling on the top floor, and more are on this level in a secret, sealed room. Eric and I can handle the few here. You take the rest on that floor."

It's risky giving orders, but he's too happy about hunting to care.

"Understood. Converge on me. T and Eric, when you're done, meet us there. Whoever has the most teeth when we leave gets off training duty for a week," Black commands.

That gets us all moving. No one wants to train the newbies. It's too much hard work and whining on top of our own hunts. I hear the quiet steps of the team moving up the winding staircase, and I tap my helmet as I see them walk past like wraiths. Eric and I turn around, and we head farther into the hallway and towards the secret room.

It's not hard to find now that I know what I'm looking for. It's through an old library, and the door looks like part of the wall. I point it out to Eric as we move into position.

Pressing my back to the wall, I share a look with Eric and start to count down on my fingers. When I drop the last one, he rips the door open, and I hurry in as he follows. I sweep the room in seconds, my finger on the trigger, and when a body lunges at me, their fangs bared in the dark, I fire. The holy water infused round goes straight through the centre of their skull, and they are dead before they hit the ground.

There's a roar, and more fly towards us from the dark. Eric and I press our backs together, our torches splashing across the room as we fire.

I drop two more in rapid succession as I move deeper into the room, firing when my torch lands on another and then another until my mag is empty.

Dropping my gun, I pull out a knife and throw it. It embeds in the vamp running at me, the force of his own trajectory slamming him against the wall like a bug. It goes silent then, and I walk over, pulling my blade free and carving out its heart before turning to check on Eric.

He's coated in blood, his gun still raised, but he doesn't seem hurt. There are four bodies at his feet, and another six—the ones I killed—are also in the room.

Sweeping my torch across the space, I ensure there are no others, nor is there anywhere else for them to hide.

I pull my mask down and blow out a happy breath. "Got ten here," I say into my earpiece.

"Good work. Going radio silent now," Black comments.

"Understood." I flick mine off as well as I look around the mess of bodies stuffed into this tiny, stinky room. Why they live like this, I will never know. Most live in courts, protected and united. Some choose to abandon that, either due to a desire to follow their own laws or start their own court. It never ends well. Then you have the ferals, though none of these are.

They killed humans though; command told us that. Hell, some were even feeding on them, and I can see the rot starting to spread under their skin. Vamps are not made to feed on our kind, but it doesn't stop the desperate from doing it—not that I'll ever tell Black how I know all this. He's firmly in the *all monsters need to die* bracket. I'm more in the middle. Those who hurt others? Absolutely. Those who are evil? Of course. Those who just want to live in this world alongside us? Nah, and I keep that part of my life closely guarded. I've made friends with monsters over the years by offering them respect and trust when no other hunter has. It gets me the intel we need and even some friendships. What my unit doesn't know won't hurt them.

"Collect the teeth. I'm going to check for stragglers," I command Eric. "We'll burn the bodies together at the end."

Pulling out a wicked knife, he nods at me. "Got it, T. Be safe."

Smirking, I pull up my mask once more. "Where is the fun in that?" I joke as he chuckles and gets to work extracting what we need. Heading out of the secret room, I sweep the rest of the floor and find half-eaten bodies of the previous hunters. I close their eyes, offering them the only respect I can. An extraction team will come in and take their bodies for purification and burial—well, whatever is left of them.

Peering into the room, I see Eric with a handful of fangs in his hand. "You done?"

He tosses me mine, and I shove them in my pocket. "Let's get moving, newbie."

"When will I stop being a newbie?" He sighs as he follows me towards the stairs.

"When another newbie comes in," I joke as I smack his shoulder. "Lighten up, I've got your back."

"I know. I don't think I would have survived this long without your help," he admits. "Especially with that wendigo."

"That's what teammates are for," I reply as we reach the stairs. I let him go first, and even as we chat, my eyes sweep the area. You can never be too careful.

A noise makes my head jerk around, and my eyes narrow on the corridor. "T?" Eric calls, stopping on the stairs.

"Go help the others," I order. "I've got this."

He nods reluctantly and heads up to join the rest of the team while I move back down the corridor.

I walk into the hall, following my instincts down a level to where the others were and through the winding corridors. Moonlight shines through the broken windows to my right, their tattered curtains fluttering in the wind. While most doors along the hallway are open, there is a stack of cardboard, rubbish, and even a wood pallet between two of the doors. Something about it catches my attention.

It's piled too perfectly. Crouching, I shine my torch into a small crevice. Eyes gleam in the light, and I jerk back, ripping away the front layer to reveal a young, terrified girl hiding there. More vamps cower behind her.

"Please," she whispers, her hands held high. She's so fucking young, she can't be much past the change. The others behind her are just teenagers, and they are all frightened. "We had nowhere else to go. That's why we are here. We have never hurt a human. Please don't kill us."

Dropping my gun, I frown. "I'm not going to kill you. We only hunt those who hurt our kind. Go now."

"They killed Emmie," she whispers, pointing down the hallway. "They enjoyed it. That's why we hid."

"What are you talking about?" I ask.

"Hunters. They want to kill us."

She must mean the other teams. I lower my gun. "Well, I don't. Go home, for fuck's sake, but remember, if you kill a human, I'm coming after you." I step back to allow them to pass.

"Thank you, thank you." She pushes the others past me, eyeing me warily. I watch them leap down the stairs with a shake of my head. What I said is true—we are hunters, but we don't hunt and kill innocents. The others here killed people, we knew that, but those teenagers didn't. I can tell.

Her words come back to me, and I hesitate before I lift my gun and move farther down where she was pointing.

There's a huge suite with an open door at the end, and I hesitantly follow a blood trail on the floor, only to stop in the doorway. My gun drops as I stare at the mess.

There is a kid on the bed—Emmie, I'm guessing. She's no older than eighteen. Her eyes are wide and terrified, and her mouth is open, her fangs gone. Her dress is ripped down the front with deep slashes across every inch of her chest.

Moving closer despite the bile crawling up my throat, I shine my torch on her clenched fist. I glance at her face as I reach out and uncurl her fingers. Her hand opens, letting me know rigor hasn't set in yet, but it's what's in her grasp that makes me gasp—black torn camouflage with a patch on it.

A hunter's patch.

They were hiding because they saw a hunter do this.

This body isn't old.

This wasn't another team.

This was tonight.

Horror washes through me, alongside denial.

I hope I'm wrong, but I have to know.

Dropping the material, I tug off my glove and hesitate for a moment. I could walk away and pretend I never saw this, but that's not my style. I need to know. I *have* to know. My life is hanging in the balance right now, the rope holding me up ready to snap and drop me through the floor.

Touching the body with a shaky, bare hand, I let the truth come to me.

Flashes fill my head of her running and screaming as masked hunters chase her. They laugh as they holster guns and pull out their knives.

"Let's have some fun, shall we?"

I know that voice—Ara.

"Nah, we aren't fucking this one. No time, just kill her quickly. You can have your fun next time."

"Fuck it."

I feel her skin split as if it were my own. The agony, the terror . . . I see it all.

I feel her die.

I recoil in horror as I stare at the bleeding corpse. My team did this. When I was on the other floor, they were here, torturing and killing this girl. They didn't care that she was innocent. They *wanted* to kill her.

They tortured her before she died. Moreover, they enjoyed it.

Who is the real monster here?

I don't know how long I stare at the body before I realise I need to move. If they find me here, I'm done for. Pulling on my glove, I stumbled from the room and towards the stairs, my brain caught on what I saw.

My world crumbles around me, and the last four years spent working and living with these men fill my head. They patched me up and looked after me when I was sick . . . . It all darkens and sets alight as I see the truth behind their actions.

I walk upstairs in a daze, stumbling into the room their voices are coming from, only to still. My eyes widen in horror once more. It wasn't a one-off or a mistake.

I've ignored so much during our hunts. Bile claws at my throat as I see the young bodies spread around, ripped apart and killed for fun. My team just stood there, laughing and joking.

This isn't about keeping our race safe. It's about killing.

The kid was right—they wanted to kill them regardless of their innocence.

"Ah, T, there you are!" Wick calls, grinning as he holds up some tiny fangs from the kid at his feet, whom he kicks with his boot as he steps over him.

I don't know why, but the fact that they assume I would be okay with this makes me angry.

I scan the room, seeing the faces of their kills. They are young, just kids, who probably came here to rebel. They didn't hurt anyone, they were just existing, and my unit played with them before murdering them. No wonder they went radio silent.

My eyes land on Eric, who's happily carving fangs from heads of the others' kills as if this is normal.

"This is wrong," I whisper.

My eyes land on our major, who holds the head of a girl so young, she still has her baby fat in his hand, ready to carve into her.

"This is wrong," I repeat, my hold on my gun wavering.

Black tilts his head, watching me from his crouched position. It's then I see the missing patch on his shoulder.

He killed the girl. He tortured her.

"They are monsters, Tate. Don't forget why we do this," he warns, his voice cold and eyes sharp as he watches me.

"I have never forgotten," I hiss, disgusted. "Have you? We do not kill innocent—"

"None of them are innocent," Ara snaps. "No matter what they look like."

"They are abominations," Wick says sadly.

Goose nods. "We are helping."

Oh god, they really believe that. I stare at the men I trusted, the men I love like family, and I wonder how they were able to hide this side of themselves from me for so long.

How did I not see it?

I stare at them, realising they all feel the same way. I'm the only one who doesn't agree with this. Maybe this is why I kept my secrets for so long. Part of me knew . . . My stomach churns as I beg them with my eyes to tell me I'm wrong. I'm frozen in horror, but they watch me with confusion.

"You're monsters," I snarl, lifting my gun and pointing it at them. "This is not what we stand for or what we do! We protect innocents. We don't kill them!" I scream, aiming my gun at Black. "We don't do this. Command will know about this, and they will stop you."

Black eyes me as he straightens, pocketing the fang he carved from the kid's head. "They know what we do, but they don't care as long as we get results. I'm sorry you feel that way, Tate. I thought you, of all people, would understand. I'm disappointed in you."

I almost laugh. He's disappointed in me?

"Knock her out. We cannot deal with her here."

"Wait—" I lift my gun, but a noise has me turning just in time to see Santos's gun heading right for my face.

"Sorry, T," is the last thing I hear before everything goes dark.

My own team is attacking me, and I plunge into the darkness feeling angry and betrayed.

CHAPTER 4

Ronan

*F*uck, fuck, fuck, fuck!

I race through the twisting halls of Stalkers' Rest. I checked Shy's office first, but he wasn't there. Sometimes I forget I can just go through the ceiling, and when I remember, I almost smack myself. Rising as quickly as I can, I head to the penthouse—the commander's apartment.

She's in big fucking trouble.

I have been watching Tate Havelock for four years at his command, and during that time, I have come to know her well. At first, I thought Shy was wrong, that she isn't the one, but he was right, as always. How annoying. She has a backbone of steel. When others would have faltered or died, she survived. She gathers secrets and friendships as easily as she breathes, using them when she needs to. She's intelligent, powerful, and one hell of a woman. If I were able to, I would have hit on her years ago.

She's beautiful, but it's more than that.

Her soul is pure and full of life. I found myself drawing closer just to feel her presence during the four years I've spent watching her and reporting to Shy as our plan sluggishly moved forward. The others, our

27

brothers spread out at the other command posts, do the same to change this from the inside out.

His grand plan all hinges on her.

One woman.

I hated her at first, thinking she would become like them, but she never did, and she seemed oblivious to their true intentions and proclivities. It almost made me pity her, but I could not interfere. Now I wish I had ignored my orders.

She's in danger. I followed her unconscious body as they drove to a black site and dumped her in the cell. She will wake up soon, and when she does, they won't hesitate to do what they need to. I know Black well enough to understand that and have watched him kill countless people who got in his way. Our plan is important, more important than anything, but for it to succeed, we need her alive.

I need her alive.

As I float through his security measures and walls, his wards flow across me, allowing me access, and I rush to his bedroom. It's late, so he will be resting, but he must sense me when I enter. We are tied together, all of us. Not even death can tear us apart—not that anyone knows.

I face Shamus as he sits up in bed, his eyes hard. "What is it?" he demands.

"Tate. She's in trouble. She found out the truth, and they turned on her. Shamus, they are going to kill her."

CHAPTER 5

I'm awake, but I pretend to be knocked out, and I use the time to catalogue my injuries. My head aches, but it's nothing I cannot handle. Nothing else seems injured, but I have lost nearly all my weapons. I shift my head slightly, as if in sleep, and I feel my wire is still there. I test my hands and feet and find them restrained, which isn't surprising.

They cannot let me escape. If I went to Commander Vilaran with this, then they wouldn't ignore it. Black and his unit would be brought up on charges or worse. No, they cannot let their dirty secret get out.

I'm their leverage, and if I had to guess from the damp, rotten smell surrounding me, we are at one of the black sites our unit uses during our hunts to interrogate monsters . . . and now me, apparently.

No one else knows about them, a unit secret, which means nobody will be coming for me. I'm on my own, facing the men I have hunted with for years—men capable of killing, torturing, and using whatever it takes to stay alive.

I need to stop thinking of them as my unit, as my family, because I know they will do whatever it takes to continue, and I am in their way.

"I know you're awake," the sharp voice comments. "I know all your tricks, Tate. You forget that I taught you most of them."

29

"Not all," I retort dryly as I lift my head, rolling it back on my sore shoulders, and face the cell. Black sits opposite me, casually sitting on a wooden chair while counting fangs in a bag. The others are spread out before the closed metal cell door. From the smell, the door, and the slightly wet walls, I would guess we are at the hangar, which is fifteen miles from Stalkers' Rest and one of the most remote and darkest secrets of our unit.

Here, no monster comes out alive, making their intentions towards me clear.

They plan to kill me so no one will ever find my body. "Let me guess, I died on the mission, yes?" I sneer as I run my gaze over them. Eric is unable to meet my eyes, hanging his head in shame. Good, he should be ashamed. Goose looks troubled, but not enough to help. The others are cold and emotionless. We might be family, but it's clear where their loyalties lie—with Black.

"A hero's death," Black says as he pockets the bag. "I'll give you that much."

"So kind," I comment sarcastically as I roll my shoulders. "Don't suppose you'd free my hands, would you? These bindings are awfully uncomfortable."

It's more of an annoyance than anything. If I'm to survive this, then I need to get free. The metal chair is welded to the floor and can hold dragon shifters, so I'm not getting out that way, and my feet are tied to the legs with barbed wire. If I try to free them, I'll bleed out before I can escape. My hands are tied with shackles, which are the weakest part of this confinement and my only shot of getting out of here alive.

They will not kill me here. I refuse to go out this way.

"I'm not that much of a fool," he scoffs.

"I'm in a locked cell in the middle of nowhere," I remind him with an innocent look that probably fools no one. They have seen me face hordes of rogues, take down a dragon, and even fight a kraken, so there is no point in acting weak, but I'll use any tools at my disposal.

"And you are one of the deadliest people alive. I won't risk it." He leans forward as he watches me with dark eyes. I haven't always liked Black, but I respected him and his drive to be the best hunter there is.

What a fucking idiot I was.

"That almost sounded like a compliment," I reply, distracting him as I snap my thumb, breaking it, and start to slide my hand free.

"Just the truth. We both know that." He tilts his head. "I don't suppose I can get you to rethink your stance on tonight?"

"Not really a rethinker," I say as I get one hand free, trying to keep my movements slow and small so they don't notice. "I'm more of a surge into action person."

He stands and heads my way just like I want.

"Yes, well, that's what I thought, but unfortunately, that leaves us with few options. Most would lie to save their life, but not you . . . never you. It's one of the reasons I like you." He stops before me, and I smirk.

"Good, then you'll understand this," I snap.

Reaching up, I grab the wire, ready to use it on them, when Black grips my hand and yanks it back. "Ah, that isn't very nice. I should have known you would have a trick up your sleeve." With his cruel eyes on me, he snaps my hand backwards. I feel the bones break and ligaments tear as he keeps pushing, and I swallow my scream before it breaks free. He grins triumphantly, dropping my ruined hand and wrapping my wire around his knuckles as he watches me.

"Cut her hair. She could be hiding something else," he orders.

Goose pulls his knife out and walks my way. Agony races through me as my ruined hand hangs at my side, but I refuse to show weakness.

It's just hair.

They are just bones.

It will regrow, and I will heal. Everything is survivable apart from death.

He fists my hair and yanks my head back. I meet his eyes boldly, refusing to look away as he slides the knife under the heavy locks. I feel the sharp edge of the blade across my nape and then he yanks it up, cutting through my hair in one sweep. Goose steps away, holding up the long locks, and I feel my hair barely brushing my neck now.

It's just hair.

It's just fucking hair.

Humiliation fills me just like he wants. He's trying to make me less human and strip me of everything I am.

"You'll have to do better than that," I tell them with a wicked grin. "Even bald and burnt, I'm still stronger and a hell of a lot hotter than all of you."

"You're right about that. We'll need to do better," Black says. "And since we are here, let's get some answers, shall we?"

I frown at that. "What answers?"

"About why you are really here," he explains like it's obvious.

"For the millionth time, I was recruited to join your unit," I gurgle through my blood.

"Yes, yes, you don't know by who. You are lying to me, Tate. You know I despise liars," Black snaps as he wipes his hands with a stained rag, trying to remove my blood, but I know it's useless. I've spilled so much in the past few hours, he will never be clean of what he has done to me.

"The only liar here is you," I rasp. "I was recruited to be one of you, and I was. I was your friend, your teammate—"

"You were recruited from the middle of nowhere, plucked directly by a commander. Explain that! I always had my worries about it, but you fell into line." Black sighs as he sits heavily. "Now that you're not, well, I might as well satisfy my curiosity."

"You can burn me, break me, or torture me, but my answer won't change." I spit a mouthful of blood onto the floor.

"Burn you . . . We haven't tried that yet." Black nods at Goose, who stoically turns to the table of goodies they set out.

I hear him move things around, and I take that time to roll out my aching muscles, ignoring the bruises and cuts. At least four of my bones are broken, but so far most have been survivable wounds. I just need to stay alive.

I run my eyes over the others, meeting every single one of their gazes. I let them see my anger and hurt. Only Eric looks away. The others aren't even ashamed. Black has their loyalty, and they believe so deeply in what they do, they don't even see how wrong this is.

A noise has me glancing back at Goose.

I hear the hum of electricity as he turns with two clamps in his hands, the wires connected to a battery.

"Tell us what we want to know, Tate, and I won't have to do this," he says reluctantly, but I know better. It's another trick.

I won't be leaving this room alive. Either I'll suffer a lot and keep my dignity until the end or I'll beg and cry and still die.

I'll take the pain, thanks.

"We aren't friends. Only my friends call me Tate," I say coolly.

He shakes his head as he stops before me, and despite my determination, I jerk back as the buzzing clamps move closer. "This is going to hurt a lot."

He clamps one onto each thigh, and the voltage slams through me. My body locks up tight and my brain fries until I can't even think. I am one giant flow of energy.

Suddenly, it stops, and I slump. My lungs scream for air as I pant and gasp. "Cut her legs open and put them inside," Black orders.

Before I can say a word, Mav steps forward with the same dagger he held when I first met him, and despite the fact that I want to beg, I do nothing, even as he buries the sharp end into my thigh. The agony is like nothing I've ever felt before, and then he slices down, cutting through muscle and skin before pulling it free and doing the same to the other one.

It takes a moment for the pain to catch up, and when it does, I have to swallow my vomit. The sight of my pulverised, skinned thighs causes me to gag, so I look away.

I have no time for a reprieve, however, as Goose steps back to my side. I don't look, but I feel everything as he pushes the ends of the clamps into my thighs, and then the battery is cranked higher.

The voltage courses through me so hard, I convulse in the chair, my bladder emptying involuntarily.

I grit my teeth, holding back my screams even as I taste blood and smell the scent of burning flesh in the air. The odour makes me want to puke, and then Eric does. He turns away, throwing up all over the corner of the room. It makes me laugh loudly, and when the current dies down, I slump.

My head hangs forward, saliva running from my mouth. My whole body aches, and a new pain crops up every second. Suddenly, a fist grabs my short hair, tugging it back, and I laugh in Black's face.

"You think I'm weak enough to break under you? Your newbie can't even handle my torture." I chuckle. "Such big, scary killers, hunting down weak and young monsters and murdering them, and now killing women?"

"You're not a woman, Tate. You're a hunter. There is a difference," Black says as he jerks my neck back harder. "Last chance. Why were you placed in my unit?"

"I told you." I pant, swallowing around the agony. "I was recruited—"

This time, my scream slips free, and I watch through narrowed eyes as Eric runs from the room, and my screams turn into laughter, even as I'm fried over and over again.

CHAPTER 6

I don't know how much time has passed. All I know is pain, the taste of my own blood, and the smell of my burning flesh as they repeat the same question each time.

"Why are you here?"

It stopped having meaning when they pulled my fingernails and toenails.

It started being hysterically funny when they shoved hot pokers into my ruined thighs to cauterise the wounds so I wouldn't die too quickly.

It started becoming a blur when they made me choke on water and I almost drowned.

"I will ask again, why are you here?"

"Why are you here? Why are you here?" I sing it, knowing my voice is hoarse from my screams. I sound like a maniac, but I don't care as I lift my head and squint at Black through my swollen eyes. "Why are you here, Black? Why did you become a hunter? I think it was because it was the only way you could kill and hunt without being locked up. I have a theory. In another life, you would have been a serial killer."

"A very good one at that," he says with a wicked grin. "Why are you here?"

"Gods, you're fucking dumb. Do you think asking the same question will get different results?" I spit my blood on his face, and he jerks back, his nostrils flaring. "Keep using it as an excuse if it makes you feel better. I'm not a traitor, Black. You are."

He raises his hand, ready to smack me, when the cell door suddenly swings open.

"We have an emergency hunt," Eric exclaims as he steps into the room. "Message from Stalkers' Rest, directly from Shamus. We have to go."

Black's nostrils flare as the others reluctantly file out, lingering outside the door. Black stays behind, watching me. Eric hesitates near the doorway, looking horrified as he meets my gaze, but he does nothing to help. He didn't participate, but he also said nothing.

He's just as much to blame as them.

"You are a traitor, Tate, to us, our kind, and what we stand for, and you will die a traitor's death. Nobody will care, will they? Not those monsters you helped or the other hunters. Nobody."

His fist slams into my ribs so hard, I feel them break, piercing my lung.

Blood fills my airways and mouth, causing me to choke, and I know this is the blow that will eventually kill me.

He knows it too.

I lift my head groggily, blood dripping from my parted lips. At least two ribs are definitely broken, maybe more. Betrayal lies thick on my tongue as I stare at the men I trusted with my life.

We are family. We have been together for years. I might not have always agreed with their methods, but I agreed with the end result—until now.

As the elite of our kind, we have survived things no others have by trusting one another and fighting side by side, but as I stare at them now, all I see are strangers—strangers willing to hurt innocents and torture and imprison me, one of their own, to get what they want.

They are corrupt. It has taken me too long to see it, and now I am left without any options or freedom. Everything we have built lies in tatters, and my dreams and hopes are broken, along with my body.

"I am sorry, Tate," Eric, one of our youngest and newest recruits, calls as he heads to the cell door.

"You will be," I snarl.

"You won't make it out of here alive," Major Black replies as he wipes his blade clean of my blood and grins at me. I knew the first time I met him that he was capable of evil, but it was aimed in the right direction, until it wasn't anymore.

"We'll see about that." I smirk, even as it causes agony to ripple through me.

He simply spares me a disgusted look. "We could have been great together, Tate, an unstoppable unit. Such a waste. Now, if you'll excuse us, we have some hunting to do." I watch him walk away, feeling such intense hatred, I'm surprised he cannot feel it.

The outer door slams shut, followed by Black's mocking laughter, and I let fury fill me.

They won't get away with this.

I won't let them.

I will hunt down every inch of evil within our house and destroy them.

It's time I become a monster rather than just hunting them.

Sometimes, it takes evil to fight evil, and before this ends, my soul will be as black as theirs.

CHAPTER 7

Tate

W hen they left, my body finally gave into the darkness, and when I wake, I want to slide back into that comforting numbness, but I know if I do, I will die.

They won't get that satisfaction from me. I am not dying here. Despite my injuries and the fact that my body is dying, I plan my escape just like I was the entire time they were torturing me.

My one ruined hand is still free, and I reach behind me, ignoring the agony this causes, and start working on the lock with the stolen bit of metal I pulled from my thigh after they beat me with pipes. It's short and jagged and should be enough to unlock the shackles. It's hard when I can't see, so I close my eyes to focus, my clumsy fingers slipping in the blood, but I force them to move anyway. It takes longer than I would like, but when the lock clicks, my eyes snap open. Tugging my hand free, I cradle my ruined one to my chest and glance at the door. It will be unlocked. The entire facility is locked down tight, so the doors stay open while prisoners are chained.

Besides, the fools were in such a rush, they left it open, like a fucking meal ticket . . . if I can get my legs to work.

I look down at the ruined meat of my thighs and take a deep breath, but I instantly regret it, having forgotten about my lung.

"This is going to fucking hurt," I say loudly, and then I throw myself forward, the shackles on my feet long gone to give them better access to cut my toes and ankles. I hit the concrete hard, and the blow reverberates through my body. I know I won't be able to walk, so I start to drag myself across the floor.

My thighs bleed with every movement, and the pain is so overwhelming, I have to stop. Turning my head, I throw up, noticing the blood before I snap my head back around and crawl forward with gritted teeth.

I'm running out of time.

If I can just get out of here, I can survive.

I have to.

I refuse to die here.

It's the one thing that keeps me going when my body wants to give in and the pain becomes overwhelming.

Each torturous inch of dragging myself to that metal door feels like fire burning on my wounds as blood smears behind me. I know I must look like pulverised meat.

All that keeps me going is the thought of revenge.

When I finally reach the metal door, I give myself a second to breathe through the agony before I slap my blood-covered hand across the door until I can reach the handle. I yank it down, but my hand slips, and I fall, hitting the floor once more.

Gritting my teeth, I press my side to the wall and start to force myself up to my feet. My legs give way at least twice before I manage to stand somewhat, though I am mostly propped up by the wall, my entire body shaking and going cold.

The chill of death flows through me, cooling the fire in my blood. I thought the pain was bad . . .

The numbness that starts to flow through me is scarier than the pain.

No, no, no.

I can almost feel the touch of death as it tries to embrace me, and with one last Herculean effort, I force the door open, my body giving way as I fall through the doorframe and right into someone's arms.

The last things I see before everything goes black are familiar dark eyes and a worried frown. Another set of brown orbs lingers over their shoulder, making my own widen for a moment.

"Hang in there, angel. I've got you."

"Shamus."

His name is a breath, a plea.

I cling to it as I fall into the darkness once more.

CHAPTER 8

Shamus

"I know, I know, Ronan. It's stupid—"

"And dangerous. They will kill you on sight," my best friend says as he floats by my side as I run.

For a moment, I glare at him as I try not to jostle the precious cargo in my arms. "Then it is a good job you are already dead and they cannot hurt you."

"Shamus, if you die, I fully die, remember? I'm tied to you," he hisses. "Is she worth the risk?"

"You tell me," I retort as we stop before a mound of rock some miles away from Stalkers' Rest. It's in the ancient magical forest. We made a truce never to cross into it—until now.

Tate groans in my arms, and we glance down at her. She is covered in blood, and I can smell death on her. A minute or two later and it would have been too late. No, I cannot let her die. This is my fault. I put her in there, knowing the dangers. I thought I was prepared to accept anything that happened, but when Ronan found me, I realised I wasn't.

Over the past few years, I have become fond of the little devil in my arms. She's my new obsession, not just because of what I need her to do without her knowing, and I'm not the only one.

Ronan's eyes linger on her, and I see sadness and pain in his gaze, alongside worry. The dead care for no one, but he cares for her greatly, even if he tries to hide it from me. It's the only way we could travel to the place they kept her. He shared his powers with me, and we moved through time and space, something we have only been able to do once before, and it was under great duress—I was dying.

This time, it was for her, so yes, he cares.

"Yes, she is worth it," he murmurs before looking up at me. "I'm just warning you. If we step through that barrier, we might not come back."

Turning to the innocuous looking rock, I pull Tate firmer into my arms, her soul slipping away with each second. "It is a risk I am willing to take." I step through the invisible barrier and then to the fae realm beyond.

We are instantly greeted by guards pointing enchanted weapons at us. A spear tip pokes into my shoulder, and a glowing flame sword is pressed to the back of my neck. I tilt my head, surveying the fae guards tasked with protecting their borders and upholding the truce.

The one I just broke.

"I seek sanctuary and a meeting with your healer. I am Shamus Vilaran, leader of Stalkers' Rest, signer of the truce, and peacemaker. I come here for your help."

They do not move, their spiked, triangular helmets only showing me their eyes, then the guards behind them part like flowing water, opening a path to a glowing, ethereal being.

"Usually begging is done on one's knees, ghost whisperer," the seductive voice calls.

Heather, or at least that is what we humans call her, is their leader, as well as the most terrifying and powerful being I have ever met.

"If I could, I would be on them," I reply carefully, knowing words have power here. You cannot lie to a fae, it is a great offence, but they are very good with word games, something I have tried to learn.

The guards part until Heather stands before me, and her bright purple eyes drop to Tate. It is hard to tell Heather's age. She is neither young nor old but somewhere in between. Her glowing hair changes from purple to grey, and her magic flows across her skin. I have to grit my teeth to stop from being consumed by it.

She is ancient and strong and not someone I want as an enemy.

Before the truce came along, she waged a war against hunters and humans, but now we live in peace—peace I have broken for Tate.

She whimpers, and I glance down at her. "Shh, hang on. You'll be okay, I promise." I kiss her head softly before looking to Heather. "I seek your healer. No earthly magic can save my hunter, but you can."

"Hunters die every day. Why is this one so important that you would break a truce and risk everything you have worked for?" Heather challenges.

I choose my words carefully. "She is . . . important."

"No human is important. You are all like stars, burning brightly for a moment and then gone, leaving only the very smallest of traces, but I know you, Shamus. You would not break this truce for anyone, not even your own life, and it intrigues me. I shall see if she is important if you'll allow it." She holds out her hand.

I don't want her to touch Tate, she could do anything with one touch, but I do not have much choice and we both know it. Either I relent or they will kill me for breaking the truce. It's a good sign I am not dead already.

Inclining my head, I hold Tate out so Heather can touch as little of me as possible. I do not want to interfere in whatever Heather has to do, and I also do not want her to touch me. I know Heather is capable of a great many things, and giving her access to my head and body as the commander of hunters would not be good.

She watches me for a moment before placing her hand across Tate's sweaty, bloody forehead.

For a moment, Heather's eyes glow before she pulls her hand away, looking at Tate. "Interesting, very interesting."

She steps back, her eyes locked on Tate, and something in her gaze makes me pull Tate closer. It almost looks like hunger. She blinks and glances up at me.

"I will allow you passage to our healer. We will speak after about the repercussions of you breaking the truce and entering our lands.

Come this way, but first, your ghost must be ironed. We cannot have him wandering around freely and getting into all sorts of trouble."

I glance at Ronan to see him floating back into the weapons, worry in his eyes.

"Ronan," I warn.

I know what this means. Iron acts as a cage to a ghost. He will not be able to float freely. His jaw jumps, an old habit, before he thrusts his arms out, allowing himself to be shackled. The iron clamps around both wrists, and suddenly his usually transparent appearance turns solid, his feet hitting the ground.

He's almost human.

"Good, then follow me. Your little seer does not have much time," Heather warns.

I fall into step at her side as we move deeper into the fae realm. "Seer?" I whisper.

"Answers have a price. You know that, ghost whisperer." She peers at me. "Do you wish to pay for the answer?"

"Not now, just take us to the healer."

She chuckles at my response, then she waves her hand and the path disappears around us. When it clears, we are inside a dark shop, the smell making my nose twitch, but I do not sneeze, since that would be rude.

Fae are big on insults.

When I was younger, I did not understand that and made the mistake of offending an older fae by mentioning their ears. I nearly ended up dead. I learned my lesson quickly.

The shelves and workbenches are covered in artifacts, herbs, and spells. Fae magic is everywhere. The roof is made of intricate stained glass, depicting the rise and fall of the fae. Those colours stream down like a kaleidoscope, providing the only light in the dimly lit room.

The magic in here is stifling and ancient.

Shuffling reaches my ears, and an older woman appears from around a corner. Her eyes narrow on me before they widen when they land on Heather, and she bows. "My queen, what brings you here? I could have come to you."

"It was urgent, my old friend," Heather murmurs softly, speaking kinder than I have ever heard her. "You must save this human."

"Human? My magic is not for them," the older fae hisses, wrinkles framing her mouth and blue eyes. Her hair is a deep blonde interwoven with grey, and it's tied back into little plaits with bones.

"It is now, just this once. I ask it of you as your queen. Save the human."

They share a look before the older one glances at me. "As you wish, my queen."

"Thank you." Heather presses her hand to the healer's shoulder before glancing at me. "You are in good hands. If anyone can save the seer, it is our healer. I will be back to collect." She vanishes, leaving Ronan, Tate, and me with the healer.

"Put her here," the older fae mutters. She waves her hand, and a stone workbench is swiftly swept clean. The dark grey slab glows ever so slightly, and I hesitate. "I mean her no harm. If you wish for me to save her, then you must do this quickly."

"Vow to me you will do everything to save her, not harm her," I demand as kindly as I can, reluctant to let Tate go. I have this weird thought that if I release her, she will slip away from me.

"Do not mistake my agreement for kindness, human," she hisses. "I do as my queen demands, not you. She ordered that I keep this human alive, so I will. Now quickly, before it's too late."

With no other choice, I step towards the glowing stone and carefully lay her down, righting her clothing, arms, and legs. She doesn't even whimper, which worries me. She is so pale and still.

The healer bustles past me, pushing me back. I stumble into Ronan, and he catches me. I keep my hold on him, needing it as we stare at the woman who has come to mean something to us.

The healer mutters as she moves around the table, gathering things and placing them on Tate's chest—a stone, a small animal skull, an empty bowl, and a dagger. Once they are placed, she stops across from us. She raises her hands, and they start to glow as she moves them slowly up and down Tate's body.

Tears start to roll down the healer's cheeks, glistening with power and pain. All her hatred and prejudice disappear. "Oh, my child, what did they do to you? So much pain and suffering. You should be dead. Your strength . . . by the old gods, your strength . . ."

"Will she survive?" I ask.

She doesn't answer me, her entire focus on Tate. The bowl starts to fill with blood, the dagger begins to spin, and the rock glows as the healer moves her hands faster and faster.

"So much agony, so much endurance . . . You are a survivor. You will survive this. That is it, fight for me. Fight to live."

Ronan and I stand silently, waiting like forgotten statues as the healer works. Time passes strangely as the bowl refills and drains into Tate five times. The stone's glow slowly dwindles until it extinguishes, and the dagger stills.

The healer's hands drop and her eyes open. She looks down at Tate, and I follow her gaze. Her chest is rising and falling slowly without restriction, and the colour is returning to her skin. She looks healthier.

That is a good sign, yes?

"Rest now, my child. You are safe," the healer whispers before clearing the objects from Tate's chest and heading our way.

The healer looks exhausted as she stops before me. "Her injuries are healing, but it is up to her to fight to stay in this body and world." She turns, her shoulders slumped as she starts to shuffle away.

I wish to say thank you, but I know it is rude. Instead, I offer my gratitude the only way I can. "I am indebted to you."

"No, you are indebted to our queen." The healer glances back at me. "Besides, losing a soul like hers from this world . . . It would be a crime. She is needed." She departs, leaving me unable to ask what she meant.

With nothing else to do, I hurry to Tate's side and kneel as I grip her hand. "Did you hear that, angel? You're needed, so wake up."

She doesn't move, and I watch as Ronan kneels on her other side, his expression hopeful before he looks at me. "The queen will come for you to pay the debt."

"I know," I murmur as I hold Tate's hand. Her gloves are gone, which she would hate. I don't know why that's my first thought, but it is. "I will pay it. When she comes, stay with Tate. I do not think they would harm her, but you can never be too sure."

"Of course. Will you be okay?" he asks.

"I have survived this long," is all I tell him. I will not lie to my friend. I know the price will be steep, but I will gladly pay it.

They are right. Tate is important and needed.

She doesn't know how much.

Ronan and I sit like sentries, keeping watch over our hunter, waiting for her to wake.

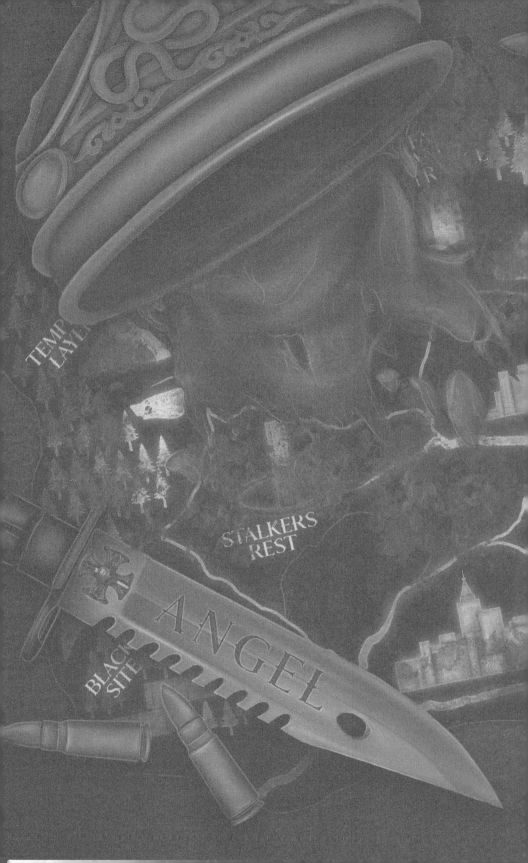

CHAPTER 9

Tate

My eyes blink open. Something soft cradles me, and it's so warm that for a minute, I revel in it before forcing myself to sit up and glance down. Vines slither back from my body, taking their soft pink and orange flowers with them. They were wrapped around me like a blanket.

Frowning, I climb to my feet and look down. My body is whole. There are no wounds or blood. My hair flows down to my ankles, decorated with flowers, and a pale yellow dress covers my body, floating in a warm breeze as I look around.

The meadow of wildflowers stretches on infinitely on either side of me. Where am I? My usual worry seems to float away in the breeze, and I can breathe deeply.

I feel warm, safe, and happy.

That cannot be real though. I grip the gauzy material of the impractical dress and trek through the meadow, searching for information. As I crest a small hill, I get my first glimpse of something other than flowers.

In the valley below is a large tree sheltering a stone, roofless structure, which is shaped like a circle, and from here I see people inside.

I slowly make my way down the hill until I come upon the structure, then I step inside and still.

It is larger inside than it appears on the outside, and it has a huge wooden table running the length of the room. The end of it connects seamlessly with the tree outside. Flowers create a soft rug.

It is the ten women surrounding the table, however, that cause me to still.

"We have been waiting for you, my daughter," one says.

I notice there is no head of the table. Here, they are all equal and all different shapes, sizes, and colours. Some have pointed ears, others are old, and a few are young.

"Me? Why? Who are you?" I step towards the table and an empty spot at the end.

"Interesting," an olive-skinned, middle-aged woman comments. "You know what that means."

"I do," another responds. She has long, icy hair and pointed ears, and she's probably younger than I am.

"Where am I?" I ask, glancing around as if that will give me some answers to this strange place. Am I dead? Is this the afterlife?

"Yes and no."

I whirl around, shocked that they answered something I did not speak aloud.

"This place is eternal. It lies within you and around you. It is our people's place."

"Our people?" I counter.

She simply smiles.

"You know what it means," someone reminds her sadly.

"Means? What does it mean?" I question.

"Anger. Good, you will need it. Do not ever let any man tame it or steal it. You are more powerful than you will ever know, daughter." They all glance at the field before blinking. "It is not your time yet. That is what we meant. Fear not, we await you. Go, your world needs you. You will see us again."

"Go," another calls.

"They need you."

"There is much to be done."

"What does that mean? Why am I here?" I ask as the edges of the vision start to fade.

"Remember, Tate Havelock, blood of ours," the blonde lady calls, "know your own heart. It can never lead you astray, and when you feel alone, find us. We will wait for you."

The flowers and brightness vanish, and my eyes open, staring up at a stained-glass window above me. A noise has me turning my head, and I meet the rounded eyes of a man next to me.

Instinct has me jerking upright with a gasp, my hand wrapping around his throat. "Who are you? Where am I?" My voice is hoarse, but he hears me.

He makes no move to free himself, and I scan his face, frowning. He isn't familiar. Where am I? Did I escape? How am I alive?

"Who are you?" I ask, tightening my grip. He should be choking, but he just arches an eyebrow.

"I'm all for a bit of choking, sweetness, but I do not need to breathe anymore. Is this the fun kind of choking or an attack? I'm down for either. I would just like to know." His voice is even and slick, like water over stones.

He is beautiful, with deep amber eyes, pouty, thick lips, and black hair. He's also bigger than any man I have ever seen. His skin is pale, and freckles dot his cheeks.

"Who are you? I demand once more. "Where am I?"

"I'm Ronan. You do not know me, but I know you," he murmurs, and something flashes in his eyes.

"How is that possible?" I hiss, tired of everyone speaking in riddles.

"You could not see me until now, which I presume is either due to the realm we are in, the magic used to save you, or simply because you almost died. I'm a ghost," he offers, and I drop my hand. "Yes, I know. I'm very attractive for a ghost."

"No, I was thinking I have never seen a ghost before," I admit as I stare at him. The realm? Ghost? What is happening?

"Well, you wouldn't have, would you? Keep up, sweetness. You're smarter than that. Anyway, you are in the fae realm. Shamus brought you here so they could save you," Ronan explains, pressing his chin to his hand and looking up at me through ridiculously long lashes.

"Shamus? As in Commander Vilaran?" I question, confused. "Why would he save me? How could he save me? Where is he now?"

He sighs. "You have many questions for someone who was very near death."

"Wait, the fae realm . . . How is that possible? The fae I know are very secretive about their homeland. They wouldn't allow a human in, never mind to save me." I look around as I speak.

"She's smart, this one," a female voice calls, and a shuffling sound comes before an attractive older lady leans against a wall, watching me. "This is my house, and I am a healer. You are, in fact, in the fae realm, child, and your commander made a deal to save your life."

"What kind of deal?" I ask as I swing my legs off the stone table I'm on.

Ronan hurries around, holding up his hands, which are bound by shackles. "You must rest—"

"What kind of deal?" I repeat, my eyes on him. He averts his gaze, and I know it cannot be good.

The fae hate humans, and they hate hunters even more. The few I know and have been able to befriend made that very clear. They also made it clear that everything has a cost. A deal to save a human?

A high price indeed.

"One you must not worry about," the fae says. "It was his choice."

"Why? Why did he make it? Why save me? How?" I ask them.

Surprisingly, it's the fae who answers. "Isn't that obvious, seer? It is the same reason men do anything. He wants you."

I frown. "Shamus hates me."

Ronan snorts. "Sure, she is right about one thing, sweetness. It isn't your problem to worry about. You need to rest. He made that clear before they came to collect him. He'll be back after he has paid, and we can leave."

"Until then, I seem to be stuck with ya," the fae remarks. "Tea?"

It is rude to turn down a drink. Sliding to my feet, I eye her. "I must find him."

"Smart indeed." She smiles crookedly. "The tea was harmless, by the way. Wait a moment." She turns away before handing me a small square. "For luck. I have a feeling you will need it, Tate Havelock. Where there is strength, there are those willing to take it."

"How do you know my full name?" I whisper.

"I know everything about you. I saved you, after all," she murmurs. "Go now." Her gaze moves to the door behind me. "If you wish to find him, follow the crowd. It's bound to be a big gathering. We do not get a human to play with very often."

Ignoring Ronan, I hurry through the small, dark shop to the glass door. A bell tinkles as I open it and step out onto a cobbled street. Shops and houses line each side, looking every bit what I imagined the fae realm would look like. Glowing magic covers it all with beautiful colours and flowers, with equally beautiful people hurrying around. I follow them with my eyes, noticing a crowd gathering at the end, and Ronan steps up beside me.

"I forgot how annoying walking is. I keep walking into doors," he mutters. "This will not end well. Shamus told me to protect you."

"Then come with me," I tell him, not really caring as I step out into the street and head towards the crowd. I hear him swear, and then he follows me. The throng gets thicker the farther we go, until we have to push our way through annoyed fae.

Ronan looks as worried as I am as we hurry through the crowd. "Who are you to him?" I ask.

"A friend," he admits. "One of his only friends . . . His longest friend."

"Wait, were you on the team he lost?"

Ronan simply turns away, but I know I'm right. How long has Ronan been haunting Shamus?

Honestly, I have so many questions, but the fae was right—we must find Shamus. I have a terrible feeling, and despite him being a pushy asshole, if what they said was true, he saved me.

That means I owe him. Even if I don't like him, I repay my debts.

We finally push through the crowd and stand at the front of a square with a stone podium in the middle. What is happening in the middle makes my stomach roll.

There, with his hands and feet chained, is Shamus, my commander. His head is tilted back, speckled with his blood, and he is pale. His eyes are tight around the corners but open, and as I stare, open-mouthed, a glowing hand waves across his back. The fae's entire arm actually glows as he uses his power like a whip and lashes Shamus's skin. It tears open his skin, adding to the many other cuts. The deep slashes bleed, and some even expose bone. He jerks from the force, grunting, but he does not scream, and the hand waves again, carving another slice.

"Oh fucking hell." I rush to the stone edge, but I'm dragged back.

"Don't." Ronan wraps me in his warm, surprisingly strong grip. "He knew the cost when he broke the treaty. If you stop this, they will have every right to kill him. Everything is survivable, but not his death. Do you understand?"

"No," I snap. "You would watch your friend suffer while being publicly tortured?"

"It was his choice. I cannot make Shamus do anything. I never could," he says, wincing as the next lash hits, the sound audible. "I do not like this either, but we are in a foreign realm where we are seen as enemies. We do not have rights here. If we interrupt, then we all end up dead."

"For a ghost, you're really afraid of death." I elbow him, and he stumbles back. Before he can stop me, I leap onto the stone podium.

Enemies or not, no matter how much I do not understand, I cannot stand by and watch another be tortured because of me.

A woman with glowing purple eyes stands before Shamus. She turns as I rush across the stone, a knowing smile tilting up her lips as she watches me advance. She raises her hands, and I glance around to see soldiers leaping up. The lashes have stopped, however, and the male with the glowing hand steps back from Shamus.

"Angel, no!" Shamus snarls, his voice laced with annoyance and agony. "Do not stop this. I must pay the price. It is the deal we made. I will survive, they ensured it. They simply wish for my pain and humiliation. They can have it."

"No, they cannot," I argue before focusing on the fae woman, knowing she is the one I need to deal with.

"I needed to be healed, so I will pay the price," I call.

"You speak of what you do not know, child," she drawls.

She nods at the man, and his glowing hand lifts again, ready to deliver another blow.

"There must be another way," I protest as I step before Shamus. "Tell me what you really want."

"I want peace. I want my people and land safe, and I had that until he broke the truce. A price must be paid. An agreement is binding, and your ignorance, while understandable, is not an excuse."

"I am ignorant of many of your ways, but I will not be ignorant and watch my commander be abused for saving me. Even if I do not like him, I want my people safe too."

"Truth, I think," she murmurs, watching me with interest. "Even those who hurt you?" I startle at that, and she prowls closer. "They are your people too. Do you wish them safety?"

"No, I wish them dead," I reply without an ounce of hesitation, and her head tips back in laughter.

"Your honesty is refreshing, and I find I like your bloodlust. I knew you would be fun." She stops before me. "Tate, is it?" She grins, brushing her fingers down my face.

I step back, refusing to cower despite her power. "Only friends call me Tate. You can choose if you will be friend or foe. Decide carefully. My enemies do not have a tendency to live long."

"No, I'm betting they don't." She grins despite my blatant threat. "I saved you."

"No, the healer saved me—"

"On my order. Your commander broke our truce, he invaded our land, so I'm within my rights to kill him or worse. He knows that, and he accepted this lesser evil to right the wrongs and make payment for it. What do you have to offer that is better than his blood and sacrifice?"

Fuck, this is not going well. They want human blood . . . . What do the fae want more than the blood of enemies?

"Fae, you crave power and oddities, yes?" I blurt, thinking on the spot.

Her head tilts as she observes me. "And what oddities and power could you possibly offer me, human?"

This is a very bad idea, but I do it anyway.

I press my ungloved hand to her cheek like she did to me, and I let myself see and hear.

There is so much power, countless years, and many memories. It flows from her to me. There were many sacrifices to our kind, then peace and happiness, until it darkens and there is a desire so strong, it breaks my heart, crippling me until my hand is ripped away.

I blink and stare into the fae's pale face. I dared to use my powers on her—a grave insult.

"That was very brave and very foolish. We fae like our secrets," she whispers.

"Yes, you have every right to kill me, but there is something you want more. Isn't there? I sensed it. Speak it and I will make it happen," I whisper.

"Such confidence," she murmurs as she presses her lips to mine. "Deal, little seer. You will grant what I want most, and if you fail, I will kill your commander and his ghost."

"Wait—" I begin as she steps back. "That was not my intention. My deal—"

She smirks. "Then you should have been specific."

I have a feeling this is what she wanted all along, as if I just played into her hands.

"Release him. Bring him and the ghost," she orders nobody in particular. "You, Tate, will come with me. You will uphold your deal."

Yeah, we are definitely fucked.

CHAPTER 10

Tate

They waste no time freeing Shamus, and he is dragged, along with Ronan, as we follow the fae.

"What have you done?" Shamus hisses.

"Truthfully, I do not know," I admit. "But it's better than your torture."

"If you cannot do whatever she wishes, we are all dead. I can endure pain—"

"I could not endure your pain," I snap. "Let us focus."

Our gazes clash, and his voice softens. "She could ask anything of you."

"I know," I murmur, "but I have a feeling this is why she allowed the healer to save me—she hopes I can help. If she believes I can, then I have to trust it's something I can do and survive."

"That's a lot of blind trust," Ronan mutters.

"Sometimes that's all we have," I retort as I glance at him. "Why did you come for me? Why did you risk it all to save me?"

"I am your commander—" Shamus begins.

"You would do this for any of your soldiers?" I interrupt incredulously.

His lips purse, and Ronan chuckles. "She got you good, brother."

59

"Shut up, Row," he mutters and nods forward. "Do not keep her waiting. The fae are not patient creatures."

"We will discuss this when we get out of here alive," I warn him.

"Yes, we will," he replies, always needing to have the last word.

Rolling my eyes, I hurry to keep up with the fae as we move through the streets, the crowd dispersing in disappointment now that human pain is off the table.

One moment, we are walking the empty streets on the outskirts of town, and the next the landscape transforms around us and we stand before the entrance of a cave.

"This is definitely where the creepy, glowing fae lady murders us . . . well, you two," Ronan supplies helpfully.

The fae glances back at us, her eyebrow arched. "I could blink and kill you. I would not spill blood here, however, so do not fear." She steps inside, and we have no choice but to follow.

I expected it to be damp, but thousands of candles cover a wall with jagged steps leading down. We descend them quickly, and at the bottom, I stare in awe at the circular room. The ceilings are so high, I cannot see the top, and light filters in through holes all around, shining on a stone slab in the middle where a body rests, unmoving.

"What is this?" I ask.

She stops at the edge of the raised dais and stares at the body for a moment before glancing back at me. "This is your payment. You must wake him."

"Wake him from what?" I ask.

"He is trapped in his mind. I worry it will warp him. You will free him." She steps back, and I stare at the man on the stone, unable to see much from here.

"Who is he?" I query, a bad feeling building in my gut. You don't wake a fae in a creepy cave, that is just rational thinking, but I suppose I don't have much choice.

"That is not important. Free him and you will all be free to go. This is your payment."

I breathe deeply, realising she will not tell me any more than that.

Tricky fae.

Glancing back at Ronan and Shamus, I see the commander narrow his eyes on me while Ronan gives me a cheeky grin and two thumbs up. Idiot ghost. I step onto the rock and still.

Something sends a shiver through me. The rock feels hungry, welcoming, as magic climbs up my legs and body, trying to devour me. Ignoring it, I head over, not stopping until I am above the man, and when I do, my mouth drops open.

I am not the kind to be swayed by beauty, but the man trapped in his mind on this stone is magnificently beautiful.

His features are delicate, almost feminine, with a small, slender nose speckled with freckles that extend across his high cheekbones. His jaw is pointed, but not too sharp, and his hair is an icy white, spread across the pillow below him, his pointed ears spearing through the strands. He looks like an angel—innocent, ethereal, and beautiful.

He wears a white and ivory fur collar doublet and trousers, and he almost looks as if he is sleeping, but when I lay my hand on his arm, I know differently.

I fall to my knees with a silent scream at the raw power, fury, and hunger.

It consumes me, pulling me deeper, like I am falling into a waiting chasm of teeth and claws. No, I am falling deeper into the darkness. I hit the bottom hard, and a sudden sharpness digs into my skin, trying to get my blood and organs.

This is not real, I remind myself.

"Oh, but it's very real, human, and now you are trapped here with me, another thing to feed on. I should thank you, as you are much more powerful than the others."

I ignore that and the wicked voice, and instead of fighting, I relax, calming my mind as I imagine I'm standing in bright sunlight.

I'm trapped in darkness in his mind. I need to free myself and hopefully him.

The teeth and claws disappear, and I am upright once more in the light that is suddenly eclipsed by darkness.

"Two can play that game." It's the voice again.

Male.

Wicked.

This was never about freeing him; this was about defeating him. I can see the bones of others scattered around. They have been fed upon in both reality and his mind. She fed me to him. I don't know if she expected me to survive or not, but either way, it's no loss to her.

Either I do or I don't.

Either way, she gets what she needs.

Tricky fae bitch.

An evil, malicious laugh echoes around my head, and I begin to wonder if I am in his head or he is in mine. Who is really in control here?

"Who are you?" I ask.

The darkness closes in around me once more, and hands slide across my skin. I gasp as something bites my neck, drawing blood, and I know it does in real life as well. That chuckle comes again, and the hands disappear.

"Oh, but you are strong. I am he, of course, the one on the stone. If you wish for my name, human, then you will have to earn it. They have power, after all."

"I am here to free you—"

He laughs again. "You are here to die, like all the others she sends. It's the price she pays for her mistake."

"What does that mean?" I ask as I spin in the darkness. I try to imagine lights to illuminate the space, but they are quickly extinguished. As powerful as I am and as good as I am at defeating people, he is better and much stronger.

If I do not win this, we will both be trapped here forever.

Closing my eyes, I gather everything in me and force the darkness back, and it slowly starts to peel away. It takes so much effort, I sweat and sway.

We are with you. Remember who you are.

The voice is from within, and I recognise it from that table with the women. They are lending me their power, and with a scream, I throw my hands out, and the darkness is burned away.

I know the control has flipped again. He's strong, but he's also hungry. He needs my power. He needs . . . me.

Either I die and feed him or I free him.

This was her play.

"Show yourself. I have defeated you," I demand, and a slow clap followed by a bone-chilling laugh comes again. A beautiful man steps out of the darkness.

He looks like a dark angel.

"That you did. Very good, human." His voice is soft and sure, sliding across my skin like a caress that leaves me gasping. He watches me for a moment as I stare back, then he begins to circle me.

"I can free you of this . . . this curse," I begin, unsure what to say now.

His laughter makes me shudder once more.

"You think I fell under a curse or spell? No, naïve human, my sister made me this way. She trapped me in my own mind out of fear and love, as she called it." He lifts my hair as he circles me. "You are beautiful." His whisper reaches me as he stops behind me, his breath wafting over my neck and ear. "And so tasty." His tongue darts out, licking down my neck, and I jerk away.

"Wait, your sister?" I frown, turning to keep him in view.

His head tilts to the side as he watches me. "You truly are naïve. Did you just follow her blindly? Silly little human. The one who brought you to me made me like this, trapping me here." He throws his arms out to encompass the shadowed area of his mind. "For my own good, she said. She thought she could free me as she wished, but magic has its own price. I have been trapped for centuries, and everyone she brings to try and free me ends up feeding my hunger." His head dips, and his eyes darken.

He looks like an angel, but there is a devil in his eyes.

This one is not the same as the other fae.

"Did she trap you because she feared you?" I ask boldly.

He laughs. "So bold and brave. Yes, human, they feared me. I am not like them. My sister and I, we are . . . How do you humans say it? Born from two sides of the same coin—one is bright and good and the other is dark and evil. We bring balance, but when I grew stronger, she feared me so she trapped me here. Now she lives with regret, loving me even now."

"You don't love her?" I ask.

"I love no one or nothing, only power and feeding." He grins slowly. "So, human, free me and I shall feed on this earth or you will die like the others."

I watch him for a moment. "I choose neither." Following an instinct I do not understand, I fling myself at him. We fall through the darkness, my hands trapping his face, and then I lift my arm, bite into it, and press it against his mouth.

I feel my blood drip into him, filling him as we hit the ground and he rolls us. He stares down at me, panting, his eyes wide and lips stained with my blood.

It's then I understand what I am doing.

I am quenching the evil.

He is powerful but so hungry it drives him mad, warping his mind.

The hunger made him do terrible, terrible things to stop the pain.

That, I can understand.

"What are you doing to me?" he rasps as my blood seems to work through him.

"Saving you for real and freeing you from your hunger. I know pain. I understand how it can change you. Let me help."

"It will hurt," he warns.

"I can handle the pain," I reply as he pulls my head to the side without any hesitation. My screams split the air as he buries his vicious teeth into my neck and feasts on the power within me—the life he so desperately needs. "I can handle it," I tell him as I wrap my hand around his head, pulling him closer as he guzzles my blood.

Pain flows through me so strongly, I scream again, even as his hands slide under my clothes. He pinches my nipple as his other hand slides into my pants, pressing firmly against my clit. I am unable to stop him, and I know he tastes the moment the pain mixes with pleasure in my blood. He snarls, gnawing at my neck as he pinches my nipple so hard it aches. My thighs part and I press into him, rolling my hips.

The pleasure grows until it explodes.

I come with a scream, and he swallows my pleasure in my blood.

He jerks backwards, falling to his hands and knees, his back bowing as he coughs up black ink. Propping myself up on my elbow, I watch him.

"What have you done?" he snarls.

"I have fed the beast within you, and now I will free you." I throw myself at him again before I chicken out, wrapping my arms around him as we fall once more. We descend through the darkness, but this time we fall right into our bodies and out of our minds.

My eyes snap open, the light so bright it hurts. My body is swaying and weak.

"Angel!" Shamus snaps from somewhere behind me.

"I'm okay," I murmur.

Slumping into the stone, I glance at the sleeping fae. He suddenly sits up, and I hear his sister gasp and rush towards us. His head turns woodenly, and he glances down at me.

My blood stains his lips as he lifts a hand and pats at it.

I have brought him back from the edge, but he is not a good fae and never will be.

He was right, he was born like this, and now I have freed him.

"You're awake!" The female fae hurries past me, her hands fluttering about before she looks at me. "You did it."

Nodding, I climb to my feet, falling back as weakness hits me. Arms catch me, and I glance up at a worried Ronan and a stern-faced Shamus.

"She did as you asked. Are we free to leave in one piece?" Shamus asks.

"Yes, go, go." She waves her hand at us, and Shamus and Ronan waste no time dragging me towards the exit of the cave. I glance back at the fae on the stone.

His eyes track me as I stumble away with them. His sister talks to him, but he doesn't move, not even to blink. He disappears then reappears before me, making us stumble to a stop.

"What?" I ask, refusing to cower.

He cocks his head as he watches me.

"Brother," she calls. "Come, we will head home—"

"You know I cannot stay, sister. They will never accept me. I will go with her. I fear it is the only way to keep this . . . madness at bay." He licks his lips—a reminder of drinking my blood.

"I was not offering," I snap. "I have enough here with an asshole commander and a ghost. I don't need a mad fae."

"Too bad," he murmurs as he steps closer. "You freed me and tied me to you. Where you go, I go."

"No, brother, the mortal realm is no place for us," the fae protests, hurrying over to us. "I will find a way to keep the hunger at bay—"

"I have found a way—her. Either I go with her or I stay here and slowly go mad again until you have to lock me away. There is no choice."

"I never said he could come," I snarl at them. "I do not need any more issues. I have my own battles to finish."

"Then you can use me to fight them." He shrugs. "Or my powers at least, and in return, you will allow me to feed on your essence so I do not go insane . . . well, any more insane." The smile he aims at me is crazed.

"This is not a good idea," Shamus murmurs. "We should leave."

"You think you can leave this realm without me stopping you?" the angel fae retorts. The entire cave is suddenly submerged in the same darkness, until all we can see is him. "I am more powerful than anything in this world or yours. I am ancient and eternal. You cannot escape me."

"I say we bring him along," Ronan says with amusement. "Who knows when a fae might come in handy? Besides, it's super annoying to have to get up to turn off the lights every night. He can just do this."

"You are a ghost. You do not sleep," I murmur, but my eyes are on the fae.

"Brother," she tries again before glancing at me. "Are you sure?

66

She's special, I can sense that, but not from this realm, and I will not be able to help you."

"I do not need your help. I need her," he declares. "Now, shall we go, humans, before you get into any more trouble in our world?"

I glance at Shamus to see his eyes narrowed on the fae. "It is your choice, Tate. Fae are trouble, and you are a hunter. You are enemies."

"If I leave, you will just follow me, won't you?" I sigh as I glance at the angelic fae.

His smirk lets me know I'm right. It's better to keep an enemy in sight rather than stalking me. I'm left with only one choice. "Let's get the hell out of this realm and then deal with this later. I'm fucking exhausted."

CHAPTER 11

Shamus

"A re you sure this is going to work? I've been at Stalkers' Rest for five years and I never knew about this," Tate mutters from my side as we crouch in the trees, peering at my command post. Technically, I could just walk in the front door, but it would raise questions, and besides, I'm not leaving Tate. She must be hidden for now. When Black discovers she escaped, he won't be happy. She needs to lie low, and what better place than right under her enemies' noses—and within reach of me.

Turning to Ronan, who keeps flickering in and out, a result of being in iron for too long, I nod at the door I just pointed out to Tate. "Go check if the tunnel is clear."

"Oh yeah, send the ghost," he snaps, but he floats off to do as he's told, appearing before the section of wall that surrounds the building that looks the same as any other. The only people who know about this are now dead—by my hand. This was always an escape plan for me and now her. The secret door allows access to tunnels that lead to an undisclosed entrance to my private elevator, which takes you to my floor. No one goes up there or is permitted to, so for now, staying there will keep her safe, as well as stop the fae at her side from causing mayhem amongst hunters.

Speaking of, I turn to see the white-haired fae, who is playing with the ends of Tate's short hair as he peers at her, not the least bit worried about the hundred or so hunters currently practicing outside. His entire focus is on her.

When he feels my gaze, he turns to me for just a moment, and then his voice is in my head, something he should not be able to do. Just how powerful and old is this fae?

Don't worry, I need her alive for now, walker.

I narrow my eyes on him, making sure to project my voice.

If you harm her, I will end your life. Do not forget I am a hunter. I might have signed the peace treaty, but if you hurt my Tate, I will be more than happy to break it.

Your Tate? His laughter is sardonic and makes my eyes feel like they are bleeding. *Does your Tate know what you are?*

A muscle jumps in my jaw, betraying me, and his laughter sounds again.

Thought not. Shall I tell her? Do you think she would follow you so willingly if she knew? The great Shamus Vilaran, grand hunter, commander of change, and hunter of monsters . . . Little do they know, you are one.

I know my eyes are burning as I glare at him. *You do not know what you speak of.*

No?

"Ahem." We both turn to see Tate. She looks between us, her brow furrowing, oblivious to what is happening in our heads. "Are you just going to stare at each other like you are debating fucking or fighting, or shall we go before we are discovered?"

Ronan pops between us, and it's only years of him doing that that makes me capable of not reacting. Tate, however, slams her dagger into where he would be if he were alive.

"Rude." He wags his finger at her. "And not very nice, considering I'm here to save your ass." He glances at me. "Tunnel is clear, and I might have caused a few . . . electrical malfunctions with the outside cameras for you, but I'd suggest moving fast."

"I agree." I glance at Tate and then the fae. "Stay close and stay low. We need to sneak in undetected, which means leaving the humans alone." I aim that at the fae.

"As long as I'm kept entertained and fed, I will leave your little band of warriors be." He smirks, eyeing Tate.

Grumbling about ghosts and fae, she climbs to her feet and pushes into a sprint, heading for the door. We have no choice but to follow.

We cover the ground quickly, the fae elegantly speeding past me and dogging her steps until I have no choice but to force myself to move faster. I do not stand a chance against an immortal magical being, but I refuse to be left behind. I have to swallow my exhaustion when we reach the door, but he shoots me a look like he knows anyway.

Immortal asshole.

Turning to the wall, I slide my hand along the surface until I hear the hum of the scanner, and then a second later, there's a click before a section of the wall swings inwards. Stepping inside, I turn on the lights and wait. Tate moves past me, followed closely by her fae, and Ronan simply pops into existence in the tunnels as the door swings shut.

"Stop fucking doing that. I'm going to get you a ghost bell or some shit," she snaps.

"Then how would I be able to spy on anyone?" he grumbles.

"Exactly my point. You wouldn't. Just how long were you spying on me anyway?" she asks, heading towards him.

He backs up, a grin on his face. "Long enough to know you're overdue for your period."

Everyone goes silent for a moment, and then Tate slowly pulls out a piece of iron she must have stolen from the fae realm. "Say one more word. I dare you, ghost boy."

"Shy, she's being mean," Ronan whines, but he's grinning.

"You two stop bickering," I tell them as I stride past them. "Angel, we will discuss Ronan when you are safe on my restricted level. For now, stop threatening to solidify him."

"Why? Then I can kick his dead ass," she mutters, but she puts the iron away after one more warning look at my friend and follows me.

The fae chuckles as he watches the entire thing. "You are vicious, human. I like it," he remarks casually.

"Okay, that's it," she snaps and pulls a blade, slamming the fae into the wall as she holds the dagger to his throat. We all know he allowed it. With one flick of his finger, she would be dead, but he leans back into the wall, his eyes heavy-lidded in hunger as he watches her.

"First and last warning, fae. I am not somebody for you to fuck with. I do not know why you decided to follow me, but if you get in my way, I will gut you from neck to balls."

"I would survive," he says calmly.

"Yes, but it would fucking hurt, and when you healed, I would do it again for as many times as it takes for me to find a way to kill you. Understand?"

"Has anyone ever told you that your bloodthirsty nature is very attractive?" the fae says.

The sigh Tate lets out has his lips twitching, and she presses the blade harder against his skin for a moment. "Remember my warning, fae."

"I shall not forget it, nor the taste of your blade anytime soon. When I do, feel free to remind me."

Leaning down, he licks the blade, and she steps away, sliding it into her pocket as I point at both of them.

"We don't have time for this," I say, "but once we are upstairs, I will happily watch you flay the annoyance open."

Turning, I head back down through the tunnel, trusting them to follow. The fae will be a problem, but if she can tame him, then she might have some of the power she needs to take care of what will happen next, but only time will tell.

At the end of the curved tunnel, I hit the button for the elevator. It appears instantly, and we climb inside and shoot upwards to the highest point in Stalkers' Rest. My ears pop since we are going so fast, but when we appear on my secure level, I lock the normal elevator and leave a message saying I am not to be disturbed.

Tate and the fae glare at each other in the hallway, so I pour myself a drink in the living room and peer out of the glass window to the world below.

The hunters surround us. Only a fool would surround themselves with enemies.

"So now what?" Tate asks, and I glance over to find Ronan sitting on the chandelier, kicking his feet, while the fae stretches out on one of my sofas. Tate lingers between us, staring at me.

"Now you need to rest. Everything else can wait for tomorrow," I murmur.

"Black—"

"Is far from here. You need all your strength to go after him," I tell her as I turn, sipping the amber liquid. "Rest, heal, and eat, and when it is time, I will help you get your revenge. Remember, Tate, we are not enemies. We are fighting the same war. You simply didn't know it."

"What does that even mean?" she snarls. "I am sick of your word games, commander."

"I swear I will tell you, but for now, you need to rest," I order.

"Rest? I was betrayed, tortured, brought back by some weird fae magic, and forced to feed his evil highness over there, and now you're telling me to rest?" she snaps.

"Yes," I respond. "Despite it all, you are human, so yes, I am telling you to rest. Revenge will still be there tomorrow, as will answers." Looking to Ronan, I nod. "Show her to the spare room." I glance at the fae. "You will be in another."

"I go where she goes." He shrugs. "You could try to stop me, but it would be pointless." He climbs to his feet, rising elegantly. "Shall we?"

"Fuck all of you. One of these days, you're going to piss me off too much and I'm going to murder you," she hisses as she heads to the door.

Smirking, I turn back to the window. "Goodnight to you too, and Ronan, make sure the fae doesn't get any ideas."

When they are gone, my shoulders slump and exhaustion fills me, pain still assaulting my body. I would have endured worse for breaking the treaty, but it does leave me weak. The body hosting this soul is not as strong as I wish. Stumbling to the sofa, I wait for Ronan to return.

He can help me clean and dress the wounds so I can rest, but I refuse to be weak in front of Tate or the fae.

They will never know how close I truly was to dying tonight.

CHAPTER 12

Ronan

"Here." I float through the door before remembering and opening it for her. "Whoops," I say with a shrug. Sometimes I forget humans cannot float through things the way I can.

Rolling her eyes, she follows me into one of the many spare rooms Shamus keeps on his floor. This one has a bed and some furniture, as well as an en suite. Technically, I also have a room, but since I'm dead and don't sleep, I mostly just watch anime in there.

"Thanks." She sits heavily on the bed, eyeing me as I continue to float. "You can leave now, ghost boy."

"No can do. I need to keep an eye—"

"Ronan." My name makes me stop since she has never really said it before. Her tone is tired and calm, which is worrying. "I'm tired. I just need some time to myself to . . . to figure out everything that happened. In the last twenty-four hours, I have been burned, stabbed, and tortured. I almost died, then I was brought back, fed to a fae, and have now moved in with my commander. I need some space." She looks at me. "Please," she pleads.

I know I shouldn't, Shamus wants me to keep an eye on her, worried she will run off half-cocked after Black and her team, but I

75

nod and float backwards through the walls. I linger long enough to see her let out a long breath and slump back, only to still at the sight of the fae.

"Not going anywhere, human," he warns.

Grumbling, she climbs under the covers, turning her back to him, and I float away. I will check on them later, but despite his nature and, well, obvious mental issues, the fae doesn't seem to want to kill Tate.

I leave them to it and find myself floating to Shamus's room. He must feel me coming because he groans.

"What have I told you about privacy?" he mutters, but he doesn't protest too much. He's stretched out on his sofa, his shirt removed to expose the extensive bleeding and weeping wounds on his back.

"Shit, I can't remember much about being human, but that can't be fun. How are you even still walking?" I ask.

"Stubbornness and pride," he admits, agony tight in his voice. "Can you get the herbs?"

"Yeah, yeah, I know the drill. You've been hurt so many times, I know where they all are by heart," I mutter as I float away. "Though, this has to be one of the worst, bar the time that troll tried to take off your head with its fists." Gathering the gifted magic and herbs, I head towards him and make myself solid as I straddle his ass and start to apply them generously across his back.

At first he groans with pain, fisting the sofa as he tries to hold it back, but as the magic works into his system, he sighs, slumping into the cushions. When I'm done, I lean back, taking a look at my handiwork. "Well, you won't win any beauty contests soon, but you'll live."

"Thank you, brother," he murmurs sleepily, snuggling deeper into the sofa. It's surprising how different Shamus can be. No one sees this soft, gentle side of him, one that was beaten, tortured, and almost ripped out of him.

"Lie like that and try to get some sleep. I'll keep an eye on your angel for you," I tell him. "Next time, we'll treat your wounds first. You die, I die, remember?"

"That's the only reason?" he jokes before becoming serious. "It was more important that she was safe. Everyone else comes second."

I find myself staring at the pale side of his face for a moment before I float down and press my chin to the edge of the sofa so I can peer into his eyes. "Why is she so important to you?"

I don't think he'll answer, his dark eyes meeting mine before he rolls his lips. "Not just to me," he admits, but he says no more. "Keep your eye on them. I don't trust the fae. If he makes one wrong move, I want to know immediately."

"What will you do?" I laugh. "They are notoriously hard to kill, the tricky bastards."

"But not impossible," Shamus replies, his voice going cold. This is the commander everyone else knows, the monster of Stalkers' Rest. "I have been hunting for a very long time, brother. Do you truly think I do not have a way to kill the fae if I must?"

"Then why haven't you?"

"He may be . . . useful. For now, as long as he does not cross the line, I will allow him to live."

"You know, sometimes you're kind of terrifying," I admit with a ghostly shiver.

"Only sometimes?" he jokes before his smile wanes. "You and I both know what I'm capable of and what I am willing to do for my duty. I think they should be more than terrified of me."

"Is it really worth all this, Shamus?" I ask, voicing something I've often wondered. I understand why he is doing all this, I've been his best friend too long not to, but I have to know.

"It has to be," he murmurs, shutting his eyes again. "Keep watch over her for me."

"Got it. Rest now, brother. Never fear, ghost boy is here!" I disappear, floating through the floor.

After all, I owe Shamus everything. He's the reason I'm still able to be here. Without him, I would just be . . .

Gone.

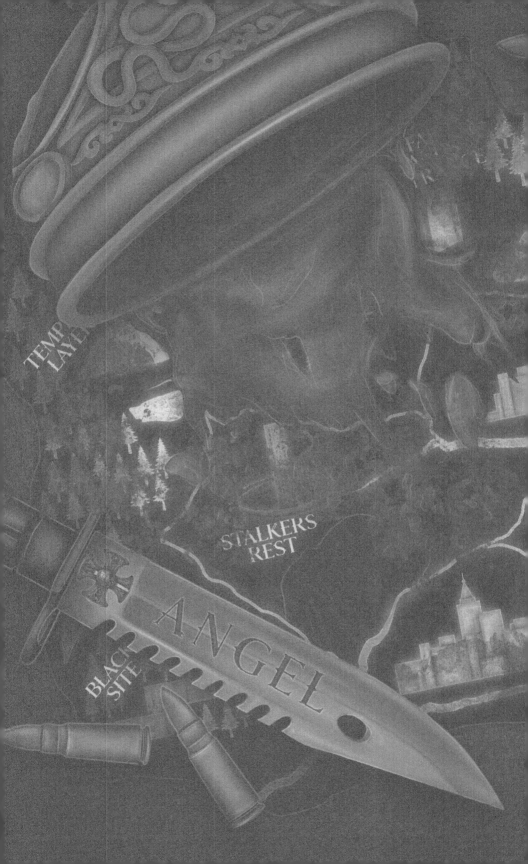

CHAPTER 13

Tate

I can feel the fae watching me, and it's unnerving. I face the window, refusing to look at him, lest that makes him strike. My eyes are open and my hand is wrapped around my dagger, which is obscured by the sheets. It will take precious seconds to free it, but it would also be an open invitation to attack if he sees me with it.

"Sleep, human. I promise not to kill you until you wake." His silken voice fills the air, and the room seems to darken, cool white filigrees and animals filling the space in an epic display of magic. A bunny hops before my eyes before disappearing and morphing into a moon with stars.

"Enough," I snap.

He chuckles, but the magic disappears. Closing my eyes, I force myself to relax, even as I swear I feel something brush across my cheek. "I will make good on my threat if you come near me, fae. I swear it."

"I have no doubt," he murmurs. "Sleep."

"I'm going to—not because you ordered me to, but because I planned to," I mutter.

"Stubborn, fierce human." He chuckles, but it sounds too close for my liking. He wants a reaction, but I don't give him one.

One by one, I force my muscles to relax.

I suppose most people wouldn't be able to fall asleep knowing an evil fae who has developed a taste for your soul and blood is watching you so closely, but I've slept around my team for years, and they craved my pain and death just as much.

I am, however, a light sleeper, so when I feel the sheets move sometime later, my eyes open.

I must have flipped to my back during the night, my dagger still held in my grip. Frowning, I try to figure out what woke me. I glance around the dark room, but I do not see the fae anywhere, and my heart starts to pound with adrenaline and fear.

Suddenly, the sheets move again, and my gaze sweeps down my body, widening when I see the bulge at the end of the bed big enough to be a person. It moves up, the sheets moving with it. Hands grip my thighs, and I am yanked down the bed and under the sheets.

A yelp escapes my mouth, but I swing my dagger, only to freeze when a hand wraps around it and I'm unable to pull back or push forward. My eyes strain in the darkness, trying to see even though I know it's the fae before his voice fills the strained, warm darkness of the cocoon under the sheets.

"You said not to get near you, nothing about touching."

Snarling, I struggle against his grip with all my strength. Luckily, he's only touching the blade, so I do not have to see into his head, but all it does is make him hiss, and then something wet drips onto my leg. I freeze, and he chuckles.

"Would you like to see?" Before I can respond, a dull, warm white glow illuminates under the sheets, which seem to blow up into a dome.

There are drops of ruby red blood on my thigh. Slowly, I drag my gaze up and meet his. His hand holds the blade, and blood slowly slides down it, hitting my thigh below.

"You made me bleed, human," he murmurs as he leans in, his hair glowing like a fucking halo, which is a lie. "Now it's my turn to make you bleed. A cut for a cut."

Before I can even suck in a breath, he is on me, pinning me to the bed, his teeth sinking into my neck.

My head slams back into the mattress as an agonising scream tries to erupt from my throat, but I bite it back, slapping at him. He sinks his teeth deeper, worrying at my neck. I feel my blood spill down across my shoulder and to the bed, and the pain makes my heart slam like a trapped bird.

Gritting my teeth, I manage to free one of my hands from between us as he drinks my blood with a deep moan.

I slide my hand down my side. Despite the agony rolling through me, I grip the dagger beside me and slam it into his ribs, twisting it as he gasps and jerks against me. "You think you're the first handsy monster I've dealt with?" I snap as I shove it deeper. It must hurt like a bitch, and I feel his blood flowing down from the deep wound, but he doesn't release my neck. If anything, he moans into the wound, and my eyes widen as his hips roll.

He forces himself against me, falling between my thighs until he's pressed against my crotch, rubbing himself against me as he feeds, all while I twist the dagger deeper, but he doesn't care.

Sick fucking fae.

I wrench my head forward, ripping my neck wound even more, and sink my teeth into his pale flesh. I feel his skin pop in my mouth, blood pouring down my neck and throat, and I jerk my head, trying to cause as much damage as I can until I have to fall back, gasping.

Choking on my own blood, I stare at him as he kneels, reaching up to trace the jagged, feral wound marring the perfection of his pale, glistening neck. The blood staining his lips and teeth betray his nature as he grins and then starts to laugh.

Coughing up blood, I fight to cover my wound, knowing it's too deep.

Shit. Shit. Shit.

"Do not say I am unkind." He waves his hand, and I feel his magic move through me. My neck wound stitches back together, the bleeding stops, and I can breathe again as he heals me. "You caused that. You would have survived my wound, but you inflicted that one yourself. I am benevolent, am I not?" He strokes his fingers across the wound on his neck like one would a cock. "But I do like this—a mark from my little human. I would be sad to see it go."

His hand glows, and he presses it to his wound. I watch the mark heal and scar over—something this fae does not have, nor any other.

A wicked scar now disfigures his neck in the shape of my teeth.

"You're mad," I whisper, dropping my hand from my neck.

"Very much so, but if I am, then so are you, human."

His tongue darts out, licking my blood on his chin and lips. It seems to extend as I watch, turning long and forked, until he can lap it all up as I recoil into the bed, searching for the dagger before I realise it's still in his side.

He sees my eyes on it and plucks it free with a groan. His eyes shut for a moment, and when they open again, they are blazing with desire and locked on me.

"Don't you dare—" The dagger sinks into the bed next to my head as he leans down, his lips nearly touching mine.

"The fae do not like to be indebted. Do you know that?" he murmurs.

I nod slowly, confused as to where that came from, until he grins. "You made me come when you ripped my neck open. It's time I returned the favour."

He grips my hips, and magic moves over me, dissolving my clothes. Horror fills me for a moment, and I grab the dagger and sit up, pressing it to his neck. "You will not fucking touch me," I bite out, forcing anger into my tone as I try to ignore the small hint of desire that sparks inside me.

I clearly need help.

"Fine." His smile only grows. "I do not need to touch you to make you come."

"Wait, what do you—" I fall back with a shout as ecstasy courses through me, lighting my blood on fire. It's all I can feel as my body convulses, writhing in the bloody sheets, the dagger dropped and forgotten. My eyes roll back into my head as my clit throbs so hard my hips come off the bed, my cunt becoming so wet I feel it drip below me.

My nipples tighten to the point of pain, as if they are being squeezed in a vice or between teeth, and I swear I feel a tongue drag along my folds before something thick and hard thrusts into me.

He uses magic to fuck me without even moving, amusement and desire dancing in his gaze as he watches me come apart from a single thought.

Another scream rips from my throat as I come harder than I ever have, and the magic still doesn't retreat. It slides through every inch of my body, flicking against nerves I didn't even know existed until I whimper and come again, my cream covering my thighs until I finally slump.

The magic still hums through me, but not as strong as it was. The covers have disappeared. I don't even know when, but I'm spread eagle on the bed, covered in blood and cum. My eyes widen when I notice Ronan observing near the ceiling.

"Well, I only came to see what the screaming was about. Now that I know it's not him murdering you, I'll go." He slowly fades backwards into the wall before popping his head through. "Carry on, don't mind me."

"Ronan," I croak, but he's gone. He won't help me. I guess he thinks I wanted this.

I'm going to wrap him in iron and kick his ass in the morning.

The magic frees me at the interruption, and it's the break I need to grab my forgotten dagger. I scramble to my knees, my body weak and overheated.

Gripping my dagger, I point it at him. "Do that again and I'll gut you."

"Haven't we established that I like your blade?" he mocks as he leans in. "Why don't we make a deal?"

"Only a fool makes a deal with a fae," I snarl. "I am no fool."

"No, you are not, but you are delicious. I think I will keep you alive to play with for a while. I debated just draining you."

"How fucking nice of you."

"Isn't it?" he replies wistfully.

"Fuck this." Sliding off the bed, I open the wardrobe and find a robe. I wrap it around my body and belt it. Holding my dagger, I grab the only intact pillow from the bed and toss the fae another glare as I head to the door.

"Where are you running off to? Trying to run from me?" he teases as he follows.

"Not running, just too fucking tired to deal with your shit right now. You got what you wanted. You ate and won the game, now leave me alone," I snarl, not sparing him a look, mortification heating my cheeks at what he made my body do.

He licks the shell of my ear, making me stumble. "Admit you enjoyed it, hunter."

"Drop dead," I snap as I open the final door in the corridor, correctly guessing it's Shamus's bedroom. It's a huge room, with a sitting room and an open sliding door to a raised bedroom at the back. Stretched out on his front on one sofa is Shamus. He lifts his head at the sound and peers at me.

"Angel?" He frowns, running his eyes down the blood splattered across my skin.

Gripping my pillow, I turn away from him and drop it onto the other leather sofa, then I throw myself down, ignoring them as I flip them off and turn to face the back of the sofa.

"Erm . . . hello?" he says, confusion lacing his tone.

The fae mocks, "If you think him being here will protect you, hunter . . ."

"Shamus, Shamus, Shamus, I caught them fucking—" Ronan cuts off, and fury explodes through me, making me sit up as they all turn to look at me.

"If I hear one more fucking word from a single one of you, I am going to chop off your balls and hang them out of the window. Okay?" I yell. "Even you, ghost boy. I will find a way. Don't tempt me!"

When I drop down with a huff, it's quiet for a moment. "You would think getting laid would make her happier. Maybe you did it wrong, fae. There's a lot of blood, but some people are into that."

"That's it—" I jerk upright, but Ronan disappears. I turn my glare on Shamus and the fae. "I mean it." I point from my eyes to them before slumping down and curling around myself.

I'm just starting to fall asleep when something soft covers me. I startle and look down at a fluffy blanket. My eyes go to Shamus's retreating back as he limps over to the other sofa.

I track his movements for a moment, something thick coating my throat before I turn away and force myself to sleep, needing the rest.

CHAPTER 14

T he robe is soft, and despite the fact that I'm naked under it, I sit cross-legged on the sofa, looking out of the windows beyond.

"Here," Shamus says, and I accept the mug, warming myself as he sits heavily on the other sofa.

"How are your wounds?" I ask.

He arches a brow, blowing over his own coffee. He's still shirtless, with some sort of herb mixture slicked down his back, and I try, I really do, not to look at his torso, but it's hard.

He's built with muscles meant for use, not just display. He's thick and strong. "Better," is all he says as he takes a sip.

I copy him, and when there's a slurping sound, we both turn to see Ronan trying to drink from a mug. The liquid slides through him to the floor below.

"Is that a puppy pad?" I ask.

"He insists on trying to drink it every single day, and I got sick of cleaning it up," Shamus answers, a blush staining his cheeks.

"I miss coffee," Ronan grumbles.

The fae isn't here. Maybe I should be worried, but Shamus doesn't seem to be, so I relax. Besides, without his constant flirting, I can relax a little. There's been too much otherworldly craziness these last few days, and this feels normal.

Well, as normal as it gets with your commanding officer and a ghost trying to drink coffee and basically pissing it onto a puppy pad.

"Can't you just solidify and drink it?" I ask curiously.

"I can, but, well, ghosts don't go to the toilet, and I have to rid myself of it straight away, so it seems like a waste," he mutters, eyeing the cup sadly. "Oh, sweet nectar of the gods, how I miss thee."

"Right." I blink and look at Shamus. "So where is that backstabbing bastard, Black? I'm not wasting any more time. I want the fucker to suffer and then die."

Shamus sips his coffee as he watches me. "I know you want revenge, Tate," he says, and hearing my full name makes me sit up taller. "Before you say anything, I am not stopping you, no. I would never be that foolish, but what I am suggesting is a smarter plan than running off after him alone. You need a new team, people who have your back. Black is ruthless and capable, you know that. You cannot take him down alone."

"What do you suggest? No hunter will go against Black's unit. That leaves us with no one. Or what? I keep collecting monsters since I already have a fae and a ghost?" I scoff angrily.

"Hey!" Ronan protests, but we both ignore him.

"It's not a bad idea," Shamus muses. "If you want to go up against evil, then use evil. I have a feeling that before this is through, it will be more than your hands that are bloody. If you want to defeat Black and your old team, then find others to fight with you."

"Who would be crazy enough to stand with me against elite hunters?"

Shamus stands and turns as he goes to walk away. "Those they hunt, of course."

Sipping my coffee, I think on his words. Although I'm a hunter, I've made it my mission not only to foster relationships with those other hunters consider monsters, but to keep them safe. If they haven't committed crimes, then they aren't my enemy, and in fact many of them are my friends. Like most, though, they hide from hunters, trying to avoid detection.

It would be a death sentence for them to actively seek out hunters and kill them, and for most, their people wouldn't allow it.

Who would be crazy enough to stand with a hunter against other hunters?

No, his plan won't work. I need Black's location.

"Hey, Tate." I glance over at Ronan, who's still holding his mug. "Go easy on him. He might not act like it, but that fae punishment almost killed him."

Pursing my lips, I eye Ronan once more. "You're trying to protect him from me? Him of all people? He's the fucking stalker, and he owns most of the hunting guild—"

"And he is still a man. You know better than most how easily power can be taken away and those around you can turn on you. Shamus has been in this game a long time, and he's had a lot of daggers in his back, so please, don't be one of them."

"Why'd he come for me and sacrifice himself?" I ask.

Ronan's smile is small and filled with knowledge. "You'll have to ask him that yourself." He nods at the door. "Go on, I won't stop you."

"Bloody ghosts," I mutter as I stand and head to where Shamus disappeared. I rip the bedroom door open, suddenly realising why Ronan was so happy. Shamus is in the bathroom, so he thinks I'll chicken out. He doesn't know me very well then.

Storming into the bathroom, I hop up on the counter as steam wafts around the room. Shamus turns to me, his mouth dropping open before he rolls his eyes and continues to scrub at his hair, both of us ignoring the fact he is naked.

"Just tell me where Black is," I demand.

"So you can run after him half-cocked and get yourself killed?" He stares at me. "No." He sticks his head under the spray, ignoring me.

"I won't get killed. I can take them—"

"Do not be foolish," Shamus snaps. "You are smarter than that.

Either they will find you are gone, know you are alive, and be expecting it or they will be on high alert. Either way, you die. Isn't suffering by their hands once enough? This time you must be smarter than them. You might not like it, but deep down, you know I'm right. You're a hunter, Tate, one of the best, but hunters work in teams for a reason. You want to torture and kill Black's entire team? Fine by me, I'll champion it, but do it with a team."

"What is your obsession with me dying?" I snap. "Hunters die every day. I'm no different—"

"You aren't allowed to die, is that understood?" His voice is low and cold.

We stare at each other for a moment, and I'm unsure what to say. I know this is my moment to ask why he saved me, why I'm important to him, but I chicken out, and he turns away, scrubbing at his body. I watch him for a moment.

Is he right? Am I blinded by hatred?

My old team is the best for a reason. Even though I know I might not make it back if I go alone, it's a risk I'm willing to take as long as it wipes them from the earth. Apparently, it is not a risk my commander is willing to take, however.

My gaze drops to his ass for a split second, but when I look up, he's peering at me with knowing eyes. "Fine, I'll find the fae and think on it," I mutter as I drop off the counter, but his voice stops me at the door.

"Running away from what you want, angel?" he purrs, sending a shiver of need through me.

Shamus is attractive and he knows it, but he's also a whole bag of complicated and someone I thought hated me until very recently.

I guess my radars are all out of whack.

Turning, I storm up to the shower and step inside with him. Water sprays down on my robe and hair, soaking me to the bone, but I ignore it, pressing against him. His eyes flare, and I feel his hard cock press against my stomach as I lean up on my tiptoes. Just when he thinks I'm about to kiss him, I move to his ear.

"I never run. If I wanted you, Shamus, I would have you." Dropping to my heels, I step back with a smirk, purposely running my eyes down every inch of his body and back up to his. "You're not my type."

His hand captures me before I can leave. He pulls me back until I'm pressed to his front, his warm breath brushing my ear as his hand glides up my robe and cups my cunt. "Liar, angel," he taunts as he squeezes me. I know I'm fucking wet. Fighting him and the sight of his body did it to me. The fucker. I elbow him, and he grunts as he hits the wall.

"Don't worry, I can take care of myself or find someone else to." I step from the shower, and undoing the sodden robe, I drop it to the floor with a wet squelch, then I walk naked from his bathroom, feeling his eyes on me the entire time.

CHAPTER 15

Shamus

I know Tate is pissed, so I give her space. She'll work it out on her own and realise I'm right. I'm not trying to stop her. In fact, I want the same thing she does—all the corrupt hunters dead—but I want to make sure she survives it.

Leaning back in my bed, I check my cameras on my phone, seeing her in the gym, the fae watching. I suppose it should worry me, but if she can sway him to her side, then that would be a whole lot of power at her back. I witnessed that power first-hand, and fae are territorial and possessive. If anyone tried to hurt what they consider theirs, then they would burn the world.

She needs him, which means she needs to win him over, so I give her space to do just that.

"Spying on her as usual." Shutting my phone, I lay it on the side table and slip farther into my sheets, ignoring Ronan, who bounces onto my bed next to me. "Does she know how often you watch her? Do you think she would find it creepy?"

"As creepy as you watching her?" I retort, arching a brow at him.

"Ah, but I was following orders." He winks.

I smirk. "Even when she was showering?"

"Don't tell her that. She'll find a way to kill me." He sighs wistfully, making me chuckle, but then he turns serious. "I'm going to go with her. I'm going to be part of her team."

That makes me sit up, and he copies my movement, seeing my confusion. Ronan has been with me since . . . well, since forever. I might have sent the others to watch the other towers, but Ronan is my constant. I could never get rid of him, even if I wanted to. Why now? He must read the question in my eyes.

"I have been with her since she got here anyway, so I'm not leaving her now," he explains. "You are right. She's important, not just to you . . . but to me. I will never be able to have a future with her since I'm dead, but I can help keep her safe while she does what needs to be done."

"Are you sure about this?" I ask. I don't own Ronan. He is my friend, my brother. Guilt assaults me at his confession. I didn't even know he thought of and wished for a future with someone. We never spoke of it, only of the job, but he's right. All that was taken from him, and it was my fault, so if he wishes to follow Tate, I will not stop him. She would be better with him by her side.

"Yes, but will you be okay?"

"Ronan, I can take care of myself, brother. Just . . . keep our girl alive, alright?"

"Our girl?" he repeats as he starts to float away. "When did Tate Havelock become our girl?"

"The moment she walked into my office," I reply. "Now, go before she kills the fae. She needs him, Ronan, do you understand?"

He nods as he watches me. "Thank you, Shamus. I'll keep her safe."

I wave him off, and when he's gone, I slump back into my bed, alone for the first time in forever.

It will be strange not having Ronan at my side, but he's right. She needs him, and he deserves his freedom.

No one deserves it more.

"Shamus!" The scream fills the air, and I hear them all around me.

My unit is dying.

They were ambushed, all because of me.

It's my fault. I led them right into this trap. I knew better, but I was tired and wanted to get back. It was our last mission before we would be sent home.

I got sloppy, and now the ground is covered in my brothers' blood.

I glance over at Ronan, who's ducked behind a crumbling building to my right. The night sky doesn't give us much light, but I can see his silhouette from here.

I hear their constant gunfire spraying the entire area. It won't be long until it sprays us too. We need to find cover quickly.

"Ronan, stay low!" I order. "Return fire."

He nods, gripping his gun, and moves to the other side of the building. I watch him go before focusing on my own task. I have to trust him to stay alive.

We have to get out of here.

We have completed eighty missions, and we have not failed a single one. This will not be the first.

We are going home, all of us.

We have to.

I return fire, then I wait until they have to reload and dive for the next crumpling building. Ronan is turned away from me, so I cup his shoulder. "Come on, we have to get out of here," I snarl. When he doesn't reply, I pull his helmet off and freeze as he falls towards me, lifeless.

His eyes are open and empty, and his hands are covered in blood. As I glance down, I see the bullet holes across his chest.

Ronan is dead.

My best friend is dead.

"Ro—" I gasp as bullets rain down on my hiding spot. They are intent on wiping us out. Swallowing, I glance over the hard-packed dirt and see my team.

Henry is still reaching for his gun, cut down while doing so.

Ezra's body is huddled where he was hunkering down, waiting to return fire.

Joe was caught trying to get to me, his commander.

Dead.

They are all dead.

My entire unit is gone.

My friends, my brothers, the ones who have been with me since I was a child . . . they are gone.

I become cold and empty at the sight as something inside me shuts down and gives up. I should get out of here to report back then help collect their bodies, but none of it matters.

I do not want to live without them.

Turning back to Ronan, I press my forehead to his. "I'm sorry, brother. In this life or the next, we will be together again." Without much thought, I stand, leaving my gun behind.

I do not need it anymore.

Stepping out into the barrage of bullets, I stare them down.

Everyone else is dead.

I am all that is left.

A fury like no other fills me and explodes outward, washing the ground clean.

I jerk awake, my body covered in a cold sweat.

Rubbing at my face, I shudder in horror, the memory clinging to my skin before the noise comes again, the one that pulled me from my nightmares and memories.

It's a hunting alert, a sound I know better than my own heartbeat.

They always come here first, unless it's an imminent threat, and I grab my phone to scroll through the report summary so I can assign it to a team before I stop.

Shit, this one is a threat, but it is also an opportunity.

Scrambling from my bed, I make it to the door when the alarm sounds, alerting the entirety of Stalkers' Rest to the emergency dispatch to deal with the danger. Usually, I'd be out there with them, barking orders, but I sprint down the corridor and burst into Tate's room.

She's already sitting up, her eyes narrowed. Her training and years of experience force her up, even though she knows she isn't one of them anymore. Her boots are on, and her clothes are firmly in place.

The fae is at her side with his head cocked. He's curious but not bothered about being surrounded by enemies.

"You hear that?" I ask.

"The alarm? No, not at all," she scoffs, rolling her eyes. I'd punish her for her sass, but we don't have time.

"I can only delay them so long while giving orders and dispatching the hunting teams. They all heard the alarm, but you must get there first," I tell her, glancing around and finding Ronan on top of the dresser. "All of you, go."

"Why?" She frowns. "I'm not a hunter anymore. Besides, I'm supposed to be dead."

"Once a hunter, always a hunter, and because if I'm right and the alarm is sounding because of who I think it is, then he's someone you will want on your side."

"What the hell are you talking about?" she snaps as she crosses her arms and faces me.

"We don't have time for this," I hiss. "Go now. I'll send you all the information. Head to the tunnel. Beat the other hunters there. Be smart and be you. Earn his trust and collect him like you have us." I turn away when I hear the buzzing of my system, letting me know they are waiting.

I glance back. "Angel, your weapons are under your bed. I had them brought here," I tell her. "Come back alive."

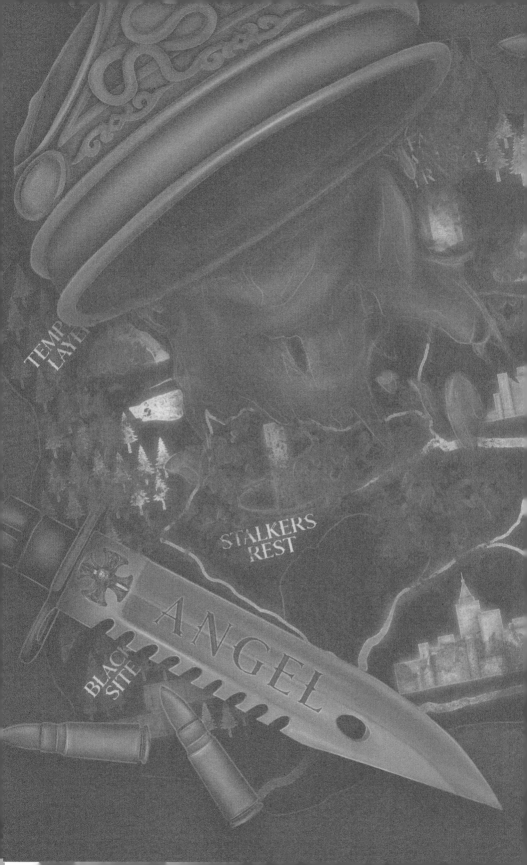

CHAPTER 16

Tate

When your commander orders you to go, you go.

I have no idea what he's talking about, but I put my trust in him. He hasn't betrayed me so far. Besides, I have never seen him so amped up or certain. We have to move fast and find whatever this is before the other hunters arrive.

It's probably a rogue vamp or something he wants me to save, and after checking the phone with the coordinates, I shove it in the bag with my weapons and arm myself before glancing at the fae and Ronan. "Let's hunt."

We make our way back down and out of the tunnel. Once in the forest, I pull out the phone and check the coordinates once more. "It's close. That's why everyone was alerted. It will take some time for the teams to form and set out, so we have a good head start, and I know a shortcut." I smirk as I glance at the fae. "Feel free to stay back if you want to."

"And miss bloodshed and death?" The wicked glint in his eyes grows. "Never."

"Fine, but stay out of my way," I order as I lift my bag higher and take off into the trees at a sprint. Shamus is right. We need to move fast if we want to save whoever this is.

Ronan floats at my side, and the fae simply appears before me every few feet. I sprint as hard as I can through familiar trails and over fallen logs, moving deeper into the forest.

Thirty minutes later, I come to a stop and drop my bag. After double-checking the coordinates, I zip up the bag, throw it over my shoulder again, and withdraw two blades. I have no idea what is in the cave, but I can never be too careful.

The opening is small and innocuous, just a black cave, one of hundreds around here, but there was an alert for a reason.

There are no tracks or signs of life, and I cannot taste any magic or see any blood. Stopping at the entrance, I place my hand on the thick stone and close my eyes.

Nothing.

Nothing has touched this or been through here in a very long time.

"I can sense something," the fae comments casually.

"What?" I ask as I open my eyes.

He shrugs, totally unbothered. "Something ancient and powerful."

"Well, that's helpful," I mutter. Ancient? What could be hiding out so close to Stalkers' Rest and be ancient? And why would Shamus send me here, so confident I needed to be here? It makes no sense, but there's no point in dwelling on it. I turn on the torch attached to the strap on my shoulder and duck into the cave without another word.

There is only one way to find out what's inside, and that's to look.

I keep my back to the cave wall as we move farther into the darkness, so that nothing can jump out at me. Stones crunch under my feet, and when I shine my light down, I realise it's not just stones, but bones as well. Whatever is here is a predator and a meat eater. I don't think these animals wandered in recently because the bones look old.

I move softly and slowly, taking my time. The light from outside soon fades, and the only way I can see is by the glow of my torch. My feet start to tilt, and I realise we are heading down.

After walking what feels like forever, we break out into a larger part of the cavern system. Unlike the fae cavern we found ourselves in, I have nothing but a bad feeling about this one.

There is nothing. The walls are smooth, as if worn by time or something else. The floor is covered in a deep, rusty sand that doesn't match any place around here, and I feel and see nothing else, bar ten ancient stone pillars placed within the sand to form a shape, and upon the top of each is an object.

Rolling my lips in, I search for threats, but there is nothing. I move forward, first one foot and then the other, and wait. When nothing springs out or attacks us, I slowly make my way to the closest pillar, eyeing the vase that stands on top. It's coated in thick dust, letting me know it's been here a while. There's a small crack down one side, intersecting, hand-painted art depicting a yawning chasm overspilling with blood and a clawed hand reaching from within. I lift my hand and gently touch the dusty surface.

Gasping, I jerk my hand away, scrubbing it on my leg.

"What is it?" Ronan asks. "This place is seriously creepy, even for a ghost."

"These are blood relics," I murmur as I glance around, realisation setting in. The tales I read from our manuals flood back—manuals Shamus made me read—and I realise who we are after. "Oh fuck, Shamus sent us here after the ancient blood tempest."

Shamus didn't want me to save them. He wanted me to tame them, the fool.

There is no taming a tempest.

There is only death.

"I thought they were all dead," Ronan whispers, looking terrified.

"No, not dead, dormant. They were deemed too evil to control, and we just walked right into its prison and rang the fucking dinner bell," I tell him as I glance back at them, opening my mouth to order them to retreat, but the surface under our feet shifts.

"It's awake."

The sand parts to create a passageway to a maze, the little tunnel carved throughout as if by magic. As I leap back to avoid it, one of the podiums starts to shake, and the blood vase topples from the tip, crashing into the sand. It splinters and cracks, and as I watch with wide-eyed fascination and horror, blood seeps from the vessel and into the maze below. It flows swiftly through the carvings in the sand, filling the maze and staining it red. Suddenly, the crust beneath our feet begins to shake, and I leap back out of the circle just as the earth rips open.

A chasm forms in the circle where I once stood, the yawning darkness leading down.

I share a look with Ronan and the fae before I look deeper in, seeing crudely carved stairs leading down into the abyss. The bloody sand slowly falls into the chasm, and an echoing groan can be heard from below.

"You know what? That doesn't sound good. How about we head back and eat ice cream or fuck instead? That sounds a whole lot more fun than whatever creep show is waiting in the ancient hole," Ronan mutters.

"I do like being eaten," I joke, and they both turn to gape at me.

"Was that a joke?" Ronan actually stumbles—well, floats backwards. "I am rubbing off on you. Wait, that's what she said. In all seriousness, do we have to go into the creepy hole?"

Grinning, I face forward and put my foot on the first step. When it doesn't crumple, I stomp down, testing each one as I go.

"I guess that's a yes. Why can't we just not chase monsters into the dark for one day and maybe go to a fair or something?" I hear Ronan mutter behind us.

"For someone who has faced death, you are very scared," the fae observes, and I glance back to see him wandering behind me, looking around without a care in the world.

"Not scared of death, just concerned a very normal amount about whatever creature needs to be trapped underground with a blood circle. In this case, you are both the weirdos," Ronan snaps.

I share a look with the fae and shrug. "He could be right." I look back at the steps leading down, and when I put my boot on the next one, it crumbles and falls away. I topple forward, ready to plummet, when arms wrap around me and yank me back. I hit a solid chest, and when I tip my head back, I meet the fae's mocking gaze.

"Every time I have to save you, it will cost you," he murmurs as he leans down and nips my ear. "Remember that, though I do think you like paying the cost, if my memory serves."

Rolling my eyes, I shove him backwards and glance down at the two missing steps. I lean back then throw myself forward, landing at least five steps farther down. Without checking to see if they follow, I continue down the winding staircase. It gets narrower the deeper we go, until it's only wide enough for half of one foot and I have to keep my hand on the wall to my left to keep my balance. Eventually, it gets so narrow that I sigh and stop, sick of this shit.

"This is wasting time," I mutter. "We need to be gone before the hunters arrive. Let's just jump down and see."

"How do we test if it's waiting to kill us?" the fae murmurs, peering over the edge into the dark. He doesn't appear afraid, more like excited.

"Like this," I reply as I kick his chest and watch as his eyes widen in shock as he falls backwards into the dark. A moment later, there is a thud and a groan. "Well? Have you been torn apart and eaten yet?"

There's a moment of silence. "No, but you are going to be, hunter."

"Did you really just try to kill him? I mean, I'm all on board with that plan, but let me know so we can get our stories straight," Ronan mutters.

"He wouldn't die, just be in a lot of pain, and he'd probably like it," I reply and leap off the edge, counting the drop like I did with him. I land a story down, bending my knees to absorb the impact.

A hand wraps around my throat, and I'm slammed back into the side of the stairs, forcing a grunt from my lungs. I do not fight back, but I do slip a blade free and press it against his groin in warning.

"That wasn't very nice, huntress," he hisses, his eyes shining in the dark.

"You didn't die, did you?" I retort, pushing the blade in deeper. "But if you try to kill me, I'll take your precious manhood with me, and we both know you like it a lot."

"I can grow it back." He smirks. "You'd still be dead."

"And you'd be left mad and hungry again," I counter.

He leans in, his eyes on me as his mouth almost touches mine. "You will pay for this later."

"I cannot wait," I hiss, refusing to back down.

"Erm, when you two are done flirting, maybe we can deal with that," Ronan whispers.

"With that?" we snap, following his gaze as we untangle ourselves. The shining orb Ronan is pointing at flickers out of existence, only to reappear again, and this time there are two.

They are floating in the air.

"Eyes," I whisper just as something snakes around my ankle and tears me across the cave. I do not scream, but I do pull another dagger.

I bend so I can reach my feet, then I slam a blade into whatever is holding me. There's a roar of pain, and I am lifted into the air. I hit something hard, my head bouncing from it, and for a moment I cannot see. Blinking to clear my vision, I crouch, holding a knife in each hand. If I'm right and this is a tempest, then the knives won't do much, but it will piss it off.

You need him. Shamus's words float in my head.

Why did he send me here?

Tempests cannot be reasoned with. They consume and kill. They are darkness and death.

Something huge slides in the shadows before me, obscuring my view of Ronan and the fae. An audible sniff fills the air, and a thick, garbled voice comes from the shadows. "Your blood smells ancient. What are you?"

"Human," I mutter as I strain my eyes, trying to make out the shape. It moves closer, so I step back, pressing deeper into a maze of tunnels leading from the pit, but I do not have much choice.

"Not entirely," the voice says, followed by another sniff.

Ignoring that, I narrow my eyes as I continue stepping back to avoid the shadows. "What's with the sniffing thing? Do I smell or something?" I ask nervously.

"Delicious. You smell delicious," it growls.

"Lovely," I mutter as I back up, the shadowy shape advancing on me like smoke but more corporeal. Is this a tempest's true form? I don't know much, but what I've read about them are legends and myths. They are not around much for anyone to figure out, and I'm not sure I will make it out to confirm what there is.

"Tate?" Ronan shouts, and the shape stills and turns, ready to head to them, so I try to draw its gaze back to me.

"Hey, tempest." It doesn't work, and the shadow moves fast to the fae and Ronan.

It seems intrigued by me and annoyed by them.

I do the only thing I can think of and draw my blade across my exposed forearm. The audible moan shakes the foundations of where we are, and I am suddenly slammed back into a wall of the tunnel.

The tempest's shadowy shape reappears, Ronan and the fae forgotten.

Something wet and warm drags along the wound—a tongue.

It's tasting me.

Gritting my teeth against the foreign yet not unpleasant feeling, I peer into the shadow. "I am not here to kill you."

"You are a hunter." The voice is sharp against my skin.

"I am, but I'm not here to hunt you," I admit, and the tongue slowly drags up my arm and across my shoulder then face. I turn my head away, but something within the shadow grips my cheek and turns it back, lapping at my lips.

"Truth," it hisses. "But they after you are."

"Yes," I answer without shame. "My commander thinks you will be useful in my hunt."

"I follow no one," it responds from the shadows. "I am a god."

"I do not need you to follow me, just work with me."

"In exchange for what?" The tongue drags across my cheek and down, sliding beneath my clothes. I slap at the shadows, but my hands are pinned to the wall as it continues its journey, shoving deeper into my clothes.

For fuck's sake, why are all monsters perverts?

I shiver as it traces the tips of my breasts.

"What do you want?" I ask, my voice even, which makes me proud.

The tongue stops for a moment, and I hesitate. "Freedom, I want my freedom. I have been trapped here for too long, only able to feed on what wanders in and send out remnants of my magic."

"Which alerted us," I muse. "If I grant you your freedom, what will you do?"

"Clever little hunter." It chuckles and withdraws. "Why don't you find out? If you want my help, then you must earn it."

It lets me go, and I frown, unsure what it means.

The shadows seem to thicken, and when I don't move, it comes closer until I have no choice but to turn and wander deeper into the labyrinth behind me. The tunnels are carved from stone, and the light is so dim, I can barely see. I choose tunnels at random, but when I pick wrong, the shadows move before me, blocking my way and turning me the way it wants.

It's leading me, and without much choice, I let it.

The air around me grows warm and humid as I walk. I'm sweating, and my muscles ache as though I've wading through water and not air. Suddenly, the tunnel opens up into a peaked archway made from stone. There is writing above it I cannot read or understand.

Well, I guess I'm heading into the creepy archway, right?

Taking a deep breath, I step through it, feeling a barrier slide across me. I shudder and hair rises on my arms, but I'm through.

Darkness surrounds me on the other side, and I turn, straining to see when flames burst to life, making me jerk back. They burn in huge basins at least three times taller than me, the flames licking at stone walls, and I turn as more burst to life around the huge chamber, filling it with an orange glow and even more warmth.

It seems to keep the shadow at bay, and when I turn, the glowing eyes peer at me from beyond the arched doorway, as if blocked.

The shadow stills and forms a limb, and it points up. Turning, I see what it gestured at.

It's a person suspended between heptagonal columns at the end of the room. Stepping closer, I crane my neck to look up.

The being is chained in the air above me.

He looks like a man.

The chain tightly crisscrosses his bare skin, causing his muscles to bulge. More hold him up by the neck, and another is across his mouth, gagging him.

Part of me pities him. Imagine being trapped like that for centuries for simply being who you are. Did anyone ever give this monster a chance?

Maybe that's why Shamus sent me here

I guess that proves one of the legends right. Tempests have the ability to project themselves.

"You were leading me here. Why?" I ask of the shadows as I glance back. "Is this you?"

"Yes," it hisses. "I am trapped. You must be strong enough to free me."

I glance back and step towards one of the columns, placing my hand on it.

My head falls back with a gasp, my eyes closing as my body jerks with power and understanding.

I rip myself away, panting as I glance from the shadow to the man. The knowledge I just stole runs through me.

To free him, I must replace those chains with my own.

Understanding dawns. A tempest needs a master. It needs someone to control it or it will go mad with power.

Shamus thought I could tame it, control it, and become its master.

What it said is true. It doesn't want to follow someone . . .

It wants to be owned by somebody.

CHAPTER 17

Tate

"That is what you want?" I ask of the shadows as the body jerks above me, the chains dancing in the air.

"Yes. A tempest without a master is uncontrollable. I was locked away when my old master died. Without one, I am doomed to this," it hisses. "If you want my help, huntress, then replace the chains. Give me my freedom and take my ownership."

Horror washes through me when I realise what he wants me to do, what Shamus sent me here to do. Did he know what it would cost?

Owning a tempest means being bound in life and death and transferring part of my soul to his. He would be mine, and there would never be peace or escape. Where I go, he goes. Yes, I have his power and support, but I will also never be alone again.

"If I do not choose this, what happens to you?" I ask.

"The hunters following you will slay me. I will not be able to protect my body forever. I will be lost," he says casually, as if he isn't speaking about his death. "It is your choice."

"You are not angry that you cannot survive without an owner? That you have been trapped, waiting for centuries just for being what you are?" I snap.

"No. It is who I am," he murmurs. "I whispered to your

commander over and over, sensing a power within the structure, one that called to me. It has taken years for him to listen to me. I called to you, mistress. Do you not understand that?"

If I don't do this, he will die, and something about an ancient creature like a tempest being slaughtered while chained fills me with sadness and regret. I know this world would suffer for it. He's a creature of power, purpose, and fate. The world would weep at his loss.

Maybe it wasn't just Shamus who led me here. The thought frightens me, but I realise Shamus is right. I need this power. To survive what is to come, I need to be invincible. The people I am going after are monster hunters, and they have faced evil every day. There will be no stopping them alone.

How far am I willing to go for revenge?

For cleansing our people?

I vowed I would give up everything if I survived that place and them.

I would give it all for revenge and to rid this world of evil. I would make a deal with the devil. I would corrupt my soul. I would shatter my life and body. I would become what I need to become.

"If I do this, you will be mine?" I ask the shadow.

He writhes with excitement and hope. "Yes, yours. I will face your enemies with you. Yours to control. To use."

"Is that what you want?" I ask, stepping closer until I can press my hand to the barrier. The shadow writhes across the other side, forming a hand to press to mine. "Do you want to belong to me?"

"Nobody has ever asked me that before," he hisses, then there's a pause. "Yes, yes, I want to belong to you. Your soul is delicious, and you are deserving. Yes, mistress, I want to be yours."

I blow out a breath and drop my hand. "Then so be it." Turning back to his body, I stop under the chained man. "How do I do this?"

"Blood. Always blood, mistress. It is how we feed. It must be freely given."

I glance down as a maze of intricate patterns forms in the sand with a circle in the middle. I drop to my knees below his body and pull the blade free, knowing and accepting the cost.

I sink the dagger into my heart, and agony tears through me as the blade plunges deep. My blood runs from the wound and down, staining the sand even as the wound seems to heal around the dagger.

Agony races through my body, tearing me apart as the dagger pulls free on its own and drops to the sand. The man above me groans, as do the shadows, as I bow over my open chest, feeling like I'm dying.

"Shattering the soul hurts," he hisses behind me. "You must be strong enough to endure it."

Panting, I glance back at the shadow with narrowed eyes. "I have endured worse. I do not fear pain."

"Nor death," it remarks. "You will do well."

The sand cracks, and I glance back as a hand punches through it. It's coated in blood.

My blood, I realise.

The claw-tipped hand turns towards me, and my body hardens in anticipation of the pain, but I cannot contain my scream.

My back arches as that bloodied hand reaches inside me, ripping through skin and muscle and reaching my soul.

"Endure it!" he roars. "You are strong enough. Find that strength, find what hides beneath you. Find what has kept you alive when others would have died."

My eyes roll back in my head as the hand drags me into the air. My legs and arms dangle below me as I hover, my blood dripping steadily to the sand. My soul tears as the claws shred it.

Find it, find it.

Strong enough.

I am. I can endure this. I have to.

I repeat it over and over, even as it feels like I die a thousand deaths. I hold on, gripping onto my life with every fibre of my strength. Even as death comes for me, I roar in its face, refusing to go.

I can taste my blood, and I can feel it filling my eyes and ears. I feel like I am drowning in it as the hand twists inside me, pulling a shard of my soul free. It starts to pull from my chest, causing pure agony as it releases me.

I hit the sand with a thump, my strings cut. My eyes are open, but my body is unable to move as the hand moves up and sinks into the tempest above me. His back arches and his mouth opens on a harrowing scream as the glowing shard of my soul is pushed deep inside him.

The chains seem to hiss as my blood slides across the links, and I watch the tempest turn slowly in the chains until he faces me.

The hand pulls back, leaving a gaping wound in his bare chest, matching mine.

Both of us are dying. His blood steadily drips down, splattering my chest, and magic fuses into my skin. When I look down, I see my skin stitching back together over the wound. My muscles heal, and my bones snap back together. I look up just in time to see his eyes open and lock on me.

"Mistress," he hisses, showing rows upon rows of sharp teeth, like a shark's. There's a roar, and I roll my head back into the sand as the barrier falls and the shadow rushes into the chamber. It brushes over me before plunging into the tempest's open mouth. He swallows the darkness, then his mouth snaps shut as the chains release him from the columns.

He falls through the air, plummeting to the sand.

He lands on his knees, blood-coated chains slithering across his skin like snakes as he kneels before me, his arms and legs trapped.

Climbing to my knees, I sway as the magic continues to heal me.

His skin is pale, like he has never seen sunlight, and he has more muscles than I have ever seen. He looks like the gods carved him, and my cheeks flame when I realise he's naked. His cock stiffens and stands at attention, throbbing and leaking what looks like blood.

As I watch in fascination and horror, a chain slithers across his throat, wrapping around it multiple times to form a collar, and then it fuses together, solidifying and turning into metal. In the middle of it is the hunters' symbol—a sign of ownership.

The man moans, his hips rolling as if he enjoys it, and I see blood seeping from the collar where it digs into his skin. Somehow, I know if I die, it will fall away, but it cannot be removed any other way.

No other can become his master now. I am until death.

"Mistress," he hisses once more as he lifts his head. Big pools of obsidian stare up at me in hunger and want.

"Did it work?" I ask, even though I know the answer. I can feel it. A throb in my chest echoes in his. I can feel him all over and in me, although I still feel weak from what happened.

"Yes, mistress," he hisses, his head tilting like an animal. "We must finish sealing the bond though."

"How?" I ask, still swaying.

"You must drink, mistress."

I frown, not understanding, and he crawls towards me, naked and chained. The sight should disturb me, but instead desire courses through me.

I fall back, but he simply crawls over me, sliding up my body. Shit. I try to scoot backwards as his hips stop above my face. A droplet of blood drips from the tip of his cock, hitting my cheek as I turn away.

"You must drink, mistress. I took you into my body, so now you must take me," he hisses, pressing towards me.

"Fuck that," I mutter.

Flipping, I grip the sand and try to drag myself away, but the chains wrap around me, yanking me under him.

"Let me serve my mistress."

I am turned over, and his cock is presented to me again.

"If you do not, our bond will break and you will die," he pleads, his eyes widening like open pools. "Please, mistress."

"Is this the only way?" I mutter.

Why does it have to be his cock, for fuck's sake?

Why are monster rituals such sexual things?

"Yes, mistress, quickly," he hisses, flashing his fangs. Another drop of blood drips down, and this time I let it hit my lip. It seems to absorb into my skin, and I shudder as power shoots through me. Another drip and I open my mouth, letting it hit my tongue.

He groans as he watches me. "Please, mistress." His hips roll desperately.

With no choice, I wrap my lips around his cock, drinking the blood from him. My hand strokes him as I suck his tip. Each drop is a burst of power, chasing away the weakness.

Pumping him harder, I drink his pleasure. When he bellows and jerks in my mouth, thrusting his cum down my throat, I swallow it down.

As I lick up every drop, he whines, his hips stuttering and pushing deeper. I release him from my mouth, all my weakness gone.

I feel stronger than I ever have, though I'm slow to admit that.

I feel . . . *powerful.*

Sitting up, I slide out from under him as he shudders, and the chains finally fall away, dropping into the sand and seeming to absorb into it. He sways on his knees, his chest heaving.

The sight he presents is incredible, but when his eyes open, I look away, not wanting the tempest to realise how truly tempting he is.

His voice is softer when he speaks. "It is done, mistress. We cannot be parted now."

Nodding, I lean back into the sand, swallowing thickly and giving myself a moment to breathe, but he seems to take that as an invitation.

He lies across my lap and purrs like a cat, arching up into me until I stroke his hair and back without meaning to. My hand seems to find his body as if it's an extension of mine, and his eyes close in bliss.

I should push him away, but something about him being close brings me comfort. It's probably my soul inside him connecting with me, or at least that's what I tell myself as the seven-foot, muscle-bound tempest curls around me.

"Well, you certainly have a way with monsters," the fae deadpans, and I look up to see him leaning casually against a column. My eyes widen, and I wonder how long he's been there. "I enjoyed the show, but unless you would like to release me long enough to kill those hunters, I suggest we leave. I believe you would be against a massacre."

Ronan floats at his side, and just then, I hear echoes from above.

"Hunters," I murmur. "They are here."

CHAPTER 18

Tem

"**H**unters like you?" I ask curiously.

"Sort of," she mutters, glancing at the ghost and the fae. Their magic is familiar and strange at the same time, but I know what they are to her through our bond. "We need to get out before they find us."

"I can kill them for you, mistress," I offer happily, but she glares at me, and I shrink back. I just wanted to make her happy, but from that soul-withering look, I don't think she would like it.

"No, they are my people. We need to get out without them seeing us," she snaps, annoyance in her tone, and I perk up. I want to prove I am useful to her and that she made the right choice in her sacrifice.

I am here to serve her. Her wants and needs matter more than my own happiness and comfort.

I want to make her proud.

I send my magic out, and it floods the entire cavern with my shadow. I hear the hunters above call out and stop as they are blinded. Turning to the columns I was trapped between, I hold out my hand and close my fist.

A hole opens in the air, tunnelling up to the earth above. She glances at me, and I smile. "Come." I step inside. She follows, and after walking up the slanted tunnel, we break out a few miles away from the entrance to my cavern. I turn to her as I close the hole so they cannot follow, leaving them lost in the shadows until they give up.

"Did I do well, mistress?" I ask excitedly as she glances around.

She looks back at me, her lips tilted down. "Sure."

I pout as I stare at her. The ghost at her side slings his arm around her shoulders, tugging her close despite her pulling some iron chains out and threatening him with them.

"Give the puppy something," Ronan, I believe his name is, jokes. "Look how cute he is right now, trying so hard to impress you."

She glances at me, her eyebrows drawing together as my pout grows and wetness builds in my lashes. I drop to my knees, my head bowed. "I am sorry, mistress. I just wanted to help."

"Fucking hell," she mutters, and a minute later, a hand lands on my head. My body reacts instantly, knowing it's her touch. Every nerve comes alive as I arch up, rubbing into her as she pats my hair. "You did good."

"Thank you, mistress." I wrap my arms around her legs and hug her. She sighs and tries to kick me away, but I wrap my whole body around her, grinning as I press my chin to her hip.

Her arms are held out at her sides as she stares at me in exasperation before looking at the fae and ghost. "Don't look to me for help." Ronan laughs. "He's your puppy."

"Let's get back before they come looking," she mutters. Reaching down awkwardly, she pats my head again. "Come on, I need to hide you for now. Can you, erm, release me?"

"Yes, mistress, whatever you wish." I release her and jump to my feet. "Shall I tear us another exit—"

"No, no, it's okay." She pats my shoulder to soften her quick words. "We will walk."

"Aww, really?" the ghost whines as she turns and heads into the forest.

The fae steps before me, eyeing me up and down before nodding. "She is mine too. Do not make me kill you."

"If you kill me, you'll kill her," I respond in confusion. "Mistress can have whomever she wishes. I will even serve you if she so asks."

He blinks, and his grin is slow. "We will get along well. Come, your mistress has a way of trying to escape those who wish to be at her side."

"She cannot escape me." I shrug. "I can simply follow my soul."

Shaking his head, he walks by my side until we reach a giant building. This is where I was whispering to.

She crouches, and I drop to my knees at her side, glancing from her to it and back. She must feel me looking because she glances at me.

"Do you have a name?" she asks me curiously.

"I am whatever you wish to call me, mistress," I supply happily, but she frowns and sighs, and I slump in defeat, hating her disappointment. "I am a tempest. We were not named. Our masters name us. Names have power, and it is theirs for the choosing."

"I want you to choose your own name," she snaps, and I recoil. Is she angry at me? "You are a person—well, sort of. You have your own will."

"Is this . . . my mistress's will?" I frown, confused.

"Yes," she retorts, and I frown harder. My old master named me to control me, to use it against me. He would take it away at will when I annoyed him. I have waited centuries for a worthy master after his death. Many have tried to claim me but were not strong enough, nor did I want them to.

Their souls felt . . . wrong.

They craved my power and body, but my new mistress does not. Yes, she wishes to use my strength, but she always wanted to free me. Now, she offers me another freedom. I am grateful and know I made the right choice.

If I did not want the bond, it would have been broken, though what I told her is true—she could claim me, but I have to accept it as well, and I did.

I wanted her.

I worry that she doesn't want me the same way though. She tasted and touched me, so that means she desires me the way I desire her, yes? I guess time will tell.

"Tem," I offer. "I like tempest. Tem is cute, I think."

She tilts her head, eyeing me, and a small smile curls her lips. "Tem, I like it. Okay then, Tem. Follow us, and please behave. No weird magic."

"Weird magic?" I sit up taller, happy that she likes my name, and she stares at me. The more she does, the more I feel my features shifting and adapting.

I adapt as I am near her, and she frowns. "What's happening?"

"I adapt to what you most desire," I reply. "Do you like it?" I slide my hand down my chest, and her lips thin, her expression cold and angry, but I feel her desire in my soul.

My smile grows.

She cannot hide from me, even if she wishes to.

"That is weird magic," she finally clarifies.

"Oh." I sigh. "Okay, mistress."

"It's going to be a long day," she mutters as she turns back and stands. "Let's go."

CHAPTER 19

"**G**lad to see you made it back alive," Shamus remarks as he steps into his office.

Tem sits on the floor at my feet. I could not make him sit at my level. I did, however, get him to wrap a blanket around his waist, though he could not understand why.

He kept asking if I did not like looking at him.

My cheeks are still red from that because damn it, of course I do. He's the epitome of beauty and he knows it. If what he said is true, then he has adapted to become what I desire, and it's working against me.

"And you brought a guest." Shamus smirks as he sits down heavily in his chair, looking at Tem.

I follow his gaze to the man sitting at my feet, one hand snaking along my leg like he cannot resist. When he feels my gaze, he glances up at me, smiling brightly. How someone like him has survived so long, I will never know.

Ronan is right. He's like a happy, little puppy, just centuries old and more powerful than any other being.

Black strands escape his tied back hair, and his features are wide and strong. His nose is thicker than when I first saw him, as is his jaw.

His eyes are bigger but just as black, and his skin is dotted with freckles. He's huge and muscular and far too pretty.

"You are lustful. Do you wish me to serve you, mistress?" he asks.

"Fucking hell." I pinch my nose and look away. "No, just, go play with Ronan or something please."

"Wait, what?" Ronan groans. "I am not your puppy sitter."

Shamus's eyebrow arches as he looks at Tem then me. "So I was right. He is a tempest. It's interesting that you managed to seal the bond."

"You knew," I snap.

"I suspected. I heard whispers in my dreams for years, magic I understood. When I felt them again tonight and heard the alarm, I knew they found him or felt his magic. It all worked out, did it not?"

"I nearly died." I lean forward, annoyed.

"But you didn't," he counters. "I knew you were strong enough to endure it."

Sitting back, I cross my arms in irritation as the fae steps behind Shamus and meets my gaze over his shoulder. He has been quiet until now, but the first words out of his mouth are batshit insane. "He insults you. Would you like me to kill him for you?"

"I can help," Tem offers.

Shamus waits, surrounded by powerful, immortal monsters who could destroy him, yet he doesn't argue or seem afraid. He stares back at me, one eyebrow slowly arching.

"No." I sigh. "If anyone ever kills this asshole, it will be me."

The fae shrugs and heads my way, kneeling at my other side, and I keep my eyes on Shamus, ignoring them. "What now?" I query.

He watches me for a moment. "I have a favour to ask."

I blink in surprise. Shamus does not seem like the type to ask for favours. "What is it?"

"Before you go after Black, I need you to go somewhere for me."

"Another to collect?" I scoff.

"Not this time," he admits, leaning forward. "I need you to do what you do best—hunt. I know you want revenge, but this is important. Monsters are turning up dead, and eyes are turning to us. In retribution, our people, good hunters, are being slaughtered. I need you to figure out what it is and make it stop. After, I will tell you everything I have on Black, and you can hunt him to your heart's desire. I will even help you."

"I am to kill whatever is doing this, yes?" I frown. "And if I do, you'll let me hunt Black and my old team?"

"Yes." He sits back and slides a tablet across to me. "You have access to my personal hunting gear and garage. Take what you need, but get this done fast. I am worried about what this means for both us and them."

"You worry an awful lot about monsters for a hunter," I murmur as I grab his iPad and scan the information.

"This world needs both of us. It needs balance. I might be a hunter, but I do not hate monsters. I simply do not want the evil ones to take over. I have my reasons like most hunters. I was born human, and I fight for my people and now theirs. I grew to a place of power to be able to do that. Now, I'm asking for your help. You're the best there is. Moreover, you are someone I can trust to do the right thing."

"You know what it is?" I ask after looking over the report. There's a map with pinpoints where the bodies are. Whatever it is, it isn't targeting a specific type of monster. There are vamps, wolves, trolls, and even a minor god, which would not be easy. It is strong and deadly, so I can understand his worry, and that many bodies will cause the monster community to be out for blood, thinking it's a rogue hunter or one of us.

"Not a clue, but every single body had one thing in common," he admits.

"What's that?" I question, lifting my head.

"They were exsanguinated," he answers.

"Vampyr?" I frown. "Though drinking from other monsters would poison them, not make them stronger."

"Exactly." Shamus nods. "I will deal with the returning hunters. Go figure out what it is and stop it before it's too late."

Standing, I glance at my new . . . team. "Are you ready to become hunters?"

"I am not wearing a uniform," the fae drawls as he stands.

"I am!" Tem exclaims.

Ronan salutes me. "Sir, yes, sir."

Looking back at Shamus in pain, I wordlessly beg for his help. He simply smiles.

That beautiful bastard.

"Good hunting, angel."

It doesn't take long to pack up. I am used to being on the go at the drop of a hat.

Heading down in Shamus's personal elevator, we stop at a different level and step out into his private armoury.

Neon lights flicker on, throwing everything into a slightly blue hue. There are silver, metal shelves built into the walls filled with every weapon imaginable. There are also clothing racks to the left and a private garage with a bulletproof SUV, a truck, and two motorbikes at the back.

I whistle as I look around. No wonder they call him the stalker.

Putting my bag down on the metal table in the middle, I rip the duffle open and browse the shelves for anything I might need.

I grab a couple of daylight grenades, just in case it is a vampyr, and some holy water and chains. I pile them in my bag with my usual weapons, ignoring the fact I have a tempest, a fae, and a ghost. I will not depend on them if I do not have to.

I was a hunter before them, and I will continue to be after them.

Pulling a new jacket down, I slip it on and braid my hair as best as I can, but it's short and finicky, and I get annoyed until the fae takes over and does it for me.

"Thanks," I mutter as I grab the keys to a car and click the fob before my eyes land on a pair of brand-new leather gloves sitting on the table.

They are too small to belong to Shamus.

Heading over, I finger them. Did he get them for me?

I slip them on, and I'm surprised when they fit perfectly, but I'm not questioning it as I zip my bag, sling it over my shoulder, and head towards the car. "Come on, time to go."

Something that is new, though, is that we do not need to spend hours travelling by car, which I did not think of.

"I am not riding in that tin box for hours." The fae snaps his fingers, opening a portal. "Let's go."

Giving the car one last look, I peer through the portal, admitting it would be easier. I guess I need to adapt, but annoyance runs through me. Didn't I just say I didn't want to rely on them? The quicker we finish this hunt, though, the quicker I can get on Black's tail.

It's the only reason I step through the portal, trusting the fae to get us where we need to go. Once I'm out the other side, I find myself in a park, the city stretching before us—the monster's hunting ground. The fae steps through, then Tem and Ronan, and it closes. I glance at them and frown. "Let's go."

"Where do we start?" Ronan asks, bouncing up and down.

"At the end, with the dead," I reply.

CHAPTER 20

Fae

I can tell Tate hates relying on anyone. It's in her attitude and refusal to ask us for help as she tracks down those who have been killed by whatever is haunting this city. I could find out easily enough, but I'm curious about her, and watching her is fun. Her mind is interesting. She thinks like a monster without even realising it.

She finds the hunting grounds easily enough, and after opening the gates, she pulls her gloves back on. "With me," she mutters.

We all follow, mainly because I suspect this will end in bloodshed and death and what is better than that? Besides, I can play along with her for now if it gets me what I want.

I have no love for hunters or other monsters. They can all kill themselves off if they want, we do not care, but when my hunter is involved, so am I.

We move a few blocks south, and she stops before what looks to be a normal coffee shop, with plants hanging outside. Gold lettering in the window proudly declares Venom Café is open all day and night, but I can sense the monsters inside.

A monster shop?

Interesting. I suppose it makes sense, though it has been a long time since I was amongst the humans like this. They seem as oblivious as always.

Us fae tend to stick to our own courts in our realm, tired of their games and greed for our magic. We rely on traditions and pure blood, although the two courts war, but that is an issue for another time.

Uncaring that she even smells like a hunter, Tate heads straight for the door and pushes inside. A bell sounds, and every eye turns to her. The music stops, and people get to their feet, gawking at her. I step inside behind her, daring them with my eyes to make a move.

They share looks, and some hurry for the back door, no doubt sensing what and who she is. Terror fills the air alongside anger, but she doesn't react to the hateful glares.

"There better be a good fucking reason for a hunter to be in my shop," a loud voice barks.

"There is," Tate replies, not the least bit scared of the ogre behind the counter glaring at her like he is going to rip her apart. With a smile, she heads past the counter and to the door next to it. "Follow me," she orders and steps inside.

I follow happily, and once she heads into what looks to be a break room, we wait. The floor shakes as the ogre heads in and slams the door. "Gods dammit, Tate, my girl, you can't be walking in like that and scaring all my customers! Do you know how bad it is for business to have a hunter in my shop?"

"Rude, I thought we were friends, Car," she says with a smile, and the ogre huffs but smiles.

"Only in secret. Can't be ruining my rep," he says as he sits heavily in a chair that groans under his weight. "What brought you here? Haven't seen you in almost a year. I have a feeling it isn't anything good."

"You hear and know everything. All types come in here. What do you know about the recent killings?"

"Eh, figured it was a hunter," he admits. "It's what they are saying, some hunter going rogue."

"Not us," she says. "We have intel it's a monster."

"Well, shit, monsters preying on other monsters now? What is the world coming to?" he mutters, leaning back. "The last one was a vamp, overheard it myself. There are some new big bad vamps around keeping order, and they are pissed, but they have their hands full elsewhere. I'd suggest getting someone on the inside and asking what they know about it."

"I can do that." She stands. "If you hear anything, let me know, okay?"

"Will do." He stands. "Oh, and Tate? Catch the fucker doing this."

"You've got it."

We head out of the back door, and once in the alley, she leans against the wall and pulls out a phone, dialling someone.

I move closer, pressing my cheek to it, curious and nosy. Tem picks up her hair and starts playing with it, and she rolls her eyes as if that will help her.

"Well, well, well, if it isn't my favourite huntress." I hear the purring words, and curiosity fills me even more.

"What's up, bloodsucker?" she replies, but she's grinning, and they chuckle, which makes my eyebrows rise.

"Don't try to sweet-talk me. You skipped our cheese night," he grouses. "My mate wanted to meet you."

"Sorry, Simon," she says sadly. "Shit came up. Speaking of, I need your help."

"Mine? Well, shit, can't say I'd look as good in leather as you, but I can try."

She smirks, even as she smacks Tem's hand away. His pout makes her sigh, and when he drops to his knees, pressing his face into her stomach, she idly strokes his hair. I find my own hand snaking across her shoulder, and she turns her glare to me in warning.

"I'm sure your mate would like you in leather, but not what I meant. I heard there's been some cross species killing in the city. Do you know anything?"

She turns away again, glancing around to check the perimeter, and I take my opportunity, licking her delicious neck. She slaps me, but I ignore her and push closer, tracing my tongue along her vein. I recall the way her blood tasted, and it has me groaning and rubbing against her side.

"I mean, I've heard some things. There have been some bodies that were fully drained. Everyone thought it was a vamp, but Al—the . . . my friend." He coughs. "She's . . . well, she's kind of in charge now, and she didn't think it was a vamp, not really, but she's busy dealing with a rogue vamp herself. Why? Are you hunting whatever it is?"

"Yeah," Tate answers, elbowing me, so I dig my teeth into her neck, making her hiss. She pulls a blade and rams it into my crotch in warning. I lean back, arching an eyebrow. Our eyes meet in a standoff.

"Everything okay? What's that noise?" Simon asks.

"Just a giant mosquito," she snarls, digging her dagger into my crotch. "You found your friend?"

"Yeah, Althea, you heard of the judges?" he whispers.

Tate frowns but nods. "A rumour. They are real?"

"Very much so. You'd get on. I'll take you to meet her one day. As for what you're hunting, there are some rumours, but I don't know how true they are."

"Anything could help," Tate replies, narrowing her eyes on me as I dart my tongue out and lick my bottom lip, wanting her blood again.

She can glare all she wants, but we both know she enjoyed it.

Silly human constraints surround what pleasure means, and it seems she is sticking to them as she warns me with a glare. Pleasure is whatever you wish it to be. It can be beautifully painful, dangerous, or dark, and I know when Tate gives into what is between us, it will be magnificent. Until then, I will keep pushing her.

How cruel it must be to be born into an existence that's so short and fleeting, where your greatest nemesis is time and yourself.

"Okay, well, most of the bodies were found near one area of the city, which led to most of the stories. There's a rumour amongst the vamps and wolves that something is hiding in the reflecting pool. The wolves have been staying clear of Meadows Park just in case," Simon offers. "But be careful. If it's true, then this thing is dangerous."

"You should warn the monster I'm just as dangerous," she

murmurs, her eyes locked on me, and something about that makes my cock harden as her eyebrow arches in challenge.

"True. After you're done, come meet Althea. Like I said, I think you'll get on well. Besides, she has something you might be able to help her with."

"Well, now I'm intrigued. Okay, I'll text you when I'm done. See you soon." She hangs up, pressing the knife deeper. "Are you going to behave?"

"Never," I admit freely, and she sighs, pulls the knife from my groin, and puts it away.

She relaxes back into the wall, still petting the tempest. Ronan floats before us, watching us with curiosity.

"Can you trust him?" Ronan asks. "He is a vamp, after all."

"And you're a ghost. What's your point?" She smirks as she puts her phone away. "Yes, I can. I met him a while ago just after his change. He was searching for his friend and got into trouble. He's a good kid. He wouldn't lie to me."

"I need to feed again," I interrupt, finding I do not like it when her eyes are not on me. Her gaze snaps to me.

"Are you fucking with me?" she snarls.

"Unless you want me to go feral and unleash my pain on this world?" I shrug, a slow smile curling my lips.

"I need to be at full strength for this hunt," she protests, her lips thinning.

Stepping closer, I press my finger to her chin and tip it up. She jerks her face from my hand, but I lean in, blowing my words across her lips. "Then let me feed on something else."

"Like what?" she asks, her voice strong, but I sense the slight tremor underneath—fear and anticipation.

My hunter wants me, even if she won't admit it to herself.

"Desire," I whisper.

She glances at my lips, her unspoken words sliding through her eyes before they shutter, trying to shield herself from me. "No." Her voice hits me like a dagger.

"Then I guess I'll feed on death and pain in the city," I drawl as I turn away.

"Fine!" She grabs the nape of my neck, tugging me back around. "If you feed from me, you won't hurt any innocents?"

"Not tonight at least," I answer truthfully. I didn't plan to anyway, nor do I need to feed, but I want to feed from her.

Her lips thin further, and her nostrils flare in anger. She hates being cornered, but she still takes control, refusing to back down. "Ronan, Tem, take watch. Make sure nobody sees or sneaks up on us," she barks out, and then she arches a brow at me. "You have five minutes. Can you make that work?"

"I can make five minutes feel like an eternity," I promise seductively, and knowing that is her permission, I slam her into the wall. My hand glides down her front and slips into her trousers, cupping her cunt while I feed at her mouth. Our lips meet in a messy kiss, our eyes open and narrowed on each other.

Sliding my fingers through her warm, soft folds, I press two inside her. Her back arches as she lifts onto her toes to escape my invading touch, a gasp slipping free, and I drink it down in victory as I add a third finger, stretching her tight, wet heat. I felt her with my magic last time I fucked her, but I can't wait to feel my cock sinking into her perfect cunt. I know if I try to fuck her now, she'll gut me, so I don't risk it. I take the scraps I am given, our tongues battling as I thumb her clit until her eyes shut on a cry. Her hands grip my shoulders, digging in like daggers, and my smile is smug as I lean back. She pants, leaning into the wall, her channel clenching around me as I keep up my quick pace. She's close, but I don't just want to feel it.

I want to taste it.

I want to taste the surrender on her skin.

I want this huntress vulnerable and weak for me. If I can't have her pain and blood right now, then I'll take that instead.

I do not kneel for anyone, however, not even for the paradise between her thighs. Instead, I hoist her up the wall and throw her legs over my shoulders as I use my magic to strip her of her trousers and panties. She's bare before me, pink and glistening, her clit throbbing for my attention as she drips.

She jerks, her eyes narrowing as she glances down, and I press my mouth to her, licking up her desire with a hum.

"Three minutes," she rasps.

"Keep counting, huntress. You'll be screaming before you reach zero," I promise as I thrust my tongue inside her, stretching it with my magic until it grows and touches her cervix. I curl it as she grinds into my face. Her muted noises of pleasure fill my ears, each one a victory. Her surrender is better than any battle I have ever won. I barely remember anything other than this little huntress now and the way her thighs tighten, trapping my face between her thighs as she rides me, using me for her pleasure.

"One minute," she gasps. Wanting to stop her from talking, I bite down on her cunt. She cries out as her body locks up, and she comes. Her pleasure slides from her core and onto my waiting tongue, but I'm not happy with this. I want more. Thrusting my fingers back inside her cunt, I circle her hole with my tongue before lashing her clit as I hold her there with my magic, and then I slip my other fingers into her tight ass. It fights me, just like she does, but I force them inside until she's riding all of me. Her cries grow louder, and just before her timer hits its mark, she screams again, coming all over me.

I drink every drop of it until I'm virtually dizzy.

Sliding her down my body, I dress her again so she won't stab me, then I kiss her once more, forcing her to taste her pleasure.

When she rips away, her face is flushed, but her lips are thin in annoyance.

"A deal's a deal. You will not hurt anyone tonight."

"I wouldn't have anyway," I admit. "I just wanted to taste your pretty pussy." I step back, letting her feet hit the cement once more as I suck on my fingers.

She gapes at me, and between one second and the next, she's flying at me with a dagger. I can't help but chuckle as I catch it and spin her so she's trapped in my arms.

"If you want to play again, all you have to do is ask," I whisper, "but you have a hunt, don't you?" Smacking her hip, I let her go and duck under her swing. "We can stay here all night with you trying to kill me. It's turning me on and will only end with you impaled on my cock, but then you won't be able to hunt. Your choice, Tate."

Her chest heaves as she debates what she wants more. Sparing me one last disgusted look, she puts her dagger away and turns, marching back into the street, ignoring my dark chuckle that chases her.

CHAPTER 21

Tate

I ignore them all as best as I can, embarrassment and anger warring inside me. I gave in to the fae too easily. I thought I was doing it to keep everyone safe, but the truth is, part of me wanted it, and I hate that he knows and uses it against me.

Now is not the time for my heightened, confused emotions though. Being distracted in a hunt is a death sentence, so I try to push them aside and focus. The information Simon gave me leads me to Meadow Park.

The black iron gates at both entrances are chained, and the park easily spans three miles, with running paths, a pond, and even a small coffee shop. During the day, it would be filled with human families and dogs, but now it remains empty and dark, a foreboding feeling coming from the trees.

The old oaks reach high into the sky, their branches casting horrific shadows across the ground. Pursuing my lips, I pull off a glove and press it to the gate.

Flashes of pain, blood, and death reach me. Something touched this gate recently, something dark. The cries of the dead call to me, striking my brain until I have to yank my hand away so I am not overwhelmed, but as always, it stains not just my brain, but my soul.

I pull my glove on and try to ignore the bile crawling up my throat. "This is the right place."

"Are you sure?" Ronan asks as he floats up, hovering over the gate. "I don't see any bodies or anything."

"Doesn't mean whatever is hunting isn't here, and it's hungry, very hungry," I murmur as I step back and eye the gate once more. The lock is thick. I could waste hours trying to cut it. If this thing hunts at night, then it should be slinking from its hiding place soon. I want to catch it before then.

"I'll climb over," I begin, eyeing the fence to the side. There are spikes on top, but I can clear them.

The fae rolls his eyes and flicks his fingers, and the lock drops free, the gate swinging open. "Or we could just do that."

Frowning, I glare at him then the gate. "Do not help. This is my hunt. I didn't need magic before, and I don't need it now."

"Is your fight not a result of magic?" he reasons. "You use that, so why not use us?"

Ignoring him and his logic, I reluctantly stomp through the gate before softening my footsteps. Whatever is here will probably sense us coming if not hear us—most monsters can. There is no way to quieten my heartbeat, breathing, or footsteps enough to fool monsters. This often leaves us without the element of surprise, but that doesn't mean I'll give up.

Heading down the winding path, I follow the cute wooden signs pointing towards the pond. Once we reach it, I stare at the still, calm water. It's a round, natural pool the park was built around.

There is a path all the way around it with a small island in the middle that seems to be for wildlife, but it's empty. There aren't even any birds or fish that I can see.

Ripples suddenly rush across the surface, as if someone is breathing under there.

Great.

This is definitely the place.

Crouching on the grassy verge, I eye the water, hesitant to reach out and touch it. Is it a water creature? Maybe it's a nymph, though I haven't heard of them being able to drain a full monster, never mind take a grown one down. Maybe it's a trapped siren or mermaid. The possibilities are endless and too many to account for.

I glance at the three men—erm, monsters behind me. "Sense anything?" I wouldn't usually ask, but I don't want to go in blind if I can help it. Whatever is hunting these monsters is strong enough to kill and drain them. I need every advantage I can get, so even though I hate relying on anyone else, I have to.

We are a team, or at least Shamus hopes we will be.

"Magic." The fae shrugs, looking bored and uninterested.

"Obviously. What kind?" I snap.

He arches his eyebrow. "The knowledge will cost you."

"Forget it," I mutter, glancing back at the water.

"It's a portal," Tem murmurs, and I glance over to see him crouching a few feet away, which is surprising since he always seems to be attached to my hip. His hand hovers over the water, where droplets slide across his palm and fingers as he seems to test it. "I can feel it. It's an old one at that." He glances at me. "It's not meant to keep anyone out, but to keep someone in. It has weakened, allowing what-ever is inside it to slip free, but it would be drawn back before long. There is blood in the portal, chaining whatever it is, very similar to my own. It's ancient magic."

"Fucking great," I mutter. "Which means it's old and powerful, or at least getting there after all the feedings, so when it's strong enough, it can break free of the portal shield."

"Very likely." Tem shrugs. "Or it could be freed by someone else."

"Will us entering break the portal?" I ask.

"It shouldn't. It seems things have gone through before—probably animals or foolish humans trying to swim. They didn't stand a chance. That's how it must have fed and become strong enough to escape it in the first place."

"Brilliant." Pulling my bag around, I tighten it so it stays on my front.

"What are you doing?" Ronan asks.

I glance at him with an incredulous expression. "Hunting, of course." Without waiting for his response, I stand and dive into the pond.

I expected it to be shallow, but the water is so deep, all I see is darkness under me. My hands cut through the water on either side of me as I float just below the surface, sparing the three observing faces one last look before I swim down.

I need to get to the portal before I run out of air. Let's hope it isn't more water on the other side or I'm fucked. Things like this were not made for humans, and my body will only be able to hold out for so long. Fighting a monster underwater could mean my death, but it has to come onto land to hunt, which means it can breathe above, and that's my only consolation.

Diving deeper into the murky water, I open my eyes and hold my breath as I swim. The closer I get to the bottom, the stronger the feeling of something sucking me towards it becomes.

It's probably how monsters of lake myths were born—a portal like this.

The magic washes over me as my lungs begin to scream, the edges of my vision blackening, but I still push forward, swimming as the magic grows.

The darkness seems to part, a glow emanating below me, and I swim towards it desperately as my body starts to give in. The glow only grows, obscuring everything, and then I fall through it.

The pressure of the water around me is gone, and instead it feels like air. I take a gasping breath, still unable to see, but I choke on the air and then hit something hard.

Pain stabs into my side, and I bite back a groan.

The air is forced from my lungs in a huff, and I lie on something sharp, the agony in my thigh making me grit my teeth. When I can finally breathe, I push my wet hair back.

As I turn, I feel something crunch, and I freeze. My eyes finally adjust, and then I peer down and swallow my horror. I'm lying on a pile of bones belonging to birds and animals, although . . . some even look human.

With dawning horror, I glance down at my leg to see a small bone protruding from the side of my thigh, my blood seeping around the old shard.

I grit my teeth and wrap my hand around the bone, yanking it free. It hurts, but as I prod the wound, I realise it's not deep, just a bleeder. Ripping a sleeve from my shirt, I tie it around the gash and then slowly get to my feet. I slip and almost fall as the pile of bones shifts beneath me.

Pulling a flare, I crack the tube and toss it, illuminating the space around me in red. Despite it being under a lake, it doesn't look like it was carved into the earth. The walls are steel and covered in rust with wires hanging down. It looks like an abandoned factory or an under-ground lab. I can't see much farther. The bones pile is higher than it is wide, but there appears to be a corridor leading deeper into the place.

Glancing up, I see the glowing portal above me, the water lapping at it dark and serene. I guess I'll have to climb if I want to . . . How did whatever this is get out?

A noise has my head jerking up again, and I see three bodies heading through the portal. I throw myself from the bones, rolling across the concrete floor and sliding to a stop in a crouch as I watch the fae and Tem hit the pile. The fae lands in a crouch before he stands and pushes his hair back, while Tem hits the bones in a belly flop. Ronan simply floats down and stands next to me.

"Took you long enough," I mutter. "I was wondering if you chick-ened out."

"Just giving you time to get eaten first." The fae smirks as he walks delicately from the bones like he's sauntering down a runway. Tem, on the other hand, just rolls and flops onto the floor before bouncing to his feet and smiling at me.

Rolling my eyes, I crack another flare and turn back, eyeing the place as I move deeper. The walls seem to drip with condensation. There's a camera, old and forgotten, high up on the corner of the wall, as well as a busted metal door before the narrow corridor. Stepping on it, I peer inside the darkened hallway beyond.

"I guess this is the way."

"I like their decorations. I never thought to use bones," Tem remarks. "It gives it more of an intimidating aura."

Ignoring him, I step into the corridor. Ronan floats behind me, and the others trail after me, discussing the pros and cons of using bones as decorations.

The passageway has a round roof and isn't very long, and when I stop at the end, the hair on the back of my neck rises. I cannot see much, but I can feel.

"Enough," I hiss, holding my hand up as I peer into the dark room beyond. "There's something in there."

"Well, obviously. Isn't that why we are here?" Ronan jokes.

Ignoring him, I pull my hand from my glove and press it to the wall. Instantly, I recoil as if scalded. Screams and death fill my vision, as do flashes of people running, white coats, and so much blood.

"Something really bad happened here," I admit.

"If you mean the lack of colour, I agree," the fae comments. "If you are going to do the creepy Gothic thing, it's all about colour."

Ignoring them, I step into the room, my senses stretching beyond. I feel the buzz of electricity so I follow it. I walk into a rolling stool and curse before fumbling across a desk. The buzz grows louder in my head, letting me know I'm close.

Putting down the red light, I spy a thick, horseshoe-shaped handle set into a square case. There's wording above it, but I can't read it. It's not any language I know, that's for sure.

As I brush my fingers across it, I feel the tingle grow, indicating there's electricity there. It's probably a bad idea, but it's better than fighting in the dark.

I grip the handle and flip it up. There's a buzz, and then light blares on above us. It's so bright, I have to shield my eyes for a moment. When I drop my hand, I glance around and find we are in some sort of control centre. Computers and screens all come back to life, some in the middle of programs as if they were abandoned. None of them look new, maybe five or so years old, but there's an immense amount of power and technology here.

What were they doing?

What is hiding down here now?

Ronan makes a noise, and I look up to see him wide-eyed as he lifts his arm.

"Erm, I think you woke him." I follow Ronan's pointing hand, and my mouth drops open.

The blazing white lights exposed the glass-fronted lab beyond, and inside, hooked to a giant machine in the middle, is a man.

No, not a man.

A machine.

A mix of both.

His blood-red eyes snap open as he snarls, flashing huge fangs as his gaze lands on us.

"Prey," he hisses in a deep, earth-shattering voice.

This was the monster from the vision, the one who killed.

"Oh fuck." Ronan groans. "I'm so glad ghosts can't be drained, but good luck, Tate."

I cannot drag my eyes away. I have never seen anything like this. It's a mix between man and machine, monster and technology. The wires tethering him to the machine seem to glow.Recharging him or imprisoning him? Chains lie at his feet, old and forgotten, with holes in the walls where they were once anchored.

His skin is deeply tanned despite being under the earth, but slashes across his chest and abs expose metal beneath his skin, and one of his hands is completely metal up to the forearm. A leg showcases more metal and wires as well.

The fucker is huge, easily eight feet, and completely naked . . . bar the blood coating his body.

This is definitely what we are here for.

"What is that?" Tem murmurs curiously. "A new friend?"

"I don't have a clue," I reply. "It looks like a mix of machine and sangui. Whatever they were doing here, they clearly created it"—I glance at the machines, realising they were monitoring it—"and watched it before it went wrong. They tried to trap it down here as a last-ditch effort, but it's failing now."

"Interesting and all, but he's moving," Ronan squeaks.

I glance back to see him disconnecting the wires from his skin before he steps down, the ground shaking under us from his weight.

"Any ideas?" I ask, but they are all silent. "Awesome. Let's try talking to it first."

"I don't think he wants to talk," Ronan mutters as he hides behind me. I stop at the glass window. There's a doorway to the left, completely open, and he could be on us in seconds. The glass won't do much, but it sure as shit makes me feel better to have it between us.

"We aren't here to harm you," I say slowly. It can obviously speak, so maybe it can understand me. "You are the one draining the monsters, right? You must be so hungry—"

He roars, and I swallow.

"I don't think he wants to talk," the fae remarks casually.

I shoot him a glare before focusing on the man, erm, machine . . . monster before me. "The thing is, you can't go around killing others and drinking their blood. It's not good. That's why I'm here. To ask you to stop."

His head tilts to the side, and his eyes narrow. His fist suddenly lashes out, hitting the glass. It splinters and smashes, and before I can react, he's reaching through, uncaring about the sharp edges carving off the skin on his arm as he grabs me and pulls me through it.

I don't scream as he turns and lifts me close to his face, roaring again.

I see a subtle blue glow in his irises, a ring inside of the darkness— more mechanics.

"I am not here to hurt you," I repeat as he lifts me higher, effortlessly holding me aloft. As I speak, I slide my hand into my bag with slow movements.

He simply bares his fangs and pulls me closer, no doubt to drain me, but I'm not in the mood for that today. Seriously, why does every monster want to eat me? Can't they just be friendly for once? I wrap my fingers around a double-edged dagger and slowly extract it as he pulls me towards his mouth.

"Fine, if you don't want to talk, then let's settle this another way," I mutter and plunge the dagger into the only place I can reach—the area between his neck and shoulder.

His eyes widen.

I don't know what I hit, but his eyes flash blue and then his head drops, his fist releasing me. I hit the floor and drop to my knees, rubbing my throat as I breathe deeply.

Peering up at him, I wait for his response, but he seems to be frozen, and I swear I hear his wires sparking.

"Well, that looked fun," the fae says.

"You're doing great," Tem adds as I glance back to see him and Ronan giving me a thumbs up. Climbing to my feet, I give the man a wide berth as I scan the room. He's not dead, so I need to find a way to kill him quickly.

If he's part machine, then maybe there's a way to shut him down.

There's a table at the back, so I head over to it and hit the keyboard, but I don't understand any of the language. Picking up a folder on the side, I scan the contents. Most is in that strange language, but some is in English.

I read the reports and glance at the now stationary man. "It seems the original king of the vampyrs wanted this experiment. They wanted to temper their weakness so they could feed from anyone and anything, becoming invincible. It went wrong, and they created . . . him. He was considered a failure, insane from merging a soul and mechanics. Well, no fucking wonder he's mad." I drop the folder. "They created him, experimented on him, and then locked him away to starve and go mad. I'd be pissed too."

"Super interesting," Ronan mutters. "Do they say how to kill it?"

"Maybe the way you kill vamps?" I suggest as I eye him. I might feel sorry for him, but I'll still kill him if I have to.

"You could use him, you know," the fae says, and I glance over, frowning. "You need all the strength you can get for what is coming. I'm not big on sharing, but this might be beneficial."

"Get to the point," I hiss.

"I could tether him to you and make it so you are linked, then he couldn't kill you without killing himself. Survival is something everyone understands, even animals like him."

"He would hate me. I would trap him like they did."

"It's a different kind of chain, and it's better than death. Your choice," the fae offers casually, as if he doesn't care either way.

I glance back at the man. Could he be saved if I have enough time? Could we free him of the madness clearly plaguing him? I hate that the fae is right. We should give him a chance. If I don't, I'm no better than Black.

We have all killed for survival.

Maybe if someone offered him a shred of decency, kindness, or a chance, he would be different. Killing him feels wrong.

"Fine, let's do it," I state.

"Magic comes with a price," the fae warns.

"Of course. What price?" I mutter as I stare at the man, swearing I see his fingers twitch.

"I want to explore your past in your mind, unchecked and uncensored. I want to feed on it," he explains.

"Fuck that," I mutter.

"What's your choice?" he counters.

There's a mechanical whir, and we all turn to see the man straightening, gearing back up, and as we watch, he reaches up and pulls the blade from his neck, tossing it aside. The skin and wires stitch back together, and his eyes blink, like a computer coming back online. "That's not good."

The fae grins. "Better decide quickly."

He turns and flashes fangs at me. He seems pissed. "That was rude, I'll admit, but you were being unreasonable," I tell him, but he appears to be done with talking.

He storms towards me, his intention clear.

He wants to feed on my blood.

Ducking under the man's arm, I avoid his meaty hands again. "Fine! Deal!" I roar as my back hits the wall, and he comes barrelling towards me. I'll kill him if I have no choice, but I want to be different than them.

I have to be.

Besides, part of me understands this monster.

Betrayal leaves its mark.

It can make you into an animal.

The fae appears behind him, and his claws plunge into the man's chest before the fae dances back as he whirls with a roar. Lifting his bloody hand, the fae offers it to me. "Blood exchange to seal the tie."

I glance at the big bastard blocking my path. I have to get past him, and it's clear the fae won't help.

Fucking fae asshole.

Glancing at the big man once more, I roll across the floor, avoiding his hands, and come up before the fae, grabbing his wrist with a wince before I suck his fingers into my mouth, swallowing the creature's blood.

"Now make him drink yours," he says as he steps back.

"Wait, how—" I am yanked backwards, my back hitting a chest as I glare at the fae.

The tricky bastard. I'll make him pay for this later.

My head is yanked to the side. I could fight him, but I don't, and instead I brace myself. A moment later, those wicked fangs sink into my neck. My body spasms from the agony, but I force myself to relax.

Just when I start to feel weak and woozy, the man removes his fangs, and I stumble forward as I look at him. I reach up and cover the wound.

His eyes flare like he's trying to fight the connection. My blood stains his mouth and chin as he reaches for me, his hands clenching and unclenching.

"It's a spell that links us. Your instincts are demanding you stop. If I die, you die," I explain. "Give me a chance to be different, to be better than them."

Taking a chance, I drop my hand and step towards him. He watches me approach, his eyes wide and scared, like an animal waiting for a blow. I press my palm to his head, and I fall inside his mind.

CHAPTER 22

Addeus

I look past the glowing darkness I am trapped in, and I see her—
the woman who dared to invade my space.

We are inside my mind. I don't know how she did it, but I
know she did. She stands before me, small and determined, her hair the
colour of fire. Her hands hang at her sides, even as I prowl her way.

"Stop," she orders. "You cannot hurt me here, so why bother?"

"Why are you doing this?" I shout, hating being trapped. I can feel
it both internally and externally, like their chains are on me again,
keeping me in the dark as I slowly starve.

She flicks her fingers, and a low light glows around us like she can
hear my thoughts. "You are not trapped, not like before. I will never do
that, but this is the only way I could stop you from dying. If you can't
be stopped, then you will need to die. I can't let someone walk around
killing innocents. This is your last chance. Either we work together or
we both die."

"Why would you risk your life?" I ask.

"Because I believe you can be saved. I believe that there is
someone inside who doesn't wish to be what they made you into. I
believe you are more than this monster, and you were never given the
chance to be anything else."

"You do not know what you speak of," I retort. How dare she?

She attacked me just like everyone else.

Does she not see I have no choice? If I do not satisfy the monster they created inside me, then the pain becomes unbearable. I do not wish to hurt others. I do not wish to be *this*.

I did not ask to be created.

Images flare between us, as if projected from her. They are of her, chained to a chair, covered in blood and being tortured.

I stare at the images, my stomach churning.

"You are not the only one who has been hurt by this world," she says softly. "You just wanted to appease them, to make them proud, didn't you? You cannot help who you are, though. None of us can. I know pain and betrayal. We are not so different. Yes, I risked my life, hoping you could be different if someone gave you a chance." She trails off, and the images fade. "My name is Tate. I am a hunter, but some of my closest friends are monsters. I kill, but I always want to save. I seek revenge and blood, but I hate the way it makes me feel. I am neither good nor bad, but something in between."

"I am evil. They told me so," I hiss. "It is not worth the risk."

"We are all evil here. We have all been abandoned, hurt, trapped, and betrayed. Together, we can be more, but it is your choice, not theirs—not this time. What you want to be is your choice."

I stare at her, wondering if this is another trick, but I can sense the sincerity in the bond tying us together. She doesn't want to kill me, but she will if she has to. She wants me to trust her. She wants me to be better, and something deep inside me wants that too.

I don't know if I can endure it—the madness is thick within my mind. I know she senses it, but she doesn't say anything.

"Name, my name is Addeus. My creators gave it to me. It means—"

"Halfling," she finishes and holds out her hand. "Would you like a different name?"

"No, I want to remember what they did to me and where I came from."

She smiles, and the darkness around us slowly fades until I am back in my body. She smiles in reality. "It's nice to meet you, Addeus. Welcome to the team."

I jerk back as a man pops up in front of me, grinning.

"Hi, I'm Tem."

"Ronan." A man waves from the back of the room, positioned as far as he can get from us.

"As lovely as this is, how about we get out of this dark, damp place? I have a debt to settle," the white-haired man remarks.

Tate rolls her eyes and grins at me. "Are you ready to leave this place for good?"

"The portal—"

"We can break it." She speaks so confidently, even I believe her. "If you are ready?"

"I'm ready." I nod, looking around at the place I was born and then trapped. The world above, even in darkness, was beautiful, unlike this place. I don't know what will happen or where Tate will take me, but if I can taste freedom, even for a moment, then it's worth it.

I follow her down the corridor, and something strange fills me as I stare at the bones piled there. I was starving after breaking the chains, able to see them in the water above but not taste them until some fell through the portal. I had no choice. Some of them were old and rotting, but I did what I had to.

"You're feeling shame," she murmurs. "Don't. We have all done what we needed to so we could survive." She glances up at the portal. "We are going to need to blast it to break it."

"If we do, it will fall, and the link to this place will disappear," the fae says. "So we better be quick."

She nods as we gather below the portal, and then she looks to Tem. "Want to do the honours?"

He grins like he's happy, waving his hand, and then the portal screams and starts to close. Sliding one arm around her waist, I push off from the ground and leap through the opening and into the lake above, powering through it like I have done many times before. This time, though, the portal doesn't try to suck me back. All I feel is a link to the woman in my arms as I swim up and breach the surface.

She sucks in air and swims to the edge. I simply push from the water and land next to her on the embankment. A moment later, the others follow, and she stands, pulling her legs from the water as we stare at it.

There's a glow within that grows brighter, yet we don't look away, and then it explodes before suddenly going dark.

"It's gone," Tem says. "The portal is closed. You're free."

"Thank you." The words feel foreign on my tongue, but I know that is the right phrase.

"You're welcome." She smiles at me. "Now let's go dry off and get you some clothes. I might know someone who can help."

The smile she gives me unnerves me.

CHAPTER 23

Tate

"When I meant you should meet Althea, I did not expect this," Simon says as he crosses his arms, looking over my ragtag team and the naked vampyr. He blinks, dragging his gaze down his body then back to his face. "Congratulations."

"Mate," the wolf at his side growls.

Simon rolls his eyes. "You're still the biggest, so calm down." He meets my eyes. "It's good to see you."

"You as well, friend. This Althea . . . I don't suppose she'll have some clothes for . . . Addeus here?" I ask.

"I mean, maybe. One of her mates is a big fucker, but this one might be bigger. Guess we'll see." He turns, and we follow him into the sprawling Gothic estate.

I'm hoping we are welcome because I really don't want to fight a horde of bloodthirsty vamps right now.

He walks through the front door without knocking, but we hesitate at the threshold. Simon looks at me, but a woman appears behind him, smiling widely.

She's stunning, with long black hair, curves to die for, and eyes that sparkle like amethysts. "Took you long enough." She smiles at Simon and then me. "You must be Tate."

"Althea?" I ask.

"That's me." When I continue to hesitate, she steps back.

"Come in. My mates are working right now, so it's just me." She smiles wider, flashing fangs.

"Are you not afraid to have this many strangers around you?" I ask as I step inside and look around. It looks like a Gothic castle, but it has a warm, homey feeling to it and a strange herbal scent that relaxes me.

"No," she replies. "I could kill you all if necessary, and besides, Simon vouches for you. Come, let us have tea."

"Tea?" Ronan whispers. "She's weird."

"Hey, that's my best friend," Simon snaps. "She isn't calling you weird for floating around."

"Enough, you two." I walk past them, following the vamp into a huge kitchen. I sit at the table, and she sets out some tea before disappearing. When she reappears, she hands me a stack of clothes. "For your mate."

"Oh, he's not my mate," I grumble, but I hand them to Addeus. "Put these on."

"Why?" he asks, confused.

"People don't walk around naked," I explain.

"I am not a person," he responds.

"Fine. Monsters don't walk around naked. It's . . . distracting, and aren't you cold?" I retort.

He frowns and looks at the clothes but shoves his chair back and dresses right in front of us. They are tight, but they cover him. I have to drag my gaze away from his bulging muscles.

I quickly remember my manners, not wanting to offend her. "Thank you, Althea."

"You are welcome, Tate." She smiles. "I have heard a lot about you from Simon. I would chitchat, but I have a feeling you are a very busy person, so I'll cut right to the chase."

I like her already. Vamps have a way of being dramatic and slow, but she seems unbothered and unafraid, even when facing a hunter in her own home.

"Simon told me about you, that you help monsters," she says as she pours me a tea and slides it over before pouring herself one.

"I'm a hunter," I correct.

"Yes, but you also help innocents—monsters and humans alike. Well, I have an innocent I want you to help. It is my gods-given duty to keep our race in line, so I cannot interfere with others' business." She rolls her eyes. "But he is innocent, and if we do not act soon, he will die."

"Why me?" I ask as I sip my tea. It's fucking amazing, and I swear I feel some of my wounds heal.

"Because your kind is hurting him. No other will dare go against them." She frowns as if she's troubled by it.

"My kind? Humans?" I question as I sip the tea again and almost come on the spot.

"Yes, but also hunters. Hunters trapped him, draining him for his magic and using it illegally. We found out from a friend of a friend, but I saw it myself." She frowns angrily. "I wish to help, but I can't."

"And you expect me to? What do I get in return?" I ask as I lean back.

She smirks at me, but it only enhances her deadly beauty, and I know she is more dangerous than she seems.

"I like her." She winks at Simon. "She's smart and unlike the other hunters I've met. Fine. If you help me with this, I will help you with what you need when the time comes."

"Who says I will need your help?" I retort.

"It can't hurt to have me as a friend, can it?" she reasons. "You are haunted. I see it, but I also see the destiny surrounding you. Yes, you will need me in the future. Do this for me and I will gladly help." She holds out her hand, and when I reach for her, she looks at my glove.

"Bare," she counters. "You can see what you wish. I will not stop you."

I freeze, my eyes widening, and she smiles. "The gods speak to me," is all she says.

Who the fuck is this woman?

Someone terribly powerful, I realise, and it seems nothing is a secret to her, which means if she is saying I will need her . . . I oddly trust her.

Taking off my glove, I lay my hand in hers, meeting her gaze, but I'm not seeing her—I'm seeing her memories. She holds nothing back, and when I lean away, I know this woman is someone I should trust.

She has earned it.

Nodding, I get to my feet. "We will go then. Where is this man you wish for me to free?"

"I couldn't see everything, but I saw a great skyscraper in the city." I know it annoys her that she can't help. She's the type who wants to save everyone, unlike me.

"The southeast tower." Ronan groans. "Great . . . It's filled with hunters."

"It was not inside. It was . . . below. Hidden," Althea offers.

"I'll figure it out." If she says this is important, then I will trust her on that. We will go, and after, we will find Black. Time is running out, and I'm growing impatient, so I nod at Simon and his mate, telling them goodbye, and head to the door, my team in tow.

"Oh, and Tate?" I glance back as she sips her tea. "Trust those you surround yourself with, no matter how hard it is. You will need to before the end. You will become so much more than a hunter. You will become our champion, our protector, and our scribe."

I don't know what she means, but when she smiles at me, I have a feeling I will find out.

CHAPTER 24

Tate

The fae rips open a portal, and we walk through, taking our time. The southwest tower is in the middle of the city, so we spy on it from the coffee shop across the road. We definitely get some looks, and I don't blame them since the guys around me are insanely beautiful and inhumanly big, but I ignore the whispers and focus on the building.

"Under it," I murmur. "A basement? Maintenance?" I muse out loud. "It would have to be hidden from the other hunters and humans around here, not to mention other monsters, but have easy access—" My eyes land on the subway and I smile.

"Tunnels." I sip my coffee as I nod. "They are hiding in the tunnels. Okay, so we—"

"Excuse me?" The quiet, unsure voice has us all whirling around. I reach for my blade while the others draw their magic, all but Ronan, who is trying very hard to drink his coffee and not let it go through him.

The girl is young, her bright blonde hair vibrant. Her cheeks heat as she glances at us. "Sorry, I was just hoping I could give you my number."

I roll my eyes and look away, assuming she means the fae, Tem, or even Addeus. "Erm, you?" she squeaks, and I look back as she thrusts a piece of paper towards me. Blinking, I take it in confusion, and she grins and giggles before hurrying off as I gape at her retreating back in shock.

Ronan snorts, and his coffee squirts all over Addeus, who grabs him with a roar. Sighing, I pocket the number and glance at the building.

"Alright, enough fighting. Let's go," I say after observing the subway entrance. I haven't seen any hunters go in or out, but that doesn't mean anything.

Standing, I throw some bills on the table and leave the boys rolling around on the floor, fighting. I walk out into the street, ignoring the traffic as I cross. Horns blare, and I flip them off as I reach the subway entrance then descend the stairs. I hear the guys hurrying after me, their footsteps chasing me. At the turnstiles, I scan my card and move through, only to stop as I glance back.

Ronan floats over it, the fae frowns, Tem hops it with a grin, and Addeus snarls at the machine, banging his fist into it. Rolling my eyes, I go to scan my card when the fae flicks his fingers and all the stalls magically open, then he walks through with a cocky grin. I throw him a glare. Poor Addeus has to move through sideways, grumbling the entire time.

This world was not made for a man of his stature.

Before we get shouted at or ticketed, I hurry down the stairs to the right and onto the platform. It's busy at this time, and I glance around, searching for what I want. People move out of our way as I walk farther down, until we are at the end of the platform. I see a small walkway leading deeper, and a few feet down is a door. It has an emergency sign, but painted under it is the hunter symbol.

Bingo.

Ignoring the gasps and calls, I hop down onto the line, my boots hitting the metal hard. I keep my back to the wall and pull my gun as I move to the door. I glance back to see the others doing the same, though Addeus is having to hunch. Smirking, I crouch before the door and look for any traps or wires. Nothing buzzes, but that doesn't mean anything.

"Addeus," I call. "Come here."

He slides past the others, knocking the fae onto the track before he is at my side. "Can you sense anything? Any traps, cameras, or tricks?" I ask. It's worth a shot, right? If the hostage inside is important, then they would at least have it wired or be able to monitor it.

"I sense people inside. I can hear their heartbeats. There are many, but they are farther in." He closes his eyes and presses his hand to the door.

His eyes glow brighter, that blue ring appearing, and I swear I hear electricity crackling through him. "There are cameras, but I have knocked them out. There is an alarm too, which I have disabled." He drops his hand. "Now it is just the people inside."

"They will have noticed," I murmur as I twist the handle, and it opens. I peer inside before looking back at the others, an idea coming to mind.

"Fae, if I make a deal with you, will you glamour all of you and hide behind me?"

The grin he gives me is evil as we hear a train barrelling towards us. "What are you offering?"

"Me, for one night, as long as I walk out alive."

"Deal." He waves his hand, and they all disappear, but I can still feel them. In one way or another, they are all tethered to me.

Standing, I put my gun away and walk inside.

The room beyond looks like a maintenance room, with a round table and a small kitchen. After a short entrance, there are two hunters who jump to their feet, their cards forgotten on the table as they eye me. I glance around, seeing the hole in the wall carved beyond, leading into darkness.

Holding my hands out, I smile calmly. "Easy. Name's Tate. I'm a new transfer from the southwest," I lie. If I say up north, they will check and find out about my team.

"What are you doing here?" the big bastard on the right snarls, his receding hair causing his scalp to shine in the light. His beady eyes dart around—he's definitely on something. My eyes flit across the table, and I see the pixie dust.

I shrug. "My friend told me to get in on this and said you were making a killing."

"Who? Give me their name," the other demands, a meaty, short guy with sharp eyes.

"Sanchez." It's someone I've run into before and a gamble. Hunters don't all know each other after all.

"Never heard of him," the short one snaps.

"So? You don't believe me? I'm one of you." I show my patch on my shoulder, and he frowns. "How else would I know you're keeping a magic user down here and draining him, hmm?" I scoff. "Look, I don't want any trouble. I'm just here for some quick cash."

They share a look, still unsure, but I would be too. After all, what they are doing is against our rules. Some might look the other way, but if brass found out about it, they would hang them, especially Shamus. Despite the rumours about him and how much he annoys me, he's determined to be a good hunter and make our people better. Considering there are people like this who fill the lower ranks, it's no wonder he's fighting a losing battle.

A bellow of pain splits the air, echoing from the darkness beyond. It's so filled with agony, it echoes my own, but I force a smile. "Looks like you guys are having all the fun."

They chuckle, relax, and share a look. "You want any dust?" the big guy offers.

"Nah, I'm good. That shit tweaks me, and I've got a briefing soon. I don't want them catching on." I chuckle.

They laugh again and sit. "Go on through. Beiz is back there right now, draining him again."

Nodding, I duck through the hole, my shoulders tightening at having them at my back, but I can feel the others behind me, so that's something. Their weapons would have to get through my team before getting to me.

The hole leads into what looks like old service tunnels. There are a few closed doors, and I know there will be more hunters in there, either high or resting.

The scream comes again, echoing down the corridor, and I follow it to the very end, where some metal steps lead down to an open room. There are pipes down each side, some of them partially submerged in water with just a metal walkway over to a man who is convulsing on a metal table. His mouth is open on a scream as glowing metal prods are driven into his chained body by three hunters standing over him. They drain into glass canisters at the end, glowing with magic.

Those are a witch's invention, ironically, to help keep magic fresh when selling spells. I've used some in the past, but this warlock is not giving his power or spells willingly. He is being tortured for them.

The hunters are too busy to notice me, and I do not have it in me to fake our way in. It's silly, but I pull my gun, unable to listen to the man's screams. His body writhes as his magic flows from him, so I aim the gun at the first hunter and pull the trigger. His head explodes, and the other two turn, pulling their prods from the warlock's body.

"What the fuck?" The one on the right drops his prod, shattering the glass, and the magic shoots back into the slumped warlock. The hunter goes to pull his gun, but I fire. It hits his chest, causing him to stagger, so I keep firing until he drops.

I hear the doors behind us open as hunters pour from their rooms to come after us. Glancing at my team on either side of me, I grin evilly. I could spend time killing all of them, cleansing our organisation, but the warlock needs me more, so I put my trust in my team like Althea said. Besides, they need this more than I do.

"Feed," I order.

I don't have to tell them twice. The fae grins and throws himself at the first man that emerges, while Addeus barrels through their masses. Tem's soft smile never drops, but he launches himself at the first man and rips his throat out with his teeth then feasts on his blood. A groan splits the air as his head tips back, and he glances at me, smiling brightly before burying his mouth back in the hunter's neck.

Leaving them to it, I head down the stairs and to the one hunter left standing, his wavering prod pointed at me. I put my gun away. I won't kill him with it. Instead, I'll turn his own weapon on him.

He throws a jar of magic at me, but Ronan suddenly appears and absorbs it for me, walking like a shield as I head for the hunter. He panics and grabs another, but I rush him, and he falls back. Catching the prod with the jar still at the end, I point it at him.

"You are a disgrace," I spit.

"You're one of us. What the fuck—"

"I am not one of you. I'm a hunter, and you? You're trash, nothing more. When I'm done, this world will have forgotten all about you. I'll wipe you and your entire likeness from our organisation."

I slam the prod into his chest before he can speak. I do not want to hear anything he says.

He's disgusting, and he deserves a painful death.

He took something sacred and corrupted it.

It might make me evil, but I'll gladly become a killer to save our kind.

He shrieks and jerks from the electricity coursing through him. His hair stands on end and his screams get higher until I pull the prod away. He slumps to his knees, drooling and gagging, so I press it to his shoulder. "How do you like it?" I ask him as more screams split the air behind me. When I pull it away again, he lifts his head, his eyes bloodshot. I flip the prod and smash the glass bottle onto him.

The magic flows down him like water, but he screams as he melts under it. It turns to acid on his skin. His flesh and muscles melt to the floor, leaving nothing but his screaming skeleton. Stepping over him, I head to the table. The warlock's head is turned away, his hair covering his face.

Eyeing the chains, I glance up at a particularly loud scream to see Addeus's hand plunge through a hunter's back and out his front as he lifts the man in the air, and then he brings him back down, breaking him, and buries his face in his chest cavity.

I turn back to the warlock and start to unwind the chains, but there are locks. Snarling, I pull out my gun and shoot them. They break, and I yank the chains off, letting them slither from his body. He doesn't move, and I worry for a moment that he's dead. The last one falls to the floor, and I lay my hand on his arm, making him jerk up, his long, tangled black hair falling back to reveal bright red, glowing eyes. I stare for a moment. He's beautiful, the kind that catches your attention, even covered in sweat and magic. His hair, a deep, obsidian black, is perfectly straight and hangs down to his waist. His face is pale, with sharp cheekbones and an even sharper jawline. He's Asian, maybe Chinese, and when his red eyes lock on me, I find myself swallowing hard. For a moment I stare at the symbol that glows on his left cheek before I force myself to focus.

"I'm not going to hurt you," I promise. "I'm here to help you." He glances at the hunters on the floor and back to me. "Come on, time to go."

He doesn't speak as I help him from the table, his head hanging forward. He struggles as I walk us to the end of the table, grunting under his weight. Suddenly, he jerks me to a stop, his blazing eyes locking on the hunters still pouring into the area, and with a gurgled scream, he throws his hand out, palm up

My eyes widen as magic fills the space, and a dragon-shaped flame smashes into the remaining hunters. Their screams fill the air as they burn to death, the smell making me retch.

When it's over, he slumps, and I catch him as he falls forward, smiling happily before he passes out.

Okay then.

"Uh, guys, a little help?" I call, and three bloodstained faces turn to me, equally as horrific and happy.

Fucking hell, when did my life get so weird?

CHAPTER 25

Ronan

The warlock is out cold, and Tate is struggling under his weight, but the tempest helps her and effortlessly lifts him, looking way too proud as he waits for her approval.

"Good boy," she praises, and his grin widens.

"We need to get him somewhere to rest before the hunters show up," I interrupt.

The fae shrugs. "I can open a portal into the little tower we stayed in."

Tate's eyes widen. "Maybe don't let other hunters know that. They might get upset." She glances at the warlock. "I have a feeling it would be a bad idea if he woke up surrounded by hunters again. No, I think we need somewhere close. We don't want him to lose it and incinerate us like he did them." She nods her head at the burnt corpses.

"Magnificent, wasn't it?" Addeus says.

Tate simply sighs, pinching the bridge of her nose and muttering to herself for a moment before focusing on us. "Right, enough talking. Let's get out of here. I'm not in the mood to fight a war today, are you?"

"Always," the fae and Addeus say at the same time, and then they share a wicked grin.

"I can help, mistress. I would win any war for you," Tem chimes in.

She looks between us then meets my gaze. "Please be the only other sane one here besides me, which is not something I ever thought I would say."

"Sorry, cupcake, but I lost my sanity a long time ago, as well as my ability to eat cheese, which I think goes hand in hand." I grin, and she turns away and starts walking, clearly done with us. With no other choice, we hurry after her, the tempest calling out along the way.

"Mistress, wait, I can be sane for you! I'll be the sanest person you've ever met!"

She simply flips us off over her shoulder, and Tem leans into me with a grin. "That means she likes us, right?"

"Yep," I answer with a choked laugh. "You should do that back to her every time she asks something. She'll love it."

"Got it. Mistress, wait!"

Floating at Tate's side, I stare at the straggly, hunched old man behind the desk of the cheap motel as he eyes Tate with lust. I came in for moral support, and Tate, well, she's the only one not covered in blood and guts. I cannot imagine asking the fae or, worse, Addeus to book a room. I have a feeling it would end with this old, wrinkled raisin man being eaten.

"How many beds, girlie?" He cracks a grin, showing crooked yellow teeth, and I shiver in revulsion. I can smell him from here. Even if I couldn't, I can see the sweat stains on his once white tank, which is barely hidden behind an oversized, also stained shirt. His hair is grey, with most of it missing on top, and it's unkempt.

"Thank fuck I will never get old. If I ever look like him, just shoot me," I mutter to Tate.

"Gladly, but I won't wait for you to get old to do that," she hisses.

"What did you say?" he asks, and she forces a fake grin.

"Two beds, please."

"I am not sharing with the tempest or fae," I snap. She ignores me as the man turns and roots through a drawer, his ass crack visible as he bends over.

My eyes rove around the cheap motel we are in. It isn't too close to the crime scene, but it isn't too far either. It's an ask no questions sort of place, which is exactly what we need since we have three blood-covered monsters outside carrying what looks like a corpse. A noise catches my attention, and as Tate strokes her blade, clearly debating murdering either me or him, I float over the desk and peer around the cracked door he exited when we entered the small, dingy reception area.

"Ronan," she hisses.

"Ya, ya, just a minute," the old man snaps with a cough.

I turn my head, and she widens her eyes at me in warning. Grinning, I duck inside the room, my eyes widening as I stare at the old-style TV and what is playing on it. I watch it for a minute before popping up right in front of Tate. She jerks back, glaring at me.

"You have to see this. He's watching porn back there. Really nasty, dirty, old-school stuff." I laugh.

"Not now," she hisses, and I turn to see the creepy guy holding out a key.

"You don't want the room?" he scoffs.

"No, I do." She reaches through me, making me shudder, and delicately takes the key so she doesn't have to touch him. He tries to stroke her skin, but she's faster, and her smile is tight as he nods at him.

She swiftly retreats to the door, sparing him a narrowed look.

"Shame all the hot ones are crazy," he grumbles.

"You have no idea," I tell him as I lean into the counter. "Is that a VHS porn tape? Would you be mad if I took it?" He heads back into the room and sits, and I frown. "That's rude! Very anti-physically able to be seen—oh, your little dick is out. I'm gone." I hurry after Tate, finding her trying to discreetly herd her monsters to the end room. Once inside, she shuts the door on me, and I have to float through. I rub my nose and glare at her, but she ignores me, focusing on the tempest as he gently lays the warlock on the horrible green and brown patterned bedspread. There's striped, green wallpaper peeling on the walls, a rickety table with only one chair, and a small bathroom with a sink outside of it, but I guess it will do.

Floating over to the warlock, I watch as his head turns in his sleep, his hair falling away to reveal his face, and I hiss. "God damn, look at that!"

"What?" Tate demands, hurrying over.

I point at the warlock as I look at her. "Boy looks like he was hit with a pretty spell. Seriously, I'm not into sausage, but how is he so pretty?" I glance down at him. "I could maybe be into sausage a little, especially if they looked like that. Damn, Tate, you should definitely fuck this one and let me watch again."

"Again?"

I turn, backing up as she narrows her eyes on me just as a groan sounds, and our eyes turn to the warlock. He doesn't wake up, but she tosses me a glare and heads over to the chair, throwing her bag onto the table with a sigh.

"It's okay, mistress," Tem says, and he flips her off with both hands.

She blinks at him, and a knife embeds in the wall by his side.

"Mistress, I'm sorry!" He falls to his knees and crawls over the nasty carpet to her. "Tell me how I have displeased you." He flips her off again when he's at her feet, and I can't help but laugh.

"He's so gullible," I remark.

"Ronan!" she yells, and another knife heads my way.

It takes over an hour for Tate to console the tempest, telling him she isn't mad or trying to kill him, but not to swear at her again. He sobs loudly the entire time, like a child.

By the time Tate calms him down, she looks like she's ready to murder me, even with her tempest clinging to her. Luckily, the warlock chooses that moment to wake up, saving me from her wrath and what I'm sure would be another death I wouldn't forget.

CHAPTER 26

Jarek

Voices surround me, and my fury returns alongside my disgust at myself for letting them catch me. How foolish I was, but they are bigger fools because I will kill them all for what they are doing to me. My eyes snap open at the same time I realise the chains are gone, and I sit up. My body betrays me, swaying with weakness, and I fall back into something soft.

Instantly, five faces, some upside down, peer down at me, and I react without thinking. My magic flies at the closest target, a beautiful, pale-haired man. It doesn't register that he doesn't look or feel like any of the hunters I know, but it's too late. His eyes narrow, and he swats my magic away like it's a fly.

Something dark enters his gaze. "That wasn't very nice. Try that again and I will tear out your throat and bathe in your blood, no matter what she says." I follow his gaze to a woman at his side.

Her face is closed down, almost cold, and her eyes are sharp and knowing. For a moment, I stare at her, wondering why she looks familiar, and it all comes back to me. "You . . ."

"Yes, me." She huffs out a breath, blowing her short hair out of her face, and her bright eyes warm slightly. She's beautiful in a deadly way, her sharp features only enhancing that. She looks like the old

165

paintings of warriors within the coven's library, as if she's about to ride into a battle covered in armour. I don't know why that comes to mind, but it does. "We saved you—"

I see the hunter patch on her coat, and with a roar, I lunge at her. A large hand wraps entirely around my throat with more strength than I have ever felt, and I am pinned to the bed with such force, I'm surprised I don't sink through it. A fierce-looking man with what looks like metal showing through his skin snarls at me, flashing fangs.

Fangs.

"She saved your life, but I will gladly end it," he warns, tightening his grip. "If you try to touch her again, you will beg for what the hunters put you through."

"Fangs," I rasp, and he glares.

"Addeus, release him," she orders, and the vamp's hand instantly unlocks with one last warning look. Sitting up, I rub my bruised skin and glance around, seeing the differences for the first time. I gently call my magic so I don't get gutted and feel what I already know.

These aren't men. They are supernaturals like me.

My eyes land back on her. There's something within her that calls to my magic, as if it's recognising its own, but she's human . . . mostly. "What do you want?" I ask, eyeing them curiously. Why is a hunter with creatures she hunts?

"Nothing," she replies.

"Everyone wants something," I snap. "Everything comes with a price. You said you saved me. I don't know if I believe that, not with that badge you wear. You want my magic, correct?"

"No." She sits on the edge of the bed, eyeing me with knowing resolve. "Someone asked me to save you. That was all. Besides, they don't represent all hunters. What they did is wrong, and they deserved to die. You're free to go." She nods her head at the door. "It's open, and we are far enough from where they kept you that you won't run into them again, but the ones inside are all dead, so you don't need to seek revenge. You can go home."

Home . . .

The word rings through my mind.

It's on the tip of my tongue to tell her I don't have a home anymore, though I don't know why I would admit that to her. It's not like she would care that my people exiled me for seeking the hunters who killed our own and taking my revenge. It is not our way. Magic is to be used for life, not death. They simply sat back and let our people be slaughtered, but I could not. I broke our laws and was exiled right before I was captured by hunters—hunters who killed my kind. I cannot go back.

"I have nowhere to go," I admit, unable to meet her eyes. These words are important, driven by an instinct that guides us all, but warlocks are more sensitive to it. Most call it intuition or a gut feeling, but the truth is, it's destiny. "I was exiled for using my magic on hunters who hurt my kind." I don't know why that slips out, but it does, and I can't take it back.

A grinning man at my side perks up, swinging his gaze from me to her. "Another friend, mistress."

My eyes widen at that, and a man floats into view. "Well, aren't we just a bag of ragtag, broken toys nobody wants." He recoils, letting out a high-pitched scream. I roll away on the bed as a small ghost boy flies through the wall and stops before the other floating ghost—er, man.

"What is it?" the woman demands, suddenly holding a sword bigger than any I have ever seen in her hand.

"Creepy ghost child!" the other floating ghost yells, a hand pressed against his chest as if his heart could have stopped.

The woman just blinks. "Um, what? Can you repeat that?"

The boy just watches us, and the ghost eyes him before heading over to the woman and touching her forehead. She abruptly jerks back, blinking. "Oh, so there is a kid. Well, fuck."

"I hate creepy ghost kids. They are always so weird," he hisses and holds out his hand. "Nice dead child, keep calm and don't go all *The Shining* on us."

"What is *The Shining*?" the one who called her mistress asks.

"You are a ghost," she snaps at the ghost man. "Ask him what he wants."

"Fuck that, you ask him," the ghost retorts.

"Can you help me?" the kid asks, making us all look at him. "I heard you talking. You helped this man, and you help people. Can you help my sister?"

"Yeah . . . we don't do that. We aren't ghostbusters," the other ghost jokes, still hiding behind the woman and making a sign of the cross.

"She's not a ghost. She's alive," he begs, his eyes wide as he looks at us. "At least for now, but she won't be much longer. Please. Please help us."

"Well, shit." The woman sighs as she puts her sword away and looks at us. "Any ideas?"

"Holy water and an exorcist," the other ghost replies.

CHAPTER 27

Tate

"Remind me again why we are helping?" the fae drawls.

"I became a hunter to help people. I cannot ignore this." I retort as I add more weapons to my body, ignoring all the unsure gazes in the room, including the warlock's on the bed who seems to be evaluating me. Ronan is still hiding from the other ghost who wants to cling to him, much to his horror.

"What about your revenge?" the fae asks casually, seemingly not bothered by what we do as long as he gets to feed and kill.

"It will still be there, but my soul might not be if I ignore this," I answer as I drop my booted foot from the rickety chair and slide my last blade into place.

The fae shrugs. "Souls are overrated."

"You are really going to help this boy?" the warlock asks.

"Why wouldn't I?" I snap, growing annoyed.

"Hunters do not help. They kill," he murmurs as he slides to the end of the bed, eyeing me. As I watch, he waves his hand. For a moment his eyes turn red, a glowing red mark appearing on his cheek before he fades back to normal. A red ribbon appears however and slides up into his hair, tying it back from his face, only exposing more of his stunning looks. I hate that Ronan is right. He really is pretty—unnaturally so.

"Not this hunter," I say. "The room is paid for tonight. Feel free to stay and figure out what you wish to do." I didn't forget the haunted look in his eyes when he admitted he had nowhere to go, but it's not my problem. I did my duty by saving him, and I'm not collecting more broken toys, as Ronan said.

"If you're really helping him, then I will too." He stands, and I narrow my eyes.

"Why would you?"

"I have nothing better to do. Besides, I've only used my magic for death recently, and magic is about balance, so it needs some life," he says as he eyes me. "If you are not like the other hunters like you say, then I need to see that too." He smiles, and it's like the sun breaking through the clouds, blinding and slightly shocking. "I'm Jarek," he shares.

"Oh god, not names! That means we are keeping him." Ronan groans before he yelps and flies up to the ceiling as the ghost moves closer to him. "Be gone, demon."

Sighing, I meet Jarek's eyes. "Tate," I reply, introducing myself. If we are hunting together, then he deserves to know. "The scaredy ghost is Ronan, and this is Tem, Addeus, and, well, the fae . . . I never got his name."

"You got his cock though," Ronan yells with a laugh before screaming when the ghost boy appears at his side.

"You shouldn't say that. My sister says it's a bad word," the boy says. "She also said anyone with a cock who isn't me should be castrated." He stumbles over the word.

"Well, your sister is stupid." Ronan sticks his tongue out. "I happen to have a very nice cock—"

"You're stupid!" The kid sticks his tongue out, and they argue.

"Ronan, stop arguing with a six-year-old," I demand as I glance at the boy. "Your sister sounds smart." I soften my tone, seeing him nod as tears form in his eyes. Whatever happened to him must be recent. He's too . . . bright to be an old ghost. It makes me worry about what his sister is going through. "Can you take us to her?"

He nods, wringing his hands together. "You'll save her?"

Crouching before him as he floats, I smile softly. "I promise I will save your sister if I can." I cross my heart then lower my voice. "She's right about the men thing. They are more of a hassle than anything."

He grins and nods as I lean back and hold out my hand. "Show us."

We don't travel far. He must have been searching for someone to help. We are only a street over in a residential neighbourhood, and we stand before a normal, blue, two-storey house. The lawn is mowed, and the drive is empty. It looks like every other house.

"Here?" I murmur in confusion, looking around as the sun shines on us. I don't want to linger here for too long. We do not blend in with our leather, weapons, and bloodstained clothes and faces.

"Here," he confirms. "I remember the number. I memorised it so I didn't forget." He points at the number fifty-five on the plaque next to the door. "The bad man isn't here at the moment. He got angry and hurt me. I don't remember much after that."

Hurt him . . . He must have killed him.

"And your sister?" I ask, checking the suburban street.

"She came after me. The bad man took me here, but she found us. He didn't like that, so he threw her down into the basement with me. She doesn't like the dark." He floats into the house, and we don't have much choice but to follow. I don't use the front door, though, just in case, and instead I walk down the driveway and to a path along the side that leads to a gate. Hoisting myself up, I climb over and drop onto gravel on the other side.

A dog barks, lunging on a chain connected to a doghouse. "Quiet," I order, and he whines and slinks back in as I walk around the patio to the sliding doors. I go to pick the lock when the door slides open, and I glance over to see Jarek shrugging. "It's easier."

Nodding, I pull out my knife and gun. "Stay behind me," I mutter as I head inside, tracking mud all over the polished kitchen floor. I glance around, but everything is clean and perfect. There's something off about it though. It seems too empty and impersonal for someone to live here, as if he tried to copy what he's seen without understanding.

There's no warmth.

The boy pokes his head through a white door under the stairs, and I head that way. The door unlocks just as quickly as the other one, and I swing it open. "You're sure he's not here?" I ask the kid.

"I don't know." He purses his little lips. "Come on, she's down here."

"Ronan, take Tem and check upstairs. Jarek, watch the back door. Fae, guard the front."

"All this for one man—"

"Now," I hiss. If someone were here, they would have heard us by now, but I'm taking no chances on someone sneaking up on us. The guys go off to do as I've ordered, and I glance at Addeus. "Stay up here and warn me if anyone comes."

He nods, guarding my back without question.

Swinging the door open, I peer down the stairs. They are concrete, with a buzzing bulb hanging above us. I get a horrifying feeling this isn't the first time he's done this. I glance at the kid. "Did he . . . do anything bad to you?"

"No." He seems confused. "He hurt me, though, and my sister said he's a . . . p-pedo—"

"Paedophile," I finish, confirming my worst thought. "Great. Were there any other kids down there?"

"No, but there were so many bones," he whispers, "I got scared."

"It's okay. You don't have to be scared anymore," I promise. "I'll protect you."

"And my sister?" He looks so hopeful, I couldn't deny him anything. He had a tragic, horrible ending to his life, yet he's trying to save his sister. He's a good kid.

"And your sister," I say as I head downstairs. At the bottom, the staircase opens into a small landing, and then there's another door there. It's padlocked, and I don't have time to break the lock. I whistle, and Addeus peers down at me. "Come break this," I order.

He jumps down the stairs, grips the metal door, and simply takes it off, leaning it to the side before nodding and heading back upstairs. "That's one way of doing it," I mutter as I step inside and scan the room.

My stomach rolls at the difference down here. It's all concrete walls and floors with scratch marks on some. There are even tallies on one wall under a stained mattress with blood specks on it and chains at the top and bottom.

There's not much else to the room, but then my eyes land on his sister, who's curled against the back wall next to a small, unmoving version of the boy next to me. His head is facing the wrong way and his eyes are wide, frozen in fear, even in death. I blow out a breath and try to rein in my anger and horror.

I run my eyes over her again, but she doesn't even notice, nor did she hear the door opening.

She seems frozen, lost in her grief.

Tears track down her pretty, heart-shaped face as she rests her head on her knees, which are dirty, as she stares at her brother's body. There's a collar around her neck, connected to the concrete wall by a chain. What I'm guessing is usually vibrant, pink hair is oily and knotted at the base of her neck. She seems small and young. If I had to guess, I would say she's maybe in her early twenties, but there's magic surrounding her.

She isn't human, I realise.

I really am the monster saviour.

The boy stares up at me sadly, his hands tugging on his striped shirt. "She won't talk to me or look at me. I tried for hours, but she couldn't see me." Tears flow down his face, and I nod. I don't know how much he understands, but I don't want him to be upset.

"It's okay, buddy. I'm here now." I walk over, putting my gun and knife away so I don't spook her, then I crouch within her eyesight, careful of the boy's body.

"I'm here to help," I tell her, but she doesn't even blink. Her deep brown eyes are open and unseeing, surrounded by long, pink-tipped lashes. "What's her name?" I ask her brother.

"Isabella, but she prefers Fang," he replies.

"Fang?" I ask, but she doesn't move, so I tread closer, holding my hands up. "Fang?" I say louder. I don't want to scare this girl, but I can't let her stay down here. It's not fair to her or her brother. "What's your name, kid?"

"Writ," he whispers.

"Isabella, Writ sent me." At his name, she jerks upright, her eyes landing on me, and she scrambles back to the wall, realising someone else is here.

"Easy," I murmur softly. "My name is Tate, and I'm here to help you."

"How did you get here?" she asks, her voice hoarse, but I have a feeling it would normally be silken.

"I had some help. We don't have time, and I will explain later, but for now, I'm going to free you, okay? To do that, I'll need to call one of my friends down to help. He'll break the chains—"

"No!" she yells at the word "he," and I freeze. Anger, hatred, and terror fill her eyes, and I nod in understanding.

"Okay, I won't, but can I try to free you?" I nod at the collar. "Then we can get out of here."

She watches me for a moment before nodding softly. Sighing, I approach her and look at the chain, trying to find a lock or something I can unhook without touching her.

"He had keys. He always takes them upstairs," she tells me, and I turn and meet her gaze from inches away. She swallows but seems braver.

"Okay—"

"They are in the kitchen," Writ says.

I stand and step back.

"I'm just going to get the keys, okay?" I tell her.

She shuffles to her knees, her eyes wide. "Please, please don't leave me here."

"I won't." I kneel before her again, taking her hands, and she doesn't pull away. "I promise, okay? I will be right back. I just need to get the keys so I can free you."

She leans closer, pressing her forehead to mine, and I let her. She blows out a breath and leans back. "Be quick."

Nodding, I hurry up the stairs, ignoring the curious looks from the others as I search the cupboards in the kitchen, taking great pleasure in ripping open doors and spilling their contents everywhere. "There," Writ murmurs, pointing at a drawer.

I hurry over, yank it open, and toss the cutlery drawer on the floor, seeing the keys under it. I grab them and dart back down. Fang's eyes are wide and her chest heaves in fear, but she relaxes a bit when she sees me.

I head back over and search for the right key. It takes a few tries, and then it finally clicks. The collar drops, and I remove it from her neck, letting it hit the floor. She rubs her throat, eyeing me. "Thank you," she whispers.

"Of course. We need to leave," I instruct softly, knowing she's struggling right now.

I help her to her feet, and she tugs on her clothes, trying to cover her curvy body. I was right. She's small, barely reaching my shoulder, and I find my gaze wandering over her delicious body appreciatively.

Fuck. I step back, wondering what the hell is wrong with me. I don't give a fuck about gender, I never did, but now is not the time to check someone out, even if she is stunningly beautiful. That's just fucked up. Luckily, she doesn't notice.

"I won't leave him here." Her voice cracks on the last word as she stares at her brother.

I see grief, heartbreak, and blame in her eyes. She faults herself for not protecting him. Writ is quiet, and I glance at him to see him looking at his body.

"We won't," I promise her, and I head over. "Can I carry him for you?"

She nods, wrapping her arms around herself, so I take my jacket off and hand it to her. She slips it on, and it drags on the floor, but it will keep her covered. I gently slide my hands under Writ's unmoving body and lift him, propping his head on my shoulder.

He watches me sadly. "I'm dead, aren't I?"

"Yes," I tell him. "But you saved her."

He nods, looking at his sister, who is staring at me in confusion. "Come on." I head to the door then hesitate. "There are men upstairs, but they will not hurt you," I promise her, but she looks scared. "They are with me. Trust them." I juggle Writ slightly as I reach down and grab a knife. "Here, to help you feel safe. If you get scared, drive it into them, okay?"

She nods, clutching the blade to her chest, and I head up the stairs. When I reach the top, I whistle to get their attention. "I want every single one of you in the living room with your backs to the wall. Do not move or speak. I mean it," I order and wait as I hear footsteps. When I think it's done, I step out. They are positioned like I asked, though the fae looks annoyed at my command.

I feel Fang step out behind me, hiding behind me, and hear her breath stutter when she sees them, but she's braver than I gave her credit for. She doesn't run or hide; she steps out at my side, glancing around. "Is he here?"

"No," I answer for them. "Let's get you and Writ out of here, and I will come back and deal with him—"

"No, you won't," she snaps, turning her fierce gaze to me. Her skin seems to glow and her hair uncurls, becoming bright and healthy, flowing down her back. Every inch of her oozes sex appeal as she watches me. "You may leave. I will wait for him. I'm going to make him pay for what he did." Her eyes drop to Writ for a moment, and I stagger back as intense power hits me.

"If you're staying, then we are staying too. This revenge is yours." That is something I understand. "But we will be here to help if you need it."

She nods and turns away as if she cannot bear to look at her brother. "Fang, may I give Writ to one of my men to hold so I can keep my hands free for weapons?"

She hesitates before nodding, and I glance at Writ. "Him." He points at the fae, and my eyes widen.

"Erm, let me hand you to Addeus—"

"Him," Writ demands, pouting. No doubt he was used to getting his way. He's a tiny version of the woman at my side.

Swallowing, I head over and stretch his body out. Surprisingly, the fae straightens, looking serious, and bows his head. "It would be an honour, little warrior." He accepts Writ's body and carefully cradles him in his arms.

When I'm sure he's okay, I turn to Fang. She sits down in an armchair facing the door, waiting, playing with the knife in one hand, and my estimation of her goes up.

Whoever this man is, he fucked with the wrong woman.

She might have been scared, starved, and locked down there, but it seems this is the true her—powerful, vengeful, and filled with wrath.

I cannot be too close to her without her power washing over my skin, making my heart race and, worse, heat pass through me.

"Succubus," Ronan tells me softly. "The boy would have been an incubus." He eyes Writ sadly, all his fear gone. "This happens far too often to their young. Their powers grow, and it attracts the wrong sort of people."

Sickness rolls through me, as does understanding, and I glance back at Fang to see her bloodthirsty eyes locked on the front door.

Shit, yeah, the man definitely fucked with the wrong person.

The hours pass slowly, and we do not move. I wander through the house, checking for entrances and exits, finding his personal information on an open letter, and then I keep watch. The entire time, she sits in the chair, running the blade through her hands.

When night is drawing near, I hear an engine and, a moment later, the telltale sound of a car pulling onto the drive. Pulling the curtains, I hide behind the door and wait, sparing Fang a look. She nods. I wind the chain I went back downstairs for around my arm.

The door unlocks and pushes open.

"Fuck, why is it so dark?" he mutters, slamming it shut as he reaches for the light switch. I step out of the shadows behind him as he freezes, and I snap the collar around his neck before unwinding the chain as I walk past, yanking him after me. He stumbles and struggles, but it's too late. I drag him closer as he shouts in confusion, then I push him down to the sofa opposite Fang. I step behind him, keeping him in place with the chain, refusing to touch a hair on his head. I don't want to see what this monster has done.

I have a feeling it is something I could never unsee.

"What the fuck?" He freezes as Fang stands and heads his way, knife in hand. "How did you get out?"

"That's your worry?" she purrs, her voice silken once more. He shudders, and I see his pants tent, making me snarl as he gasps for breath.

"You took her and the boy, didn't you?" I ask him.

When he doesn't answer, I tighten the chain, waiting as his face turns purple and he slaps at the collar. I release it, and he sucks in desperate gulps of air, glancing up at me with terrified eyes. I don't know what I expected, but it wasn't this normal-looking man. He would blend in with a crowd. He's middle-aged, not fat or thin, with short blond hair and brown eyes.

"I usually kill them. I don't like them old, but this one . . ." He shakes his head. "I couldn't resist."

It's her powers. I'm starting to think that's also the reason she hates all men.

Men are weak as it is, especially human men, and with a beauty like her who also has her kind of power, I'm guessing this isn't the first man who has tried to take her by force.

She stops in front of him, and we focus on her. This is her revenge, not mine. I'm just here to ensure she doesn't get hurt, though I have a feeling the only one getting hurt will be him.

She slides the knife gently across his face before lashing out. Fang carves off his nose as he howls, and with a wicked look, she grabs his open mouth and reaches inside with the knife, slicing off his tongue. His screams sound different as she tosses it away and steps back, putting the knife away as she wipes her hands.

Suddenly, she presses her hands on either side of his face, gripping his head, and his screams grow louder, his whole body shaking from whatever she is doing. Her eyes turn black, and when her voice comes, it's seductive and deeper. "Succubi don't just feed on pleasure. We can feed on pain, too, if we wish—two sides of the same coin."

He continues to writhe and scream as her fingers seem to dent his skin, and her smile grows as she watches him, an evil look overtaking her face.

This woman is dangerous, maybe more so than any other being in this room.

Suddenly, she releases him, stepping back as he slumps, still screaming and clawing at his face. She watches him, her eyes slowly turning back to their normal deep brown. "It will never be enough for what you have done, but I will make sure you never do it again."

Pulling the knife out again, she slams it into his cock and steps back, all of us observing as he dies slowly and painfully.

His screams and moans fill the air until he becomes silent, and when I look up, I find Ronan has his hand over Writ's eyes and Tem has his over Writ's ears, and something about that makes my heart skip a beat. I glance at Fang as she pants, staring at the dead body.

"Do you feel better?" I ask, genuinely curious as one woman seeking vengeance to another.

"No," she replies as she stares at her brother's body. "Not even a little bit, but it's a start."

I have nothing to say to that.

"Would you like me to take you home? Maybe to your family?"

"We have no other family. It was just . . . us." She breaks on the last word. "Just me now, I guess."

"I'm sorry, Fang. I wish I could bring him back for you."

"It's not your fault. You saved me. How did you do that? How did you know my name?" It seems to click, and I offer a sad smile.

"Ronan, can you help?"

He steps forward, nodding, and I glance at Fang.

"There will be a small touch, don't worry." Her eyes widen, but before she can react, Ronan touches her head and steps back, his hand on Writ's shoulders. She blinks and looks around.

"What—" Her voice breaks off, her eyes widening as she stumbles over to Writ and falls to her knees before him. "Writ, Writ—" Tears flow down her cheeks.

"Hi, sissy. I made some new friends. Hope that's okay. I know you always told me to stay close, and I'm sorry I didn't listen."

She sobs, and my heart breaks for her. So much pain is contained in her body, it leaks out to us.

"No, no, it's okay. It was my fault, buddy. It was all my fault." She hiccups and trembles as she breaks. "Writ, I'm so sorry. I'm so sorry I didn't protect you." Her sobs shake her body. "I'm sorry I couldn't save you."

He steps forward, wrapping his little arms around her and kissing her head. "It's okay, sissy. You protected me for so long. This wasn't your fault. Don't blame yourself like you did with Mum and Dad, okay? I don't want you to be sad forever."

"Writ." Fang presses her face to his chest. She holds him and cries, and then he steps back.

"I think . . . I think there's a light here for me."

"No, please stay," she begs before she swallows her words, closing her eyes. "Yeah, buddy, that will be for you. You're right. It's okay. You can go through."

"What will happen?" he asks, scared.

"Nothing. You'll be safe, and Mum and Dad will be there, okay?" she promises. "They'll take care of you, and then I'll join you."

"Soon?" He frowns.

"Do you want me to be there with you?" Something serious fills her tone, and I freeze.

He frowns, watching her. "Not yet. It's not your time." He looks older for a moment, and then he smiles, looking like a kid once more. "Don't join me too soon, okay? We can wait. We'll wait for you, sissy." He glances at me. "Take care of my sister please?"

I nod. What else can I do?

He looks back at his sister and presses his hand to her face. She covers it with hers, watching him. "Bye, sissy."

"Bye, buddy," she whispers, holding it together. He smiles and then, seeing something we don't, he heads towards it. I step forward, my hand landing on her shoulder, and we watch as he turns back, grinning.

"You're right! They are here. Bye, sissy! Love you!" Suddenly, he's gone.

"I love you," she croaks, and then she falls back into me, sobs ripping through her. Kneeling behind her, I hold her as she cries. Her nails dig into my arms, drawing blood, but I don't complain as she breaks.

Ronan was right.

She's lost, alone, and broken.

We are all broken toys. Maybe that's why we found each other.

When her screams taper off, her sobs turning into quiet whimpers of pain, I gently slide my arms under her and lift, all my weight training paying off as I carry her to the door, my men following silently. Once outside, we turn back to the house, and Jarek steps forward.

"May I?" he asks.

She nods, and flames burst through the house.

We watch it consume the place before we turn and walk away. A portal opens before us, and we step through and out into a beautiful field.

"Where are we?" I ask as Fang clings to me.

"It is where we bury our dead—a sacred place," the fae answers as he carries the boy. He waves his hand, and a fresh grave appears. Fang sobs harder, burying her face in my chest, and the fae carefully lays the boy down, arranging him so he looks like he is sleeping. I head over, and Fang looks, sniffling.

When she's ready, the fae covers him with dirt and grass.

We don't speak, honouring the boy the only way we can. He saved his sister. He was strong and determined enough to fight off death until she was safe.

The fae is correct. This is the right place for a fighter like him.

Flowers grow over the grave, and I glance at the fae to see his fingers twisting at his side. He meets my gaze. "He deserves a warrior's burial." The fae looks at Fang. "Any time you wish to see him, just ask. I can bring you here. No deals. No charge."

"Why?" she croaks. "The fae don't do anything without cause."

"He gave his life for you. How could I do anything but? I might be cruel and evil, but that little boy had more strength in his body than any of us have in our entire souls. He was a warrior. He deserves this, and so do you. No deal needed. Not this time."

"Thank you," I whisper to him.

He nods and turns away, walking amongst the flowers like the prince he is, and I understand now why his sister wanted to save him so badly.

There's something in him, something good, even if it's usually hidden.

The fae isn't as evil as he seems, and we are not alone in this.

Neither is she.

I made her brother a promise, one I will keep.

The fae is right. Writ deserves it.

He died to protect his sister, and I will live to protect her in whatever way she needs.

CHAPTER 28

Fang

I let the woman carry me wherever she wants, all of my fight gone. The last reserves of my strength and power were used on the bastard who kidnapped Writ and me.

Writ . . . Even his name sends fresh agony coursing through me, and I bury my face into her neck, sucking in her unique, calming scent. It's odd, we are strangers, but something about this feels right as she carries me, and as I press my face to her skin, it seems to help settle my heartache a little.

I feel safe.

My eyes close, and when I wake, I'm in a bed. I jerk upright, scrambling back, and she's there, sitting on the edge with her hands out. "It's okay. You're safe," she assures me in a soft voice.

I glance around the room, but I see no one else, and I relax.

It's clearly a hotel, a nice one at that. I'm lying on a huge, white, fluffy bed with a canopy above me. There's a chair and table to the right, with open curtains showing the city and darkened sky.

It's still night.

There's a soft glow of a lamp, just enough to see her by. She's in a tank top that displays impressive arm muscles intersected by scars and some loose shorts. She watches me carefully, like I'm a wild animal.

I know she is a hunter, but I cannot seem to care.

She saved me and helped me say goodbye to Writ.

Writ . . . I bend over, gasping in agony, and her hand rubs circles on my back. "It's okay, it's okay," she soothes, and I find myself leaning into her again, her scent wrapping around me.

We stay like this for a while, and then she moves back, taking her warmth and scent with her. "Do you want some water or something to eat? You look weak."

I hate that she's right. I feel it.

I drained myself while trying to save Writ and free myself.

I'm running on empty, which is a dangerous place to be. It means my powers will soon spark out and start luring anyone close to me so I can feed. It happened once, and it's the reason I hate men.

I tell myself he couldn't help himself, it was my power, but even after he didn't stop. I screamed and begged, and he cried and apologised, but he didn't stop.

I hate men's lust, and I hate men in general, but I don't usually have much choice. I need to feed to stay alive and to keep Writ . . . Well, to stay alive.

Anger and hatred fill me as I admit the truth. "It won't help. I need to feed."

Her eyes widen, but she understands what I mean and hesitates. "Okay, how do we do that?"

I look away, shame filling me. "I can feed off anyone's lust. I can go find a club or a willing man." Even the thought sends a shudder of horror through me, but it's the truth. Men are strong enough to withstand my feeding, plus I don't mind draining them even if I hate the taste. They deserve it.

I don't know what she sees, but she frowns. "You said you hated men, right? I saw your fear of them, so it cannot be pleasant."

"It's not, but I don't have much choice. If I don't feed, it will call out to them anyway." Horror fills me. "It's better to be in control of it."

"Okay . . . Maybe I can help." I jerk upright, and she watches me then seems to decide something as she nods. "Could you feed on my lust?"

I nod, something pounding in my heart as she observes me. She's quiet, and I hesitate. We both know what the other isn't saying.

She could fuck me so I can feed.

She might not want that though. I have a feeling she is the type to sacrifice her own wants and needs to help others. For some reason, the idea that she could fuck me to help me without wanting me makes me want to cry.

"I can feed as you . . . fuck someone if you want. It doesn't have to be me," I admit.

She frowns. "But you don't like it, do you? Being that close to a male's pleasure."

"Not really," I reply, "but I think I would hate forcing you to serve me without wanting it even more. I never want to force anyone, but especially you. I don't want to use my powers on you. I want something . . . real."

She's quiet again for a moment, and shame heats my cheeks.

"I never said I didn't want this, Isabella." Something about hearing my full name on her lips makes me shiver. No one calls me that, not even my parents. I always hated that name, thinking it made me seem weak. It's why I chose Fang, but on her lips, it sounds like something to cherish.

I clench my thighs together under the duvet, desire coursing through me. I haven't felt desire since I was a teenager and didn't know better. I fed on pleasure, but the truth is, I have never felt my own. Something about this woman makes me wet, waking my body.

"You want me?" I glance at the door. "Those men—"

"Are my . . . team," she finishes. "I have never bothered with gender before. I like both men and women." She slides closer and slowly cups my cheek with her warm hand. It's rough, calloused, and strong, and I lean into it. My mouth parts on an inhale as I have the insane urge to taste her skin.

I should feed on her lust, but I'm too focused on my own.

"Do you want this? Do you want me? If not, we can find another way."

"I want this," I blurt. "I've never wanted anything so much as to feed on you."

She smiles, and it changes her face, making my heart hammer at her beauty. She's deadly, strong, and so confident, and I want to rub myself against her and let her protect me. "Then feel my truth. You can taste lust, yes? See the truth."

I close my eyes and focus on it, feeling it thick in the air. There is so much lust that my clit throbs in agony, my pussy turning warm and wet. When my eyes open, I know they are black, but she smiles wider.

"Then fuck me," I purr.

I am usually in control, playing with my prey like puppets, but not this time.

This human hunter has me in her snare, and I cannot seem to care.

Her hand drops, and I feel the loss keenly, climbing to my knees as if to chase her touch. The duvet falls to my knees, puddling around me.

I think she's changed her mind when she stands and heads to the door, and I slump, resignation filling for me what I will have to do. Suddenly, there's a click, and I glance up, seeing her slide a lock into place before she turns back to me. "They won't disturb us this way. I don't want you to be scared."

My heart stops and then races as she saunters my way. Climbing onto the bed softly, she kneels above me, and I anticipate what she will do next. Her hands slide down, and I gasp, waiting for her touch, but she simply grabs the duvet and yanks it away, stripping the bed so we are kneeling on the bottom sheet.

Lust wraps around us, and I suck it down. It strengthens my own, my nipples pebbling behind my torn shirt.

I'm shaking with expectation when she reaches out, pressing her thumb to my lips and making them part. My tongue darts out to taste her skin, and I whimper as her flavour explodes across my taste buds.

"You want to feed from me, yes? Then you will do as I say." My eyes widen at her order. "Open your pretty mouth."

I part it, and she narrows her eyes. "Wider," she demands, and I would do anything to make her happy. I open it as wide as I can, and she nods.

"Good girl." Her praise washes over me, and I swear my cunt clamps in a way it never has before. I can feel my own wetness filling my panties.

"Do I need to call you mistress?" I joke, remembering the other man calling her that.

She smirks, gripping my chin as I wait there, mouth open. "If I let you."

She grips my chin harder, the pinch of pain flowing through me, muddling with the pleasure in a way I didn't know I would like, but I find it only enhances what I am feeling.

I arch up. "I don't even know your name."

"Tate," she murmurs, sliding her thumb across my lips again before pressing it into my mouth. She watches me as she slides it deeper into my mouth. I close my lips around it, sucking. Her eyes narrow, this time in desire, and I suck harder, clutching her wrist to hold her to me. She pulls it free and sucks her thumb into her mouth, tasting me like I tasted her.

I crash into her. She catches me, gripping my arms as I press my lips to hers. She chuckles, but it turns into a moan as I sweep my tongue into her mouth, tangling it with hers. Her hands slide down to my hips and drag me closer so I'm pressed against her. Her mouth isn't like a man's. It's soft and warm as she slants her head. My hand slides up into her hair, fisting it as I rub against her. My other hand sinks down, undoing my trousers.

I need . . . I need . . .

Fuck, I need to come.

"Greedy," she says as she pulls back and knocks my hand away. Snarling, I bite her lip, and she kisses me again. She's distracted by dominating my mouth, so I glide my hand down her front, squeezing her breast, and then across hard muscles to her shorts. I shove my hand inside them, desperate to feel her skin. She lets me, and I move lower as her legs part to give me access when I brush across soft, smooth skin and then lower. When I feel her wet pussy, I part her lips and slide my fingers down her folds. Memorising the feel of her cunt, I circle her hole and then sweep back up, rubbing her clit the way I like to rub mine.

She groans into my mouth, and I pull back, pulling my hand free. I keep my eyes on hers and press my two glistening fingers into my mouth, sucking them clean.

"Delicious," I purr, and her eyes narrow.

It's the only warning I get.

I gasp when her hands hook under my knees and she drags me down the bed so my ass is pressed to her groin, and then she licks up my neck, making my back arch.

"Please, Tate," I beg, ripping at her shirt. She leans back and tugs her tank off, throwing it away, and then she unhooks her bra so she's naked from the waist up and so fucking sexy.

Her high, tight breasts are tipped with rosy nipples. She looks so fucking beautiful and strong, my complete opposite, but she doesn't seem to care as she cuts my shirt away with a knife and tosses it aside, exposing my plump breasts and rounded stomach.

Her eyes dilate with lust, and it triples in the air, making me gasp and arch up as I feed on it.

She wraps her lips around one of my nipples through the lace cup, and she sucks while massaging my other breast, building my pleasure.

"Tate, please," I implore, words tumbling from my lips as I wrap my legs around her waist and grind against her thigh. There's material between us, but I don't care. I need to come, and she keeps sucking and biting.

I come with an embarrassing moan.

My legs shake as I ride the waves of pleasure. Grinning, she lifts her head and cuts my bra off before she moves back, and I start to panic, thinking she's leaving, but she presses her hand against my chest and pushes me back down. Gripping my trousers, she yanks them down and off, and then my panties before sitting at my feet as she looks me over.

"You look like a goddess," she murmurs as she lifts my leg and licks a line down my calf, raising it as she goes until it's over her shoulder. She kisses my inner thigh and murmurs, "So fucking soft. Look at these curves. I'm going to fuck and taste each and every one. There will not be a place I leave untouched on your body."

My eyes widen, and suddenly her hand slides under my ass, gripping my plump cheek. She hoists me to her mouth, her tongue darting out and tasting my cream.

My head falls back before I raise it again, wanting to watch her. She licks me leisurely, tasting every inch of my folds before I toss my other leg over her shoulder, clamping my thighs around her head. She chuckles and grabs my ass as she buries her head between my thighs.

"You smell so sweet," she murmurs as her tongue traces my clit. "You taste even better. You're the sweetest thing I've ever had on my tongue. You were made to be worshipped, Isabella, until you're dripping with your own release and can't walk. I'll do just that. Feed as I fuck you because I plan to take my time."

My eyes widen at her words, but then they quickly roll back in my head as her teeth clamp around my clit. It throbs in time with my pounding heart, and I lift my hands, rolling my nipples as I rock into her mouth.

She releases my clit and laps along my folds, sliding two fingers inside me, and I cry out again as she licks around her fingers as she begins to fuck me.

Her tongue alternates between sliding in with her fingers and attacking my clit until I just grind against her face, chasing another release.

Lust and pleasure bombard me, only heightening my desire in a way I've never felt.

I'm wild and wicked with it, claiming what I want as I grind into her hand and mouth until I tumble over the edge again with a scream. She licks my cunt as I come around her fingers, and when I slump, she slowly pulls them free, laying a soft kiss on my clit before lowering my shaking thighs to the bed. Panting, I watch as she widens her thighs and slips her fingers inside her core, fucking herself with my cum.

My desire slams back into me, making me arch up. I can taste her lust, and I want more. I want to feed on it as I taste her. I want it to pour into me as she uses me the way I want.

Sitting up, I reach for her. "Please, please, I want to taste you."

She grips my head, tugging it up until I look at her. "You want to taste me?"

I nod, and she lets go, moving around to lie against the headboard, and then she crooks her finger. "Come here then, my good girl. Come taste what you made."

Crawling over the bed, I lie between her spread thighs, a moment of shyness assaulting me. I've never been with a woman. I've fantasised about it a lot, and it's what I dream of when I'm with men, but actually doing it is different. She doesn't let me hesitate, however, lifting one knee and tugging me up so my face is pressed to her cunt. "Do you want to taste me?"

I nod.

"Then you can't do it wrong. Do what you want—explore, touch me, taste me . . . Do what feels good."

Desire replaces my shyness, and I sweep my tongue out, dragging it along her pussy. Her taste explodes across my tongue, and I groan, gripping her hips as I drag her to my mouth.

"That's it, princess, just like that, just like how I ate your pretty cunt. That's all for you. Look what you did to me."

I slide my fingers inside her like she did to me. "Like that?" I murmur as I blow over her clit, and she groans, pressing into my hands and mouth.

"Like that, princess, just like that."

I drop my head, dragging my tongue along her folds, and she moans when I slowly flick her clit. When I speed up, however, she cries out, so I do that again. "That's it, good girl, learn what I like. If you're good and get me off, I'll bend your pretty ass over and fuck you until you're so full you won't need to feed ever again."

I whimper at her filthy words, gripping her harder, but she doesn't care and neither do I. Her wetness slides down my fingers as I fuck her with them, my tongue attacking her clit, and when she reaches down and grips my hair, directing me to speed up, I love it.

I drink down her lust as she gasps. "Isabella, I'm close, so close. That's it, just—" She cries out, her pussy clenching on my fingers, and I dive down, licking up her cum as I drink her pleasure. She slumps back, pushing me away, and I fall beside her.

She pants next to me, and we lie like this for a moment before I turn my head and meet her gaze. She rolls on top of me, pinning my arms above me as she kisses me again, tasting her own cum.

"I promised to fuck you, and I meant it. Can you handle it?"

"Yes," I murmur, arching up to rub against her.

She reaches down and directs my body, lifting my leg and spreading me to the point of pain. We somehow slot together, and I feel her cunt press against me.

"I don't have any toys with me, so I'm going to fuck you like this for now," she murmurs as she licks my cheek and down my neck before biting, and then she leans back, rubbing her cunt against mine. "You feel so good, and you look even better below me."

I arch up. It's strange feeling her against me, almost not enough to get me there, but when I look into her eyes, I almost come all over again.

"That's it, eyes on me. You'll watch me fuck you. You'll know I'm here with you. Can you feel how wet I am for you?"

"Please," I beg as I hold her as hard as I can as her hips roll, grinding her cunt into mine. It's harsh, and my channel aches, wanting to be filled. When she catches my clit again, I scream as another orgasm rips through me. I writhe below her, yet she doesn't stop. She keeps grinding into me until I hear her groan and pleasure explodes across my skin. I drown in her pleasure until every inch of me is filled and overflowing, another orgasm tearing through me at the strength of the feeding until I just whine below her.

Her lips touch mine, rough and wild, and I kiss her back, power flowing between us until she yanks herself away, releasing us and breaking the circuit.

She slumps down next to me, panting, but when her head turns and she meets my gaze, a smile tilts up her bruised lips. Exhaustion suddenly weighs on me—not the physical kind, but the emotional—and I find myself seeking her warmth.

I snuggle into her side, and I feel her stroke my hair.

Tears escape my closed eyes, and Tate simply kisses them away.

"Shh, I have you," she vows. "You're safe with me. I'll keep you safe. I'll never let anything bad happen to you again."

I believe her.

CHAPTER 29

Tate

I sleep on and off. Isabella sleeps deeply, curled into my side, holding me as if she cannot bear to let me go, and I don't mind it one bit.

Fang is a strange mix of innocence, fear, and brilliant power, and there is something so addictive about that. She could flay me alive with a touch, but instead she kisses me softly, seeking my guidance and strength.

A noise has my head jerking up.

I pull my gun from under the pillow where I hid it, pointing it at the intruder even as I tug the covers over Fang when she yelps and hides.

"Tem," I snap.

"Mistress." He climbs on the bed, careful not to touch Fang, and cuddles against my other side. "I missed you."

Rolling my eyes, I drop my gun, making sure he doesn't touch Isabella. She peeks up and startles a little, but she doesn't complain, just curls back into my side.

"Can I join?" Ronan jokes, and I glance up as the door opens. They all crowd the doorway. Fang's eyes widen in fear, and I snarl.

"Out, all of you." When they hesitate, I narrow my eyes. "Now, or I will turn all of your balls into oven mitts."

That gets them moving, the door shutting behind them. "It's okay. They are gone," I murmur, lifting the covers. She lifts her head, and I kiss her rosy lips softly.

"Go shower, Isabella," I tell her, smacking her hip. "I'll order you some food and have a talk with my boys."

Climbing from bed, I dress and head out, giving her some privacy. She's been through a lot recently, and she will need that time. Crossing my arms, I face my men, who all sit on the sofas across from me, blinking innocently.

Tem pouts. "She got to play with you."

"She got to taste you before I did," Addeus mutters.

"And me," Ronan adds.

"I've tasted her. She's delicious," the fae comments.

Jarek looks between them and me. "I'd like to find out."

I slash my hand through the air. "Do not embarrass her. She has been through enough. I mean it or no one will be tasting me again because you'll be dead."

"Fine," they mutter.

"Is she staying with us?" Ronan asks. "A succubus could be helpful."

"I don't know. That's her choice. It will be dangerous where we're going, and she might want peace." I head to the coffee maker and ignore the way my gut twists at the idea of losing Isabella. She isn't mine in any way, but I feel protective of her.

Sitting down with them, I nurse my coffee as they talk amongst themselves.

I expect Isabella to come out shyly and meekly, but she stomps out, looking defiant, daring them to shame her or make her scared.

That's my girl.

"Coffee?" Tem hops up. "I learned how to make it today."

"Er, sure." She sits on the sofa, eyeing us all. "So what are you, like, a monster team?"

"I like her." Ronan nods. "She stays."

"No." I laugh, ignoring him as usual. "Just . . . thrown together."

"Okay, so are you all monsters?" She looks us over once more.

Ah, that's right. We didn't make introductions.

"That is Tem. He's a tempest," I tell her.

"Mistress rescued me." He smiles and hands her the coffee. Surprising me, she takes it.

"This is Ronan, and he's a ghost. I had no choice," I continue.

He grins. "I'm her stalker."

"This is Addeus." I nod at the big vamp trying his best to be as small as possible and squeeze next to me.

He inclines his head to her. "Tate rescued me as well."

"Me too," Jarek adds. "I'm Jarek, a warlock."

"This is . . . the fae." I shrug, still having no better way to introduce him. Maybe I should name him like a stray puppy.

"She woke me up and fed me." He smirks. "She's delicious, isn't she?"

Isabella blushes at that but nods as she looks around.

"Okay . . . so that's all of you?" she asks, trying to take in all the information.

"Oh, there's Shamus too," Ronan says, and I whirl around to look at him.

"Shamus?" she asks.

"The hunter commander," Ronan supplies helpfully.

I cough. "Shamus is not . . . one of the team."

Ronan snorts and shoots me a look of disbelief. "Sure."

Isabella blinks, looking around. "So Tate just . . . saved all of us? I'm seeing a theme here."

"Don't go thinking I'm some sort of hero because I'm really not," I murmur as I drain my coffee. "I have my own revenge to get."

"Revenge?" she murmurs.

Nodding, I look around, seeing them all sober at the reminder. "My team, fellow hunters, betrayed and tortured me then left me for dead. The only reason I'm alive is because Shamus came and had the fae heal me. I plan to hunt them down and make them pay."

It's quiet for a moment, then Isabella smiles. "You helped me with my revenge, so it only seems fair I help you with yours."

Jarek nods, drawing my gaze. "I'm all for hunting corrupt hunters. I hate them all. I'm with you."

"It is not that easy. They are elite hunters for a reason and very dangerous," I protest.

"I can handle danger," Isabella says.

"Me as well. Besides, we are all supernatural creatures here. I think we are the dangerous ones." Jarek chuckles. "Though, I do believe the most dangerous person in this room is you, Tate."

"Me? I'm human," I reply incredulously.

"Yet you have saved all of us. It is not simply the power you hold that makes you dangerous, nor your weapons, but the people supporting you as well."

"A vampyr hybrid, a ghost, a tempest, a succubus, a warlock, a fae, and a hunter . . . Will that be enough for your revenge?"

I sweep my gaze over them and then nod. "It will have to be. I'm tired of waiting. It's time."

CHAPTER 30

Tate

I need a moment of silence to think and plan.

I'm used to working on a team, but my old one . . . Well, we all had our strengths and could plan together, while my new team looks to me for guidance, like I'm their leader. It's something I'm not used to and quite overwhelming. If I am going to hunt Black and the others, then I will need my wits about me, which means I need to focus.

I leave them bickering and strip off, climbing into the shower. I press my hands to the wall as the scalding hot water sluices down my body, unlocking my tired, aching muscles.

The creak of the door has me spinning and reaching for my blades on the toilet, but I relax when I see Tem. "What's wrong?" I ask tiredly, probably more waspish than I mean to. He considers me for a moment but doesn't speak, but I'm too tired for that so I turn and ignore him. He'll talk when he's ready.

Out of all the monsters surrounding me, he is the oddest. It's like he cannot exist without me. He looks to me for constant approval and happiness, as if his every emotion depends on me. That kind of devotion is terrifying. What if I mess up?

What if he gets hurt or killed?

Nobody looks at anyone else the way Tem looks at me. He would slaughter millions for me, his power for me to control.

One could go crazy with that kind of dominion over another being, and I think that's what truly terrifies me. No doubt his old master did, considering he said they weren't good.

I refuse to be like them.

Tem is his own person, even if he doesn't realise it.

I don't want a slave. I want something . . . more.

TEM

She dismisses me, and something inside me cracks. Fear courses through me—fear she will toss me aside like all the others.

I am not good enough. It's why all my masters abandoned me.

I am not disciplined enough, powerful enough, or tame enough.

I do not want my mistress to leave me too. I never wanted to please my master so badly. I hated their orders, but not hers. I want her small smile when she looks at me when I've done well. I want her approval and attention.

I crave her need of me, need others demanded while she simply allowed me to choose.

I have chosen her, but she doesn't seem to understand that.

She was strong enough to free me, yet she has not claimed me.

It's what spins around and around in my head.

I shed the clothes she gave me with a simple spark of magic and step inside the cubicle she bathes in. I do not stop until I am pressed against her warm back, and I sigh happily. She stiffens, however, and whirls, pushing me back.

"Tem," she snaps. "What are you doing?"

Searching her gaze, I see her displeasure, and it cuts through me like a knife. Does my touch repulse her that much?

I fall to my knees before her. I do not have the strength to stand anymore, not when I am once again not good enough.

"Tem," she barks when I do not speak. "Words. Explain."

"Have I displeased you, mistress? Am I not good enough?" I peer up at her, panic building in my chest. Sliding my hands around her legs, I press my face against her thighs as she grunts. I shuffle closer, trying to bind myself to her so she cannot let me go. My other masters chose me, but I am choosing her. "I can be better. I can be whatever you want, mistress."

I press my face to her pussy. "I can serve you however you wish. Please command me, just do not release me. I choose you, mistress. I choose you. I want you. I can be whatever will pleasure you." I let my magic flow over me, shifting to look like a blonde-haired female. Maybe she will enjoy that, since some of my old masters did. Her eyes widen, and not in pleasure, so I quickly change to a big, muscular male, and when I speak, my voice is deeper. "I can be whoever you wish me to be. Simply tell me." I change again, my body adapting with my different faces. I hope to see a spark of desire for one of them.

She reaches down and cups my face, stopping the transformation. Her expression almost looks sad as she watches me. "I do not want any of that."

"Then what do you want?" I ask in confusion. For all my age and power, this mistress of mine is a total conundrum. I can't figure her out.

She lowers to her knees before me. I try to flatten myself further because we are not equal, but she simply holds me in place until I am level with her, as if I have the right to be.

"I want . . . I want something real," she murmurs. "No magic. I want you how you are. No master or chains. I want a being, not a slave. You are a being, Tem, an incredibly powerful and ancient being. Surely you want more than to just be mine?"

"I want nothing more than to be yours," I admit. She frowns, clearly struggling with my confession. "I want to make you happy. I want to be at your side every day. I want to wake with you needing me and sleep in your arms. Is that not okay?"

She blinks but slowly nods. "I suppose, though I have never had that before. To be happy, you simply wish to . . . be with me?"

"Yes, mistress," I reply. "It is not a compulsion or an effect of the bond like you believe it is, though it is what drew me to you. I never felt this way with my other masters. I am my own being, but I wish to be a part of your life. I don't need your entire focus, mistress, because I know you have great things to do, but I simply wish for a small speck of your attention. I just wish to be involved and important to you."

"You do not want freedom to follow your dreams, see the world, or have a family?" It is clear she is trying to understand me.

"I know my mistress is a determined, strong hunter. You have big dreams for this world, but all I have is you. It's all I want. I have seen this world a thousand times, mistress, and it is not what kept me going. It was the hope that someday, someone would come along worth serving, someone who would keep me safe. I do not want anything else, mistress. I just want a home with you."

She runs her eyes across me as if she is truly seeing me for the first time. "I suppose I am no better than your previous masters, only seeing your worth and what you are capable of, not the real you. Those chains bind us, but you chose me, didn't you? If you wanted, you could break this."

"Yes," I admit truthfully, voicing something I have never admitted to another before for fear of what would happen. "Yes, I could break this, but I do not want to. I am right where I want to be."

"Then what do you want right now, Tem?" she asks.

"I want you," I answer without hesitation. "I want you to look at me the way you look at the others. I want you to reach for me. I want you to touch me. I want you to taste me. I want you to make me scream the way you made the succubus shout. I want to be yours in every way. It is all I think about, wishing you would look at me the way you look at them with desire and need. I want to be needed by you, mistress. I want to be yours."

It is then I see the desire in her eyes. It's for me in this body, not the others.

None of my old masters ever wished to take me in this form.

They wanted perfection, their ideal mate.

She slowly reaches out and slides her fingers down my cheek and chest. I sigh, leaning into her touch, my skin coming alive everywhere she caresses. "You're beautiful, Tem, do you know that? In this form, your true form, you are stunning. Every inch of you is perfect."

"I am glad it pleases you, mistress." I gasp as her hand circles my cock and squeezes. My hips jerk forward as a whine leaves my throat, and the small smirk she aims my way makes me growl.

"It pleases me, though you don't have to call me mistress," she says as she pulls me closer. "Take what you want, Tem."

She gave me permission, and I can't resist. I tackle her to the cold cubicle floor. She laughs, but it changes to a sigh as I lick her throat and bare chest. I have wanted to taste her since the moment I saw her.

"Can I still call you mistress? I like the way it rolls off my tongue," I murmur as I taste her skin again.

She shivers, which lets me know she likes it. "Only if you want to."

"I want to," I respond instantly. "I want to scream it while you claim me. I want everyone to know I belong to you."

"Possessive little thing, aren't you?" She grins, stroking my back, and I gasp when her nails dig into my ass and yank me closer so I fall between her splayed thighs. "Then show me how much you want your mistress."

I couldn't hold back even if she demanded it of me now. If she wants to know what I want, then I will show her until she never doubts it again.

Running my tongue down her chest, I drink in her reactions. I want her to scream in pleasure like she did with the succubus. I want to be everything she craves.

"Teach me how to please you, mistress," I murmur as I slide my tongue down and lap at her cunt. "Teach me what you like. I want to be the best I can be for you."

The water sprays over my back, but my skin is already hot, and as I roll my eyes up to her, I see flames reflected in hers. "Take me as you want. I promise you I'll enjoy it."

I search her face for the truth, but she simply waits, and my chains slip away, all bar the collar that belongs to her as I unleash my desire for my mistress on her body.

My hands grip her thighs, tossing them over my shoulders as I bury my face in her pussy. She smells delicious, but as I dart my tongue out and lick her cunt, I realise she tastes even better, so I thrust it inside her. Her essence coats my tongue as her hips rock. She tangles her fingers in my long, wet hair and drags me closer. I go willingly, lapping at her deeply.

Her thigh twitches when I twist my tongue around her clit, so I repeat it until she cries out, lifting her hips so she's fucking my face. I drag her closer, burying my mouth in her cunt as her pleasure detonates. More of that delicious cream drips from her hole, so I lap it up as she pants and slumps in my hands.

She tugs at my hair. "Tem."

I resist until I drink my fill, and then I slide up her body and stick my tongue out as her heavy-lidded eyes watch me. "Taste yourself. You're delicious. I want more, mistress, please."

Leaning up, she sucks my tongue into her mouth, and I groan. When she releases me, she slides her hands down my head until she can fist my hair, and then she tugs until it hurts. Leaning forward, she kisses my collar, sending a shiver through me. "Then fuck me," she orders. "Come on, tempest. Show me what you can do. I want all of it." Her mouth slides up my throat to my ear. "Show your mistress how badly you want her. That's an order."

CHAPTER 31

Tate

My words seem to snap any last shred of humanity and control Tem has. He bares his sharp teeth as his hands grip me, his desire evident. This is what I wanted.

His long hair is wet from the shower, his stunning caramel skin stretched over perfect muscles. I wrap my legs around his waist, loving how much control I have over a beast like this.

His hand wraps around my throat, making my eyes widen as he climbs to his feet, lifting me effortlessly before slamming me back into the glass screen. My breath is knocked out of me, and I feel the glass crack, but he doesn't care as he hoists me higher and drops me, impaling me on his cock.

It hurts so badly, I cry out, yet I grip him, wanting more.

My head falls back into the glass as he starts to move with cruel, hard thrusts, forcing me to keep up as I bounce on him. I dig my nails into his shoulders as I ride him, meeting him thrust for thrust as his dark eyes pin me in place.

His thrusts are so hard, the glass shatters behind me. He spins me and slams me into the tiled wall, the force hurting my muscles, but I don't care. I love how he doesn't treat me gently, but as an equal.

My eyes widen, however, when I see the glass from the screen floating in the air behind him before my eyes meet his.

He lowers his beautiful head as he fucks me harder, his cruel mouth latching onto my nipple. The threat of his sharp teeth makes me cry out and clench around his invading cock, my clit throbbing in time with my pounding heart. His teeth pierce my skin, drawing blood, but pleasure still rocks through me as he sucks my nipple. He turns his head and abuses my other bud until my eyes roll back in my head, and an orgasm rips through me.

My cunt clenches around his cock as I ride out the waves of pleasure, shaking against him from the force.

When my vision returns, it's to see him right in front of me, my blood staining his teeth.

"Delicious," he hisses, more beast than man as his hips drive into mine, the slap of our skin loud over the thundering shower. He fucks me through my release, building my pleasure once more, but a noise has my head falling back in confusion.

My eyes widen as blood bubbles on the crack in the ceiling, and then it slides down the shower walls, turning everything red. It drips over us until we are coated in it, and yet we don't stop.

The shower spray itself turns red.

Blood is all I taste and see, red obscuring my vision as he drives into me until the tile behind us cracks and the room seems to shake.

No, the Earth is sensing his power.

It should terrify me, but I drag him closer and sweep my tongue up his throat, tasting the blood as I drive myself down, taking him deeper.

In this moment, I'm not Tate Havelock or a hunter. I am not even a survivor.

I'm just his woman.

He claims my body, his cock hitting so deep I will never get rid of the feel of him, but it's clear it isn't enough for him as something expands inside me. My eyes widen as I meet his gaze. Something moves and wiggles, growing from his cock, and slides deeper inside me, anchoring in my womb as he drives into me. It's unnerving, yet it feels so fucking good, my eyes cross and I beg for more. That thing inside me grows until he can barely move, just rocking his hips until there is not one inch of room left in me. It hurts so badly, it feels good.

The wiggling sensation only increases as his cock swells and his head drops forward as he sinks his sharp teeth into my neck. He drives into me once more, pushing himself so far inside me, I shatter again.

An orgasm rips through me, alarming me with its strength, and I squirt around him. My blood mixes with the crimson liquid dripping everywhere, my cunt milking him and that thing inside me.

His teeth slip from my neck as he pulls me deeper onto him, my cunt still tightening around his length.

He throws his head back and he roars like a beast as he pumps me full of his cum. His seed comes in a never-ending stream that fills me so abundantly, I know I'll never get him out of me.

He holds me in place as blood continues to rain down on me, and then he tilts his head forward, his dark eyes meeting mine, and despite the incredible abuse he just put me through, he kisses me softly as I whimper.

"Mistress," he murmurs. "Mine."

"Yours," I rasp. Every inch of my body should hurt, but if anything, I feel great.

I feel reborn.

I don't know what the fuck just happened, but I want it again.

No wonder tempests are worshipped.

CHAPTER 32

Shamus

Everything is . . . *messy.*

I hate messy.

After reading over the latest report on Black and his team, I close it and pinch my nose, knowing sooner or later, Tate will be back. Black and his team have been out of control for so long, I was growing desperate. I needed to stop them, but as a commander, I am bound by duty and laws. I needed someone who could move silently and stealthily, giving me the evidence I needed. I knew Tate Havelock was perfect the first moment I met her, and I also knew it wouldn't be easy, but I never imagined Black would take it this far.

I should have, but I didn't. I underestimated him, and because of it, she nearly died. I blame myself, and maybe that's why I'm blocking her from going after him, but I know I can't stop her forever, nor would I want to. It will only end once Black is gone. This is my whole purpose, the whole reason I am here, and Tate will be my weapon, carving away the dead, infected flesh of the hunters and remaking them into the grand warriors they used to be.

I cannot protect her forever, nor should I try because if there is one thing I know, it's that Tate Havelock needs no man's protection, nor does she want it.

As if my thoughts have summoned her, a portal rips open in front of my desk and Tate stalks out, followed by a merry bunch of monsters. Blinking incredulously, I glance at Ronan as he floats to sit on my desk. He raises his brows as if to say he doesn't have a clue either.

I scan the newcomers in the group. It seems my angel has been very busy collecting a new team. Good, she will need it. I refuse to underestimate Black again, but it's not just Black I will need her help with. The hunters need to be cleansed from the inside out, and to do that, I need people who are willing to darken their souls and hands with the blood of their brethren.

"It seems you've forgotten how to knock," I tease as I lean back in my seat.

She scoffs as she sits in the chair before me, propping her muddy boots on my desk. I eye them then her, and her smirk only grows. The others spread out across the room. A pink-haired female eyes me angrily, keeping a wary distance from everyone else.

"You have been busy," I comment when she says nothing.

"I did as you asked. Now it's time for you to keep your end of the bargain. Where is Black and my old team?" she demands.

"Angel," I begin, and her eyes narrow. Suddenly, she's around the desk, pressing a blade to my neck, and I arch a brow at her. If she expected to frighten me, she was very wrong. Instead, I feel respect . . . as well as something much more dangerous—desire.

Tate is the only person to ever stand up to me, as well as the only person skilled enough to be able to. No other has ever gotten this close. Some might say I let her, but they would be wrong. She is simply that fucking good.

"Do not fuck with me, Shamus," she warns. "I want his location now or I'll leave and never come back, and whatever fucked-up plans you have will die with him."

I lean into the blade and let it cut my skin, drawing a drop of blood.

She watches it roll down my neck, and when it drips down, I catch it without her noticing and press it to a cut in the side of her trousers where her skin is exposed. My blood soaks into her skin like I needed —another added protection.

Some would say it's a waste of energy, but I do not care.

I need Tate Havelock alive—no, it's not a need. It's a want.

I sense the monsters with her bristling, eyeing me like I'm a threat, all bar Ronan who simply watches while tossing fake popcorn into his mouth as he wiggles his eyebrows at me.

"I was simply going to tell you that it will not be as easy as you think." I nod at the folder on my desk. "Read that."

Removing her blade, she keeps her narrowed eyes on me before scooping up the folder and sitting on the desk, her legs spread on either side of mine as she flips through the information.

I see realisation hit her, and when she jerks her head up, she appears worried. "The pack they are going after . . . he will slaughter them. Innocents will die."

"I know. I have tried to recall them and stop the hunters in that area, but they are ignoring commands. Black heard about it and dispatched himself without asking. It's a small sector of hunters refusing directives and hunting for fun."

Someone snorts, and I look at the man who made the noise. He seems angry and bitter, and I taste his power in the air. Warlock? "Most hunters trap and hunt our kinds for fun."

"But not all," I counter. "I am aware I'm fighting what seems to be a losing battle, but I will not give up. These hunters are acting of their own accord, warping our laws and rules."

"We have to do something," Tate begins.

"I am," I assure her. "Do you think I would let him get away with this? I've been fighting this for a very long time, Tate, and I have been playing the long game. I'm giving you his location. I want you to stop him before it's too late."

She searches my eyes. "Why now?"

"It's time," I reply.

Her eyes narrow on me, distrust gleaming in her gaze. "What skin do you have in this game, Shamus? Why recruit me? Why place me with Black? Why make me collect a team? What are your plans?" she demands. I do not look away, but I feel the others watching me. She might trust them, but there are only five people in this world I trust— her and my brothers. I will not jeopardise everything I have built and worked for, not when we are so close.

"Leave us for a moment," I tell the others in the room.

Nobody moves, however, not even Ronan, and then without looking, Tate raises her hand. "Leave. Ronan, show them to our room for now."

They shuffle to the door, and then they are gone. It should make me angry that they ignored my commands in my house, but if anything, I am grateful because it means they are loyal to her, not the cause or me.

Perfect.

I wonder if she knows that if she commanded me in such a way, I would follow her as well.

Leaning back, I run my eyes across her. "Ask your questions, the ones you have wanted answers to."

"You won't answer," she snaps, putting the folder down and sitting stiffly on my desk.

I can't resist teasing her a little. I look up at her through my lashes as she stares back at me.

"Ask and see," I challenge.

"What are you, Shamus, or *who* are you?" she asks, her eyebrows drawn together in annoyance and confusion.

"Would you like to know?" I murmur softly.

"I've wanted to know for years," she grumbles.

"But you never asked." Her mouth drops open as she thinks through the past, and I smirk when she comes to the realisation she never did. "All you ever need to do is ask, Tate. I hide nothing from you with malice. We are in this together, even if you do not realise it." I hold my hand out.

She looks from it to me before carefully laying her palm in mine. I slowly peel off the glove I gave her, desire spiralling through me, but I ignore it. Leaning down, I kiss her palm gently, unable to stop myself, and her eyes widen a fraction. Before she can hit me, I lift her bare hand and press it to my cheek. I could simply let her touch my hand, but I seem to crave her touch, and this is a way for me to get it without asking or her realising the truth.

"See for yourself," I murmur.

I don't look away from her. Her eyes seem to go far away, distant, like she is trapped in her own head. In this moment, she looks vulnerable, and I don't like it. Nothing will touch her while I am around, but the thought of someone attacking her while she uses this in the field makes me decide to mention it to Ronan so he can protect her better.

I don't know what she sees, but I do not bother to fight it. I let her into my mind, sharing memories spanning thousands of years. I let her see the truth of what and who I am. I will never hide it from her. She deserves to know. She didn't play a part in my years before this life, but she has a role in this one and is quickly becoming the most important component of it.

For millennia, I have walked alone, doing my duty, but not this time.

She stumbles back, holding her hand to her chest like it's burnt. Hooking my legs around hers, I draw my chair closer to the desk so I'm positioned between her spread legs. My hands are propped on either side of the desk, framing her thighs, as I lean in.

"Did you see what you needed to?" I whisper, sliding my pinkie across the outer corner of her trousers, needing contact.

She swallows, her eyes blown wide as she watches me. "What are you?"

"Hmm . . ." I think as I stare at her. "To answer that, I must ask you something first. Do you believe in reincarnation? I didn't, not until the moment I lost my best friends, my brothers in battle. I was already a hunter by then, one of the elite on my way to the top when everything was ruined. Death came so quickly, and it touched me, bringing back the truth and my memories. Everything clicked in my soul, allowing me to save their souls and keep them in this world. Selfish, yes, but I did it. Death and I are old friends, but life and I are as well. Each lifetime is different. I know some from an early age, and others, I learn later. The truth comes when I'm ready, but even before, I can sense the difference in me—places feel familiar, I see flashes of memories I do not understand, and recall battles I don't remember fighting. Lifetimes of skills, sometimes magical, give me powers and knowledge others could never possess."

"What are you?" she demands once more.

"I am no more human than you are, Tate. This body may be human in design, but my soul is not. I have been reborn many times since the start of this world. Each time, I have a duty. Some have names for me, like fate or karma, while others call me justice, but it matters not. It is my duty to better this world and keep the balance. I am a wanderer, a warrior, and a lost soul. I am older than every monster born into this world, older even than most gods, yet I take no sides. I am this world's reaper, and with your help in this lifetime, I will continue to do that."

"I don't understand." She works through my words. "How can you be karma or fate or whatever when you trust evil and monsters?"

"Some evil is necessary—that is a lesson I have learned through my lifetimes. It's all about balance. Most monsters have been hurt and betrayed. They are not born evil; they are *made* evil. It is my job to stop that from happening, and I failed, so instead I embrace the darkness, or rather I ask you to. You are the bridge, Tate. You are the saviour, not me. I am simply the compass pointing you in the right direction. I always thought my purpose in this reincarnation was to stop the mass killings of monsters, but I was wrong. This lifetime, I was brought back to help you do that. I was brought back to be yours."

"No, this isn't real." She tries to move away, but I don't allow it. I won't let her run from this.

"You cannot run from the truth, angel, nor what is inside you," I caution softly.

"I'm human—"

"Are you?" I challenge. "No humans have the gifts you possess. You are touched by magic. It could have originated centuries ago and been watered down through your lineage, but you are born from wild magic, Tate Havelock. That is why monsters trust you. That is why the fae recognised you. You are not human, Tate. You are the best of both worlds—or the worst depending on what this world needs. My soul found yours out of billions of people because I need you. This world needs you. You are important, do you not see that?"

"Why?" she croaks.

"Because I need you, Tate, like I have never needed anyone. I cannot do this alone. Will you help me bring the hunting guild back to its former glory and cleanse it of evil with me? This world requires balance, and death is part of that. Hunters are needed as much as monsters are. We are two sides of the same coin. Will you be my sword?" I wait for her answer as she considers my words.

"Why choose me out of everyone?" She seems concerned.

"Because you're a fighter. I have walked this world alongside some of the best warriors it has to offer, but you? You were born to be one. You have the strength to do this, and moreover, you have the ability to make people trust you. We need that. We cannot do this alone. They weren't meant to follow me, Tate. It was you. I built all this for you, waiting for the day you would arrive. Now it is time. Take your revenge and cleanse this earth of Black and the betrayers and then come back to me." Getting to my feet, I grip her chin as I lean closer. "Come back to me and stand at my side while we make the hunters great again."

"If I say no?" she whispers. "If I don't want to be the righter of wrongs?"

"Then you can go. I will not force you, but you cannot lie to me. I see it in you. You want this. You want to make this place great, for yourself, the father you lost, and the monsters that could have been saved. It is your choice, Tate. Which path do you want to walk?" I ask her. "I will support you either way, but I will not lie—I want you with me on this."

"Why?" she asks again, dissecting everything so she can assess it, which is exactly why I chose her. Although Tate relies on emotion, she's also logical, and despite her words and actions, she is good down to her soul.

"Because I trust you." She startles at that. "No matter what you do to finish this, I know you will never hurt an innocent. You will never betray this world. I want you, Tate, because you are a good person . . .

because where others would run scared or choose the easy path, you never will. You are filled with a righteous fire that I want to burn in," I admit. I glance at her lips before I drag my gaze back up. "So, angel, are you with me?"

She watches me for a moment before she seems to decide something, and when Tate makes a decision, she sticks to it, but her next move shocks me.

Gripping the back of my head, she pulls me close, and for a second time tonight, she gets the drop on me. "Then let's do this together." She slants her lips over mine, kissing me hard and fast. I taste my own blood with the knock of our teeth, and then she pulls back, smirking. "To seal the deal." She pushes away from me and tries to escape, but I cannot let her.

I was going to before she kissed me.

Grabbing her arm, I jerk her back and wrap my arms around her, my mouth brushing her ear. "You cannot escape me, angel. You forget how I got this position."

"And you forget who I am." The move is quick as she frees herself and tries to throw me, but I dodge it and slip my arm around her, spinning her until she's bent over the desk.

"I have watched you fight for years, Tate. I know all your moves." I hold her face against the desk as I press against her from behind. Nobody spars with me, plays with me, or challenges me, and I want this.

I want her under me and over me. I want Tate in a way I've never wanted anyone in any of my lifetimes. I have been drawn to her since the moment I laid eyes on her, and for years, I have resisted, trying to keep this line between us, but she won't let me anymore, and honestly, I'm glad. I'm tired of fighting this. I know all too well how short our life spans are, so I will make this one count with her.

"Not all of them," she says, and then she seems to relax into my hold. It could be a trap though, so I don't let go, but a groan slips free as she presses back into me, rubbing her perfect ass against my cock, which is ridiculously hard from sparring with her.

Nobody stands up to me like her. Nobody dares to speak to me like her.

That fire and bravery is so fucking attractive.

"Angel," I warn, my voice a growl as I try to ignore my body. Tate still hates me in a way, and she probably doesn't even trust me to a certain degree, so I should take this slowly and win her trust before I take her body, but I can't ignore the way she rubs against me.

"Isn't this what you want? I see the way you look at me when you think I'm not looking," she purrs, arching back to rub against me. I remind myself she's a weapon, but I'm helpless against her. I always have been.

With my guard dropping, she takes advantage, and before I know it, I'm pinned to my chair. She swings her leg over mine and straddles my lap, her lips tilted in a cocky, victorious smirk. She leans in and brushes her lips across mine until I chase after her. "I feel the same," she whispers. "I hate that I want you, but neither of us can ignore this. We'll probably end up dead before all this is through, so fuck it."

Her mouth crashes against mine again. Groaning, I tug her down so she's pressed against me, my hands sliding down to her ass as her tongue invades my mouth.

Both of us battle for dominance. Our teeth snap together, our lips bleed, and we still don't stop until she abruptly pulls away.

"We'll finish this when I'm back," she murmurs, her tongue darting out to trace my lips. "Maybe take some more fighting lessons, commander. You'll need them if you want to win me."

Sliding from my lap, she strolls towards the door, leaving me there.

"Fuck it," I mutter, leaping to my feet. I slam into her, letting go of all my control. I stop pretending to be the good guy, and instead I show her the warrior we both know I am.

She hits the wall, but before I can pin her, she slips under my arm, her foot going to the back of my knees, making them crumple. I spin and reach for her when she leaps back, out of the way.

Smirking, she wags her finger at me. I prowl before her, feeling like an animal rather than a man. "You think you can get past me to the door?" I spread my arms. "Make it and you're safe. Otherwise, when I catch you, you're mine."

Her tongue presses to the side of her cheek as she watches me. "Weapons?"

"None." I smirk. "Unless you're scared, angel?"

"Never," she replies, rolling her shoulders back. "Fine. Bring it, commander. Let's see if you are as ruthless as they say or if sitting behind that desk has made you . . ." Her eyes drop to my crotch. "Limp."

She's taunting me, but all it does is make me more determined. She feints left and then right before moving left again, but I catch her and push her back. "You'll have to do better than that, angel."

I see the moment she snaps. She isn't playing anymore.

She dives right at me, slamming her fist into my face before sliding to her knees and through my legs. She takes two steps, no doubt seeing her path to the door, when I wrap my arm around her waist, lift her into the air, and drag her back. I turn and toss her across the room. She lands hard on the floor, rolling before pushing to her knees in a slick move, and then she is on me again. Her legs wrap around my neck and knock me down to the floor before she scrambles up and leaps for the door once more.

Snarling, I grip her ankle, and she hits the floor, hard. I crawl over her body then flip her, but her legs wrap around my waist, and she flips us until she's on top. I roll us again, and we end up tumbling across the floor, fighting for control. She smacks into the table, and something crashes from the top. She catches it—a tray, I realise—and tries to bring it down on my head. I lift my arm at the last minute, blocking it, and it breaks across my forearm. The resounding pain makes my arm ache, but I don't care.

She's worth it.

I throw her again and come down on top of her, managing to pin her wrists above her in one hand.

I shove my hands into her pants as she fights me. "I'm not letting you into my bed," she growls.

Licking a line up her neck to her ear, I can't help but grin. "This isn't your bed, though, is it, angel?" I tug her underwear aside and slide my fingers along her wet cunt, feeling her warmth and desire even as she struggles. "You want this just like me. Look how wet you are." Lifting my fingers, I lick them clean as I watch her. "You like fighting with me? Does fighting with me turn you on, angel?"

"Who said I like it?" she snaps.

"Your body, angel. You can fight me all you want, but this can't lie to me. Keep running your pretty mouth though." I lick a line down her neck to her chest, addicted to the taste of her skin. "I like when you fight me, and I like your sharp tongue. Neither will make me stop, but it will make me all the more determined to get inside you."

"You bastard, I'm going to gut you when my hands are free."

I shove my hand back into her pants, sliding my fingers inside her with a thrust that has her crying out and her hips arching into the air.

"Go ahead. You could carve me with your blade and I wouldn't stop, not right now, when I have you where I want you." I press my lips to hers, silencing what would have been a cutting retort.

Instead, she bites down on my tongue, making me groan in ecstasy as I taste my own blood. She gives as good as she gets, even as her hips roll and she rides my fingers. I swipe my thumb over her clit, swallowing her cry, but I want more. I need more. I need her to know. I need Tate Havelock like I've never needed another, and I'm tired of fighting it.

Pulling my hand free of her clinging cunt, I grip her trousers and rip them open before tugging them down. I slide down her body, and before she can fight me, I quickly seal my mouth to her cunt as her cries fill the air.

She grabs my hair, her grip brutal and hard, but rather than push me away, she drags me closer. Her legs hook over my shoulders and her back bows as her cream drips across my tongue. I hold her tighter for my assault, thrusting my tongue inside her before flicking her clit.

"Fingers," she demands.

Rolling my eyes at her command, I slide my hand between us and thrust two back into her, knowing we both want it. She's so wet, she's dripping, turned on from our sparring match just like I am, but I ignore my hard cock. Instead, I lash her clit, adding a third finger and forcing her to take me as I fuck her with them until she locks up and her moan fills the air as she comes all over my hand and tongue.

Victory fills me, and I grin as I kiss her swollen clit and slide my fingers free. I lick them clean as she slumps to my office floor. She's so fucking beautiful, it hurts. When she opens her eyes, she catches me watching her. I know what she wants, what we both want, but I don't plan to give her it, not yet, even if it's the hardest thing I've ever done.

Tugging her trousers up, I button them and sit back before standing.

She licks her swollen lips as I move away with a vicious smile. "Go make him pay. Come back alive and I'll give you what you want. I'll be waiting." I turn away from her and walk back to my desk like nothing happened.

Like my entire world did not just shift all because I got a taste of her.

CHAPTER 33

Tate

That fucking prick.

I storm from his office, his laughter chasing me.

His fucking smirk haunts me as I stomp down the corridor, only to jerk to a stop as Ronan pops into view before me. "Fucking ghosts," I mutter as I march through him.

"What happened?" Ronan chuckles, completely unbothered by my anger. "You look like you got fucked or tried to kill each other—or maybe both."

"Shut it," I warn.

I know I'm being unreasonable, but I'm annoyed at myself. I would have fucked him if he hadn't stopped us. Why did he? Shit, I'm a mess, and I need to focus on the hunt ahead, not my annoyance at that smirking asshole sitting behind his desk.

Black is all that matters.

"Ronan," I warn as he appears in front of me again, and I come to a stop.

"Tate, listen to me." His serious tone makes me swallow my next rant. "Whatever Shamus did or said, you should know he's not the kind of man to do something without thinking through every angle of it. He chose you for a reason. You can trust him."

"You trust him blindly—"

"Not blindly. He earned it," he replies. "He earned it with every battle and year spent by my side, and when I died . . . he was lost. He brought us back, fighting death itself for it. He's the strongest and most trustworthy person I have ever met. He does everything for other people. His entire life is for someone else, so if he took something for himself, know that it took something major to make him. I'm not saying he's perfect, but he's a good man, Tate."

I hold his gaze, relaxing a little at his words. "Are you angry you died?"

"I used to be," he admits. "Not anymore. It was nobody's fault. It was just a matter of life. We all die eventually. My time was simply a lot earlier than some, but I'm lucky. Shamus gave me a second chance, and most do not get that." He's as serious as I've ever seen him.

I shrug. "You're loyal to him."

"I am, but I'm also loyal to you," he says. "You've earned it. I spent years watching you, Tate, and reporting to him. You may not like it, but we know you. We trust you. I'm loyal to Shamus, yes, but to you as well. You are the only two people in his world I care about. I'm with you."

"Until he orders you not to be," I snap as I walk past him, and something about Ronan leaving causes me to feel a sense of unease. I didn't know he was there before, but knowing I wasn't alone, even in my darkest times, it's . . . comforting. There is no embarrassment between us, but maybe there should be. He's seen me at my worst, my most vulnerable, but there's just this bond I can't explain.

He stops before me, suddenly turning solid, and grips my arm to stop me. "Not even then. I'm loyal to him, yes, but he cannot order me away from you. Nobody can, not even you. I will not go."

"Not even if I order you to?" I challenge.

"Not even then. You're stuck with me, Tate." He grins. "I've seen everything about your life. There are no secrets between us, and there never will be. The others will be jealous of our connection."

I snort at that before something clicks.

"Wait." My eyes narrow. "Did you watch me shower?"

His eyes widen, and he suddenly goes back to being incorporeal.

"Ronan!" I roar as he ducks and floats away. "You fucking pervy ghost! Get back here now!"

I chase him down the corridor, but he's gone, the floating invisible fuck. When I get my hands on him, I'm going to make him wish he were never brought back.

I'm all packed for the hunt. Shamus provided us with transport, so we'll drive the truck through the portal. We are all ready. The others didn't need much prep, and they all know what we are doing now.

They are joining me on my journey for revenge.

As I stare at myself in the mirror of the safe room, wearing my hunter leathers, I realise I look wrong. Something is missing, and I know what it is. The wire is before me, the one I usually keep in my hair. It's silly, but I feel naked without it.

I stare at my hair in annoyance. I can't plait it back into my usual hunting braid, and I finger the short strands in a bit of irritation and shame. It's just hair, but they did this to me, and I don't feel like I can hunt them like this, as if they have a hold over me. I need to make this weakness a strength.

"I could grow it for you," the fae offers, reading my expression.

"No." Even if it wouldn't cost me, I wouldn't do it. "I refuse to show weakness. It's just hair, but I do need to change it from what they did to something of my choosing."

I pluck a small dagger from my waist and carefully grab a chunk of my hair on the left, putting the sharp edge under and slicing through. The red strands fall to the floor, leaving short, rough ends behind, and I frown, wishing I had a razor. One appears before me, and I glance back to see the warlock nodding at me.

"Whatever happened, your body should always be your own."

"Thank you," I say as I pick up the portable razor and buzz the left side of my hair above my ear and push the other side over so it falls jaggedly. It looks better. The fae appears, and without a word, he clicks his fingers and a small braid appears at the top of the left side, flopping over to the right, and he weaves the wire through it before stepping back.

"That one was for free." He winks.

I turn and face them. Fang is sitting on the bonnet of the truck, waiting, and she gives me two thumbs up when I catch her eyes. "It looks hot."

I wink and carry on looking them over. "If anyone wants to back out, now is the time. This is my revenge, not yours."

"We're a team," Tem says. "Aren't we?"

"Yes, we are all going with you," Addeus confirms.

Jarek simply grins as Ronan smiles from a safe distance.

"Okay then." Taking a deep breath, I grab my bag, throw it in the back of the truck, and toss the keys to Fang. "You drive, hot stuff."

She blinks but grins as she slips down from the bonnet, and as I pass her to head to the passenger side, she smacks my ass and kisses my cheek. "Let's kick some ass. By the way, speaking of ass, yours looks great in those pants."

I gawk as she whistles and heads to the driver's seat.

Ronan nods. "She's right."

"I can't see it well enough." Tem crouches and eyes me, and I storm away, embarrassed but smiling as the others join in, talking about my ass until my face is bright red.

Once everyone piles into the car, with Tem sitting on Addeus's knees and Ronan floating in the boot with Jarek, I glance at Fang. "Let's do this."

I show them the location, and a portal big enough for the car opens. She drives through with a confident look, and then we are on the other side, the portal closing behind us. We are on a wide road with trees surrounding us on either side.

"Where are we?" she asks.

"Wild country," I reply. "Be careful. Wolves call this place home, and they won't be too happy seeing hunters. The hunters are holed up at a local two-storey building, and that's where Black will be, at HQ.

Head that way, but stay off the road at the end. We need to scout it first."

"Got it." She blows a bubble with her gum, and we drive for a little while before she pulls off, hiding the truck in the trees.

I grab my bag and glance back. "We are on foot from here. Fang, you're with me. Ronan, scout ahead. The rest of you will stay here. I'll call if I need you."

Tem pouts. "Aww."

"Just for now," I promise, "until we know what we are dealing with." I turn forward, refusing to admit I don't trust them not to storm in and slaughter everyone. I want to speak to Black first. I want him to see me coming.

Fang and I climb out while Ronan disappears into the forest.

Keeping my eyes peeled and a gun out, I glance at Fang as she moves silently at my side. "Do you want a weapon?"

"Nah, I'm good. I am a weapon." She winks.

Snorting, I look forward before crouching.

"What is it?" she murmurs, glancing over my shoulder.

"You see that?" I nod at the print. "That's a wolf paw."

"Shit, we might be too late," she says.

"I hope not." Standing, we tread farther into the forest, but it feels strange.

"There are more tracks—not just wolves, but many others. See that? Something big trampled through here," I whisper. "It's . . . weird. This many monsters near hunters?" A bad feeling builds within me.

A few days ago, there was a blood moon, and I swear I woke with something hammering in my chest, and that feeling comes back now, like a call.

Ronan suddenly appears, his eyes wide. "You are going to want to see this," he says.

I lift my gun, and he shakes his head. "You won't need it. Let's head back to the car."

"What do you mean?" I ask, but he ignores me.

Following Ronan's advice, we go back to the car. I hate going in uncovered, but he asked me to trust him, so we drive slowly down the road. Every one of us is on edge in case hunters jump out at us, but when we pull into a parking lot before the two-storey building, I get my first glimpse of what he saw, and I understand what he meant.

It's a battlefield filled with bodies and death. Wild animals eat the corpses, until gravel crunches under our tires and they scatter. The front doors are blown open, and there are bullet holes everywhere.

More shell casings cover every inch of the ground.

Fang stops the car, and we get out. I step over limbs, puddles of blood, and rotting bodies, searching every face for someone I recognise, but they are all too badly destroyed. I don't see Black or the others, nor do I see any monsters, only hunters.

"What the fuck happened here?" Jarek asks.

"I don't know," I say as I glance at the busted door. Lifting my gun, I head that way, ducking inside in case anyone fires, but no one does.

There's more blood here, more bodies and bullets too, and I follow them to a door that leads down. I tap my side and gesture for Ronan. He heads down and calls up a moment later.

"All dead here."

Following after him, I keep my gun raised just in case, but he's right. There's nothing living here, just more blood and bodies—all hunters. We pass through the room and follow a narrow corridor marred with claw marks, finding rooms holding more bodies.

Wolves. It seems the hunters picked a fight with the wrong people.

There's a cage in the back room that draws my attention. It's empty, the door hanging off its hinges with claw marks and blood leading away from it. Clearly, it held a wolf.

Turning around, I scan the room. "There was a big battle here, and the hunters lost." From the smell, I know it has to be a few days old, maybe even weeks.

"I smell wolves, a lot of them," Addeus remarks, and I nod. I see the signs as well, even if my senses are not as good as his.

"It seems they picked a fight with someone they couldn't win against," I murmur.

I stand in the midst of what was once a hunter HQ. All that is left is death and destruction. I wonder where and how Black fits in when my eyes land on the computer room, and I walk inside. A video is loaded on the screens, so I hit play.

A determined, grim-faced woman starts to speak. There's something about her eyes . . . She's a wolf.

"Last night, my pack and I killed every hunter in this area. We didn't do it unprovoked. Hunters came into my home, burnt my family alive, and chopped my father's head off before my eyes. They killed so many, the blood cannot be washed away, even today. They also went after children, innocents who had never done anything wrong. Along with this email, which I am sending to every hunter whose email address is in this laptop, I will attach the videos I found that show their crimes—not just against wolves, but against every beast, as you call us. You vowed to protect human life and innocents, but you are just using it to cover your sick tendencies, like rape and torture. You aren't soldiers, you are serial killers, and this is your warning. We will rise. We will not accept this anymore. Every monster will be made aware. You have two choices—die for your crimes or clean house. Stop the madness. Kill those who hurt innocents, not those who are innocent. I know from my mates, who were hunters, that you did not start this to be evil, but to help, so do that. If you don't, and if this doesn't stop, mark my words—I will hunt every single one of you down and rip out your hearts."

The date is from a week ago. What does this mean?

Is Black dead?

I didn't see his body outside, nor the others', but that doesn't mean anything. He could have been ripped apart, eaten, or simply be somewhere else.

Is my revenge gone?

It's a bitter pill to swallow.

"Tate?" Ronan murmurs. "I think we should leave."

I nod, knowing he's right, but as I look around, I know I cannot leave without answers. Pulling off my glove, I press my hand to the closest bloodstained wall and watch. Agony, pain, and death ricochet around my chest. A female . . . A wolf . . . It's her memories. She's angry and so very strong.

Love fills her every action, and respect fills me as I wander through and up the building, touching every surface I can, searching for Black and my old team.

At the front door, I finally see what I need to.

Black's voice rings through my head, igniting my fury. I wish I were here that night to end him—not just for me, but for all the wolves huddled around, scared and tired of fighting. I can feel this she-wolf's need for peace.

She never wanted this, just like me.

I follow the trail outside and lay my hand on the ground, closing my eyes as I watch what went down. I see my team fall, and then Black.

Standing, I slide my glove back on and turn around to find them all watching me.

"They are dead. It's over," I announce.

I hate those words so much, but it's the truth.

Black and my team are gone, and so is my revenge.

It's a good thing they have been stopped, but I can't help feeling like it was stolen from me.

CHAPTER 34

Tate

We have nowhere else to go. I don't want to go back yet, and I can't move forward. I'm almost listless, so when Fang steps up and we find ourselves in a hotel room, I'm almost thankful, but I will admit I'm in a bad fucking mood.

I hear them whispering, but I focus on cleaning the blade in my hand, trying to relax with the rhythmic movements, but if anything, it's only making it worse.

I hear one of them yelp, and my head jerks up as Ronan is pushed before me. "Hey there—" he starts, but I throw the knife. It soars right through him as he shouts and hides behind Fang, who sighs.

"You go as our ambassador," he hisses. "She scares me."

"So you want her to scare me?" Fang grouses as I pick up my next knife and start to clean it.

"You're a brave succubus. Seduce her into being happy or something." Ronan pushes her forward, and Fang mutters insults but stomps over and kneels before me so I have no choice but to look at her.

"Tate," she murmurs softly. "It's over. They are gone. You said so yourself."

"I didn't get to kill them," I mutter. That's what keeps echoing in my head. "I didn't get to make them pay."

"But they are dead, and that's what matters, right? Not who delivered their deaths, but that they cannot be around to cause any more," she reasons.

I don't want that. I know she's right, but I feel . . . slighted.

"You got your revenge," I mutter, and she flinches. "I didn't get mine. I suffered, and I almost died. For what? It was all for nothing. Everything I have done to get here was for nothing." I pull my hands away when she reaches for me. "We were all for nothing."

I see pain bloom in her eyes, and I regret the words as soon as I speak them, but I cannot take them back. I used my words like a weapon, and I will deal with the consequences.

"Alright, enough fucking moping," she snaps, changing tactics, and my eyes widen at her harsh tone. "They are dead. Get the fuck over it and put your big-girl panties on. This was not all for nothing. We were brought together for a reason. Maybe it isn't the one you want, but that doesn't matter. You don't always get what you want in life, Tate. You are better than this. Do not let them ruin another minute of your life."

She snaps her mouth shut as we stare at each other, and before I realise it, my blade is at her throat. She doesn't react other than a slight widening of her eyes. She digs her chin into the blade until she bleeds.

"Go ahead, punish me if it will make you feel better. I owe you my life, so it's yours to take." Her voice is silky. "If this is what you need, then take it."

I stare into her eyes that were filled with pleasure a day ago and see a desperate sort of fear.

For me or *of* me?

I'm not sure, and I hate that I put it there.

I don't want that either. It's not her fault he's dead. Removing the blade, I stand before I take my frustration out on her. She shouldn't have to deal with my bad mood, none of them should. They've all suffered at the hands of men and the blades of hunters. I will not add to that.

I will be better than the other hunters

I will be better than men.

Fang especially has suffered at the hands of men for years. I will not add to her list. I recognise her willingness to be whatever I need her to be right now, but I will not.

I drop the blade and move past her. I'm not good to be around right now, and they all deserve better.

"Oh, good job, Fang," Ronan mutters as he shoots her a thumbs up. The others struggle to copy the gesture, not used to it, and I roll my eyes and slam the door shut behind me before opening it to give them an order.

"Stay inside," I snap, still worried about them. I don't want them wandering about and getting killed by a rogue hunter.

Taking a deep breath, I wander down the second storey of the hotel. The rooms face the woods, and I lean over the railing at the very end, but I still feel trapped.

Catching the edge of the roof, I haul myself up and lie back, staring up at the stars.

I don't expect anyone to come after me, not with the mood I'm in, so when someone lies down next to me, I startle. He's the last person I would expect, but the fae stares at me from inches away.

"It's okay to be angry, to want to be the one who ended their miserable existences. It was stolen from you. I understand," he says, and I blink, unsure what to say. "My name is Zeev."

I jerk as the name wraps around me with power and purpose.

A fae's name gives you power over them. It's an offering, a way to tell you they trust you.

"Zeev," I whisper. He shuffles next to me, his eyes tightening as I roll it over my tongue. "Why are you telling me?"

"You have earned it," he answers as he stares up at the stars, but I still look at him, so he turns his head and meets my gaze again. "I have been around a very long time. I have known great leaders able to kill with a thought, but I have never met anyone else with convictions as strong as yours, Tate Havelock. You have the determination to survive, but not at the price of your soul. You have resilience and strength I admire, but it is your soul I crave. You freed me when no other could, and you saved all of those in that room without asking for anything in return. You are a true warrior. You were born to wield the blade, and I would like to be at your side as you do so."

"The fae offer no loyalty to anyone but their own kind," I whisper, reciting what I know.

"We offer loyalty to those we choose to, those who earn it," he retorts.

"Your sister—"

"Is a queen. My place was never at her side. I never fit into that world because I was never strong enough to resist the darkness, but at your side, I can. It is purely a selfish reason, so do not read anything into it." He turns away, but there's a smile dancing on his perfect lips.

"Selfish, huh?" I ask as I look at the sky, but it's working. He's distracting me from my bad mood.

"Yes, no other reason." His smile grows, and I cannot contain mine. I never expected a truce between us, and I don't particularly like Zeev, but I can't deny there is a connection between us that is stronger than anything I've ever felt. There are no lies or illusions, and we are our worst selves when we are around each other.

We are each other's worst half, and when we are together, they only seem to explode.

There is a feral kind of need between us, the kind that reaches past love. It's so strong, we cannot resist. I still hate him, but it doesn't change that.

Maybe that's why I feel like I can be myself, because he will never judge me. He will never be disgusted. He understands. He lives in the darkness with the part of me I hide.

His monster is the same as my own.

"Zeev," I whisper. I don't know what he hears in my voice, but he sits up, watching me. "Fuck me."

He blinks once, and then he snarls and rolls above me, slamming my hands to the roof above my head. We both know if I wanted to, I could break free, but I relax beneath him, needing this. He searches my face and must see that because he leans down. I close my eyes, expecting his kiss, but his lips brush over my cheek at the last second, making me flinch.

"You wouldn't use her, but you will use me, hunter. I like pain. I like it to hurt . . . . I want you to rip me apart and feast on my flesh, desire, and blood. That is where we are different. I will offer you this— no deal or lies between us, just shared need. Use me, Tate Havelock. Take your revenge out on me."

He leans back, straddling my thighs, a smirk playing on his lips.

"You want to fuck me? Then do it," he taunts. "Unless you're scared? All talk?"

Sitting up, I search his eyes, but all I see is a cold sort of patience. He's curious about what I will do. Most would be afraid to dare a hunter, but not him. He fears nothing, and maybe it's that or the fact that I can't hold back my hatred anymore.

Wrapping my legs around him, I flip us so he's below me. I draw my dagger and run it across his perfect face. He leans into it without a flinch, his smirk only growing, and when I rub the metal across his lips, his tongue darts out and wraps around the sharp end, cutting him. Tugging it away, I lean down and kiss him hard and fast.

We both groan, our tongues tangling.

I break the kiss, both of us panting. The darkness spilled out of me at the first taste of his blood. I'm a hunter, so it's my job to protect innocents, but he is not innocent, and neither am I.

I slam the dagger into his chest, burying it deep, and then my eyes widen as I still, my hands falling away as it protrudes from his chest, blood pooling around the wound.

He gasps and closes his eyes, and for a moment, horror fills me at what I've done . . . at what I have become. His eyes suddenly snap open, on fire with desire.

"That's the best you have? I'm an immortal fae, a god in your world, and you think this will hurt me?" He wraps his hand around the hilt and slowly pulls it out, groaning the entire time.

The sound isn't born from pain. It's from desire, and my fear is swallowed by my darkness.

There's an understanding in the darkness, an acceptance of who I am, allowing me to release my feelings across his perfect skin.

He lifts the dagger to my mouth, and without hesitation, I sweep my tongue down the sharp edge, tasting his blood and surrender. He watches me hungrily before he licks the blade too, tasting his blood now mixed with mine before he flips it and offers it to me, cutting his palm.

I know if I take the blade again, I'm accepting this and who I am deep inside.

Wrapping my hand around the dagger, I take it.

"Do your worst, huntress. I can take it." He stretches his arms above his head like an offering, his lips stained with our blood.

I am not Black, and this is a willing partner. I might enjoy hurting him, but he does as well.

We are different, and Black is dead.

Anger fills me once more, and Zeev only encourages it. I slice out, tearing up his skin with the blade. I keep slicing, my vision completely red. All of my anger and hatred slip free until I just carve him up.

He laughs, even as blood splatters us all, and it's only when my arm grows tired and heavy that I stop and look at the mess below me. One of his eyes is almost gone, and his chest is a mess of slashes, more ruined meat than person. For a moment, horror fills me, as does panic, but as I watch, the cuts start to heal, and then his face is perfect once more.

"I'm still waiting. Impress me," he taunts, licking his lips.

My chest heaves, my anger still riding me, and his taunts don't help that. I know he's pushing me over the edge of sanity for a reason, but I give over to it. I stab the blade into his chest again, even as he reaches down and presses his cock to my entrance. He holds my gaze, and when I pull the blade free, he slides into me with the same rhythm.

I stretch around his ice-cold cock. I try to lift off him, but he drives me back down and holds me there as pleasure rolls through me, mixing with my fury and helplessness. I slam the blade into him again, and he pulls out. When I free the blade, he slams back into me, and I get it, so I drive it into him faster, and he keeps up as blood covers us both.

His icy length hits spots inside me that change the pain to pure ecstasy, and I stab him just to get him to move faster. Each feral thrust drives me higher so nothing else matters.

I'm free of all this . . . human entanglement.

I slice through his throat and freeze, panicking for a moment. He laughs around it, the sound horrid, then plucks it free, and my eyes widen.

Flipping us, he slams the dagger into the roof next to my head, and then he pushes my head to the left and bites my neck until I feel blood. I swallow my screams of agony, even as I lift my hips to meet his thrusts. The stars sparkle above me as my nails slice his back, cutting it to ribbons before digging into his flexing ass. He releases my neck, my blood dripping down his chin to my skin below. His blond hair is unbound and flowing in the wind, and his eyes are bright.

He's so beautiful, it hurts as he drives into me, his ice-cold length spearing me over and over.

"Zeev!" His name slips free, and it only seems to urge him on. His cock warms inside me, no longer painful but still rock-hard and huge, and I love it.

I lift my body, using his as he uses mine, and when his lips meet mine, I taste our blood. Our hearts hammer in sync, our bodies slick with blood and desire, and then it all becomes too much.

I rip my head away as ecstasy ripples through me, stealing the sight of him, which I hate. My muscles lock up, my legs jerking as I come so hard he groans.

When my vision clears, I find the stars shining brightly.

"Don't look at the stars, mortal, for I am much more beautiful and powerful," he warns as he rises above me, lifting my hips into the air and driving into me from a new angle. He fucks me through the after-shocks and right into another orgasm, and he still doesn't stop. His cock is so warm now, it's like a hot poker.

"Zeev, please." I don't know what I'm asking for, but it doesn't matter. The prince turns wild as he takes my body brutally, and when he leans down and kisses me once more, I tip over the edge again, coming around his length.

He grunts into my mouth, his cock jerking inside me, and scalding hot cum splashes deep within my channel, making me whine. He swallows that noise, our messy kiss turning slow and languid as he falls into the cradle of my thighs. We break apart, both of us panting, and for once the fae looks affected.

His heaving chest is covered in blood, and even his hair is stained at the tips, but it's the look in his eyes—possessive.

"My mortal," he growls as his hand slides around my throat, and he jerks me up to kiss me again. "No matter what, you are my mortal, and I am your Zeev. Only yours. No matter what this world hands you, I will be at your side to lessen the burden and fight with you. Never doubt that."

His words unlock something inside me, and despite the strange bond between us, I wrap my arms around him and bury my head in his chest. He sighs, and I expect him to push me away, but he awkwardly pats my back before stroking it.

CHAPTER 35

Addeus

The door opens a little while later. We waited, trusting her to come back in one piece. She slips in behind the fae, both of them sharing a knowing look as she treads deeper into the room. It's quiet as she looks around, and it's clear she's uncomfortable.

She's a strong warrior, but everyone has a weakness.

I understand the need for revenge, and when that is stolen, it changes your world. I do not blame her for her reaction, I'm even thankful for it. All this time, she has been cool, calm, and in control, so it was nice seeing her let go.

It proved we are not so different after all.

"Your small machine was ringing. We did not wish to interrupt though." I hold out the device, and she smiles.

"My phone, thank you."

I run my eyes down hers and the fae's torn, bloodied clothes. "I seem to have missed a good time."

She grins even as she blushes, but her device rings again. She answers it, heading over to the bed before hesitating. Tem runs off and comes back, placing a towel down, and she sits carefully on it, trying not to drip blood anywhere. I sniff at it before climbing on behind her, dragging my nose over her as I try to figure out if it's hers or his. Is she hurt?

She gives me a confused look but focuses on the phone, her conversation audible for us thanks to our enhanced senses.

"Simon, hi," she greets. "It's nice to hear from you."

"So formal, I thought we were besties," the guy jokes. "I just wanted to pass on a message from Althea. She said to tell you thank you for her help. She hopes the person she sent you for is what you are looking for, and she is ready to talk whenever you are. There will be peace between the vampyrs and you when you know what that means. Okay, enough mystic shit."

"Mystic shit," she scoffs as I lap at her neck. She startles, turning her gaze to me.

"You know it, so I'll tell her I told you. Are you still there, Tate?"

"I'm here." She narrows her eyes on me in warning. Sliding my hands up her thighs, I caress her body, searching for any wounds.

"Do you know anything about a wolf pack close to the red mountains?" she asks as she slaps at my hands, but she leans back into me despite that protest. Resting my chin on her shoulder, I inhale once more. Some of it is her blood, but not a lot. She's okay. It's mostly the fae's, though he doesn't seem worse for wear because of it.

"Yeah, there's a big pack out there. You're not hunting them, are you? They are good people. I know them," Simon hedges.

"No, I want to meet them. We have a common enemy—or did," she admits. "I won't hurt them, I promise."

"Oh, well, the alpha's name is Jang. He's a good guy. He has a daughter called Quinn who's a badass she-wolf. They are deep in the woods before the mountain, with lots of families and kids. They keep to themselves, but they are one of the strongest packs there is—" There's a grunt. "Yes, except yours, mate."

"Would they kill me on sight?" she asks curiously.

"Hmm, I'm not sure, to be honest," he answers.

"No worries, I'll figure it out. Go be with your mate. I can hear him panting in the background. Speak soon." She hangs up and tilts her head to look at me. "Finished feeling me up?"

"You smell like blood," I say, my hunger evident even as I fight it off.

"Uh-huh, are we going to have a feral to deal with as well?" Ronan grouses as he eyes me. The warlock leaps back, magic forming in his hands. Tem just drops to the floor, watching us inquisitively. Fang seems more curious than anything, and the fae just smiles as he lies on the other bed, content and lazy.

"No," I growl, but it does sound more animalistic than human.

Tate's eyes narrow on me, looking deep within and seeing the things in the darkness I hide from. "Jarek," she drawls.

"Yes?" he hedges.

"Do me a favour and bind Addeus to the bed." She says it so casually, it doesn't click at first. When it does, I snap my teeth at her, but metal suddenly slides across my skin and I'm yanked down onto the bed, my arms pulled up to the headboard as my legs are spread and chained. Roaring, I buck and writhe until Tate swings her leg over me and perches on my waist, her eyebrow arched.

"Stop," she demands, and I slump into the mattress. My fangs ache with the need to bite her, my mechanical side battling for dominance at being restrained again. "I will let you go when you calm down. I am not them, Addeus. This is not a trap to keep you in, but I will not let you hurt what is mine."

"Yours?" I hiss.

"Everyone in this room is mine for better or worse," she says, placing her hands on my chest as she watches me like I am nothing more than something for her to tame and control . . . and she would be right. My body hums at being so close to her, my circuits popping and frying.

She might be human, but she is the most dangerous person in this room filled with monsters.

Her nails dig into my chest, and the slight sting makes me hiss and snap at the air again.

"Are you going to behave?"

"If I don't?" I retort.

The smirk she aims at me goes right to my cock, and I roll my hips, trying to force her down for some pressure.

Her eyes narrow, and she leans down to me, her scent clinging to my skin.

Arching up, I try to press as close as I can, and she rewards me by dragging her tongue up my neck to my ear where she bites down, making my back bow as a howl of pleasure erupts from me. "Good boys get rewards. Bad ones get punished. Tell me, which do you want?"

My circuits are firing so hard, my chip cannot compute.

"Punishment it is," she purrs as she sits back.

Her hand wraps around my length, and even that slight pressure makes me howl like a trapped animal. I drive into her hand as she grips me, jerking my length until I almost spill, and then she just lets go. I slump into the bed, confused as I come down, my desire cooling as she slides off me. She removes her clothes and then crawls up my body, stopping to wrap her mouth around my length. My hands grip the chains as she slides her mouth all the way down and then off.

"You taste like metal and blood. It's nice," she murmurs as she grips my length and slides her mouth back down. The sight is so incredible, I come off the bed, wanting more, but the more I push up, the more she retreats, until I just slump and let her work me over with her mouth. When I'm about to come, she pulls back again.

Punishment, I realise.

Straddling my body, she teases me with her cunt, rubbing it across my length.

"Ah." She wags her finger. "I didn't say you could come—" She gasps as I surge up from the bed, my hips lifting her high into the air. Her hands scramble to grab me as the magical metal snaps away, and I roll us, driving into her with a brutal thrust. I power into her as she cries out, her nails clawing my back until I feel it strip away to reveal the metal underneath, but I don't stop.

I hammer into her tight, wet cunt, feeling it grip me deliciously. The others draw nearer, watching me, but she doesn't care, and neither do I. I would never hurt her. I'd rather pluck out my own fangs.

I show her just how badly she teased me, forcing my length deep inside her repeatedly as she cries out words that make no sense. My circuits fire as too much information overloads me.

The need to feed rides me as hard as the need to fill her belly with my cum. It's an animal instinct driving me to move faster until the bloodlust becomes too much. The scent of her blood is still in the air, and I can't hold back.

When I sink my fangs into her neck, I feel her scream vibrate against my skin, echoing from her throat as I drink her blood. It tastes of pleasure and lust and so much power, I feel my body expanding. I am too big for this little human, but she doesn't care. She recklessly clings to me, riding me from below as I drain her.

Her power fills me as I continue to thrust into her tight, hot body until her channel clenches around me as she screams. I feel her come below me, her ecstasy exploding in her blood, and I am helpless to resist the cling of her cunt. It milks me, and I oblige, driving as deep inside her as I can and unleashing my release. It fills her tight womb, and I order more to be made and pumped into her as I slow my feeding and then swipe the wound with my tongue.

She's limp below me, her eyes closed and skin flushed, but she twitches as I force more cum into her. Finally, I shut down those systems and slowly pull from her fluttering cunt. Her eyes open, and I heave a relieved breath at the lax contentment on her face. She's always so strong, brave, and fearless, but she's so defenceless and trusting in this moment that I gather her into my arms.

Curling into my chest, she pants against me. "Remind me next time not to taunt you."

"I am only tame for so long, especially when it comes to you. I would obey every command unless it has to do with your pleasure." She shivers against me, and I purr in happiness.

"Bravo. Ten out of ten, no notes." We lean up to see Ronan floating above us, slowly clapping as he eyes us. "Bit bloodier than I'm into, but I can admit it was very hot. I do have a question. Since you drink that much blood, is your pee red? No? Like, where do you store all the blood? And you're part machine, so is it, like . . . lube for the machine parts? Like, do you sweat blood when you are too full? Do you get stomach cramps—"

He yelps as my little one pulls a blade and tosses it through him.

"That wasn't nice! Just because I cannot feel doesn't mean it doesn't hurt my feelings." He wags his finger at her, pouts, and then disappears.

She groans and slumps back into me. "I'll pay for that later. He'll probably jump out at me when I'm on the toilet again."

I can't help but chuckle. My life was so quiet before her and those that surround her. Now, I do not know a moment of quiet or peace. For some, it might be too much, but for me, I enjoy it. I spent centuries locked away and alone, but now I never am.

It's nice.

Tate is not one to lie around, so just ten minutes after I've cleaned her, she is on her feet.

Tate insisted on showering, since she didn't appreciate the blood covering her like we do, and she's just strapping up her boots when Ronan appears, looking frazzled as he lingers near the door.

"Eh, Tate," he begins.

"What now, Ronan?" She sighs. "I don't know if my blood mixes with his to make a super soldier."

"Yep, no, not that. Just thought you ought to know there are like five men in all black heading to the room," he says casually. "And they seem mad as hell."

She blinks at him before leaping to her feet and diving for her bag. She just grabs a gun when the door splinters open and chaos explodes.

CHAPTER 36

Tate

Rolling away from the exploding hotel door, I duck behind the closest chair, taking aim with my pistol. My body goes cold, however, when I get a good look at our attackers.

They aren't monsters, or maybe they are, but they are familiar either way.

They are men I hunted with for years.

It's the men who betrayed me.

It's our elite team, still in their shredded, bloodied black hunting gear. There are no guns or weapons in sight, however, as they sweep deeper into the room. I sit frozen like a child as I gape.

They died . . .

I saw it.

I felt it.

"Kill them all," comes a gruff order.

"Protect our mistress!"

Tem roars and throws himself at them. Addeus joining him, while Jarek begins to conjure. Fang is at his side, holding a blade, and Ronan stands beside her. Zeev appears behind them, and they turn to attack, my old team lunging at my new family. Black isn't here, but he must be close. Their eyes land on me where I'm staring in shock.

Goose.

Except . . . this isn't the Goose I remember.

His skin is pale, the colour of death, with black veins crawling over his pallid face and up to bloodshot eyes.

"There you are," he says.

My eyes widen as Goose heads towards me. He backhands a chair out of the way, and it flies across the room with inhuman strength, smashing into the wall and breaking into pieces.

Tightening my grip on the gun, I get to one knee and fire, my shock wearing off in the face of impending danger. His body jerks as it's riddled with bullets, and I continue to fire, but he doesn't stop, not until he's grinning before me. He smacks the gun away and reaches for me. I roll forward and slam a dagger into the artery in his thigh as I slide through his legs, coming up behind him. I wrap myself around his back and slam another blade into his neck for safe measure.

Roaring, he spins and reaches for me, but blood doesn't squirt from the wounds like normal. Instead, a thick, blackish substance slowly rolls from the wounds and across his skin, confusing me for a moment, and then I'm airborne. I hit the wall hard, and he's on me. He wraps his hand around my throat and lifts me into the air with inhuman strength.

"Hello, Tate." He grins. "Miss us?"

I cannot spare the others a look, but I hear them fighting. I just hope they are doing better than I am.

There's nothing human left in Goose's gaze. "You're dead. You should have stayed dead," I hiss as he jerks me forward.

"Where's the fun in that? I've always wondered how you would taste. I bet you're delicious. Let's find out." He pulls me towards his mouth.

I slam my dagger into his arm and rip it up, tearing through tendons and muscles, but he doesn't even blink, just gives me a creepy grin with teeth covered in blood and black inkiness. His eyes are soulless.

There is no spark of warmth or life there.

Pulling the dagger free, I slam it into him again, hoping to loosen his grip, but if anything, he just seems amused by my attempts. He should be dead. They are all fatal wounds for a human.

He isn't human, though, not anymore, and I do not have a fucking clue what he is.

This isn't working; he won't fucking die. Bullets didn't stop him, and he won't bleed out. I can hit him with everything I have, but unless I know what he is now and how to kill him, we are at a disadvantage and could sustain losses.

A good hunter knows when to retreat.

This battle cannot be won, not like this, and I have more to think about than just me. Death doesn't scare me, I welcome it, but those around me deserve better. They have been failed far too often.

I will not let them down.

He tugs me closer to his gaping mouth, and I know I won't survive what he has planned, but he forgot one thing—I'm not that easy to kill. I lunge, taking him by surprise as I wrap around him from the front.

I sink my teeth into his neck, feeling his veins burst before I rip my head back, wanting to gag as that tar-like blood fills my mouth. He roars as I'm dropped to the floor. I hit it hard, spitting out his skin and that disgusting slimy substance, then I scramble to my feet and dive towards my bag. I grab it and glance around the room.

We are losing. Magic is flying everywhere, blood as well.

Fang screams as she's thrown onto the bed, Mav coming down on top of her with a wicked laugh. Tugging my shotgun free, I fire as I walk over. He jerks and rolls away. Grabbing Fang, I keep hold of her hand as I take out a grenade and glance at her.

She looks around before nodding at me. Both of us know what we have to do.

"Let's go!" I roar to my men. Trusting them to follow and survive, I shoot a path to the door. Once outside, I toss the grenade back into the room, keep hold of Fang, and start to run.

I hear more footsteps behind me, but when I glance back, I see it's Addeus, Jarek, Tem and Zeev. Ronan pops up in front of me, and just as we turn the corner, the grenade goes off. The gas will fill the room, choking them and hopefully knocking them out. We use it for big nests so we can head in without being attacked, and I hope like fuck it works on whatever they are now.

Keeping hold of Fang's hand, I dive into the truck and spin the tires as the others dive into the back, and I peel away before their doors are even shut.

When I fishtail out onto the empty, dark road, the headlights of the truck splash across a figure in the middle waiting for us. I slow and then stop as he lifts his head, a knowing grin on his face.

Black.

I stare at my old major, or what he has become, my heart hammering as his eyes light up with a wicked gleam I know far too well.

It's a trap.

"Back it up! Turn around!" Fang yells.

He grins wider, and I grip the wheel tighter, my nostrils flaring in fury. "No." It's what he wants. Jerking the truck into gear, I slam my foot on the gas and barrel towards him. We grow closer and closer, but he doesn't dive out of the way, and when we hit him, he goes up and over the vehicle, cracking the windshield as he hits the top.

I speed off, glancing in the rearview for him, but I don't see him. Suddenly, my window smashes and a hand grips my throat, trying to jerk me from my seat. "Take the wheel," I hiss at Fang, and when she grips it, I stab my dagger into Black's arm. It does nothing but piss him off, and I'm slammed into the door. A grunt escapes me at the pain as I feel the others reaching for him.

"He's mine," I hiss, truly pissed off now. Not only did this bastard torture and try to kill me, but he also made me think he was dead and didn't even have the decency to stay dead. "Fang, drive." It's all the warning I give her as I kick my door open, knocking his arm away and gripping the edge of the doorframe. I haul myself up and onto the roof, crouching as the car swerves, and I glare at Black.

He kneels before me, his arm extended and twisted at his side from where it just broke.

Pulling another dagger from my side, I brandish one in each hand, panting as I wait.

He snaps his arm into place, and within seconds his fingers flex, even crushed and facing the wrong way.

"What the fuck are you?" I demand. "What did you do to yourself, Black?"

"What I had to." He chuckles, the sound like nails on a chalkboard. "Now it's time to finish this. You should be dead, Tate."

"So the fuck should you, but I guess we are both disappointments," I retort.

"Enough talking." He dives at me.

I slide to avoid him, and he almost tumbles from the roof, but he catches himself at the last minute as the truck jerks to the side. I use it to throw myself at him, one blade aimed at his chest and the other going towards his neck to carve off his head.

No fucker can survive that, so it's a safe bet.

As I'm sawing through his neck, his arm comes up and snaps onto my wrist. My fingers open reflexively, and he kicks me back. I hit the roof hard, the breath gone from my lungs, and then his hand is in my hair, dragging me up until I hang over the edge of the front windscreen. I manage to bring my arms up just in time as his fist slams into them. He rains punches across me, my arms aching with the force, and I grit my teeth as I try to block him, but he gets tired of it. Growling, he grips one of my arms and yanks it out and to the left. I feel it pop out of its socket, and I swallow my scream as it instantly goes numb. His hand slides around my throat as he grins down at me, tightening his hold and cutting off my oxygen.

I choke even as I kick out, trying to dislodge him. It would have worked before, but not now. Whatever Black is, it's something with a huge amount of strength.

"I'm going to rip your head from your body and feast on your insides," he threatens, "and then I'll do the same to the ones helping you before I go back to Stalkers' Rest and kill every single one of them."

I kick out once more. His hand loosens, and I scramble for anything. I need to get rid of him and fast.

"I'll make this world dark like my soul," he snaps.

My head rolls to the side and then back, and I see what I need to— the bridge. Turning back to him, I grip his ruined shirt and grin in his face as I jerk him closer. "See you in hell then," I snarl, and I count down. Just as we reach the bridge, I kick and push with all my might, lifting him off me. He hits the bridge and flies from the top of the truck.

Lying as flat as I can, I wait for us to clear it and then groan and roll over, gripping the passenger door. My other arm isn't working, so I have to reach down, open the door, and slide in with one arm. It's hard work, but I make it happen and slam it shut. My hand goes to my shoulder, feeling it. It's dislocated, and I can't fight like this, but it's clear Black and the others aren't going to give up.

Numerous voices reach me. "Are you okay?"

I nod, gritting my teeth as I extend my arm and, with a jerk, snap it back into place. A hiss escapes my lips, and I test my grip. Luckily, it's working, just sore. Glancing at Fang, I grin. "Great driving, babe."

"Sure," she replies, her eyes wide and locked on the front window.

Reaching over, I lay my hand over hers. "It's okay. You can ease up a little. Head somewhere deep into the forest. We need to lie low for a bit."

She nods jerkily, and I make sure she is okay before I look at the others crowded in the back. "You guys okay?"

"You should have let us help," Jarek snarls.

I shrug. "Nah, I had him."

"Let me fix your arm," Tem offers.

"It's fine, honestly. Let's just get somewhere safe," I mutter.

"Is anywhere safe? What was that?" Addeus murmurs.

"That was your old team, no?" Zeev asks.

"It was." I nod as I glance back at them and then into the darkness beyond the cracked windscreen. "You're right. Nowhere will be safe."

"Why?" Fang asks, glancing at me before looking back at the road.

"We are being hunted," I inform them.

"What do you mean we are being hunted?" Fang asks, pacing before me as I set out what I have in my bags. It won't be enough for whatever they are now. I need a fucking tank and an armoury, not just some guns, grenades, and wire.

Lifting my head, I watch her pace. The truck is idling, its lights splashing across us. The others sit next to us, their heads slowly tilting from side to side as they watch Fang before me.

"That was my old team. Clearly, they have become something else," I admit, "and now are hunting us. They probably picked up my scent from HQ when they went back and followed it. Dumb. I was fucking dumb."

"Well, it was fun to see the old gang," Ronan remarks, and my anger flares at him . . . at everything. I leap to my feet and head towards him, getting right in his face as his eyes widen.

"You could have told me who it was!" I roar.

"I didn't know!" Ronan snaps. "I couldn't see their faces, and I panicked and had to warn you, okay? It was more important you were alive!"

"It is not your responsibility to keep me alive—"

"Yes, it is! I have done it for years, watching your back and protecting you. I will not stop now. No matter what you think of me, everything I have ever done is for you!" he shouts, more serious than I've ever seen him.

I stare at him for a moment, unsure what to say. "They died, I saw them, so what were they?" I whisper.

"Ghouls," Jarek says, and I step back from Ronan, breaking the tension between us. "They were ghouls."

"Shit," we all say at once as I rub my head.

"I've never hunted ghouls. They are really fucking rare," I mutter. I don't like not knowing things, and this is even worse. I cannot hunt what I do not understand. "I don't even know how they are—" A noise has me spinning, raising a knife and a gun as I scan the area. I gesture for them to get down, then I crouch and wait.

"Anyone see anything?" I hiss.

"Movement in the trees, fifty feet ahead," Addeus murmurs. "They are . . . wrong. Dead, whoever it is."

"Great. Be prepared," I mutter, and the next minute is filled with tension as I wait for another attack. The trees rustle, twigs snap loudly, and then a body emerges from the darkness. I fire automatically, and they jerk, falling to the ground. I head over, scanning the area, but I don't see anyone else.

Suddenly, they lurch to their feet, and I still as their head lifts. I know that pale, innocent face—Eric, the baby of the group and the person I was closest to, the one who did nothing to stop what happened to me.

He's weak, always has been, but not anymore as the bullet hole in his chest continues to leak black fluid.

"Please help me, Tate," Eric pleads, his eyes wide as he falls to his knees. Blood coats his mouth and hands. "Something is wrong. I woke up like . . . this, and I'm just so hungry and lost. Please, Tate, please help me." He collapses forward.

My eyes are wide as I keep my gun pointed at him. "Tem, check if he's alive or awake or something."

Tem treads closer, hesitantly kneeling at his side, and rolls him over. Eric's eyes are closed, and his skin is pale with black veins bulging across his neck and stretching into his face. "He's out cold," Tem says. I move back, and without removing my eyes from Eric since we can't be too careful, I toss some rope at Tem. It won't hold for long, but it's the best we have and will give us some warning.

"Tie him to the tree," I order. He didn't attack on sight. It could be a trap, but he sounded scared and lost. Black hates weakness, and Eric is just that, even in this form.

Tem and Addeus drag him to the nearest tree and wrap the rope around him and the trunk before Jarek touches the rope, nodding at me. "Should be unbreakable now."

"Thank you," I murmur as they walk back to me. Addeus, however, stays close to Eric, not trusting him, and that gives me a little relief.

I'm still pissed at Ronan, but he's right. It's not his fault they attacked, and he's not a hunter or a soldier like I am. We are all doing the best we can in this situation. I run my eyes over Ronan, and he looks away. Sighing, I make a note to talk to him later, but right now we have more important things to deal with.

"So they are ghouls." I prop my hands on my hips as I stare at Eric. "I don't know shit about them. How the fuck did they even become ghouls?" I ask, bewildered.

"Ghouls are said to be created from a soul so bleak and black that even the afterlife rejects them. They must consume the dead's blood," Jarek answers. "Or so I read when I was doing research on species and their helpful properties."

"Consume the dead's blood? When the fuck did they have time to do that?" I huff.

"We all did," Eric rasps as his head rolls back, his soulless eyes staring at me, but he seems tired and afraid. "Even you, Tate."

"We never drank blood—the tracking liquid," I whisper with dawning horror, realising what this means. If I'd died when they tried to kill me, then I might have become one too.

"Tracking liquid?" Fang asks, confused.

I head to my bag and search through. I don't usually carry any, but Black always stocked our bag with extras. My hands are frantic as I search. "It's a glowing blue liquid. Black told us it was for tracking within our team in case we were captured or worse." I tug out the silver vial at the bottom of the bag. "We were always told to stock up each time and ordered to drink it before each mission. It was the only thing we all consumed." Uncorking the top, I sniff it before handing it over to Addeus.

He takes a strong inhale and hands it over to Zeev. "That is blood. Moreover, that is dead blood. Has been for a while."

I turn and gag. He had us drinking blood from the dead in case we died so we would come back.

"It makes sense." Eric groans, and my head snaps up to see him leaning back into the tree, his eyes bloodshot. "Black never wanted to die. He wanted to live forever. He always claimed he was eternal and untouchable. I guess he was right."

"He always had a backup plan for everything," I whisper in shock. "He even wanted to cheat death."

Eric nods, and I crouch before him, shocked and confused. "So they are ghouls?" I glance at Jarek. "How do we kill a ghoul?"

"I don't know," he admits.

"Fuck!" I roar as I pace. "They are going to go after Stalkers' Rest, and it won't end there. Thousands will die. Black was bad enough when he was human. It won't just be monsters he hunts for fun now."

"We need to warn Shamus," Ronan whispers.

"No, we need to do better than that. We need to kill them all and protect not just Stalkers' Rest, but everyone else in this world." I glance at Ronan. "Warn Shamus and find out how we kill a ghoul, then find us again."

"But—"

"Please," I grit out, and he swallows, nods, and disappears. "The rest of us need to buy time and safety," I mutter as an idea comes to mind. I head over to Eric and untie him, handing the rope to Addeus before I walk towards the truck.

Opening the gas tank, I pull what I need and toss the delayed grenade in the tank. "What the fuck, Tate?" Fang demands, backing away.

"They will be able to track it. If you want to survive until dawn, listen to me and do everything I say." I glance back to Eric. "I know these men better than anyone. Right now, they will be hunting that truck. We need to burn it and find a defensible position for when they attack so they don't catch us off guard. Let's go." Slinging my bag over my shoulder, I walk into the trees, taking the rope from Addeus which tugs tight as Eric stumbles behind me at the end of it.

An explosion rocks the earth minutes later, but I don't look back.

It seems I will have my revenge after all.

CHAPTER 37

Tem

We head deeper into the trees, and I stick close to my mistress's side, not liking the ghoul being this close to her.

"Do we even know where we are going?" Fang mutters, stumbling over a twig with a disgusted look.

"There has to be someplace we can fortify," Tate murmurs.

"What about going to the pack of wolves Simon mentioned?" Addeus suggests.

"No, I won't take our troubles to them. They have faced enough. This is my team, my problem. Besides, if some of the most dangerous monsters in the world cannot defeat five ghouls, then we don't deserve to be alive," she snaps, scanning our surroundings at all times.

"There's an old electricity station about two miles up," the ghoul says. We all look at him, and he ducks his head. "We scouted the area for the pack for a while and found it then. It had a fence and was locked to stop trespassers."

"Why would you help us?" the fae asks.

He looks at Tate then, who glares. "I should have helped back then. I was weak and scared, but I'm trying to atone for that now."

"We cannot trust him, mistress," I admit quietly.

"No, but we don't have much choice. We will scout it first." She nods. "Okay, lead the way, Eric."

He nods and slides past me, giving me a wide berth, and heads farther into the trees. Everyone is quiet, but then the ghoul's voice fills the air again. "I have to ask, how did you survive? I was sure you were dead when Black came out. I thought he killed you."

"He tried." She smirks at him before her eyes go to the trees. "He didn't succeed then, and he won't now."

He nods, glancing at her and stumbling over rocks before righting himself. "And the monsters you're with? I always knew you sympathised with some, but Tate, they are the enemy."

"No, my enemies are the very people I was supposed to trust who tortured me and left me for dead." She glances at him, snarling, "You might not have driven the blades into my skin, Eric, but you watched and did nothing. A bystander is just as bad as those doing the act. You never once tried to help me despite being my teammate and friend. These people around me have fought by my side without me asking. They would die for me, so no, they aren't the enemy. Monsters never were. It is our duty to cleanse evil from this world, but not all monsters are evil. I guess you will know now, though, since you're one of them. Ironic, isn't it? The man who hated monsters so much chose to become one just to cheat death. Tell me, Eric, where's your stubbornness and belief now? Your unwavering dedication to Black's belief that all monsters are evil and deserve to die when you are one?"

"I didn't know this was what he planned," he whispers.

"And that makes it better? You are not a child, Eric. Grow up. You cannot be innocent in this. You are as bad as Black," she warns, tugging his rope to make him stumble. "Now focus and get us there quickly."

Heading towards my mistress, I slide my hand over her side, offering comfort. This man betrayed her, and she trusted him. He was a friend, now he's an enemy, and that is wearing on her, not that she will ever show anyone.

"Are you okay, mistress?" I ask quietly, hoping the ghoul does not hear. She doesn't like to appear weak, priding herself on being so strong nothing can hurt her.

"Fine," she snaps, and then her expression softens as she glances at me. "Thanks, Tem. Can you help me keep an eye on him?"

I know what it cost her to ask that, so I stand taller, proud to be able to help her. "Always, mistress." I walk at his side, feeling her eyes on me, and when I glance back, she's grinning as she glances around the woods.

I burst at the seams, knowing I could cheer her up, and nearly skip.

The ghoul glances at me. "So what are you?" he asks.

I don't respond, and his eyes narrow. For a moment, I see something in the darkness, the veins crawling farther across his face. He might have been an innocent, weak human before, but he certainly isn't anymore.

He's a monster, and we cannot forget that.

"Answer me."

"I only answer to my mistress." I shrug.

"Mistress . . . Tate?" he scoffs. "Jesus, she really has lost it."

My good mood disappears, and I feel the transformation come over me. My shadows pour from me, expanding into the woods and wrapping around him as I change before him. He falls to the ground, his eyes wide in horror as I roar in his face, shadows covering every inch of him.

I might be easy-going, and the others might look at me like I am nothing but a puppy to our mistress, but nobody, and I mean *nobody*, will ever hurt her emotionally or physically when I am around.

I am hers in every sense, and I am the most powerful being to ever walk this Earth, and she controls me. It's time they realise that.

"What are you?" he exclaims, gaping up at me as my shadows dive into his skin and start to pull him apart from the inside out.

"Your worst nightmare. I am the hand in the dark, the evil in the shadows, and she is mine!" I roar.

He nods, his mouth opening to speak, but my shadows invade him. We might not know how to kill ghouls, but I can keep trying until we figure it out.

"Tem," Tate calls, and I turn to see her walking through my shadows without hesitation. They allow her passage, caressing her skin as she stops next to me. She reaches up, her hand cupping where my cheek would be. "We need him alive. If we didn't, I would let you rip him to pieces. Can you let him go for me?"

"He insulted you," I hiss.

"He has done worse than that, but we need him for now." Her voice is soft. "Release him for me, please."

I instantly shrink, put my shadows away, and step back from him and into her as she smiles. "Good boy."

"Anything for you, mistress," I say as I kiss her softly. She lets me and even takes my hand.

"Come on, let's get moving." She keeps hold of my hand as she tugs the rope and Eric is dragged forward. "Either get to your feet or be dragged. Don't slow us down or I will let Tem eat you."

He scrambles up, and this time he keeps a wide berth from me as I walk at my mistress's side. Fang chuckles behind me, and I wink at her as she shoots me that same gesture again with the thumbs.

We stand in the trees that seem to surround the abandoned electrical station. It's overgrown, and there are no signs of life. There's a huge barbed-wire fence the entire way around the one-storey building, a pylon to the right of it, though the wires are cut.

"It will do." Tate nods, and I know she hates it, but she glances at the ghoul, clearly not wanting to trust him or leave him with us. "Addeus, Zee—fae, go scout it for any signs of life."

They nod and head out. "Tem, take Fang and scout the woods. Check for any signs of life anywhere. We don't want to bring trouble to anyone or vice versa."

"Yes, mistress." I nod, and Fang and I slip away, heading through the woods. I stretch out my senses, even as I check with my eyes, wanting to be sure.

"You're doing good, you know, to get her to fall for you," Fang remarks.

"Fall for me?" I repeat in confusion.

"You know, to make her love you," she scoffs, her gaze on the woods.

"Mistress already loves me. She saved me." I shrug.

"Right." Fang coughs with a smile.

"Have you always enjoyed the company of other women?" I ask.

She snorts, laughing even as she looks around. "Yes, they are better than men. Men are just walking idiots. No offense."

"I am not a man. I'm an ancient tempest."

"Good to know, but yes, I've always enjoyed the company of other women." She grins. "They are just soft, sexy, and so much fun. It's like your best friend and partner rolled into one."

I nod. "I like my mistress. She's sweet and soft and tasty too."

"That she is." She grins. "But she's also strong. She makes me feel safe when no other has."

"You are important to my mistress, therefore I will protect you. She cares for you," I say. "Nobody will hurt you again, Fang."

"Family," she blurts. "That's the word you are looking for. We are a family."

"Family . . . I have never had one of those."

"Me neither, apart from my brother," she says. "I like it, even if we are trekking through the woods and avoiding ghouls."

"Life is never boring with my mistress." I grin.

"Say that again." She chuckles. "Would you like to be friends, Tem?"

"Friends . . . Best friends?" I ask as I stop, hope blooming in my chest.

"Sure, best friends." She grins. "I'll help you make Tate love you and vice versa. We will have each other's backs."

"What else is required?" I murmur as I scan the ground. "I want to make sure I am a good best friend."

"Erm, you comfort me when I'm sad, help me if I'm in trouble, watch movies with me, eat with me, support my delusions, and help me hide bodies."

"Very good, I can do all of that," I respond, and she laughs. We become quiet for a moment. "What is a movie?"

"I'll show you." She smirks. "They have some great ones you will really like with men and women embracing."

"I like the sound of that. What are they called?" I'm learning so much about this world through my mistress's people. I like it.

"Porn. Ask your mistress about it," she says.

"I will." We circle back around, and when we come upon Tate, I shake my head. "There are no signs of life anywhere."

"Good, we'll wait for the others then go in," she murmurs, and I glance at Fang, and she raises her eyebrows at me.

"Mistress, do you like to watch porn as well? We could watch it together."

Her head slowly turns towards me, and she stares at me incredulously as I tilt my head at her.

Fang bursts into laughter, and we both glance at her. "Another thing besties do, Tem, is tease each other."

"Tease? Mistress doesn't like porn?" I frown.

Fang grins. "Maybe she does. I bet she's into the kinky stuff."

"Kinky porn?" I repeat.

"Oh my god, stop saying porn!" Tate gapes. "It's like kicking a puppy, Fang."

"Sorry, I couldn't resist." Fang giggles and moves to my side. "Ask her again later."

"I will." I nod, still confused.

The others come back with the same news, and Jarek simply breaks the lock on the gate. Once we walk through the fence, he and the fae stand side by side, working their magic and laying barriers of protection before we head inside through the open front door. It's dark in here before Tate and Fang set out some lights in the engineering room.

The ghoul is tied to a pole in the back while the others spread out, resting and relaxing as we wait for our next orders. I munch on some fruit from Tate's bag, sharing with Fang as Tate watches the ghoul and he watches her right back.

Fang gives me a confused look, and we all wait quietly until Tate sits forward in the rolling chair, her hands hanging between her parted thighs, a knife in one.

"What will you do with me?" he asks.

"I'm still deciding that," she replies.

He nods, looking around. "How long will we stay here for?"

"However long I want," she snaps then turns to us. "I want one of you out front and one out back at all times. Decide between yourselves who is first."

Addeus climbs to his feet along with Jarek, and they head out without a word, leaving us with Tate and the ghoul.

Time passes slowly as we wait for Ronan. "So you woke up like this?" Tate asks, filling the silence.

Eric nods carefully. "In the parking lot I died in. I don't know how much time passed, but I was so hungry, and the next thing I remember was devouring a rabbit, covered in blood, when Black and the others found me. I stuck with them because I didn't have much choice."

"Even though he wants to attack Stalkers' Rest and our people?" she snaps.

"I didn't have a choice. I was scared, Tate. I didn't know what I was and what was happening, and Black seemed to."

"He's controlling you the way he always did, with fear, power, and knowledge," she scoffs.

"He wanted to go after the wolves. That's why we went back to the lot, and then he smelled you," he says, leaning back.

"Smelled me?" Her brows draw together as she watches him.

"You smell." Eric nods. "It's a distinctive scent, and he knew it was you, so we followed it right to your door."

Her lips purse as she stares at him.

"I'm scared. Tate," he says, and it seems to soften something in her.

"Eric, we will find a way to help you, but in the meantime, tell us how to stop them," she demands. "Okay?" She crouches before him. "You can rectify your wrongs now by being like you used to be, but better."

He nods, lowering his head as he sniffles like he's crying, and she lays a hand on his shoulder in comfort despite everything he did to her. Suddenly, that sniffling grows louder, and I realise he's not crying.

He's laughing.

He starts to laugh loudly, and she frowns as his head lifts. "The old Eric is dead, and you fell right into our trap. Sweet, kind Tate, always trying to save everyone. We knew you would try to save me, even now after everything. We've been waiting for you." His grin is pure malice as he leans back into the wall. "They will be here any minute. You came just like I said you would." He pouts his lips. "Poor, defenceless Eric needs protection, and big bad Tate always wants to be the saviour. You couldn't even save your own daddy, though, could you?" She flinches, stands, and steps back as I get to my feet. "And you won't save any of them either."

Just then, an explosion rocks the earth.

"Time's up, Tate. Welcome to the end," he says with a smirk, the veins crawling over his entire face.

CHAPTER 38

Tate

Rushing towards the front door, I nudge it open and peek out. Addeus and Jarek wave smoke from their faces as they crouch behind an old metal barrel. The front fence is down, clearly blown inwards, with smoke billowing around it. I don't see anyone, but that doesn't mean anything. They could have blown the front doors, but they didn't.

"Back inside," I call, and they hurry past me. I close the door and dash back into the room, my eyes narrowed on Eric.

I'm furious at myself for falling for his tricks. I played right into their hands.

"Is that them?" Fang asks, looking out the window before she lets the blinds fall back into place.

"Yes," I answer without looking away. "If they are making noise like that, then it's a distraction to draw our attention away. Tem, Addeus, check for other exits and entrances. Zeev, Jarek, split up and go with them. Spell any you find. They will try to sneak up on us, surround us, then stab us in the back."

They rush away, but I keep my focus on Eric.

Pulling out a blade, I stalk his way and crouch before him. He smiles as he leans back, totally unbothered. The crying, unsure, anxious boy who followed me around is gone. Turning him into a ghoul seems to have completely changed him. This is a soulless killer.

"Tell me everything you know," I demand.

"Why would I do that, Tate? You're smarter than this. You know you can't win, so why try?" he counters.

"You also thought I was going to die, so it seems you're always wrong." I grin. "I will win, and I will kill you all. The only choice you have is how much you'll suffer before that occurs."

"You won't hurt me, Tate. You're a good person," he sneers. "Protecting the little guy, doing no wrong—"

"You might have lost your soul, but so did I." I drive the blade into his thigh, and he roars in agony. "You might not be able to die, but I'm betting I can make it hurt. In fact, I can make it hurt over and over without you dying. Isn't that nice? Tell me everything you know."

Pulling the dagger free, I watch him jerk and hiss before I drive the dagger into his other leg, then I twist it as he shouts. Something full of joy unfurls in me at his pain, and I yank the blade out and slide it down, cutting his thigh open like they did to me. When both are carved open and he's howling, I drop my knife back to my side and glance to my right to see my open bag. I can feel their gazes on me, but I don't care.

"Hand me that taser." I hold out my hand towards my bag, and then I worry what they will think of me for a moment.

I might not be a monster like they are, but I sure as shit am acting like one.

Fang doesn't hesitate and gladly hands it over with a grin. "I'm in the category of kill all men. They are guilty until proven innocent, so go ahead and have your fun."

Turning back to Eric, I press the taser into the meat of his thigh and arch a brow. "Do you remember how you vomited when they did this to me? Let's see if you're as strong as I was then." I turn it on and watch as the current courses through his body. His bellows ring out as he jerks in the chains, the smell of burnt flesh filling the air. I let the current flow for a while before flicking it off and pulling back. He slumps into the wall, breathing heavily as he watches me, the black veins crawling farther across his face.

"You can't win," he wheezes. "You're weak—"

"No, you are. You always were, and so is Black. You're all weak, scared, little men afraid of dying, so you turned yourselves into the very thing you hated, and yet you're still scared, otherwise you wouldn't be hunting me. Don't you see, Eric? Your precious major is terrified of me, even now when he's a monster because he knows I'm stronger than him and I'll win. Even when he was human, he was scared of me. I'll show you why soon enough."

"You're wrong. They'll be here soon, and you'll be dead," he hisses.

"Fine, don't tell me anything because you just told me everything I need to know." I stand as he blinks. "They aren't all here yet. They are buying time, trying to trap us, which gives us the time we need to prepare a defence."

I head over to Fang to check on her. Compared to the others, she is not used to this kind of thing, but she seems to be thriving, going through my weapons and picking some out. I crouch at her side and take the knife she chose then hand her another. It's more ornate than the others, and it was my father's. "It will be better for your smaller hand," I explain. "You're little and quick, but they are trained, so stay out of their reach as much as you can and throw it if you need to."

She nods, covering my hand on the knife. "I'll be fine, babe. Stop worrying, okay?"

"I'm sorry I dragged you into this. You're still grieving your brother—"

"He's gone, Tate. Nothing can change that. I'm very lucky I got to say goodbye thanks to you. I'll meet him again someday, but that's not today, so until then, I plan to live my life to the fullest and tell him all about it." She smiles softly. "I'm not sad. Okay, I'm a little sad, but I got to spend so much of my life with him. I won't regret that or dishonour his sacrifice for me. He came to you, Tate, for a reason, and now so am I. I'm not going anywhere. We will kick these small-dicked hunters' asses, and then I'll follow you everywhere."

I can't help but smile despite the situation. "Fine. Remind me to teach you some fighting moves when we have time."

"Having you touch me all over and pin me down?" She wiggles her eyebrows. "Looking forward to it."

Shaking my head, I kiss her gently. "Stay behind me today. Don't fucking die."

"You've got it." She returns to the weapons as I stand, just as the others return.

Jarek grins as I look to him. "We spelled all but one vent entrance. I figured we can let them think they won. I might have even set a few traps."

"That's smart," I say.

"Don't sound so surprised." He grins. "Let me show you."

I nod and glance at the others. "I want someone watching Eric at all times, two on the door, and two on the back entrance. They won't move without us knowing."

"So we just wait?" Jarek asks as he falls into step beside me.

"For now. There's no point in trying to fight our way out. Besides, I want them all here. They think they are trapping us, but it will be the other way around." I smirk.

"Good plan." He points at the vent and the corridor before it. "You can't see much, but they will have to walk through here. We'll know about it, and so will they."

"Great, anything else?" I ask as I turn to Jarek.

"One more thing. This way." He turns and strides down another corridor, pointing at a double door to the right.

"In here." He swings a metal door open, and I step in, scanning the room, but I see nothing.

"What is it?" I turn just as he barrels into me. My hands automatically go up to his throat as I hit the desk hard behind me. His face is above mine, yet I don't feel any fear. "What are you doing?" I ask.

"We might die tonight." He shrugs, his sneer turning cocky and confident. "I figured if I'm about to die, then I might as well do the one thing I've wanted to."

"What's that?" I hedge, feeling something pulse deep within me as I stare into his eyes.

"Fuck you, hunter. Isn't that obvious?" His lips crash onto mine.

It takes me by surprise, but I melt into the kiss, desire coursing through me as he lifts me up onto the desk. Magic flows across my skin, and my clothes disappear. I jerk away, my eyes wide. "The attack—"

He grins. "You're talented enough to listen for them while I fuck you."

"Jarek," I warn.

"We'll be quick." He smirks. "Don't you want that?" His magic strokes over my pussy with fluttering touches, driving my desire higher, but he's not wrong. Violence and sex have always gone hand in hand for me, and all my anger and frustration only ramps me up more. Grabbing his head, I yank him down and silence him with a kiss.

Our teeth clash together, our tongues tangling as I slide my hands down his body, feeling the power flowing through it as his magic continues to tease me, slipping inside me like a cock as it presses to my clit until I cry into his mouth.

His magic flows across my breasts, twisting my nipples. He notches his cock at my entrance, and with a dark look at me, he thrusts inside me, filling me with his powerful length. One of his hands presses against my back to keep me in the half-bent position, so that every thrust hits that spot that has me biting down on cries of pleasure. All the while, his magic strokes my skin like a million hands, building my desire and pleasure higher. Both of us work hard and fast, knowing we don't have a lot of time. The impending attack only seems to make us wilder for it, until our lips crush together again as his magic slides inside my other hole. My eyes widen in shock, but he doesn't let me pull away.

He rocks into my cunt, claiming it with his cock as his magic moves deeper into my ass, stretching it until I feel like I'm being fucked by two people. It shouldn't feel good, but it does, and I just hand myself over to it. I lift my hips to meet his as his magic twists my nipples and rocks across my clit.

His hand covers my mouth, silencing my cries of pleasure as his magic works deep inside me, stroking every nerve ending in a way I've never felt as his cock pummels my pussy.

I can't even feel where I end and he begins, and despite the fact that I should pay attention just in case, all I feel is bone-deep, numbing pleasure. The desk rocks from the force of us fucking, and his magic pulses inside me until neither of us can take it anymore.

We shatter apart with muffled cries, my release triggering his. I feel his cum flowing deep inside my pussy as his magic continues to lash my clit and nipples. My whine grows as the release barrels on. Ecstasy rolls through me so strong, I fall back and tremble with it until finally, his magic pulls back and releases me.

Panting, I try to remember how to breathe, and when I open my eyes, I see him grinning at me. "Now I can die a happy man," he murmurs.

Rolling my eyes with a laugh, I look down at myself. "You better conjure my clothes or no amount of magic will save you."

"I will in a moment. I just want to look at you first," he says, his hungry eyes sweeping down my body like he's already thinking about the next time, and honestly, so am I.

I lie back, stretching out, and let him look his fill. He's right, we could die tonight, so why not enjoy it while we can?

I don't know if everyone knows what we did, but I refuse to be ashamed as I walk back into the main room.

I check the front door and the window. Waiting is the worst.

"What are they waiting for?" Tem asks.

"To get into position. They want us to feel relaxed and safe so they can catch us off guard. It's an age-old tactic, lulling us into a false sense of security. When we slip up, that's when they will attack." I shrug. "It's what I would do."

"You're kind of . . ." Tem trails off, and I tense. "Incredible."

I smirk at that and wink. "Hunters' knowledge, sweetie."

"More like your father's knowledge," Eric calls. "Where is your daddy now, Tate? Oh, that's right. He's dead because of you, just like your whore of a mother—"

There's a yelp, and I turn around to see Zeev holding Eric's tongue in his hand. My eyebrows rise, and he shrugs. "Only I get to speak badly of you."

"Oh, that's fucked up. You don't bring someone's parents into it unless it's a funny dead dad joke," Fang mutters.

"Don't worry. He's going to be as dead as my dad soon," I deadpan.

Everyone in the room gapes apart from Fang, who bursts into laughter. "Oh, what about knock-knock jokes? Who's there? Not your dad."

I bite my lip, trying to stop my smile. Most people would look at me with pity, but not her. She makes me laugh. "Someone asked me once how much taller I am than my mom. I said six feet or so."

"Oh, I have one! Your dad, he's dead," Tem says excitedly before frowning. "Wait, did I do that right?"

"Close enough, buddy." I nod, and Fang gives him a thumbs up just as Addeus's eyes flare, turning bright before he glances at me

"They are coming," he tells me.

"Do we run?" Tem asks in confusion.

Unsheathing my sword, I grin at him. "No, we fight." I rock my head from side to side, loosening my muscles. "I was part of their team, remember? Let's remind them of that. Tonight, the hunters become the hunted."

Just then, there's a loud scream from the corridor, and I cannot help but smirk.

CHAPTER 39

Zeev

Their screams are music to our ears. As Tate mentioned, it won't kill them, but it will hurt. I can taste their pain in the air, and I feed on it. It's not as delicious as hers nor her surrender, but it will do. I linger in the shadows, waiting.

I do not need a weapon because I am a weapon—one she wields even if she does not know it.

It has been too long since I have experienced battle, the high of trading blows and stealing lives. I should thank her for bringing me with her and allowing me this freedom to kill and slaughter.

Ronan, the ghost fool, pops into existence in the middle of the room. He looks uncharacteristically stoic as he holds out his hand, revealing a dagger on his palm. The hilt is twisted golden metal that hums with magic, inlaid with glowing red stones.

It possesses strong, ancient magic. In fact, from the feel of it, it appears to be death magic.

"This is how you kill a ghoul, with an enchanted blade. You must remove the head from their body," he murmurs. "Shamus sends his regards."

Tate grips the dagger and nods at Ronan. "Thank you. Good work."

"Make it worthwhile. Shamus had to give a lot to get that," he murmurs, and she frowns but turns back as the screams taper off. They are silent, or at least they must think they are, but I can hear the pitter-patter of their feet like scurrying rats.

Do they really think they stand a chance?

They took us by surprise in the hotel room, and if she allowed it, I would have ripped them apart until I learned how to kill them, but I did not want to leave her unprotected. Now, however, she is giving us free rein. She looks at us and grins.

"Kill them or make it hurt so much they beg us to." She holds up the dagger. "And I'll end their miserable lives."

"Monsters killing hunters," Jarek scoffs. "I love the irony."

They appear around the corner, and I don't wait any longer.

I am showing off a little since I rarely get to, but I can't resist.

I appear in their midst, and they turn, but it's too late. I move like air, faster than they can follow, wielding my magic like a weapon. I slice and cut them apart, dancing as their bellows of outrage and agony fill the air. Their tainted blood spills across me, staining my perfect skin and hair, but I do not stop.

My hand slams into one of their chests, and I grip their heart and yank it out, dropping it to the floor before moving on to the next. They reach for me, but they move too slowly. I let out all my rage and darkness, everything that made my own people fear me.

I am the creature they speak of when they tell tales of the evil unseelie. I am the reason they fear the dark, and it has been far too long since I reminded the world of it. I feel the air darken around me, reacting to my magic. The earth calls me home, offering me its strength, but I do not need it.

I rip them apart like butterfly wings as they flutter to the ground around me, torn apart in a macabre offering.

Covered in blood, I turn and look at Tate. She smirks at me, and I see no fear in her gaze, unlike everyone else who has ever seen my darkness and fury. She watches me like I am magnificent, and as I meet her eyes, I know I will be hers until my last breath. There's a groan, and I glance down as they start to put themselves back together again.

I walk to her side, and we watch as they mend their broken bodies until a leering Black stands before us. "You cannot kill us," he reminds her.

"Want to bet?" She walks over to Eric, jerks him up, and forces him to kneel before her as she faces Black.

She presses the dagger against Eric's neck. The enchanted blade glows, the magic calling to my own as I watch curiously. "You brought him back, Black, so you must care a little, but I'll kill him."

"Do it." Black shrugs. "He's nothing to me and never has been. They are all expendable, just like you, Tate. You were just another stupid blade."

"Sir," Eric rasps, struggling in Tate's hold, but Black ignores him, keeping his eyes on Tate. He thinks she won't follow through. He thinks she's weak.

He's a fool who can't see past his own ego.

Her eyes remain on Black as she leans down, her mouth near Eric's ear. "See what your loyalty gets you? You sullied your soul for a devil who doesn't care if you live or die. I want you to remember that while you burn." She cuts with the dagger, and it glows brightly at the first drop of blood, and the slash widens. Tate slices again, cutting his head off and tossing it at Black's feet. Eric's now headless, lifeless body falls to the side, and we all wait with bated breath, but he doesn't move.

Holding up the dagger, she grins. "You always told me to be prepared." She eyes the bloodied blade and glances at Black. "You're next."

"Get the blade!" he roars.

CHAPTER 40

Mav lunges forward at Black's command. His bright smile and dazzling blue eyes are gone. All the joy and life he carried with him is drained, and now he's just a shell of a man intent on following orders. Before he can reach me, Tem tackles him from the side, growing in size and strength as his shadows and beast come out to play. I leave him to it as Goose, Wick, Santos, and Ara head towards me while Black lingers at the back. Ara has no blade, but I see his hands twitch and I brace myself.

One way or another, they will die tonight.

Magic soars past me like a whip, wrapping around Goose and yanking him past me to Jarek.

They will incapacitate them, and I'll kill them.

It will work, but Black?

Black is mine.

I duck under Wick's meaty fist, and Addeus drags him away. Santos suddenly disappears, undoubtedly from Zeev's magic. Ara steps before me, but Ronan and Fang distract him and lead him away, giving me a clear shot to Black.

Flipping the dagger to face inwards, I head towards him. He waits with a cocky grin on his face, but it falters briefly when I step over Eric's body. He's not so sure anymore, and I can use that. I feint a swipe, and when he ducks under it, I kick out, sending him sprawling back. He recovers quickly, and his boot hits my side hard enough that I feel my ribs crack. Ignoring it, I dance out of his reach, which is the only thing that saves me as his fist comes up. I duck and weave, recalling moves we have done a million times in sparring matches.

We were always equal then, but we aren't now.

He has a weakness. He's scared of dying, and I am not.

I use that, making risky movements and leaning into hits that could kill me, but it pays off when he stumbles back. I dive at him, knocking him to the floor, and raise the dagger in a killing blow when my name splits the air in a panicked yell.

"Tate!" I turn at Ronan's shout to see them struggling with Ara. I look at Black and debate killing him before I turn and hurry to help. Black can wait. I will not lose my people due to my revenge.

I leap onto Ara's back as Fang holds one arm, Ronan the other, and drive the blade in deep, cutting his head off. He loved knives so much, at least he'd appreciate the irony of it.

Hopping off his corpse, I nod at them but sense movement behind me, then I see their eyes widen in horror.

Arms grab me from behind, and I fly through the air. I stop abruptly, then I'm lowered gently. When I glance over my shoulder, I nod my thanks to Jarek, who turns his attention back to his own battle. The dagger is done, knocked away in the attack, but I spy the glowing stones and dive at it, only to be blocked by Black. He grips the back of my shirt, lifts me in the air, and tosses me at the ceiling. I hit the panels hard, agony blooming in my back as I drop and hit the floor. I roll at the last second to stop him from breaking my face.

He's on me again, gripping my neck as he flips me, cutting off my air as he grins above me. Black liquid drips from his lips and hits me, making me buck in disgust as I try to dislodge him, but he's too strong. He's going to break my neck.

Panting for breath under him, I watch as Ronan takes a running slide, grabs the dagger, and tosses it to me. I catch it with my extended hand, and with my last bit of strength, I slam it up. I can only reach his side, but he roars and falls off me. I see terror in Black's eyes as he scrambles across the floor until his back hits the wall.

He covers the wound with his hand, eyeing the blade before he looks around, seeing they are losing, then he leaps to his feet and stumbles down the corridor, leaving a blood trail.

Rolling to my knees then my feet, I grip the blade and notice Goose is the closest. Furious, I leap at him and slice, gutting him before I sweep the blade across his neck. He falls down, dead like the others.

The blade is doing its thing, and it's so hot in my hand it almost burns, but I don't let go.

Turning, I find Wick on his knees with Addeus behind him. "It's your kill."

I walk over, staring into Wick's soulless eyes. "I hope you never find peace," I tell him as I stab the blade in and jerk it to the left and out. His head falls from his shoulders.

There's a noise, and I turn to see Santos escaping Zeev's choking grip. I smirk and head after him as he trips over Eric's body and falls. Turning, he sees me coming, his eyes widening with true fear in those soulless depths.

"Wait, wait, Tate, please!" Santos screams as he crawls backwards to avoid me.

I ignore his pleas as I grab his hair and slice his head off, killing him.

Looking around, I find my entire team dead, their heads and bodies scattered around like broken dolls—all but Black. My eyes return to the trail of blood, and I know if I let him get away now, it will be worse, so I head after him.

"Tate, wait!" I ignore their calls as I run down the corridor, tracking the blood and smeared handprints on the wall that lead to the back door. I step out into the fresh air, seeing a pool of blood, but there's no more after. It clicks into place as I sense it.

I roll forward to avoid him as he drops from the roof, his black blood spilling from his foaming mouth. He kicks the door that I came through shut and grabs a dumpster, blocking it as he heads towards me. "There's no one to help you now, little girl."

I grin. "Nor you."

"You think you're so strong with that dagger and those monsters behind you, but you're nothing more than a hole to stick a dick into. Even when you were a hunter, you were weak with sentiment, too fragile and hormonal. I knew you wouldn't last, but I was curious how much I could push you. I wanted to see you cross the line. I made a bet that I could make you do those things and you wouldn't be able to forgive yourself. Oh well, you'll die either way. No one will care, and it will change nothing."

"You've got it wrong, Black. That sentiment that you think makes me weak actually makes me strong. It makes people want to follow me —not out of fear, but out of trust and loyalty. It makes me stronger than you will ever be, and no one will remember you. You're weak, Black, always have been. You're nothing without a team, without someone to order around. You're an old man the world doesn't care about, and you can't stand that you are weaker than the monsters you hate so much— weak mind, heart, and stomach." I hold out my arms. "Kill me if you can."

His eyes narrow, and he rushes me, all fury and hunger.

I duck under his hands, driving the dagger up, but he dances away and backhands me. I spin from the force, and he grabs me, yanking me back, and sharp pain blossoms in my left arm.

His teeth close around the flesh there, and he takes a chunk of it with him, making me roar. I stumble back, covering the wound in disgust as he chews on my skin and muscle and swallows it. "I'm going to eat every inch of you."

"I'm going to put your head on a pike," I retort sweetly as I drop my hand and tighten my grip on the dagger. This time, I don't wait for him, and I dive at him with a flurry of perfectly practiced movements.

I've been fighting monsters since I was a child.

I never lose, and I won't start now.

He might wear a familiar face, but he is just another kill.

His hand hits my thigh as I bring it up in a kick, and it goes dead, but I fight through it, bringing the dagger across like I planned. It slices his cheek, and he falls back. I keep driving him backwards with determination and strength created by his brutality and pain.

He manages to land a few solid blows on my face, bursting my nose and lip too. I know my eyes will swell as well, but I don't care.

I use the pain as a reminder of what he did to me and the agony he put me through. As I move faster and with more force, I see fear enter his eyes as he realises I won't be as easy to kill as he thought.

He got lucky last time, but not this time.

My hands seem to move faster than I've ever been able to before, as if something is guiding them. Power moves through me like when I use my gift, and when I smash my fist into his face, he staggers, his eyes going far away.

He's locked in his mind . . . in his past.

His hands come up, clawing at his face as his memories assault him, and my eyes widen. Did I do that? I usually read memories, but did I give them back?

It's the moment I need though. I kick him, and he hits the metal edge of the door the dumpster doesn't cover. Just as he shakes his head and seems to come back to himself, I step right in front of him.

"Eat this," I snarl as I drive the dagger into him. It pierces through his neck and stabs into the door behind him. His eyes widen and his mouth flops open before his face goes blank.

Dead.

Pulling the dagger free with a smirk, I watch his head fall from his body, then step past him, kick the dumpster out of the way, and open the door to see my team there. "It's done," I tell them.

They step out, surrounding me.

Putting the scalding dagger away, I flex my palm, feeling the tight skin. I wipe it on my jeans before I see the burn on my hand in the shape of the stones and ornate handle.

As I look at Black, I can't help but chuckle. "You know, they say revenge doesn't help, but I sure as shit feel a lot better." I wipe my face on my sleeve before I pull my phone out and dial Shamus.

"It's done. Cleanup at my location and also the one I will send you." I hang up.

"Now what?" Ronan asks as he crouches before Black. "You know, he always seemed bigger. Maybe it's the missing head."

"This is just the beginning. They aren't the only corrupt ones in the guild. It's time we showed them what being a monster truly is," I say.

CHAPTER 41

Ronan

<p>ate doesn't seem to want to wait for cleanup, and none of us say anything as she gathers the heads, the dagger on display at her side. "Portal. Drop us right before the entrance of Stalkers' Rest."

"Are you sure? It will be morning by the time we are there. Drills—" I start.

She eyes me. "I want everyone there to witness this."

"Let me heal you," the fae offers.

She shakes her head, standing tall even while covered in blood and guts. "No, I wear them as a warrior's badges of honour. Let them see what I'm willing to do and take to prove my point. Portal. Stand behind me. I will not let them touch you, but do not make any moves on hunters. Do you understand?"

"Yes, mistress," Tem replies happily.

I nod while the others offer their agreement, and then the fae summons the portal. It glows and swirls before us, displaying a muted, wobbly vision of Stalkers' Rest bracketed by the rising sun on the other side. She stares at it for a moment before stepping through, and we follow her.

Our feet hit the path leading up to the closed gate of Stalkers' Rest.

I know the moment they spot us. A shout goes up, and guns are aimed at us. Tate rolls her eyes at the guards. "Tell Commander Vilaran that Tate Havelock is back."

There's muttering, and then we wait. She doesn't move, so neither do we, and five minutes later, the gate slowly opens.

She walks inside like she has no fear, even as guards swarm us, their guns aimed at us. She waits as those training inside all turn, drawn by the commotion.

A crowd begins to form, and whispers spread like wildfire as they jostle to see better. They glance from Tate to the monsters surrounding her.

"What is this, Havelock?" someone yells. "Have you betrayed us?"

"Are you a fucking monster lover now?"

"Kill them and her!"

The crowd starts to scream for blood, and weapons are drawn. She stands tall before it all, one eyebrow arched. "Any man who takes a step towards me before I have spoken to the commander will meet the same fate as those who dared to betray us. Choose your actions and words carefully," she calls out.

It's enough to make them hesitate. Everyone knows Tate means what she says. Black might have been the elite's leader, but Tate? Everyone knew she was his right-hand man—er, woman, and his greatest weapon. She has defeated every hunter here at least once in training. She wouldn't be able to take them all when they are together like this, not alone, but her confidence is enough to make them waver.

The crowd parts, and Shamus barges through until he stands at the front. For a moment, I see his eyes soften in relief before he masks it. He was so worried when I appeared and demanded to know how to kill ghouls, but as soon as I mentioned Tate was in trouble, he moved. He made a deal with an old foe to get her that blade and paid the price dearly, even as he swore me to secrecy.

Does she know just what Shamus is willing to do for her?

She still thinks of him as an enemy, but he has always been on her side. There is no one here he would betray his cause and his people for bar her. His hands move to his weapons ever so gently, making it look casual, but I know differently. He's preparing in case he needs to defend her.

"Angel," he calls, and the crowd falls silent, all waiting with bated breath. "You're back. I take it your mission was a success?"

Clever Shamus. With one sentence, he's letting them all know she's still on their side and that he sent her. The fact that he's not reacting to those behind her seems to unsettle and confuse the hunters, but none are brazen enough to question the commander—not in his own nest.

"You could say that." Her voice carries, and I sense a bit of magical intervention. When I glance back, I see Jarek's fingers moving at his sides before he winks at me. It's not only Shamus who has her back.

A whole army stands before her, but there's an unstoppable force right behind her that could wipe them out without even breaking a sweat if they so much as blinked at her wrong. Does she understand the level of devotion she inspires?

All my life, I've followed Shamus, but we both know if he asked me to choose now, I'd choose her.

I'd remain at her side until she could join me in this form.

She lifts the heads in her hands, and gasps ring out. Smirking, she tosses them at Shamus's feet, and everyone watches as they roll with a sickening sucking sound before stopping. The faces of her team are evident, their eyes still black and skin covered in inky veins.

She eyes the hunters like she's preparing for war, and they eye her like she's now the enemy.

This could get bad very quickly.

"My mission was a success. Major Black and his team have been cleansed from this world for their crimes." A roar of anger begins, and she waits for it to quieten, not the least bit intimidated. "Look at what your great major has turned into and look closely. He is not a human. He is a monster." She narrows her gaze on the crowd.

"We all know of his deeds, though few speak of them, but the time is now. There will be no more secrets, hidden hunts, or killing innocents. Let their deaths be a warning to you all. Everything will be done by the rules now. We hunt monsters, not innocents!" she roars, and I see their nervous expressions. "We do not hunt innocents of any race," she carries on, tilting her head back. "And to ensure it stays that way, I will hunt down any man or woman who has ever or will ever touch an innocent. Your secrets are not safe from me. I will find them, and you will pay. This is your only warning." She looks to Shamus. "This is your house, Commander Vilaran, and your people, but I will not let it happen anymore. You wanted me to do this, but I'm doing this my way. I will cleanse the hunters of those who give us a bad name. I will remake us into what we once were. I swear that on my soul, and anyone who gets in my way will face my wrath."

There's a moment of silence before all hell breaks loose. "Commander!"

"Commander!"

"What does this mean?"

"Commander, what are your orders?"

Everyone looks to Shamus for answers, and Tate waits, her eyes daring Shamus to betray her and say she speaks alone.

I know he won't, but it surprises me when he steps forward, holding his hand in the air to silence everyone. He never once looks away from her, nor does he speak as he covers the distance between them. When he is level with Tate, he kneels before her, his arm over his chest in a hunter promise.

Commander Vilaran has never kneeled to anyone, not even death, yet he kneels to her.

It gives them all the answer they need to know.

He supports her.

He follows her.

He trusts her.

Either they will as well or they will leave before she finds their truths.

I have never been prouder of my friend.

He would stand against his own people, his own purpose, for her.

We remain silent until we reach Shamus's office, and once the door is shut, we all relax, all except Tate who paces before him. The fae is stretched out on the sofa like he owns the place, and he swiftly falls asleep. Jarek looks over the books. Addeus is staring out of the window, no doubt looking into the security software in this room without even touching it. Fang and Tem stand at my side while Shamus leans into his desk, watching her pace before he grows bored.

"Why did you do that?" she asks when he steps into her path and stops her.

"It was the only way to defuse the situation. It would have ended in you slaughtering them all if not." He shrugs casually, as if him kneeling before anyone isn't a big deal. She could have killed him while he was unprotected, but he trusted her not to.

"So you did it to smooth things over?" she mutters, crossing her arms.

His smile is crooked and knowing. "I did it because it was the truth, but that was a bonus. They see their commander kneeling to you then they trust you. They understand I will support you and will not go against you—not openly at least. I also did it for you, Tate." He reaches over and uncrosses her arms as she narrows her eyes on him. Neither of them like to back down, and it's always entertaining when they clash.

"For me?" she repeats.

"Yes, you were questioning my loyalty after the reminder of those who have betrayed you. I will not allow that. If I have to kneel for you to understand that I will always be by your side, then I will." Her eyes flare, and he steps closer, gripping her chin as his head lowers, and I want to squeal and cheer for them.

Why would I not want my best friend and the love of my life to be happy? There's no need for jealousy, not here.

"You can make up your own reasons, but the truth, angel? I have had your back since day one and you know it. I will never betray you or leave you. I would carve out my own heart before I let anyone else hurt you. I have and will give my life for yours. This place grew because of me, but it was made for you. I've been reborn many times, but this is the only life I care about. You are what I care about."

She's quiet as she searches his eyes for answers. He remains still, letting her read everything on his face.

I feel like I should look away, like I'm intruding on their personal moment, but I also feel like I should have popcorn so I can watch them.

Fang leans into me and Tem. "Is it just me, or do those two need to fuck already? I could cut their sexual tension with a knife."

Both Tate's and Shamus's heads jerk around. Shamus grins, and Tate looks annoyed.

"Oops," Fang whispers as Tem and I chuckle.

The moment is broken, however, and she pushes Shamus away. "Whatever reason you did it, it worked. They won't come for my head for a little while. That buys me some time. I meant what I said, Shamus. My revenge is over, but this is just the beginning. You were right. We need to clear up the hunters before we are too far gone and the monsters stand up to us. We need to stop a war before it begins. Your actions will prove if you're telling the truth or not."

He grins. "Then we'll see."

She nods and turns away, but he catches her arm.

"Are you okay? Not just physically, you've been through a lot—"

She tugs her arm free, her face cold. It's Tate's go-to mask when she is trying to cover how she feels. "Never better."

He leans in, and I only hear his words because I'm close when he whispers, "Liar, angel, such a liar, but I'll pretend I believe you for now." He lets her go and heads back to his desk.

She watches him for a moment before turning to us. "We'll take the elites' old floor since it's the most secure and away from everyone." She opens the door and slips out, and we have no choice but to follow.

CHAPTER 42

Tate

W hen the elevator opens, I automatically duck. Goose was usually there practicing his knife throwing, but it's empty now and the lights are off. Straightening, I ignore their curious looks as I step out and the lights turn on. Heading down the corridor, I open the doors of the living area.

"Kitchen is there, and the gym is down there. There are plenty of rooms upstairs, so feel free to sleep wherever you want. I'm going to shower," I call without looking at them. I need a minute to myself. I haven't been alone since before Black betrayed me. I'm always with them, and I find I even like the lack of quiet, but right now I'm a little overwhelmed and need a minute to gather myself.

I head down the corridor to my room, unlocking it with my finger-print since I didn't trust them not to leave booby traps in my bed for fun. I shut the door and lock it behind me, pressing my back to it. My double bed is made and pushed against the back wall. My shelves above are filled with manuals and maps I used. My desk is to the left with the lamp switched off. My other wall has four windows, which are currently closed with curtains pulled.

My room is still the same, and nothing has been touched. It's strange being back here. The last time I stayed in this room was the night before our hunt when everything changed. Everything around us has done just that, changed, but this has stayed the same. It was never home, just a room, but as I hear my new team's laughter filling the air, I realise it's starting to feel like it.

So many memories haunt this floor, good and bad, and it's all too much.

Closing my eyes, I breathe deeply before ripping the bathroom door open then slamming it behind me. I strip from my bloodstained clothes, knowing they are beyond saving, and chuck them towards the bin before I carefully lay my weapons on the counter to clean later. My LED mirror flickers on, displaying the temperature and any hunting alerts, but I turn on the walk-in shower. The glass screen steams up quickly, so I step inside and walk to the end, where the two shower-heads are, both aimed at me.

Everything is state-of-the-art, but this shower was always my haven. The hard spray unknots my sore muscles after hunts.

My hands press to the wall as I stare at the drain, watching the red-tinted water flow down it. My body will be clean, but my soul never will be, not after the things I have done to survive, but I can live with it.

I can live with being this version of myself as long as it puts people like Black in a grave.

I feel the air behind me change, and I glance back to find Ronan there. He looks serious for once. I'm too tired to scold him, so I simply offer what I should have earlier, but before I can, he speaks.

"I'm sorry about the motel."

"It wasn't your fault. I was too hard." I shrug as I turn away and close my eyes. Maybe it should bother me that he's in here with me, but honestly, Ronan has seen worse, and if he's been watching me for years like he said, then he's seen every inch of my body. There is no point in feeling shame or embarrassment, and I am too drained for that.

"You're not okay." His voice is so close, it startles me, and I feel him behind me, not quite solid but not weak either. "Not just physically. You look exhausted by life and what it has forced you to do.

Killing your team, no matter what they did, has worn on you, Tate. Let me help."

"Why would you?" I murmur.

"Because I couldn't do anything before, but I can now. I have always been with you, Tate. You just didn't know it. I've seen your comedowns after hunts, and this is different. You're hurting. Let me make it better." His voice is soft and prying.

I lift my eyes again, looking over my shoulder, and meet his searching gaze.

He sees too much, but there's no escaping Ronan. Wherever I go, he can simply follow, and he will. I cannot rid myself of this nosy ghost.

"Did Shamus send you?" I ask.

His smile is small. "No. I have no doubt he would have, but he didn't need to. I know when you're struggling, Tate. I know you better than you even know yourself. There's no one else here, so there's no need to put on a mask. Let me help you."

"How?" I whisper.

"By reminding you that you're not alone and making you think of anything other than what has happened."

My brows furrow as I try to decipher his meaning.

He suddenly disappears, and my eyes widen as I search for him behind me, but he's just gone. Is this how he hid before now? It literally feels like I'm alone.

I go to turn when hands grip mine and slam them to the wall, something pressing to my ear. "Stay right there." His voice, dark and hungry, fills my ear, but I still can't see him.

A hand slides across my shoulders, massaging my stiff muscles, and I jerk. He chuckles, and his other hand roves down my arm, massaging as he goes, working the tension from my body. He keeps it up, touching every part of me.

"That's so fucking weird," I murmur. I can't see him, but I can feel him. I startle at each unexpected touch since I can't prepare for it, and his chuckle fills my ear.

"Close your eyes, Tate," he murmurs, and I obey. My eyes close as his hands slide across my body like he owns it, turning my muscles to jelly.

His touch is warm despite him being dead, and my thighs part in invitation as his hand crests over my mound, but he keeps going, massaging my thighs, down, and then back up, teasing me. I ignore my own desire and frustration and just give myself over to him. Every muscle in my body relaxes as he touches me.

"Ronan." His name slips from my lips in a blissful sigh, and his touch becomes harder, stronger, as his fingers trail down my sides, making me shiver. I almost giggle at the ticklish feeling, but that soon disappears as he moves lower.

His palms slide across my thighs, and he pushes them farther apart. I shouldn't let him, but I do. I'm so tired of being strong. I let him control me however he wants, and when fingers thrust inside me, I groan.

My eyes flutter open, but I still can't see him, and for some reason, I like that. Leaning back into the tiles, I roll my hips into his invading fingers. Thick and strong, they curl inside me, building up the slow desire that I have no control over. Something plucks at my clit, slow and sure, in a rhythm that is familiar. It's one I use on myself. I freeze for a moment, knowing what that means.

He watched me touch myself.

It should piss me off, but I really don't care, not when it feels so good. Everything else disappears. It's just sensation, and Ronan being invisible helps. I just focus on the feeling, rocking my hips as he slowly fucks me with his fingers, building my desire into a slow, crashing wave that finally takes me under. My gasps of pleasure fill the air as I quake, the slow release leaving me languid and more relaxed than ever.

Slumping back into the wall, I pant as my eyes open once more to find him rising to his feet, his eyes hungry and dark as he sucks his fingers into his mouth. "I've wanted to do that for years. Watching you with others, watching you touch yourself, I imagined how you would feel a thousand times."

"Perv," I mutter, licking my dry lips, and he follows the movement with his gaze before stepping closer so he's pressed against me. I can feel every inch of him, although the water goes through him, which is odd to see as his hand slides across my collarbone and wraps around my throat. My eyes widen as he pulls me from the wall and presses his lips to mine in a soft, leisurely kiss. My lips part on a happy sigh. His tongue wraps around mine and strokes teasingly, making me shiver. It's odd. I can feel and taste him, yet he doesn't feel . . . solid. It's a strange sensation, but not necessarily bad.

We kiss for so long, I struggle to breathe, and when I pull back, I'm panting and filled with lust again.

"That's not the only thing I wanted to do though," he warns, and before my brain can process his words, he spins me and presses me to the wall.

My hands slap against the slippery tiles as his mouth drags down my neck. "I want your taste in my mouth. I want to know what brought my best friend to his knees. I want to know the heaven the others found between your thighs. Try to stop me, Tate, but you won't be able to. You can't fight what you can't see." The truth is, I don't want to stop him. The idea of him doing this when I can't see or find him to fight him has my cunt clenching. His lips tilt like he knows that, and they drag down my spine and across my ass. He kicks my legs apart, and his lips continue their journey lower, and he licks my cunt from behind.

Groaning, I press my overheated face to the tiles as I curl my nails into the cracks between them, holding on as his tongue sweeps over every inch of me. He tastes my cunt thoroughly, like he doesn't want to leave any part untouched, and my legs widen of their own accord to give him better access, making him chuckle.

"I've seen you tear apart monsters three times your size and fight off armies, and yet look at you, so soft and submissive for my tongue."

"Shut up," I mutter, closing my eyes. I don't want to think about anything else. I don't want to be a hunter in this moment. I don't even want to be Tate. I just want to forget. I just want to feel. He must know it because his voice stops and his tongue flicks across my clit, making me cry out.

His hands dent my hips, pulling me back to his hungry mouth as his tongue slides inside me, thrusting deeply before pulling out. He fucks me with it, and the thought of him inside me, fucking me, makes me moan and grind into his face for more. My skin overheats, and it's not from the water, even as the steam wraps around us, his talented tongue alternating between torturing my throbbing clit and fucking me.

My nipples drag along the wall, the abrasive tiles making me moan as my eyes close, and I hand myself over to him, letting him build up my desire once more until I can't handle it.

I need more.

I want him inside me.

"Stop," I tell him, but he doesn't, so I reach down and push him away.

Turning, I swallow hard around my desire as I lean back into the wall, my eyes sweeping down his body as he gets to his feet, licking his lips. "Can you even . . ." I glance down at him meaningfully.

His smirk grows, and suddenly he's very real, turning solid. The water that passed through him before now wets his hair and clothes. "I can do whatever you need me to, Tate. I have been watching you for years, wishing I could touch you. Do you really think I wouldn't have figured out a way to do that?"

"Then fuck me," I demand as I reach for him. No more words pass between us as our lips crush together. I taste myself there as he lifts me up. Like we have been doing this for years, I wrap my legs around his waist as I feel his cock press against me.

He's warm despite being dead, and his length feels big. Neither of us speak as he reaches between us, and I lift up, helping him as he presses to my entrance. I slowly sink down, taking all of him, stretching around him. He's curved, and when I settle on his length, it rubs a spot inside me that has me leaning back with a moan. My eyes meet his dark gaze as we pant and shiver, both of us adjusting to being locked together.

The world behind him is obscured by the stream, making it feel like we are in our own world, and then he starts to move. His hand slaps into the wall as he holds me there and pulls from my body before thrusting back in. My groans fill the air unchecked as our lips meet once more. Our joining speeds up as I use the wall and his body to ride him until I'm meeting him halfway, bouncing on him as he fucks me. His kiss is messy, and I love it. I give as good as I get, using him like he's using me, but under it all, it feels like more. It feels like coming home. It feels like safety. I know then Ronan has always been here.

My cunt clenches around his cock until he grunts and his thrusts speed up. Both of us breathe heavily, our bodies slick with water and sweat, and then our kiss breaks as I scream.

My release slams through me with such force, it takes me by surprise. My channel clenches around him, and he snarls into my skin as he presses his head to my neck. I grab his hair, holding him as ecstasy washes through me, locking me to him. Groaning into my skin, he bites it as he pulls from my core, thrusts back in, and stills. I feel him coming, but I can't feel it spilling inside me, which is odd, but he's panting and still locked against me. When he lifts his head, his eyes are filled with blissful pleasure.

"Worth the wait," he murmurs breathlessly. I smile as I lean back and just let him hold me.

When we can finally move, he helps me down and starts to wash me, and I let him. How many times did he watch me break in this shower and wish he could reach for me?

Probably as many times as I wished someone were here to hold me, but he is this time, and both of us make the most of it.

Honestly, I've gotten so used to Ronan being around, I don't bother kicking him out as I dress, and when I head back into the common area, I freeze. Mattresses, blankets, and bedding have been arranged between all the sofas to make a giant pit. "What is this?"

"Well, none of us wanted to sleep in the rooms of those who hurt you," Jarek answers.

"And we didn't want to sleep alone," Tem adds.

"So . . . a puppy pile?" Fang says with a huff. "But I told them if they touch me, you'll kick their ass." She heads over to me. "I'm going to borrow some clothes."

I nod and watch her go before turning back to the others. The TV is on, and Addeus and the fae play with it, seemingly amazed. Shaking my head, I step over the blankets and sink into the huge bed. Tem and Ronan dive to be next to me, and I let them, wearing a small smile on my lips.

How did they know I needed this to replace those memories?

I never would have trusted my previous unit enough to sleep out here before, but I trust these monsters with my life.

Addeus turns back and rolls his eyes as he walks over and simply drops on Tem and Ronan until they have to drag themselves from under him. He lies back, grinning widely at getting the spot next to me.

Jarek rolls his eyes and climbs next to him, Zeev lounges across my legs, and Tem and Ronan fight for snacks on the side.

There is a huff and shuffling sound, and I glance back as Fang walks from my room, her hair knotted on her head in a bun.

As Fang saunters over, she tugs down a pair of my shorts. "Babe, you're way too fucking skinny." She huffs. "My ass barely fits in your shorts." I nod because when she turns to show me, I nearly swallow my tongue. The bottom of her ass is hanging out, my oversized shirt isn't down to her knees like it is on me, and she tied it under her breasts, showing her golden stomach. Possessiveness fills me.

"Everyone, look away," I bark.

She turns, shaking her head, but she grins when she realises I'm sitting up, watching her. I pat the space next to me I saved for her, placing me between her and the others. She prowls over, her powers making everything she does seductive, and when she sinks down next to me, I debate ripping those shorts down and discovering if she's bare underneath, but instead I cover her with the duvet. When her eyes widen, I push her back and tuck her in up to her chin.

"Nobody else needs to see what's mine," I mutter.

Her smile is so wide, dimples flash.

"What?" I ask.

"Most would have pounced on me, but you tucked me in." She bites her lip adorably. "You're so cute."

Rolling my eyes, I lie back, and she scoots closer, pressing her face into my side. I lift my arm and let her lie on it, even as I lean my head into Addeus, my legs acting as pillows for Zeev. They all seem to move closer as the lights dim, and when I glance over, Jarek winks. "Magic, beautiful."

"Handy." I grin before I focus on the TV and the film they put on. I soak in their warmth around me, their comfort. They said they were doing this for them, but I know it was for me, and I can't even explain how grateful it makes me feel.

In this place, where I should feel alone and unsafe, I feel comfortable and protected enough to drift off to sleep, surrounded by my new family.

CHAPTER 43

Shamus

I have lots to do, so I'm up before sunrise. Black's and his team's heads have been spiked on the wall. A macabre idea, yes, but I hope it reminds them of Tate's and my promise. I spent my morning reassuring the commanders that as long as they are not doing anything wrong, they have no reason to worry, and they should get back to hunting and training.

It seems Tate has everyone on edge. One woman has the ability to topple this empire, and I couldn't be prouder, so I seek her out. I checked in on her using the cameras a few times during the night, and what I saw warmed my heart. She was surrounded by her new team. I don't know if she's even aware that they took turns keeping watch over her and the area to protect her while she rested. She didn't order them to, but they did it without asking.

She might have built this team for revenge, but it seems a bond has formed.

I wonder if I'll fit at all. I don't plan to let her go either way, but I need to find a way to fit in with them. They are clearly important to her, as she is to them. I need to earn their trust as well as hers because Tate Havelock means everything to me.

Her location shouldn't surprise me when I find her, but it does.

Most would hide after that declaration or be planning or resting, but not my angel. She strides into the gym like she owns it, uncaring about the others training there. The fact that she chose the basement floor gym speaks volumes. She wants to show them she's not afraid, and the monsters tailing her only add to that.

Leaning into the observation platform above, I can't help but watch her. She is magnificent. Every eye is on her, but she doesn't care or even look their way. She wanders through the gym like she owns it as she heads to the machines at the back.

I watch her as she warms up and then jumps on the treadmill. Her eyes remain stoically forward as she runs. Tem runs on the one next to her, keeping pace and grinning at her as he does. The big guy, Addeus, picks up the weightlifting machine and starts pressing it rather than the weights, as hunters stumble away in horror.

Ronan floats around grinning, and the fae lounges on the mats, watching Tate's ass move with Fang at his side. Jarek does squats near Addeus, all of them ignoring the looks and hatred thrown their way.

It finally boils over, and a brave hunter heads their way, slamming his hand into the emergency stop on Tate's machine. She slows and stops, turning her gaze to him. I can't hear what they are saying from here, but she smirks and turns her back on him, heading to the mats in the middle.

Ah, he challenged her.

I knew it would happen, and I settle in to watch Tate Havelock kick his ass. The only reason Black and his team won before is because they took her by surprise. Otherwise, they would have lost as well.

Tate does not give up, and it's not conceited to say, but she is the best fighter the hunters have. She's even better than I am . . . well, *almost.*

I need to get a better look at this, so I head down and blend into the crowd, watching amongst them as they gather around the mats where Tate and the hunter face off. She bows out of respect, but he spits at her feet, and I know he will pay for his disrespect. Some of the crowd cheers him on, booing her. She doesn't let it show, but I know it hurts her. She has given her life to these hunters, so the disrespect is insane.

She has faced more than most due to her gender as it is, but she showed them time and time again that she deserves her status, and now they are back to judging her and tearing her down.

This is necessary to remind them who she is.

She waits for him to move, and he doesn't disappoint. He's acting on anger, thinking he's in the right, but it makes him clumsy and stupid. Oh, don't get me wrong, he's trained and could kick most people's asses, but she is not most people.

She ducks under his punches then dances out of the way, letting him tire himself out.

Her movements are fluid, and she dodges before they can even react, leaving him standing there as she dances circles around him. Tate is playing with him, and he knows it. It infuriates him, his face twisting as he lashes out angrily.

His movements start to slow as the crowd laughs at him, and that's when she strikes. Slipping under his guard, she sweeps his leg out, knocking him down and into her waiting knee. His head slams into it, and he's unconscious before he even hits the mat.

She steps over his body and faces the crowd, which is now silent.

"Anyone else?" she calls.

At least six other hunters step forward, and she grins. "Fine, but I don't have a lot of time, so let's make this quick and take care of all of you at once."

She gestures for them to step onto the mat, and they share looks and nods as they circle her, ready to attack.

"Wait, wait . . ." She holds up her hand, and the crowd laughs, thinking she's scared, but I see amusement in her gaze. "Let's make this interesting, shall we?" She pulls her shirt up and off, exposing her sports bra and creamy marred skin, then she wraps it around her eyes as a blindfold. "There, now it's almost even. Let's begin."

She waits with her hands at her sides, her gloves off. They hesitate only for a moment before diving at her two at a time. She ducks under a punch and knocks someone else's leg away. They stumble back-wards, but another launches at her back. She spins, and he flies past her.

Mid spin, she catches the leg of a man aiming a brutal kick at her stomach, and she uses it to yank him closer, smashing her forehead into his. He falls backwards, hitting the floor hard, and she pounces on him, slamming her fist into his face twice before knocking him out then rolling away to avoid a boot. Sliding up behind them, she slaps the edge of her hand between one's shoulder and neck, and when he crumples, she grips another's neck and knocks him out. There's a yell as two run at her again, and she chuckles as she ducks under their attacks. They become brutal, trying to kill her, but when she ducks from between them, they hit each other instead and go down in a tangle of limbs, leaving only two left.

They are smarter and more patient. They circle her, and she tilts her head, listening as her body relaxes. Unlike most, she has virtually no telltale signs on when she will act. I only notice the slight twist of her fingers before she leaps, but to others, it would be unnoticeable. She pivots, kicks into the air, and slams her foot across one of their faces. He goes down hard, knocked out before they hit the mat, and she rolls under the second, coming up behind him and swinging her legs around his neck. She flips him into the mat and follows him down, her hands on his cheeks as she smashes his head into it over and over until he stops moving.

Climbing to her feet, she waits for a moment before tugging her blindfold off to see them all unconscious or groaning around her.

Not one of them touched her.

The crowd cheers for her now, and none are louder than her monsters who clap and whistle the loudest. She winks at them, and I step onto the mat. "I challenge you."

Shock ripples around the crowd as she gapes at me. I have never challenged anyone. I don't even spar with hunters here, since I'm too busy and don't want to lose face, but they need to see that I won't go easy on her and that she's earned my loyalty.

Stepping onto the mat, I tug my shirt off and toss it to the side so I'm in nothing but my trousers and socks. Her eyes narrow on me as I wait.

"Unless you're scared, angel?"

"Of you? You wish. You've gone soft sitting behind a desk. Stalker? More like staller," she says, stepping back into the middle. I join her, standing opposite, and we bow to each other before her feet slide back and her hands come up. Unlike with the others, she's serious and more hesitant.

She knows I'm strong, and she's not about to lose face by underestimating me. Luckily for me, I know how she fights, and I know exactly what to expect—or at least I think I do as I rush her. She dances back, avoiding my punches, before I feint left and bring my right fist up in a brutal jab.

Her head jerks to the side with the blow. I hold nothing back, giving her my full strength, and when she turns back to me, she spits her blood in my face. It blinds me for a moment, then she's on me, utilising that weakness. It's dirty fighting, and I can't help but smile.

That's my fucking girl.

We hit the mat hard, and she manages to land four good punches before I buck her off, and she gets back to her feet.

She stands before me, panting, and smiles. Narrowing my eyes, I reach up and find my cheek split and bleeding.

She's the first person to ever land a hit on me.

Climbing to my feet, I suck my fingers clean of the blood, not allowing a drop to fall. You can never be too careful. Blood is a life force, and in the wrong hands, it can be used for anything. She doesn't care as she eyes me.

"Come on!" someone yells.

She glances to the right, a rookie mistake, and I sweep her legs out. She goes down hard, but she flips to her front, gripping the mat. Holding her hips, I yank her back, and she rolls and kicks me in the face. I fall back, and she snarls at me as she climbs to her feet. She's panting and mad as I dive at her, knocking her back. Her fists hammer into my back before she wraps her body around me and flips us, throwing me across the mat. I recover as fast as I can to see her standing once more. She knows she's losing, and she can't have that. Her eyes dart away for a second, and I see it the moment she does—her shirt.

I rush her, but she manages to kick it up, catching it midair, and duck under my punch before coming up behind me. She kicks me down, and I hit the mats again.

She uses her shirt as a weapon, winding it around my neck and yanking me up onto my knees. Most would lift their hands to grab it, but instead, I reach back, clutch her thighs, and flip us forward. It loosens her hold as she hits the mat, and I let the shirt drop as I slam her hands above her.

"Give up, angel?" I pant into her face.

Her eyes are narrowed, her lips thin. "Never." Her head jerks up and slams into mine. The force makes me see stars, and I don't let go, but she manages to flip us, and I lift my hands at the last minute to protect my face as she rains brutal punches to my arms until they ache.

Kicking up, I wrap my legs around her waist and roll us again. "Not the face, angel." I lean down so only she hears me. "How will you ride it later if you hurt it?"

That pisses her off just like I wanted.

Her elbow comes up, hitting my chin, and I actually fall back from the force. She's on me then, her hands on my cheeks, and my eyes widen as memories assault me—no, not memories. These are thoughts.

She throws them at me like a physical block, blinding me.

I see her on top of me, our bodies writhing together in ecstasy.

I am not sure if they are her wants or mine, but it does the trick, and when I manage to shake off the stupor, my face aches and she's hammering into it.

Rolling away with a groan, I kick her, and she hits the mat, breathing heavily. She holds her side as she climbs to her feet and faces off with me again. "I see you're getting stronger." I'm careful about what I say, but I mean her abilities.

Her lips tighten, and I don't know if she meant to control it or if it just happened. Either way, it worked in her favour. I'm dripping blood, my face hurts, and exhaustion is setting in, but she's leaning to the side and bleeding too. She won't give in, and neither will I. If we continue this way, one of us will end up dead.

"Draw?" I ask.

"Fuck that." She flies at me again, and I catch her fist and spin her so her back is to my front. "Draw, angel, before one of us kills the other."

"Then kill me." She elbows back and spins, kneeing me in the groin. I go down with a groan, clutching my prized possessions. Agony races through me as she smirks, and she uses my weakness. Her knee comes up, and I feel my nose burst, but I manage to block her next blow. She hits the mat hard as I wrap my hands around her throat. She narrows her eyes as her legs come up and circle my neck.

Both of us clench hard, choking the other.

It's now a game of who has the most courage.

Dots dance in my vision, and she's breathing heavily from the earlier hit. She'll let me kill her before she gives in, but I don't want that. I don't care about looking weak, but I care about hurting her, so I loosen my hands and she takes it, thinking I'm losing. She flips me, looping her arm around my neck. "Give up?"

"I give up." I tap out, and she leaps to her feet, raising her hands in victory.

I watch her with a smile on my face as Ronan grins at me, floating upside down. "You let her win."

"She deserved it," I mutter as I climb to my feet, touching my battered face, knowing she did a number on it. When she glances back at me, though, I know it was all worth it.

CHAPTER 44

Tate

Heading away from Shamus and the crowd around us, I keep my eyes on my monsters. I ignore the congratulations and the fact that those who were looking at me with suspicion now look at me with awe. Humans are truly fickle creatures.

It's always like this with hunters. They respect strength, not knowledge, and you earn loyalty through blood, sweat, and gritted teeth. Shamus gave me that opportunity, so I should probably thank him for that and the fact I finally got to smack his pretty face.

It was satisfying as hell to see him bleed. The shock in his gaze when I landed that hit, yeah, I'll admit it made me wet as hell.

There's something about taking a man down a peg that does that to me.

Watching the realisation setting in that they might have been the top of the food chain before, but with me, they aren't is addicting. Since I was brought back and embraced the darkness to hunt down Black, I've noticed these thoughts a lot more. It's as if whatever restrained me previously doesn't now.

Maybe I lost my morality or soul along the way, but I can't seem to care as my monsters grin and cheer for me as I walk their way. The gym is filled with so much excitement, people even chatter near my monsters without throwing them dirty looks.

My eyes narrow, however, when a hunter gets too close to Fang where she sits on top of a bench by a weight press. She eyes him disdainfully and looks away, her eyes meeting mine as I head towards her. Uncaring about her reaction, he leans closer, gripping her hair and jerking her head around. Her eyes widen in fear as his other hand reaches for her shoulder to pull her towards him, and I lose it.

I see red. His hands are on her, on what's mine, and a male is touching her when I know she hates it. I appear next to them, and the gym goes quiet, no doubt sensing my change in mood—all but him.

The cheers die down as he leans closer, his gaze on her lips. "Want to have some fun? Maybe all monsters aren't bad—"

I grab his hand before it can make contact with her shoulder. She jerks back, tugging her hair free with a wince. Her eyes are wide in anger and fear, but I step in front of her, blocking his view of her and forcing him back. His eyes narrow as he twists his wrist, trying to free himself from my grip.

"Shit, Havelock, you scared me," he grumbles, still trying to look past me.

This dumb fuck does not get it.

I snap his hand back, breaking his wrist. His scream fills the air as I keep my eyes on him. When I release his mangled wrist, he stumbles back a step, his face pale as he holds it to his chest while I circle him. Once I'm behind him, I kick the back of his knee, and he crumples to the floor. Reaching over him, I grab his other hand as my mouth meets his ear. "You touched her with both hands." Lifting his other hand, I hold it for her and everyone else to see.

"No, no, no," he chants as I grip his thick fingers in both hands and then snap them all sideways. His howls of agony fill the air as I meet Fang's gaze, her eyes filled with desire as she watches me.

Squeezing his ruined fingers, I listen to his screams of pain crescendo before I release him and grab his chin, tilting his head back until his eyes meet mine. "Do not ever touch what is mine, understood?" He nods rapidly, his eyes wide and bloodshot. I release him and let him fall prone before I step over his body and gently lift Fang's chin. "Are you okay?" I murmur.

"Yes, babe, I'm fine," she replies, her tongue darting out to lick her lips. "That was hot as fuck. Feel free to claim me anytime."

"You're right, I should." I turn and face the stunned crowd as I lay my foot on the hunter's back when he tries to crawl away. "Let me make one thing very fucking clear. Any attack on my team is an attack on me. If you try to hurt one of them, I will repay the favour tenfold. They are behaving and holding back, otherwise you would all be dead, but I will not. Any scrape or, hell, even a fucking bruise and I will make you wish you were dead. Every single one of them is mine in every way, and I do not fucking share or allow what is mine to be hurt. Is that understood?" There's not much noise, and I narrow my eyes. "Any slight on them is a slight on me, even emotionally. You will treat them with respect and dignity or I will make you wish you had."

I look back at my monsters, and without a word, I head towards the crowd. They part for us, my monsters following like I knew they would. I'm pissed as we ride the lift up to our rooms so I can shower.

When we reach our floor, I let them file out first. They eye me worriedly, but I lift my arm and block Fang's exit. Her eyes swing to me. "Go ahead," I tell the others as I pluck my dagger and wedge it at the base of the door so it won't shut. The elevator pings a warning. Taking my sweaty shirt from my shoulder, I reach up and cover the camera calmly before I turn to her.

Her eyes are wide as she watches me worriedly. "Tate—"

I slam my hand into the wall, and she hits the metal with her back as I tilt my head and run my gaze over her. "You let him touch what's mine."

"I didn't want to cause trouble—"

I cover her mouth with my hand. "Next time, break every bone in their body before they touch you, understand? I know their touch makes you uncomfortable. Do not hold back on my account. I would allow you to murder them before I let you feel uneasy." Sliding my hand from her mouth, I grip her chin. "Tell me you understand."

"I understand," she whispers, glancing between my eyes and lips.

"I do not share, Fang. Let me make that very clear." I watch her swallow as I lean in and lick her juicy, perfect lips. "And he touched you. You stink of him."

"I'm sorry." She gapes as I pull back and drop to my knees before her. "Tate, what are you doing?"

"It's obvious, isn't it? I'm making you smell like me again. I'm reminding you whom you belong to." My bloodstained hands grip her perfect, unmarred thighs, knowing it will bruise, and desire flames in her eyes. She loves when I'm mean with her, and I like it too. I love the feel of her soft, supple flesh denting under my touch, easy to tame and tease.

I throw her up the wall, and she gasps as I hook her legs over my shoulders and shove my face into her cunt, inhaling through the fabric of her shorts.

"People could see," she says, but she drags me closer, her hand in my hair.

"Then I'll pluck out their eyeballs," I murmur as I kiss her cunt through her shorts. "Only I get to see you like this."

Holding her there with one arm, I unsheathe a hidden dagger from my side and slide it up the side of her shorts, tugging away as I lean back. She jerks, her eyes narrowing.

"I liked those," she grumbles.

"They were mine anyway. I'll buy a hundred more so I can cut them off," I reply as I lay a kiss over her mound. "Unless you want me to stop?"

She shakes her head, her thighs clenching around my ears, and I chuckle as I run my nose down her pussy and back up, her scent invading every atom of my being. Gripping her ass, I force her higher, ignoring the ache in my knees as I part her lips and look at her glistening, pink cunt.

"Looks like somebody is feeling needy. Is this for me?" I ask as I lick her cunt, taking the path I did with my nose. Her moan echoes around us, but I pull back and wait.

"Yes, yes, okay? Fuck, Tate, please," she begs.

Chuckling, I drag my tongue up her cunt and circle her throbbing bundle of nerves before I flick it with my tongue. She jerks in my hold, rolling her hips to push her cunt closer until I feel her desire smear across my face. I lick it up as I move down to her greedy hole and thrust my tongue inside her.

She cries out, clamping her thighs around my head as I fuck her with it.

"Tate, oh gods," she pants, her chest thrusting out as she grips me. I love how needy she is and how I can feel her feeding even as I force her pleasure higher. Her soft, pretty cunt is so warm against my tongue and face. Her delicious cream covers every inch of my mouth as I juggle her, holding her with one hand and sliding my other down so I can slip my fingers inside her. Her tight channel clenches around them as she cries out, her clit pressing to my tongue as I lap at her, fucking her hard with my fingers.

She's so hot and tight, but I force a third into her, and she drips around my knuckles, her hips moving restlessly as I lash her clit, feeling how close she is.

Pulling back a little, I lick my lips, tasting her cream. "You know what's good about being with a woman? We know exactly how we want to be touched, don't we? I could have you coming within a minute, and you'd love it and beg for more, so remember that the next time someone else tries to touch what I own."

My own desire is growing, and I know she's feeding as I fuck her. I don't mind. I actually like knowing she can taste how much I love this. Her pretty pink tongue darts out as her chest heaves, her full breasts straining against her stolen shirt.

"Lift your shirt," I order as I look up at her. "Let me see your pretty tits bouncing while I fuck you."

Groaning, she fumbles with her shirt, ripping it up and exposing her flushed chest and perfect tits, her nipples tight and ripe. She grips them, playing with them as they bounce with the force of my touch.

Fuck, the sight makes my cunt hot and slick, but I ignore my own wants as I fuck her with my fingers and tongue. Her cries fill the elevator as my own need fills my panties, but it's her desire I focus on.

Curling my fingers, I force her tight cunt wider, even as I suck her clit, creating a pressure that has her panting above me as she reaches for her release—one I deny her as I stop.

Her whine fills the air, and I release her clit, kissing it. "Say you're mine, Fang, and I'll let you come. Say that you belong to Tate Havelock and you will let no one else touch you."

"Tate," she begs.

"Speak or I'll stop," I counter.

Her eyes narrow in anger, her power rising to stoke my own desire, but I ignore it and wait. "I could find someone else to get me off," she snaps in annoyance.

I blow my breath over her wet cunt, and she shudders. "You could try, but I'd kill them as soon as they looked at you, and we would be right back here. Now say it and you can get what you want . . . what we both want."

Her nostrils flare, her stubbornness fighting her desperation, until her voice comes, quick and annoyed. "I belong to Tate Havelock and I will never let anyone else touch me. Happy?"

"Yes, very," I purr as I seal my lips around her clit and fuck her with my fingers. I set a quick pace, feeling her clench around me, and I know she's close.

Smirking against her wet flesh, I bite down on her clit, and she screams.

Her eyes roll into the back of her head as she holds me to her cunt, winding her hips as she rides my face through her release.

I fuck her through it, and when she slumps back into the wall, I kiss her pretty cunt and pull my fingers out. As I suck them clean, I let her shaking legs lower to the floor, and then I stand up, catching her before she falls. Her eyes open, clashing with mine as I grin at her.

"That's better, isn't it, my good girl?" I murmur as I lean into her.

"I'm an entity of sexual pleasure and desire. I am immortal and the embodiment of beauty," she grumbles.

"Yes, you are." I smirk as I rub my thumb across her smudged lips. "You're also my good girl."

Her lips part, and then she pouts. "Fine, I want chocolate."

"Okay, let's get you some chocolate, babe." Holding her hand, I tug her from the elevator, kicking my knife up and catching it one-handed before sliding it back in its sheath as she gapes at me. I wink, and she blushes.

Everyone is sleeping, but I can't, so I climb from the puppy pile. I know they sense me leaving, but they let me go, knowing better than to stop me.

I find myself in front of his door, and before my hand is even raised to knock, it opens. He leans into the doorframe in some low-slung pyjama pants and nothing more. I run my eyes across his bruised abs before bringing my gaze up to his injured face to see him grinning.

"Is this a booty call, angel?" he teases.

My eyes catch on his split lip and black eye, and I snort as I push past him. "You wish," I say as I head into his apartment.

I swear I hear him say, "Damn right I do," but I ignore it as I turn to face him, crossing my arms as he shuts the door and follows me into his living room. He looks tired, and the bruises and cuts are not helping, but if he didn't want to get hurt, then he shouldn't have stepped into the ring with me. He knew what would happen.

I have no doubt about why he did it, but there is one thing I don't understand. "I know you let me win at the end. Why?" I ask.

"I don't know what you mean," he hedges, an annoying smile curling his lips and driving me crazy. I hate the fact I notice and remember how they feel.

"Yes, you do. You let me win," I snap. "I want to know why."

"No one else suspected I let us draw," he starts, and I narrow my eyes as I press my finger into his chest.

"They do not matter to me. Why you did it bothers me. Why did you let me win?" I hiss.

He wraps his hand around my finger and presses my palm to his chest, and I swear I feel his heart racing. "I didn't let you win, angel." When I go to pull away, he circles his arm around me, stopping my movements, and my eyes jerk back to his. "I didn't. We could have kept fighting, and you would have won, but the message had been sent, so I just let the inevitable outcome happen. You think I would be able to kill you?" he murmurs, frustration in his tone. "That is what it would have come down to. You would kill me to win, I know that, but I would never be able to kill you, not even to win. So yes, I stepped back. I let you have the win instead of the draw."

"Why?" I murmur.

"Don't you see, angel? Everyone else does. You're my fucking weakness, my soft spot, and always have been."

I stare into his eyes for a moment, reading the stark truth there. "You're such a liar, Shamus. You just let me win." I tug away, feeling annoyance as well as something else I don't want to look at.

I try to turn away, but I'm slammed back to the sofa, and he's above me with his hands on either side of my head, pinning me. My eyes widen as he leans in. "I have never and will never lie to you, angel. You are the only person in this world who could ask anything of me and I would do it without thinking. Not even Ronan can say that, and he has been with me all my life. You're my weakness, Tate Havelock, in every sense of the word. How do you not see that? One look from you and I'm weak. One word from you and I'm running to your side. My life and blade are yours. I'd give you this entire organisation if you asked. I'd let you kill all of them if it would make you feel better. If that isn't weakness, then what is?"

"Why? Why am I your weakness? I'm just a hunter," I press.

"You were never just a hunter, and you know it, so stop lying to yourself. From the moment you stepped foot in my office, you became mine." My eyes narrow at that, and he grins. "In more ways than one. I would do anything for you, angel. I would break truces, risk death, face torture and punishment, make deals for weapons, and fight my own people. When will you see what is right in front of you?"

I don't know what to say to that, so I remain silent, staring up into his dark eyes and finally seeing the truth in them, the one I never wanted to see.

The devotion.

The obsession.

He broke the fae's truce to save my life.

He made his best friend haunt me to keep me safe.

He made a deal to give me a blade to end my enemies' lives.

He kneeled before his people for me.

He let me beat him, surrendering when he never has before.

I think back on all our arguments over the years, the push and shove and the way I would force myself to hate him because it was easier to do than admit I wanted him. I might have hated him as well, but somewhere along the way, that hate changed.

He trusts me, values my input, respects my strength, and has never held me back.

How could I not want him?

I couldn't let myself, though, so I buried it so deep down I would never act on it, hidden in dreams and veiled arguments, and he waited. He never pushed, but now he's above me, telling me everything I didn't know I wanted to hear, making me look at myself.

I was reborn because of him. Can I finally allow myself to take what I want?

Him?

"Do you want me to believe you came here for answers? No, you can lie to yourself, but you can't lie to me. You know why I did it. You just wanted an excuse to come here, didn't you?"

"Fuck off!" I go to push him, but his hand grips me tighter and jerks my chin back to him.

"Don't lie, angel. It isn't your strong suit. You've always been brutally honest, so why hide from it now? You want me. You came here to fuck me, to finish what we started. You're letting me pin you now. You could get out of this if you really wanted to, but you don't." He lets go and sits astride me. His built chest rolls with the movement, mesmerising me for a moment.

Shamus really is a fucking machine. His brain is built for leading, but his body was built for fighting . . . and fucking.

He's right, fuck.

I hate that he always sees through me.

"So what will it be, angel? Going to claim what you want, or are you too scared?"

"Nothing scares me," I snap.

"Then prove it," he growls.

Blowing out a breath, I jerk up and kick him off, and he rolls away. He was right. If I wanted to, I could have gotten out of it. We tumble to the floor, me on top of him, and before he can speak and piss me off more, I crush my lips to his.

He groans into my mouth, sliding his hand up my back and gripping my hair. Our kiss turns brutal, and I taste blood. I pull back, seeing his lip's split open again. "You're bleeding."

"I don't fucking care, but if you don't kiss me again, I'll fucking lose it," he snarls below me.

Grinning, I lean down and lick the blood from his chin and soothe the cut on his lip with my tongue. Shamus isn't below me anymore, it's the stalker, and I love it. I want the being they all fear. I want his power, strength, and obsession.

If we are doing this, I want my equal, not someone to control.

As if he hears my thoughts, he spins us so I'm below him, his teeth sinking into my lip until my blood fills my mouth, and then he crushes his lips to mine, our blood mingling with our tongues. Our hands slide over each other's bodies as we tumble across the floor, fighting for dominance just like last time, only this time neither of us has any intention of stopping.

I end up above him again, and I break away, ripping off my bra, and he sits up, sliding his hands up my back and dragging me to his lap as his mouth brushes over my breasts before he sucks my nipple. My head falls back in pleasure, desire rolling through me hard and strong. My need for him roars through me like a flame, burning me alive, and only his touch can cool it.

My moans fill the air as he turns his head and sucks my nipple, rolling it between his teeth. My clit throbs as his hands slide up into my loose shorts and grip my ass cheeks, his fingers digging in until I know it will bruise. He lifts me up, effortlessly standing, and drops me onto the sofa, my head falling back into the cushions. Gripping the waistband of my shorts, he tugs them off and kneels between my thighs.

His mouth comes down on my cunt like he's a starving man. Lifting my head, I watch as he grips my thighs, forces them wider, and drags his tongue down my folds and then back up. He flicks my clit until I'm moaning and riding his tongue, and then his fingers slip inside me, finding me dripping wet. His eyes meet mine as he seals his lips around my clit and sucks, making my back bow as ecstasy courses through me.

Gripping the sofa cushion, I ride his face. Seeing my commander, the leader of the hunters, on his knees for me is a heady type of power, and it has me moving faster. I chase a release I have denied myself for so long, one he wants to claim. His face glistens with my desire as he brutally twists his fingers, stretching me as he sucks my clit harder, and it's enough to throw me into an orgasm.

I cry out as I grind into his face, riding the waves of pleasure as he kisses and licks me through it until I slump. He finally pulls back, sucking his fingers as he watches me lie on his sofa before he gets to his feet. His eyes are filled with flames of lust so strong, I'm surprised he's not burning in them. His chest and face are flushed and glistening with my cum.

He's so fucking beautiful. I want him.

Standing before me, he grips the waistband of his pants, pushes them down slowly, and steps out of them, his huge, hard cock springing free. Shamus might be human compared to the others in my bed, but he is not lacking. Licking my lips, I eye his large cock, desperate to feel it inside me, but I see something that makes me sit up.

Above his cock, tattooed in black lettering, are two words.

ANGEL'S PROPERTY

My eyes jerk up to his as he smirks, his hand circling his cock as he watches me. "I got that the day we met. I knew you would be mine. I've been very fucking patient, angel. I think I deserve a reward."

Leaping at him, I crush my lips to his as he catches me, and we stumble into his bedroom, falling into his sheets, naked and fighting to get closer. He stills above me, his features highlighted by shadows.

"I want you raw, angel. I want to feel every inch of your perfect cunt. Say yes." He groans as I feel his cock between my thighs. "Say yes or I might fucking die."

"Yes," I answer without hesitation.

It unleashes the monster he hides deep within, one that echoes my own, and his hands grip me tightly.

He throws me across the bed and comes down on my back, pulling my hips up and back as he impales me on his cock. My face presses to the bedding as I fist the sheets and push back to take him.

My body is forced to adjust to his size, the slight pain disappearing as he takes me. The edge turns into nothing but pleasure as I flip my hair back, and he grabs it, using it as an anchor to drag me on and off his cock. The shadows steal our pleasured moans as he snarls behind me, the slapping of our skin loud as we come together. My heart pounds so fast in my chest, I struggle to breathe, and when he reaches between us and pinches my clit, I shatter once more.

Lifting me up onto my knees, he forces himself through my milking cunt, snarling in my ear. "You're so fucking beautiful when you come for me, angel. The way you surrender to pleasure . . ." His lips drag along my pounding pulse. "I want to see it every moment of every day. I want to be buried this deep inside you at all times so there is no space between us."

Panting, I lean back into him until I recover, and then I fall forward, dragging myself off him. He snarls, reaching for me, and I roll him onto his back and straddle his thighs. I look back over my shoulder at his narrowing eyes and reach down, grip his wet cock, and press him to my entrance before I sit down on his length once more. His groan fills the air as he reaches for my hips and helps me ride his length. His eyes are focused between my legs, where he's thrusting in and out of my cunt.

My head falls back as I anchor my hands on his thighs, digging my nails in as I ride him, wanting to feel him come.

All this time, he's touched me and made me feel pleasure, but I've never felt his, so when he speeds up, I know he's close.

Lifting off his cock, I turn quickly and hold his jerking length to my mouth. I open my lips and roll my eyes up to him as he squirts across my tongue. He snarls, lifting his hips as he rides out his release, and when he collapses back, I swallow his release as he watches me through heavy-lidded eyes.

"I wanted to know how you taste too, commander," I purr as I slide up his body and lie on his chest, sweaty and satisfied. "Next time, I want you to come down my throat."

"Shit, angel," he growls as he drags me closer. "You'll be the death of me."

"But what a way to go," I tease.

CHAPTER 45

Shamus

I wake up before dawn like always, even though I was up all night fucking my angel and making her realise just how much I want her. I half expected her to sneak away during the early hours, but when a soft breath wafts over my chest, I look down. Her leg is thrown over mine, her arm is draped across my chest, and her head is notched just below my chin. I don't move, don't even dare to breathe.

Her face is relaxed, making her appear so much younger and softer without the weight of her alertness on her. In sleep, she is at peace, able to rest and let down her guard. The fact that she feels safe enough to do that in my arms makes me want to roar in victory, but instead, I wrap my arms around her and kiss the top of her head. My eyes slide shut once more as I bask in the happiness I feel.

I have a never-ending list to do as a commander, but for once, I ignore it and put myself first. They can all fucking wait. I won't wake my girl for anything.

I laze around until she moves closer, rubbing against my morning wood. My eyes snap open, narrowing on her. Her breathing is the same, and her body is still relaxed, but she rubs across me teasingly, and my eyes narrow further.

It's either an innocent touch or she's playing with me.

Knowing Tate, I know which it is.

"I know you're awake, so unless you want me to fuck your pretty cunt, stop teasing me," I growl, trying my best to ignore my hard cock.

I feel her smile against my skin, and then the little devil rubs herself over me again. I snarl in warning, and she chuckles and lifts her head, her eyes bright.

I expected to have to hunt my angel down and demand she not run after she gave into this thing between us, but she just stretches with a yawn before kissing my chin. "Morning."

"Morning," I whisper.

"Your bed is comfy." She groans as she rolls to her back and stretches further. I watch the magnificence that is my girl and her incredible, toned body.

"Then have it, but I want you to know that it comes with me in it." She opens her eyes and rolls them at me. "Besides, you slept on me all night, so how would you know?"

"Are you complaining, commander?" she taunts.

I roll above her as she grins up at me. "Keep flirting with me, angel, and I'll chain you to this bed so you can never leave."

"I know how to pick locks," she says casually. "Now feed me. I'm hungry, and I mean for food, not your cock."

"Demanding little thing," I mutter, but I grin and steal a kiss, rolling from the bed as she goes to hit me. I pad into my kitchen naked to cook for her while she lounges in my bed, right where she belongs.

I watch as she shoves another forkful into her mouth. Propping my chin on my hands, I debate how to broach the subject. I don't want to ruin this peace between us, but she deserves to know.

"Tate, we need to talk about what happened during the fight."

Her fork pauses, and something passes through her eyes. "You mean how I kicked your ass?" she jokes.

"No," I reply seriously, and her jaw ticks. "The visions you gave me."

"I don't know what you mean," she mutters, but she won't meet my gaze.

"I know your gift, angel, so there is no point in pretending otherwise, but I've never seen you do that before. Is shoving visions into others' heads new?" I wait, hoping she'll trust me enough to tell me.

"It's new," she finally says. "I didn't even know I could do it. It just happened." Her voice is small and hesitant.

"I expected as much. Do you know much about your ability?" I ask. It's something I've wanted to know for a while, but Tate keeps her cards close to her chest.

"Not really. I was born with it. My father helped me control it and gave me things to help, like gloves. I wondered why I was born with this ability, but after a while, I stopped thinking of it as a curse and stopped questioning. It's just part of me," she admits, and the fact that she trusts me with that makes me smile.

"I agree. It's a gift." I debate how to proceed, but Tate values truth over everything else. "Do you remember what the fae called you the day you woke up?"

"Seer," she murmurs.

"I was curious why the fae called you that. They do not give titles lightly." I look at her hands knowingly, and she pales. "I did some secret digging and research." Her eyes narrow, and I hold my hand up. "So I could help you. You are the type that likes the truth, so I figured you would want it too."

"Fine." She sits back. "And what did you find?"

"I traced your bloodline back. Your gifts, Tate, are not a freak accident. You are a descendant of an ancient, powerful fae lineage. It has been filtered down through your blood, lessened and weakened by human blood, but it's there." She gapes at me, and I smile. "You're part fae, Tate, at least enough to receive some of their power and gifts. You're still human," I say, heading off that train of thought. "Now you simply know."

She watches me for a moment, and I brace for her anger or sadness, but she just watches me, something gleaming in her eyes.

"What is it?" I ask, hoping she will trust me enough to share what is worrying her. I want to be her partner, her safe place. I want Tate to come to me with anything, not just about hunters, but about her life. She got her revenge and is planning an overhaul of the hunters, but there is more to her life than killing.

"When I was dying, I went to a place . . . . I thought it was the afterlife or a weird dream. There were these women, and they claimed I was one of them, but it was not my time . . . . I think they were my family. I think I am their descendant," she shares softly, her voice almost worshipful.

"Makes sense. Fae often have visions, and coupled with your gift, you probably reached out to them beyond the grave. It does make me curious about how strong your gift could truly be. You have spent your entire life repressing and hiding it, so maybe it's time to embrace it and train. You're not just a hunter anymore. You are so much more. You're a bridge to the monsters. You will need every inch of strength you have to continue that. I want to keep you safe. I want you to win." I offer her my hand, and she lays hers in it, reading the truth in my memories. "I think we should start to train it. Let's make you invincible."

She looks at my hand and then to me and nods. "I think you're right. I will probably need it for what is to come." Her eyes go far away.

"What do you mean?" I ask, worry tightening my chest.

She blinks and looks at me. "I don't know. I just get this feeling we need to be as strong as we can possibly be."

Those words hammer into my chest, laced with foresight and prophecy.

Something is coming. Something we need to be prepared for.

That thought alone gets me moving.

CHAPTER 46

Tate

I sit across from Shamus on his bed, cross-legged, as he holds his hand out again. "Focus, Tate," he snaps, and my eyes narrow in annoyance at his use of my name. I'm accustomed to the endearment he always uses when speaking to me, and I find it hard to hear my name on his lips now.

Pressing my palm above his, I close my eyes and focus on the vision I want to throw at him, and then I touch him. This time he jerks back with a laugh, and I open my eyes, grinning. "Did you see it?"

"You slapping me? Yes, good. Try again, but more detailed this time. Shove more at me, as long as you can," he murmurs.

Nodding, I close my eyes and visualise what I want him to see. I struggled at first to get the details just right, but we found intense emotions seem to work best, such as fury, love, and lust. I focused on the first half, so now, with a wicked grin, I focus on the last.

I just can't resist. I press my hands to his, and his groan fills the air as my eyes open to observe him. His eyes are almost glazed over as he watches my visions pouring into his head of my lips wrapped around his cock. I send him more visions as they come to me, and when I remove my hand, he startles, his cheeks red.

"Angel," he growls.

"Yes, commander?" I tease, blinking innocently. "Did my visions work? Maybe I'm getting better."

"You better not ever show anyone else visions like that," he warns.

"Or what?" I murmur as I press my hand to his leg and throw another one at him. His teeth flash in warning before he's on me.

Our lips meet in a flurry as we tumble to the bed, the visions making us both hot and bothered, but then we hear a chuckle.

"I bet them I'd find you both still in bed." We jerk apart, swinging our heads around to see Ronan floating close by, wiggling his eyebrows. "Looks like I got here at the right time. Don't let me stop you. I'll enjoy the show."

My eyes narrow on him, but Shamus grips my chin and turns me back, his lips crushing to mine once more. He doesn't care that his best friend is watching us, and honestly, I don't care either. I've fucked both Shamus and Ronan, and I have nothing to be ashamed of.

I kiss him back, sliding my hands down his abs before I sit on my heels, eyeing him below me, then I wrap my lips around his cock. I did say I wanted him in my mouth, after all. His groan fills the air, and he thrusts down my throat, letting me set the pace as he fills my throat, and I bob on his cock, getting it nice and wet. When he's had enough, he rips me up, and our lips meet again as he drags me down and impales me on his cock, swallowing my gasp of surprise and pleasure as he stretches me. I sink all the way down his length, my nails digging into his chest as we break apart, and then he pulls from my body and thrusts back inside me. His hand slides possessively down my body, and he rubs my clit until I cry out and roll my hips.

I ride him hard, but then I hear a noise. Glancing back with a smirk, I meet Ronan's dark, hungry gaze as he watches me. "You sure you just want to watch, Ronan?"

His eyes flare, snapping up to mine. I offer him my hand with a wicked grin. "You've been inseparable with Shamus since, well, forever, so why start now?" I glance at Shamus to see him smirking, gripping my hips and urging me to move.

"Take her hand, fool," he tells Ronan. "I won't last long in her cunt. She feels so good."

Ronan disappears, but I feel him behind me, and then a hand grips my neck, turning my head, and invisible lips meet mine. My eyes widen as I clench around Shamus, but I hand myself over to him even though I can't see him, and big hands cup my breasts from behind, tweaking my nipples. Shamus rubs my clit until I cry out into Ronan's mouth.

Groaning, Ronan pulls away, and I search for him as he pushes me forward so I'm lying across Shamus, who stops moving. I still can't see Ronan, but I feel him. His cock presses against my pussy, knocking into Shamus's. Neither of them seems to care, and I jerk with a cry as he pushes into me, filling me alongside Shamus, forcing my pussy to stretch so wide it hurts. I bite Shamus's chest in punishment, and he grunts and jerks inside me, and then Ronan moves, pulling from my body and pushing back as he and Shamus find a rhythm. They pin me between them as they use me—one in, one out—filling my pussy over and over. Ronan's hand is on my neck, pinning me, and Shamus's are on my hips, my teeth digging into his chest.

"Shit, she feels good like this." Ronan's voice fills my ear, and I shudder. "You should see her, all stretched around us. It's fucking incredible."

"I can feel it," Shamus growls. "She's dripping for us. You like it, don't you, angel? Like us sharing you?"

Fuck, fuck, fuck.

He's not wrong, and his words go straight to my already throbbing body, pleasure coursing through every inch of me as they surround me. Their cocks build my pleasure until I can't handle it anymore.

I shatter, screaming into Shamus's skin.

My cunt clenches on them, and Shamus groans, burying deep inside me. I feel his release filling me. Ronan huffs into my skin, biting the nape of my neck as he hammers into me before stilling as he follows us into ecstasy.

The pleasure continues to flow through me, making me twitch

between them, and when it finally lets me go, I slump into Shamus, covered in sweat and cum but oh so fucking satisfied.

I guess you should mix business with pleasure, especially if it's at the hands of your dangerous commander and his mischievous ghost.

CHAPTER 47

Jarek

"Are you sure about this?" I ask Tate as she sits on the floor of the room we claimed. The others are scattered around, watching curiously. She came back this morning, smelling of sex and magic, and explained about her heritage. It doesn't shock me, since she has always felt like old magic to me, but this could go wrong, and I would hate for her to grow frustrated with her powers.

"Magic has a way of disrupting other magical gifts, and you are still learning—"

"I'm sure. I need to learn to harness these skills, and the best way is to practice. I don't go up against humans all the time, so I need to test them on as many supernaturals as possible."

"Luckily for you, you have a whole buffet to choose from," Ronan calls with a laugh.

Ignoring them, she places her hands above mine. "I'm sure."

I nod and wait. I feel her push, and then her mind brushes across mine, soft at first before it grows more confident. I keep my door open, something we learn when we are younger. If it's shut, no magic can enter my mind and use me like a puppet. Every powerful warlock knows this skill, but it's strange to open up to another.

I let her inside, and her vision fills my head. It's blurry but grows more detailed. "Again," I tell her as she lets go.

She practices a few more times until they grow clear, as if they are happening before me. "Good," I praise happily.

I let her vision wash through me for a moment, and she grins victoriously, but then I twist the vision, morphing it, and shove it back at her. She shudders, her eyes widen, and her smile drops. Her vision changed from her dying my hair to her on her back below me.

"Don't give up. Keep going. Using magic on another is like fencing. You must always be willing to fight back. Give and take," I say, and her vision changes to me on my back with her looking down at me.

We volley back and forth like this, changing the other's vision and shoving it back. I see her growing tired. Magic is draining, even for an older practitioner like me, but her strength is astonishing. Usually, new users cannot even last one round, never mind this many.

She truly is a creature of beauty and strength.

She is a warrior through and through.

Even now, she grits her teeth, fighting that weakness.

"You need to rest—"

"I don't have time to rest. I need to practice," she mutters, clearly annoyed. "Stupid human body."

"We have ways around that," the fae says, and we both look at him. "A boost, if you will. You have us all here, so use our blood, magic, and power. Take it from us and fuel yourself. If it works, you can do it in battle as well."

"How?" she asks.

"There are many ways." He looks her over. "But the only way I'm offering right now is with payment of your body." She freezes, and he chuckles darkly. "You smell like sex and magic, mortal, my two favourite things. If you want my strength and energy, then you pay for it."

"You can have my blood," Addeus offers.

She looks between them as Fang chimes in. "And my strength, too, if we can find a way."

"Me, mistress, drain me! Take it all," Tem exclaims, so happy he's almost bouncing.

Ronan groans. "She drained me this morning, but I guess I could go again."

She looks to me, and I smile. "My strength is yours if you can take it. Choose which you wish."

She looks us over. "How about all?"

Lying back on the floor, she tilts her head as she leans on her elbows. "The more power, the better, right? Fine. I'll use you all, and you can use me." She glances at the fae. "I accept your offer."

It gets us moving, and my lips crash onto hers as I order my magic to strip her of her clothes so she's bare below me. She chuckles against my lips, but it ends in a moan as I slide down her body, wrapping my lips around her hard nipple and sucking. Popping it free, I blow a breath over the tight bud and turn my head to give the other one the same treatment, all while I slide my magic down her body and slip it inside her. She gasps, her back arching as her hips work. I lean back as her legs open wide, showing me her pink, glistening cunt.

My eyes catch on something, and I see Fang quietly slip away. I hesitate. She is just as much one of us as the others. None of us want her, we only want Tate, but Tate wants her like she wants us. We need to find a way to make Fang comfortable enough to stay. Leaning down, I grip Tate and drag her up so she's kneeling.

"You want us all, yes? Then you'll start with me since you teased me. I'm going to take your pretty pussy from behind, and while I do, you're going to fuck your succubus." I feel her clench in want around my magic and grin. "You want that, don't you?"

"Fuck yes," she responds, glancing away to see Fang, and her eyes narrow. "Where the hell do you think you're going?"

"Oh, erm—" Fang stutters. "I didn't want to get in the way."

"You're mine, and I want you. Get your sexy ass back here," Tate orders, and Fang hesitates for a second before walking back over and kneeling before Tate, who grabs her and kisses her girl. Turning her, I give them better access, and Tate pushes Fang back with her body, pinning her to the floor before she breaks the kiss and slides down, lifting her oversized shirt as she looks up at Fang's wide eyes. "Are you okay with Jarek fucking me while I fuck you?"

Fang's eyes widen farther, but she nods rapidly, and Tate wastes no time burying her head under the shirt so we can't see what she's doing. Fang's back arches with a scream, and I drag Tate's hips into the air then press my cock to her entrance. I pull my magic free then bury myself inside her in one thrust.

Her muffled groan of pleasure reaches me as Fang grips her hair, drags her closer, and raises her legs to give her better access. I focus on Tate, my eyes locked on her cunt as she pulses around my cock when I pull from her body and slam back in.

I'm careful as my magic moves over Tate's skin so I don't accidentally touch Fang, and then I tweak her nipples and rub her clit until she groans, her head moving faster under Fang's shirt, who's panting and writhing.

Grunting, I let go of everything and just hand it to her. My power flows into her alongside my cock, giving her everything she needs. Her muscles lock up as I pummel into her, and Fang screams, arching up off the floor. Her eyes close, and I feel the rush of her power slam into Tate, who cries out.

Her orgasm rips through her, her cunt milking me until I can't stop my own. With a groan, I pump her full of both my magic and cum, giving her every drop as she presses her panting face into Fang's stomach over her shirt, twitching around me as I groan.

I fall away, drained of both magic and cum, and watch with lazy eyes as Tem crawls to his mistress, ready to be used just like the others, and I smile.

CHAPTER 48

I can still taste Fang in my mouth, her delicious cum staining my lips and tongue. Jarek's drips from my cunt, and I'm breathing heavily, but as Tem crawls over to me, my body lights up. His long hair is bunched on his head in a bun, with strands framing his incredible face. His eyes lock me in place as he crawls up my body, stopping to lick my lips.

"Is it my turn to feed you now, mistress?" he asks.

I wrap my leg around his hip and roll us so he's below me. "Yes," I reply. I want them all, and I need their power, so why not have some fun? Leaning down, I press my lips to his teasingly. "Have you ever had your cock sucked, my tempest?"

His eyes widen, and he shakes his head. "I served my masters, not the other way around."

That's a damn fucking shame, but as I slide down his body, undo his trousers, and palm his cock, the wonder and disbelief in his eyes makes it all better for me. When I first press my lips to his cock, he cries out, and then I slide my mouth all the way down his magical length. My ass is high in the air, enticing the others, and I hope one of them takes the offer. When big hands grip my hips, I almost grin. They are warm but solid, and I know without looking it's Addeus.

Wiggling my ass, I push back as I swallow Tem all the way down, his wild eyes locked on me even as his hips lift and he pushes down my throat. Wrapping my hand around the base of his cock, I pump him as Addeus's cock presses to my pussy, and he pushes inside me, helped by Jarek's cum and my cream. His massive length spears me, and I gasp around Tem's cock.

"Mistress," he rasps.

"Does it feel good?" Ronan teases. "She's good at sucking cock. Just don't blow too early, she likes to tease."

"Her mouth," Tem growls, his head banging back to the floor. "It feels too good, mistress, please! I can't. I won't last."

"Want my help?" Ronan chuckles as Addeus thrusts in and out of me with a slow roll of his hips. It's not enough to get either of us off, and I snarl, tightening my lips. Tem whines and lifts his head.

"Please," he begs Ronan.

"I've got you, mate, don't worry. Between us, we can satisfy our woman." He disappears from my side, and the only reason I know he's there is because I feel him. My eyes widen as his lips wrap around my clit and suck, making me clench down on Addeus, who grunts and pulls from my pussy. I pop my mouth off Tem and glance back in annoyance.

"Take her ass, big guy, just don't hurt her too much." Ronan chuckles as he teases my clit, and I feel him slide up my body below me, his mouth wrapping around my nipple and sucking before he lets go. "I'll take her cunt. She likes to be shared. She'll come in seconds with us all in her, won't you?"

"Fuck off," I grumble, but the idea has me wiggling back, wanting just that.

Addeus's wet cock presses against my ass, and I freeze. "I'm big," he warns me, his voice dark and feral, and when I glance back, his fangs are so long I'm surprised they aren't hurting.

"I can take you," I tell him, pushing back and taking him an inch inside me. Snarling, he thrusts into me, forcing himself deep into my ass before pulling back and working deeper inside me. Dropping my head to Tem's stomach, I breathe through the burning pain and pleasure as he sets a slow rhythm. When I get used to it and push back to take him, I feel Ronan's mouth working my nipples again as his warm cock presses against my pussy, and when Addeus pushes inside me, he pushes me onto Ronan's waiting cock. I cry out into Tem's abs, which clench, his cock leaking across me, so I suck it, taking it out on him. I meet his eyes, wanting him to enjoy this since it's the first time someone has thought about his pleasure rather than theirs.

I hollow my cheeks as I swallow him, taking him all the way to the back of my throat, and he cries out. He's close to coming as I suck and slurp him.

Addeus's slow thrusts push me onto Ronan's cock, and they work together, one thrusting inside me while the other pulls out. The burning stretch turns to delicious pleasure, driving me wild, until pleasure is all I know.

Tem's cock expands, and that wiggling tip slides down my throat, tickling me, but I keep swallowing him deeper as Addeus speeds up, hammering into my ass as Ronan bites my nipple, and my release explodes through me. I scream around Tem as I come, but they don't stop. They fight my clinging body as I drool and pant around Tem's cock.

When I've recovered enough, I suck his cock deeper into my mouth, his hips lifting wildly as that wiggling edge slides deeper each time I take him deep. I'm dripping around their cocks, and I can't help but push back, offering them more, and they lose control.

I feel their powers flood me as Addeus pounds into my ass, forcing himself so deep it hurts, his unbending, metal cock like a rod, while Ronan's curved cock slides over the nerves in my channel that have me lighting up once more.

With a sudden roar, Addeus leans into me and bites into my shoulder, and I cry out, exploding once more at the sudden pain, dragging them with me.

I feel Addeus spill inside my ass as Ronan thrusts up, burying deep inside me, his cock pulsing his release in my cunt.

Addeus slumps into me before pulling from my ass and falling back, leaving me speared on Ronan's softening cock before he's gone too. Tem grabs my head and shoves his cock deep into my mouth, and that confident, wild mood makes me happy, knowing he didn't ask or hesitate. He just took what he wanted.

That wiggling end expands in my throat, and my eyes widen. I want to gag, but I can't seem to. The squirming tip of his cock presses to my throat, opening it wider than ever before, and his cum squirts down it, forcing it deep into my throat and stomach.

I have no choice but to take it, and when he withdraws his cock, I gasp, rolling to my side and swallowing repeatedly as I stare at him in wonder and shock. He looks completely drained, wearing a crazed smile on his lips while his eyes are closed.

Zeev appears above me, one eyebrow arched. "Don't tell me you're too tired for me?"

I lick my sore lips as I stare up at him. I can feel cum leaking from my ass and pussy, but despite their use of me and what I wanted, their powers flow through me, and rather than exhaustion, I feel . . .

Powerful.

I kneel and look up at him through my lashes. "Never," I purr. "Are you going to play nice this time?"

He reaches down and strokes my hair, almost petting me before he fists it and drags me to my feet, and I go willingly. "Never," he growls as he turns me and throws me over the coffee table.

I hit the wood hard, and my ribs ache, but I don't have time to complain because his hand is back in my hair, dragging my head up as he grabs my hip with his other hand and impales me on his cock.

I cry out, but he keeps me pinned, trapped as he claims my body with brutal, hard thrusts. "If you want my magic, then you will have to earn it."

I swallow and push back, taking him deeper. His magic flows across my skin, his ice-cold cock soothing the ache deep inside me. "You know I will," I rasp. "Give me your worst."

He does, using my body for his pleasure.

His cruel magic slides over every inch of my skin, creating cuts as he bleeds me. It wraps around my throat until my mouth opens, and it slips inside, silencing me as it flows deeper. More sweeps across my skin, tightening on my nipples to the point of pain as I feel it slip lower, clamping around my clit and then past his cock and into my sore ass.

Every inch of me is filled by him, and I love it.

Pleasure and pain mix, his icy cock warming inside me as he ruts into me. The angelic fae becomes the demon I know and love.

Hands touch my body, and the others move closer, all of them stroking my skin, even Fang. They caress me as he fucks me, and my eyes close in bliss as I give myself over to the sensations. Zeev turns downright feral, his magic ripping me apart inside and out as his cock burns inside me.

I can't take it anymore.

It's too much.

As my release slams through me, their blood and magic fuel me, filling me and overspilling so I explode.

Every inch of my body comes apart until I'm floating, the pleasure a never-ending wave mixed with power that's so strong, I realise I'm not in the living room anymore.

No, I'm standing on the grass before Stalkers' Rest. The full moon is above me, which isn't due for another three weeks, and heading towards me with a furious war cry are legions of hunters with their weapons raised.

I lift my arms to brace when suddenly, I feel like I'm spinning, and then I land back on my feet, my eyes opening to see the familiar stone table once more where the women watch me curiously.

"Interesting. Your powers are growing if you have managed to visit us," the younger one remarks.

A fae.

This must be the original one I am descended from.

"You're fae, and I am also part fae," I say.

"Very good," she replies. "You're learning. Why have you sought us?"

"I didn't mean to. I saw something that hasn't happened." I stumble over the words, unsure how to explain what I saw. Was it fear or a vision?

"The future," she murmurs. "Very rare indeed. It was my gift once, but none of my line have possessed it in over a hundred years. I knew you would. It's a dangerous gift, Tate, but if used wisely, it can save many lives. Remember, the future can always change. There are always choices that lead us down different roads. It is up to you to decipher them." She looks me over. "I fear your time here is running out. I offer you one last piece of advice, daughter of ours—embrace your gifts because they will save you one day, and let those like you stand at your side. Love will always win against hate, Tate, always."

I'm thrown back into my body, jerking up with a gasp and wide eyes.

"Tate." Shamus is before me, shaking my shoulders worriedly. "There you are. Fuck, you were gone for an hour. What happened?"

Swallowing, I peer into his eyes. "I saw the future," I whisper.

I hold a mug between my hands to warm them, feeling their eyes on me as we sit around the table.

"The future, huh?" Ronan says, breaking the silence. "Cool. Was I still as handsome?"

I smile and silently thank him for it.

"Tate, what happened?" Fang asks nervously.

"I think the power flooded me, and my gifts turned it outwards so I didn't burn out. Apparently, the fae in my lineage had the same gift. It's rare but there. I saw the future, or one possible future. I don't know." I rub my aching head. "She said futures can change with choices, so it's not set in stone." I glance around, hoping that's true, because what I saw . . . "Right? It might not happen."

"What might not?" Shamus asks, an order in his tone before he softens his voice. "What did you see, angel? I have never seen terror in your eyes before."

He's right. I'm scared. If what I saw happens, then everything and everyone will be lost. The hunters walk the line of this world, and if we are at war with each other, then it will descend into anarchy without rules.

"War," I croak. "I saw a war coming for us."

He sits back, his face closed down. "I see." That's all he says. "Do you know when?"

"When the moon is full," I murmur. "Shamus, it wasn't the monsters coming for us. It was our own kind. It was hunters."

He watches me, giving nothing away, and I soak in his confidence and strength. "Then we need to prepare."

It's all he says, even faced with the impending betrayal and end of his organisation, but I see the pain in his gaze at the thought. Will friends turn into foes again? Will I be forced to hurt our own people?

"She's right. The future can always change," Zeev says, no doubt sensing my unease. "It's not always what happens. Sometimes seeing it is enough for you to make the decisions that lead to it transpiring, like a self-fulfilling prophecy. Sometimes it's enough to swerve off that path. There is one thing for sure—you cannot control the future. Nobody can, not even the gods. All we can do is endure it and wait." He smiles gently at me, which is worrying in itself. "Time stops for no man."

"I am not a man," I snarl, my fear turning into anger at once again being betrayed by my own people. "And I will not let that happen."

CHAPTER 49

Fang

Sipping fresh orange juice, I lean back into my seat and watch my girl. She barely slept last night after what she saw, and I know it's weighing her down. We watch as she paces back and forth, her eyes a million miles away. She doesn't even notice when Shamus slips into the room and sits with us at the table where breakfast is spread.

"How long has she been like this?" he asks worriedly.

"An hour," I respond as I reach for some fruit. Jarek does at the same time, and our fingers brush, but he instantly jerks back.

"I am so sorry!" He drops to his knees before me, his head bowed. "That was an accident. I truly mean it." He lifts his hand, and before I can even say anything, magic wraps around the fingers he touched me with and he breaks them. Cradling his injured hand to his chest, he continues to kneel.

"Jarek, it was an accident," I murmur. "It's fine." They are all very good about giving me space without making me feel like an outsider. They joke and laugh with me like I am one of the guys, but they are very careful not to touch me. I even saw Tem fall over yesterday so he didn't brush against me. It's nice. I know Tate is behind it, and it only makes me care for her more.

Jarek rises, looking completely ashamed, so I put some fruit in a bowl and slide it towards him. "Heal your fingers and eat. We have more important things to deal with than an accidental touch."

"Tate will not forgive me, accident or not," he whispers.

"She will, but we won't tell her. Eat," I order, my eyes going back to Tate as she continues to pace, lost in her own world.

"What do we do?" Ronan murmurs. "She's going to wear a hole in the carpet."

"I could tie her up," the fae suggests leisurely as he throws a grape and catches it in his mouth. Out of all of us, he's the most unbothered —no, that's not the right word.

Excited. He wants this war. He wants bloodshed and death.

Tate is right, he's evil, but he seems to be obsessed with her and she with him, so I cannot complain. I am just glad he's on our side.

"I know you are worried about what you saw," Shamus begins, trying to stop her pacing.

"Worried? We all should be," she snaps. Tem paces at her side so she isn't alone, and Addeus reaches up and hands her some toast, which she accepts without a word and begins to eat as she moves.

"The best way to avoid what you saw is to make them fear you, fear us, and show them we mean what we say, which means you need to hunt down all those who would stand against us." Shamus catches her hand, stilling her movements, and he rises elegantly. His hand grips her chin possessively as her eyes flare. "Do what you do best, angel."

"I don't see how that will help." Her eyes widen when he kisses her, and I giggle for her as she blushes, something I've never seen her do.

"Then trust me, angel. Do as I ask and let me worry about what you saw, okay? You do trust me, yes?" He waits, his hand cupping her cheek.

"Yes," she whispers softly.

"Good." He kisses her again before dragging her down onto his lap and sliding his iPad in front of her. "Then start here. I have been keeping dossiers." I lean over, trying to read upside down, so he tilts it slightly so I can see, accommodating me without a word.

"He's not a complete prick like you said," I comment to Tate.

"Is that what she called me?" he scoffs. "I'm disappointed, angel. I expected more colourful words from you."

She rolls her eyes, ignoring us as she scrolls through the folders. "This one." She pulls up a burly, middle-aged man with a scraggly beard and hair. "I met him when I was a kid. I'd remember his face anywhere. I figured he was dead by now. He was a total asshole. My dad gave him that wicked scar on his face when he used me as bait without warning. I almost died."

Shamus's expression closes down as he scans the face. "I remember this one. I coded him red—extremely dangerous. He's killed many innocents, I just can't prove it, but his hunts are sloppy. It isn't just monsters getting hurt, but humans too. He doesn't care who gets in his way. He simply likes killing."

"Then let's give him what he wants." Tate nods as she closes the file and looks at us. "I want you all showered and dressed and ready to go in ten."

"This hair takes more than ten minutes, mortal," the fae drawls.

"Then we'll leave you behind and no murder for you," she retorts.

"I can make it work." He flicks his fingers and his hair is plaited back. His face now sparkles as if diamonds are trapped in his skin, and his casual clothes have been replaced by battle wear with a sword at his side. "Ready."

"Show off," I mutter.

"You too," she warns me. "You don't need to fuck around with your eyeliner again. Hurry up."

"It's my battle makeup," I whine.

"I'll help." Jarek leans over, and magic slides across my face. A mirror appears, showing me my perfectly done makeup. I look like I normally do, only better. "As an apology."

"Apology for what?" Tate's voice is deadly cold, and I swear the room drops two degrees.

"I accidentally touched—" Jarek begins before I shove an apple in his mouth to silence him.

"Touched her?" Tate rises. "What did I say would happen if you did?"

His eyes widen, but he sits and accepts his fate, so I shove him from the chair. "Run, you fool, while we calm her down."

Shamus wraps himself around Tate as she pulls a dagger, and I spread my arms, blocking her as Jarek rushes away. "It was an accident. No! Not the sword!"

We eventually calm her down, but she's glaring daggers at a very sad looking Jarek. It's especially worrying since she's strapped to high heaven with weapons. When she goes to grab a blade, Ronan snatches it. "I'll hold this for you." He shoves it in a bag he appears with. She doesn't look away from Jarek as she grabs for her shotgun. "And this."

By the time she's done, the bag is filled with weapons, and Jarek is even more pale.

"It was an accident, babe," I murmur as I step in front of her, stroking my hands down her shirt and straightening it under her jacket.

"I warned them," she hisses.

"And he apologized." I grip her chin and drag her gaze to mine. Her eyes are so cold, I swear I feel frostbite, but I don't back down. This is a hunter's gaze, not a lover's, but the fact that her anger is on my behalf makes me want to kiss the shit out of her, so I do. When I pull back, the ice has melted slightly. "He also broke the fingers he brushed my hand with as an apology. Let it go. Accidents will happen. I trust them, Tate, because you do. Don't punish him like this. Look at the man, he appears ready to gut himself on an altar for you."

She glances at Jarek and sighs deeply.

"We need to work as one, not fight each other. Now go apologize for threatening him with the dagger . . . and the sword . . . and the flamethrower."

"No." She huffs.

"Now," I order. "Or else I will never let you touch me again." She gapes at me, and I point at Jarek. "Go."

Muttering to herself, she marches his way. "I am sorry for throwing the knife at you. And for using my sword. And for threatening to obliterate you with a flamethrower." Each word is pulled from deep inside her, and I have to bite my lips to hide my smile as she glances at me. I give her an encouraging thumbs up, and she looks back at him. "Fang tells me it was an accident, and I trust you. I know you wouldn't do it on purpose. I just didn't like the idea that she was hurt. I reacted badly. I'm sorry."

"It's me who's sorry," he murmurs, staring at her like she's the entire fucking world. I get it, I do. Tate has that effect on people. I can't imagine my life without her now. She's helping fill the hole my brother left behind, and it's never boring at her side. "It was a genuine accident, but I will do better." He drops to his knees, a sword appearing across his raised hands. "If you wish, you can cut off my hands so I may never do it again."

She grips the blade, inspecting it, and I start to worry, but she suddenly presses it to her chest and kneels before him. "Then you have the right to carve out my heart for doubting you. You have stood by me with nothing but loyalty and a helping hand. I never should have doubted you or your intentions. I truly am sorry, Jarek."

They stare at each other for a moment, and I grip Tem at my side and turn him around to give them privacy. I do peek back, though, to see their hands in each other's hair, their foreheads pressed together before they kiss softly.

"Eight out of ten, use more tongue!" Ronan calls, and the sword flies right through where he was. "Angel!" he yells. "You'll pay for that later."

She snorts, and when we turn around, she's holding Jarek's hand and he's smiling widely. "Alright, enough playing around. Are we ready?"

"We are now." Shamus steps back into the room in full hunting gear, something I've never seen him in.

Her eyes widen, and she's speechless for once. "What? You cannot go with us," she murmurs. "You're needed here—"

"We will be gone and back before they know it. Besides, this man is dangerous—"

"And I can look after myself—"

"I know you can," he assures her. "But I need to sharpen my skills. Not all of us are as good of a warrior as you, angel. Some of us have been sitting behind desks as you so helpfully reminded me. I'd be honoured if you would let me join your hunt."

She stares at him for a moment before groaning. "I'm in charge."

"Just how I like it." He winks, and I groan in disgust.

"Fine. Zeev," she calls, and a portal appears. "Remember, he's very dangerous," she warns us, "and his hatred for monsters is all that drives him. He will kill you if he has a chance. Don't give him one." She steps through the portal.

I sigh wistfully. "She's so fucking cool."

"Cool? Is she sick? Should we bring her back and warm her up?" Tem asks nervously.

"Oh, my little bloodthirsty friend, I have much to teach you." I sigh. "Come on, dummy, let's go hunting."

I follow my girl through the portal.

CHAPTER 50

Tate

George Brown, or Demon, as the other hunters call him, is the epitome of what I hate. He hunts anything and everything, regardless of what their crimes are. He is relentless and messy. If Shamus's research is anything to go by, then he doesn't care who gets hurt in the process, which doesn't surprise me. I still remember the hardness of his gun at my temple as he marched me into the abandoned bakery to leave me as bait for the troll we were hunting. Well, my father and George were hunting, but not together—it just so happened they'd run into each other. My dad made a friendly bet, as most hunters do, and George made it unfriendly. He didn't care if I lived or died.

It was only because of the skills my father had taught me that I survived that encounter. The troll got away, and George was so angry, he backhanded me. When my father turned up with the troll's head, he was furious, and for the first time ever, I saw fear in George's eyes. He managed to escape my father's wrath, not without that scar, but I knew then what lingered inside a man like that—bloodlust, the type that is never satisfied.

He feels no sanctity for human life nor monsters, just a need to kill. He isn't a hunter because he wants to protect humans. He's a hunter because he'd be a serial killer otherwise. He's gotten away with it for a long time, mainly because his superiors are too scared to say anything so they cover for him.

Not anymore.

He doesn't scare me. He's just a man with murderous intent—one that will learn there's always someone bigger and stronger than him.

I'll make him regret his ways and show the other hunters how serious I am when I return with his head in tow.

The portal spits us out in a small town in the middle of nowhere. "What is he hunting here?" I ask curiously.

"His superior reports he is chasing down a wendigo," Shamus replies as he appears at my side.

"Then he'll be in the woods. I know how men like him think. He'll be watching and waiting, probably luring locals or hikers in as a trap. Let's go." We cross the small, empty road and head into the woods that border this tiny town. Its population cannot be more than a thousand, but the woods seem to span many miles—perfect for a wendigo to hide.

Once they have tasted flesh, there is no going back. He is hunting an actual monster for once, but it's how he's hunting it that worries me.

There is a ripped tent six miles into the vast forest, just off the hiking trail. Reaching down, I press my fingers to the cinders of the fire. "Still warm. They haven't been gone long."

"Boot tracks," Shamus points out. "Big, has to be him. Two smaller ones are near it. He probably led them away."

I nod as I scan the area before placing my hand on the tent to see it. I have to be sure I don't just rely on my training anymore, but my powers as well. I'll use every advantage I can get.

Gritting my teeth against the terror that saturates the images, I focus on the flashing, distorted visions. They are tainted by panic and adrenaline, which makes them harder to understand.

"Two women," I say. "They were sleeping this morning when he slashed open their tent, tied them together, and frog-marched them away. He explained in detail what would happen to them. He wants their fear." Pulling my hand away, I point in the direction they went. "Let's go." I pull out my shotgun and set off into the trees.

Fury fills me. Nobody should be made to feel fear like that. They are innocent. They weren't hurting anyone, just enjoying nature and their time together, and now it will always be tainted by this memory.

My team spreads out around me, and every now and then, I touch a tree in passing and alter our course accordingly. We move silently, Shamus knowing exactly where to move and how to work at my side even without working together before. His steps are silent, and he moves like a wraith. Even in the bright sun and knowing where he is, he's hard to spot, using the coverage perfectly.

No wonder they call him a stalker.

It's strange seeing him in this mode. He will always be the commander to me, sitting behind his desk while pulling the strings, so it's easy to forget he is a hunter too. Now that I see him in action, I realise there is a reason they all fear and respect him. He earned it.

Letting out a low whistle, I grab his attention and alter our course farther north. The trees are older and bigger here, the foliage growing everywhere. This is true wilderness, not a hiking trail or path. It's clear that aside from George, his captives, and us, it's not been explored or walked through in many, many years. It's a perfect place for a wendigo to hide. Its den must be deep in the woods, below the earth, where they feel safe.

Another mile in and Addeus catches my arm, his voice low. "I smell blood. Fresh. Human."

"He's right," Tem supplies, closing his eyes as he sways. "Female, young, definitely human."

"Which way?" I ask. They both point in the same direction, and Shamus appears at my side.

"We are close," I tell him, and he nods. "George will have set a trap, and we can't spring it. We need to be unseen as we creep up on him. I want you all to spread out. Use every power you have, but I don't want anyone to be seen at all. The humans are to be left alone. They are innocent. George is mine, but capture him if you must."

"And the wendigo?" Shamus asks, trusting me to take charge like we agreed.

"Let's hope we get there first. Deal with the hunter then the monster." I shrug. "Shamus, you're with me. I want silence from the rest of you. Close in, leave no room for escape."

They nod and fade into the wilderness.

"Let's go," I murmur to Shamus.

"You're hot when you're hunting," he responds quietly.

"No flirting on hunts," I murmur, but a smile curves my lips.

"Whose dumb rule is that?" He winks as I roll my eyes, but he falls into silence then, moving away so we create a net. We walk in sync, not even breaking branches under our weight.

Ten minutes later, I hold up my hand, and he stops. I point at the ground, seeing the trail, and he nods as we search the area. They seem to disappear, and I glance up, realising why. I jerk my thumb up in explanation, and he nods in understanding. He holds a knife between his teeth as he starts to scale a nearby tree, and I do the same. We need to see him before we act. I have to trust the others to follow my orders and focus on George.

The tree is wide, but it's easy to climb, and just below the canopy, I inch along a branch. I perch there and scan the area. The trees open up slightly, and I only see him because of my training.

He's in all green and brown, pressed against the trunk of the tree, holding a sniper rifle in his hand. It's aimed at the clearing in the woods below, where moss and fallen trees seem to create a natural break in the foliage.

That's where I see his trap and bait.

The women are tied to a tree stump with deep cuts across their necks. The scent of their blood fills the air, no doubt to lure the wendigo. He must have tracked its den to around here and hoped that would be enough. Even now, filled with fear and hopelessness, they hold hands, their heads pressed together and eyes closed as their mouths move, speaking just for them.

They must know death is coming, yet they face it together.

My gaze goes back to George before I find Shamus. I point at the women and back to him. He nods in understanding. He's going to save them. George is mine.

Creeping across the branch, I leap over the short distance to the next tree. The branch trembles under my weight, so I quickly cross to the trunk and scale around it before moving down the next branch and over to the subsequent tree. I repeat it three times more before I'm behind George on a tree. I need to get across without him hearing me, so I head down a few branches and leap. The tree sways, and I press to the trunk, waiting. He either doesn't notice, which means he's not as good of a hunter as he thinks, or he ignores it. Either way, it means he's getting old and his hearing isn't good. It's a trait with hunters from too many explosions or weapons firing near our ears. We don't have long shelf lives.

When I'm sure he's not heard me, I silently make my way up to the branch he's lying across. There are a few bundled together, creating a perfect arch for his body, which is probably why he chose it. It also allows me to creep up behind him and perch directly next to him. I expect him to turn, sensing me, but he's so focused on the scope, he doesn't even move.

I follow his gaze to the clearing below in time to see Shamus emerge from the trees.

He moves into the clearing brazenly, trusting me to take care of the issue. His back is to the sniper rifle as he crouches in front of the now struggling women, their eyes wide with terror at the sight he makes.

George snarls and swears, his finger tightening on the trigger as he takes aim.

He will not get to pull it. "Hey, George," I whisper behind him, tapping his shoulder with my blade. He whirls, and I slam my hand into the rifle so it's pointed at the sky just as it goes off. I snatch it from his grip and toss it away as he stares at me in shock. "Remember me?" I grin.

"Havelock," he hisses. Despite the fact that the last time he saw me was over ten years ago, he clearly remembers my face. "You look more and more like that bastard who did this to me, but now I get to return the favour. It's a shame he died before I could." I see the flash of silver before he jerks his arm up, and I knock it away.

"You're getting slow in your old age." I grab the branch above me and kick him from his perch. He flies backwards, a yelp escaping his lips, and I hear the moment he hits the ground with a grunt.

Swinging down the branches, I roll when I hit the ground and stop before him where he's sprawled in the clearing.

Crouching, I tap his leg. "Don't tell me you're already dead. I came all this way. It would be such a disappointment."

He blinks and slowly lifts his head before he seems to realise what happened and scrambles to his knees. "You bitch."

"Really? I expected something much wittier." I sigh. "Oh well, I guess I could give you the spiel I gave the other hunters, but the truth is, you're not worth wasting my breath. George Brown, I sentence you to death for your crimes." I reach for my blade, but he's already coming for me faster than I expected.

I lift my arm to block the blow, and his blade pierces it. The pain is sharp, but I don't let it show. He laughs as he falls backwards, but I arch my brow, grip the slippery handle with my blood, and pull it free, holding it in my other hand. There's a huge wound, a through and through, but it's bleeding a lot. I hold it up, however, trusting them to understand, and with my eyes on George, I feel the magic move across my skin and heal it like it never happened.

"How?" he exclaims, his eyes wide. "You're fucking one of them! You're a monster!" he roars.

"Not quite, though I guess maybe I am half monster, but would you like to meet some true monsters?" I tease. I whistle, and then I feel them appear behind me. He tries to grab a weapon that isn't there. Zeev dances out of reach with a laugh as he tosses his blade into the forest.

George spins, taking in my monsters surrounding him. "What is this?"

"The new elite team," Shamus says as he steps from the forest. "Specifically created to hunt scum like you—those who betray the code of hunters, flaunt the laws, and hurt innocents. I'm sure you remember Tate Havelock. Well, she's their commander."

He looks from Shamus to me. "I'm one of you!"

"No, you're a killer with a patch." I grip his arm, ripping the patch off then holding it up for him. "And that patch does not protect you anymore. You are no longer a hunter, which just makes you a killer. Would you prefer to die on your knees like the weakling you are or on your feet? It's your choice."

"You want me dead? You'll have to fight for it," he bellows as he leaps at me. I sidestep him and hold up my hand to stop the others who are moving forward.

"He's mine. Keep your eyes out for the wendigo," I call as George turns, his gaze landing on me again. He knows I'm smarter, faster, and stronger. He's at a disadvantage, and he recognises it.

"I hear your dad died screaming your name," he hisses. "He was eaten, and there was nothing left. I bet it hurt."

I know he's trying to make me sloppy, so I rein in my anger, arching a brow. I know how my father died. It haunts me to this day.

"Did he cry like a little bitch? Beg? I bet he did. He always was a pussy. You loved your daddy, didn't you? Loved him a little too much. It was always strange how he wouldn't let you out of his sight. Tell me, Tate, did your daddy love you a lot? Did he love his precious daughter in all the right ways?" He leers at me. "Did the great William Havelock like little kids? I bet he did."

My nostrils flare as Shamus's voice fills the air. "I wouldn't," he warns George. "You're just making it worse for yourself."

"He's right," I agree, my voice dead and cold. "I was going to kill you quickly. Now, I'm going to make it hurt."

I hold daggers in both hands as I head towards him. His eyes track my movements, and when I get close, I feint left then right and spin around him. Gripping the back of his head, I shove him to his knees. He struggles, but I dig my thumb into his mouth and force it open, slipping my blade inside as he screams and fights

"I hate hearing his name from your mouth," I snarl as I rip out his tongue. "Now, I never have to hear it again."

Stepping back as he screams, I hold his tongue up. "Now your mouth is as useless as the rest of you." He covers his mouth, his face pale. "You can dish out pain, but you can't take it. You're the weak one. Look at you. One little wound and you're down. I expected more." I look to Shamus with a laugh. "You tagged him red for nothing. He's pathetic."

He crashes into me, and I laugh as he tackles me to the ground. His fist pummels into my side, and I let him. My ribs crack, but I let him get his best shot in before I jerk my fist up. It hits him square in the face, bursting his nose as he falls backwards, and I sit up. "Is that really the best you have?"

The noise that leaves him is a mixture of a laugh and a cough, and I follow his gaze to the dagger sticking from my side. I didn't even feel it thanks to the layers I'm wearing. "Really? This is my favourite shirt," I snap as I tug it free and throw it at him with a flick of my fingers. It embeds in his bicep, and he makes that horrible screaming noise again as he holds up his arm.

Sighing, I climb to my knees. "This is just boring. I expected more."

"Then stop playing with your food." Zeev chuckles. "Play with us instead."

"Fine." Reaching over, I pull the dagger from his arm and grip his chin. "This is for my father." I drive it into his eye. It doesn't go as deep as one would think, but as he falls to the ground, writhing, I drive my boot into the handle over and over until he stops moving.

Reaching over my shoulder, I tug my father's sword free. It seems apt that it will deliver the final blow. Hoisting George up, I grip his hair as I press the sharp edge of the blade to his neck and start to carve. His arteries burst, spraying his hot blood across my face.

It's not as easy as one might think to cut off a head. It's messy and tiring, but when it's done, I pry the last string of muscle keeping it on his spine away and hold it up victoriously, just as a mighty bellow fills the air.

"That would be the wendigo," Shamus casually remarks.

"Shit." I glance down at the head and drop it, keeping hold of the sword. "Anyone remember how to kill a wendigo? I'm a little rusty."

"Silver to the heart is the best bet," Shamus answers instantly.

"Do you have any pure silver?"

"Of course." He grins as the trees shake on the other end of the clearing and then finally part to reveal the wendigo.

"Good, we're going to need it," I mutter as I stare at the monster. This one is old and too far gone to care what or who is on its land. Its head lifts, scenting the blood. It's more monster than man, which is why I can guess its age. Its huge, talon-tipped hands drag along the ground, its skeleton head lifting to show me black, soulless eyes. Fur covers its warped back and limbs. I can see its ribs protruding from its side, and I even see a flash of bone where someone tried to kill it before. This one won't be easy.

It roars again, swinging its head to me. Of fucking course.

It barrels towards me, and I realise why—I'm covered in blood.

"It wants the blood. I'll be bait!" I shout to Shamus. "Make sure to aim true."

I whistle loudly when it jerks to a stop as Fang throws something at it, catching its attention again, but only for a moment before it turns to Addeus. Snarling, I grab my dagger and slice my palm. The cut bleeds, and I squeeze it, then it turns. "That's right. You want me. I'm tasty. Come and get it, you cannibal."

"Angel," Shamus yells.

"I'm trusting you!" I shout back. "Don't let me die, stalker!"

He nods and races to catch up to the wendigo as it heads towards me. I stand with my hand out, using myself as bait, trusting Shamus to keep me safe. My instincts scream for me to run, but I stand still, eyeing the monster who could kill me with one blow.

It's almost on me when Shamus flies through the air, holding a long silver spear in his hand. His eyes are hard and determined.

Shamus leaps onto its back and stabs the silver spike into its spine. It roars and spins, throwing him off, the weapon still impaled in its body. It turns back to me.

Fuck!

Shamus climbs to his feet unsteadily and sees it the moment I do—its claws are coming towards me. Shamus leaps quicker than I could anticipate and lands before me. Its claws swipe through him, and I watch with wide eyes as he goes flying, but within seconds, he's on his feet. I throw my blade at the wendigo, and his attention is back on me. Rushing towards it, I duck under its arm and slash its chest, opening a shallow wound that seems to annoy it rather than hurt it. It plucks me from the ground and flings me around in the air until I feel my brain rattle in my skull. It lifts me higher, and I glance down to see its mouth opening to swallow me whole.

Fuck that.

I drive a blade into its hand, and it drops me, then I roll to avoid its feet.

His arm comes up for another brutal strike when Shamus appears. He rolls across its back, pulling his spear with him, and then dances under its swing. It spins to keep him in sight, and I watch as he avoids those wicked claws until he can drive the spear into its ribs at the side. It tries to run away, but with a mighty yell, Shamus slams it in deeper, and the wendigo freezes. Its whole body contracts before it falls to the side, dead, the spike sticking from its corpse.

Clapping fills the air as Shamus stumbles towards me and takes us both to the dirty ground with a groan.

Chest heaving, I turn my head on Shamus's chest, and our eyes meet. My lips curl into a smile, and I burst into laughter. He laughs with me before he groans. "Shit, that wendigo hit hard."

My laughter cuts off, and I sit up, opening his shirt to see the epic claw mark across his perfect chest. "Shamus—"

"It's not life-threatening. Besides, I have plenty of scars." He grins up at me. "It's nice to see you worried for me though."

"I'm not worried. I just don't want to be blamed for your death," I grumble as I touch the ragged wound. "Let me ask Zeev to heal it—" I look for him, but Shamus catches my hand.

"No."

I jerk my gaze back to him.

"It's not because I don't trust them, but I got this saving you, the person I love. I'll wear them with honour."

"You bloody fool," I snap, even as I twine our hands together.

"Rude, your commander is injured. Kiss it better," he teases.

I scoff at that as Zeev appears at my side. "He's right. They are warrior wounds earned while protecting someone he loves. He should wear them. Not doing so would be a dishonour to his feelings for you. I, however, can heal them enough that they will scar, but you will be able to move like normal." He looks to me. "Shall I, little mortal?"

I sigh. "What's the cost?"

"No cost. Anyone willing to sacrifice their life for yours deserves my magic." He nods seriously as he looks at Shamus. "May I?"

He nods, and within seconds, the wounds have closed, looking months old rather than fresh. Shamus blinks incredulously as he touches the scars and looks to Zeev. "I would thank you, but I know better."

"No thanks needed. You protected the only thing that is important to me." Reaching over, I grip Zeev's neck, tug him closer, and kiss him. His smile is charming and soft, even if his eyes are still cold, and I glance up and around.

"Let's clean this up and get back." I look to Shamus. "Get up, commander. Don't be such a pussy." I go to stand when I'm yanked back down and his mouth crashes onto mine in a possessive, hungry kiss that leaves me gasping.

"My thanks," he murmurs.

CHAPTER 51

Addeus

The whole of Stalkers' Rest is gathered, watching as another warning is added to the wall alongside Tate's old team. George's head is spiked next to theirs, and I scan the crowd. I can sense anger, disgust, and fear as well as respect. It's a volatile mix, and I worry about what it means. Shamus was hoping fear would keep them in line, but what if it sends them the other way and makes her vision come true?

Could she survive her people turning on her again?

Could we survive a war?

They still don't respect her decision to have us here, and most of the hunters think she has bewitched their commander, and now this. Suspicion and mistrust are rife. I spent the night invading the electronics of Stalkers' Rest, reading text messages and watching them through cameras. There are whispers, nothing concrete yet but enough to have me worried, so when Tate goes in to shower, I slip away. I wander the halls of Stalkers' Rest, tracking those I need to. Half my brain is locked on the cameras I have invaded, following their movements back to a storage room. The mics pick up the whispers, and I enhance them so I can listen as I move silently.

"She's out of control. We will be next!"

"We need to stop her before it's too late." They look around nervously at the servers and weapons filling the room, and they have no idea I'm right there with them.

"We should sneak in tonight while she's sleeping and slit her throat." I mark that one to die first.

"With those monsters around, we don't stand a chance," another mutters.

"If we can lure them away, I can lock them in a room from the control centre." This is from a man wearing glasses. He's not a hunter, he's too skinny, but he looks just as angry.

"I still don't get why he's here," another says.

"He has just as much to lose. If she starts looking into it, she'll find he helped cover us more than once," the leader replies. "It's a plan. We'll strike tonight."

"And the commander? He won't be happy. It's obvious he's whipped," one scoffs.

"Then we end him as well, if need be, and take control ourselves. He's gone weak and soft because of her. We'll spike their heads with their victims' and take control of the hunters."

I reach the door, and despite it being locked, I simply switch it in my head and it slides open. I step in and relock it behind me. They all turn, their eyes wide. "What the fuck? How did you get in here?"

I point at the camera blinking in the corner. "You should have been more careful. I am everywhere, and I hear and see everything."

They draw their weapons as I grin.

"You're going to need them. Not one of you is leaving this room alive. Nobody touches what is mine."

"Kill him first," Glasses orders. "I can use him as bait to lure them and lock them here."

One pulls a gun and aims it at me. He fires twice—one into my skull and one into my heart—but I do not even jerk from the impact.

I stare down at the bullet hole in my chest then raise my eyes back to them. "Pathetic." I smirk. "Many have tried to kill me." The bullets wiggle free from my skin as it heals, and I catch them and fling them faster than their guns can. They embed in the skull and chest of the one who shot me and he falls to the ground, dead.

The others roar and leap at me with raised blades. I let them, batting them away like flies, but one climbs onto my back and saws at my head. My circuits fizzle and my vision goes out for a moment. When my eyes come back online, my head falls to the side, almost detached. My vision flashes from colour to black and white as I reach behind me, pluck him from my back, and toss him into the wall. He hits it hard, and when he crumples to the floor, I know he is dead. I cannot sense his heartbeat anymore.

My head hangs from my body, more annoying than anything, so I lift it up, put it back into place, and feel my body mend as I advance on them. They are wide-eyed and terrified, backing into the wall.

"Please, we're sorry!" the leader shouts. "We'll leave her alone—"

"Yes, you will. I will hand your bodies to her as an apology for you."

Ripping his head up, I sink my fangs into his neck and tear out his throat. He falls, and I turn to Glasses as he pulls out a tablet and unlocks the door, rushing towards it. I lock it with my mind, and he slams into the door, pounding uselessly against it as I advance on him.

"Your skills will not save you now. I am the heart of this building. It obeys me, not you." He taps on his tablet before gripping it against his chest as he watches me.

"I can help—"

"I need no help." My hand wraps around his skinny neck as I lift him into the air. He turns red then purple, beating at me before I snap his neck and drop him. Glancing around, I find they are all dead. I wipe my mouth clean of their disgusting blood since I only want hers, and then I get to work.

It doesn't take much force to rip their heads from their bodies, and then I unlock the door with a blink, my vision finally fixing and returning to colour as I heal. These hunters were useless. My girl put up more of a fight than all of them together. It's no wonder she won my trust and loyalty.

Keeping their heads in my hand, I wander through the corridors.

Hunters see me coming and gape in shock. I locate her by using the cameras and call the elevator in my mind. When I step inside with some horrified techs, they scramble to get out. I skip the floors I don't need and get off at the gym where she is with the others.

It falls silent when I walk in, and she senses it and turns, her mouth dropping open. I don't stop until I stand before her, lowering to my knees and holding up their heads. "My love, I bring the heads of those who would do you harm."

"Addeus." She blinks at me as Shamus moves to her side.

A crowd forms, and I feel their anger.

"You cannot just kill us!" someone roars. "Look, it's been allowed to kill our own!"

Without a word, I project the scene in the storage room, their malicious intent and words flowing through the air as they plot to kill her and the commander.

"Well, shit." Shamus laughs as he looks at me. "I guess it pays being half machine. Alright, let's add them to the wall." He clears his throat as he steps past me, but I keep my eyes on her. "Enough. Disband and take this as a warning. Anyone who plots to harm Tate or me will face our wrath. We are everywhere. Go now."

"How did you know?" she asks me.

"I have been keeping an eye on everyone for you. I know you were worried about your vision, so I wanted to make sure it did not come to fruition." She grips my chin and jerks my head up. I stare lovingly into her eyes. "If I have displeased you, you may take my head with theirs."

"Displeased?" she repeats as she looks at me. "No, I'm not displeased, Addeus. I'm honoured you thought to protect me like that." She kisses my head. "Thank you for keeping us safe."

"Always," I vow. "No matter what."

Her thumb rubs over my lip and lifts to show me blood. "Did you feed on them?" Her eyebrow arches accusingly.

"No, I ripped out his throat. I did not even let a drop roll down my throat. It was nasty," I sneer, and she grins.

"You're healing. There's a line on your neck. Did they injure you?" she asks, and I nod. "Then feed and heal, my protector."

"You need your strength," I protest, hating the weakness in me that wants her blood. There isn't a moment when I don't want it or her, not since I tasted her when she freed me. Maybe it is me she should fear, but I would rather die than harm a hair on her head.

My eyes widen as she grips one of her daggers and slices her neck. "I said feed," she snaps.

The scent of her blood fills the air, and before I know it, the heads roll from my hands and I tackle her back to the mats. My mouth seals over the cut and I suck, worrying on it like an animal before I slide my fangs into her vein. The addictive taste of her blood explodes in my mouth, lighting me on fire from the inside out. I drag her under me, needing everything she is.

I roll my hips against her, seeking her warmth and body.

Shamus's hand tangles in my hair, yanking my head up. "Not too much. She will need her strength," he warns, and his logic winds through my head.

I slow my feeding, enjoying her blood as she groans beneath me, clutching me tightly. As I pull my fangs free, I sense her confusion, but I slide down and her clothes disappear. I feel the magic and know it was either Jarek or the fae, and I make a note to thank them later as I force her legs open and slam my fangs into her inner thigh, somewhere I've always wanted to feed from her.

She screams, but I pin her as her delicious, powerful blood slides through me, her glistening cunt inches away. I shove my fingers deep inside her as I feed, feeling her clench around them, and I grunt into her skin, sinking my fangs deeper before pulling them out and biting her other thigh while I fuck her with my fingers. I keep biting, covering both thighs with my marks. Her hips lift and her cunt clenches on my fingers as I carefully slide my fangs into her sensitive flesh on either side of her clit, and she yells.

Her pussy clamps around my fingers as she comes. Humming happily, I carefully extract my fangs and lick it better as I slide my fingers from her channel. I lick her cream from my digits as I sit back.

Lifting my head, I stare down at her dazed, happy expression before glancing at the others. Shamus nods and steps away, letting me know he was there in case anything happened, and I respect him for that. My eyes find the others and widen.

Ronan has the heads propped up so their unseeing eyes watch us as he throws popcorn into his mouth. The fae reaches over them from the other side, grabbing some kernels as he, too, observes us.

Tate sighs and sits up, touching the wound as her eyes rove over the room. She must spy it at the same time I do because she groans and buries her head in my chest as I chuckle.

"Damn pervs, all of you."

CHAPTER 52

Zeev

Days pass without incident, but we can all feel the tension in the air, and it keeps us all on edge, especially Tate. Something is coming. Even the commander, Shamus, does not allow us to go on any hunts. He keeps her close, feeling it as well.

Tate's or Addeus's actions have tipped the scales, and my magic tells me before this week is out, her vision will come true. It is not even the full moon yet, but we all know how the future can easily change. Everything she has tried to avoid will come to fruition, and the hunters she believed in will turn against her. She now wears her battle gear to the gym, no doubt sensing it as well. She's withdrawn and barely sleeping or eating.

All that hard-won peace and rest was gone in an instant. Her friends became enemies, and everyone is a threat. I hate seeing it, and I hate even more that there is nothing I can do for her yet.

War is on the horizon, I feel it in my blood, and when it comes, we must be ready.

While she prepares, we do as well.

We put out the call to everyone we can. If we are to win this and keep her alive, then we will need all the help we can get. She will never ask for it, so we ask in her place.

As night falls and exhaustion settles heavily on my bones from the sacrifice I made today, I find her lingering in the dim living room. Her eyes are locked on the hill outside the window—the hill where she saw an army come towards her.

"My vision is going to come true," she murmurs without looking at me. "I keep seeing a million different variations, but one thing is always the same—the hunters turn on us. There is so much death. It's a battle no one wins." She looks at me, seeming so isolated and alone. "I cannot stop it. I have tried everything."

"Then we'll face it together," I tell her as I stop at her side.

"I gave everything to these people. I died for them, for what I believed in, and now it will get me killed again." She releases a bitter, haunting laugh that carves something out of my chest. She tames the madness inside me, but in turn, she has taken part of the darkness into her.

She has become what she hunted, but it is not that which bothers her. It isn't the price she paid. It's the people she did it for.

What happens when you find out those you were willing to die to protect would not do the same for you?

It's a bitter truth I have faced before, and it's a question I cannot answer, nor a fact I can protect her from.

"Tate, you are not alone," I remind her.

"I have never felt more alone in my entire life. Everything I became, everything I lost, it won't matter. We will be ruined. Even if I survive what is to come, we will never recover from the loss." She meets my eyes. "I am a hunter, Zeev. It is all I am, it is what I was born to be, and yet I have never hated it more than I do in this moment. My soul is ruined, bleeding from a thousand tiny cuts they made. One day, there will be nothing left of me. Being a hunter won't kill me, but trusting people will."

"Then I will be your shield and your medic. I will heal those cuts and protect your soul," I vow.

Her smile is soft and sorrowful. "I had such fire in me, such belief in who I was and what I was doing . . . . They extinguished that and plunged me into the darkness, and in that darkness I found the monsters who called me home. I found you, and now I'm scared," she admits. "I'm scared I will lose you, that I have led you to your death and that your belief in me will be your end, just like my belief in this place will be mine."

"We will not let it happen. We would all gladly die for you, but our deaths will not be today or tomorrow. Whatever comes next, we'll face it together and then pick up the pieces in the ashes. You cannot stop hate, but you can prevail against it. Yes, you were born to be a hunter, which means you were born to face this. Everything you have survived and endured does not end here. *We* do not end here. Let them try to take the loyalty and strength from you. I will be your shield, your medic, and the blade in the shadows slaying your enemies. Where you go, I go. I knew it from the moment I tasted your blood—not just because you tamed the madness, but because you embraced it. This was always my purpose, and now I know a few weeks at your side is not enough. Ten lifetimes will not be enough, but I vow this to you. Tate Havelock, monster tamer, I will not let your life end here, so bring on the future. I am ready. Are you?"

She stares into my eyes, putting herself back together. "I'm scared." I know how much that cost her to admit.

Tugging her to me, I slide my hand into her hair as I press my forehead to hers. "Then let me be your strength. Do not let fear stop you. Embrace it like you do everything else."

"I don't know if I have it in me to slaughter our own people," she whispers.

"You do. You have the capability to do anything, and they stop being our people the moment they raise a weapon against us." The voice fills the dark room, and she pulls away to see Shamus.

"He's right. We are your people, not them," Fang says.

"Those in this room," Ronan adds, all of them standing there, loving her.

"No matter what happens," Jarek says.

Tem smiles. "Wherever you go, mistress, we are with you."

"Trust in us the way we trust in you," Addeus implores.

"They are right. The creatures in this fucked-up family are your people, not those who are willing to harm you for trying to save lives. Some of them will turn against you, but it means you are walking the right path. When the battle comes, remember who stands at your side and who stands opposite it," I tell her.

A flare fills the night sky, and we all turn to see it.

"It's here," she croaks before she clears her throat. "They are early. I didn't see it happening tonight."

"Something changed," Shamus murmurs. "It doesn't matter. Whether it's tonight or tomorrow, we are ready." He looks to her. "We will kill any who turn against us. We keep this place safe and rebuild after. First, we need to survive the night." He grabs her then and kisses her solidly. "Do not die or I will bring you back and tie you to me like I did that fool."

"You too." She looks at us. "That goes for all of you. Nobody dies tonight—not one of us, at least. Everyone else? Kill them. I give you free rein to slay whoever would harm us or our cause."

"You just unleashed monsters," Fang jokes. "Let's hope they are ready for that."

"It doesn't matter if they are not," I reply as an explosion rocks the building. "They are coming either way." I look at Tate, we all do, and she composes herself before our very eyes.

"This is our last stand, right here. We'll make our way through the building and outside. We'll give ourselves room to manoeuvre and work as a team. Addeus," she snaps. "I want constant reports on what is happening. Keep every door locked bar the ones we need. Ronan, go get their numbers and report back. Fang, stay behind me, and when I say, call them to us. Tem, change and block their vision with your shadows. Jarek, I want shields for all of us. Focus on them and keep us safe. Shamus, we need every weapon you have."

"And me?" I ask.

She looks at me. "You're my general. Let's go to war."

Ronan reported that the siege is from inside and outside. They had been gathering quietly, collecting weapons to take us by surprise. Hunters from all over approach Stalkers' Rest, their lights illuminating the outside area in case we make it out.

"At least we'll clean up your hunters all in one night." I chuckle as we walk from the apartment to the stairs at the end. Addeus shut down the elevator so they cannot take us by surprise.

"That's one way to look at it," she mutters.

"Those who are not involved are locked in their rooms. Shouldn't we let them help?" Addeus suggests.

"No, it is not their fight. It is ours. They could get hurt or die, and we will need their numbers to keep our guild alive when this is through," she reasons as she opens the door and peeks into the stairwell beyond.

"Addeus is right. We should let them fight," Shamus suggests. "Not all are against us, Tate. This is their home too."

She looks back at him, debating it. "And if they die?"

"We're hunters. We face death daily. At least they would die protecting something important. They have trained for this, so let them fight."

I know she hates the thought of any more blood being spilled because of her, but sometimes leaders make hard choices. "Unlock their doors and let them choose. They can either wait it out or fight with us. I will not force them to, but I won't take their choices away. Now let's move before they blow the whole building while trying to get to us."

Just then, small explosions meant to fill us with fear rock the building. Ronan has already reported that they are not causing major damage, just trying to spread our forces thin so they can pick us off one by one.

"Can you get me on the speakers?" she asks Addeus. He simply nods and holds out his hands. She clasps his, and he nods.

She clears her throat, and it echoes around the hallway from the speakers. "Fellow hunters, this is Tate. I am with Commander Vilaran. Tonight, we are under attack by a very familiar evil—those within our own ranks who wish to betray our commander, our laws, and the very fabric of what it means to be a hunter. They want their crimes to be kept hidden, and they want to get away with murdering innocents in the name of our guild. Now, because our commander and I would not let that happen, they seek to end us all. I will not ask you to fight, since this is a war I started, but your doors are unlocked. You can stay inside and wait to see who wins, or you can pick up a blade and fight. It is your choice. No one will order you to. Tonight, you must choose for yourself who you wish to be.

"I, like most, have lived, breathed, and suffered for this cause, for the belief that what we do has merit. We are hunters. We are the shield between good and evil. We bloody our souls to keep the world safe. We are the line between humans and supernaturals, but we are not indiscriminate killers. Some among us are, however, and they are afraid of what I will do when I find out they are no better than the monsters we hunt. Well, they should be. Tonight, I will cleanse this organisation of the evil that has rotted its core. For those who are here to do us harm, I only have one thing to say—you have come to die and we salute you." She nods at Addeus, and he cuts off the transmission.

Without a moment of hesitation, she kicks the door open and stalks down the stairs, her footsteps loud. She is not hiding, and neither are they. We barely reach the next flight before the door bursts open, and a surge of angry hunters pours from within—a trap.

She simply laughs, grips the railing, and flings herself over it, letting those who would grab her fall to their deaths. When she lands on the other side of Tem, her eyebrow arches as she reverses their trap. "Foolish men." She nods at me. "General, these are yours."

I know my smile is cruel as my bloodlust takes over, and all I see is red. I unleash everything inside me, everything my sister tried to lock away. I become the blade Tate wields. I will be the evil they fear.

I will be the reminder that humanity is not the strongest race out there.

We are.

Their blood splatters across their sacred halls, their screams echoing for all to hear as I carve through their masses like a well-aimed gun. My magic tears them apart as easily as my hands, shredding them like tissue paper. My laughter fills the air like a haunting melody as their screams reach a crescendo. They attempt to flee back into the hallway, but the door shuts, and Tem grins at them. They try to move down the stairs, but my girl is there.

Her hand darts out and smacks into the wall, creating a barrier. "Uh-uh, where do you think you're going?" She grins, and when they lunge left, she does the same, grinning all the while. "Didn't you want to fight? I warned you that whoever stood against me would die." She looks at me where I stand in their masses. "Continue."

A knife soars towards my face, and I stop it with a blink, freezing the person on the spot as I duck under the frozen blade and move their arm. I point it at their own face and unfreeze them. They see it coming, their eyes widening, but their momentum will not allow them to stop it as they drive it into their own face and fall into the crowd, only to be trampled.

A bullet hits my side, but the slight sting is barely felt, more like an irritating tickle, but it gets my attention, and I grip the man's neck, lifting him into the air as he turns a myriad of colours. The hunters freeze, their eyes widening as they watch. I know my eyes glow, as well as my hair and skin, as my magic moves through me, down my arm, and into him. Thousands of tiny shards of glass cut him from the inside out, tearing through his organs, muscles, and veins, and when his mouth opens to scream, blood pours out, not sound. More streams from his eyes, nose, and ears as he kicks and moans. Finally, he bursts like an overripe fruit, all within seconds.

All from a single touch.

I turn back to the others, just a fraction of their numbers remaining, and I smile pleasantly. "I would run if I were you."

One throws himself over the stairs to avoid me, but I simply click my fingers and bring him back with my magic. When he floats in the air before my girl, I force him to his knees. The others fight to get past as I laugh, and then I do the same to them, capturing them with my magic and forcing them to their knees as she watches. I move through them, opening their mouths. "We are sorry. We are nothing but fools meant to die." I control their words, and her eyebrow arches at me as I dive into their brains and tear them to pieces.

I make them into nothing but empty shells, ripping out every thought, memory, and feeling, and I let them choke on who they are. When I finally stop their hearts with a thought, I let them crumple down the stairs like broken toys.

I stand amongst their bloody bodies. "Shall we continue?"

"Let's." She opens the door to the floor and steps inside, and we follow.

The hallway is empty, tinted orange by a flashing alarm and lined with open doors. I hear whispers and shuffling, and so must she.

Her knife drags along the wall of the corridor as she prowls down it. "Come out, come out, little mice. I can hear you scurrying around."

At an open door, she tilts her head and looks inside. "Ah, there you are."

"You traitorous bitch!" comes a roar, and a body hits her, knocking her back into the opposite wall. She holds up her hand to stop us from intervening, and I lean casually into the wall to watch as the huge woman smashes her fist into Tate's face.

Her tongue darts out, tasting the blood on her lip from the hit. "That is the only blow anyone will land on me tonight," Tate says before she grips the woman's face. She starts to scream as she stumbles backwards, and when she hits the opposite wall, her eyes are muddled, giving Tate an opening she doesn't waste.

She doesn't hesitate as she embeds her knife in the woman's chest, letting her view her own death as Tate looks back at us with a grim, determined smile.

"Let's go."

CHAPTER 53

Tem

Floor by floor, we work our way down the building.

I follow my mistress happily, my shadows obscuring the halls and stairs.

The top five floors are pretty much empty, bar a few lingering assailants. All the doors are open, and we see signs of a struggle, but no other hunters—not until we reach level twenty-five. The door is open and screams and shouts come from the corridor leading to the living quarters. Bloodied hand and footprints are on the walls and floor as we follow my mistress. We pass one room with a dead hunter lying in his bed where he had obviously been sleeping.

"Our hunters must have heard the call and joined," Shamus murmurs. "They will be slaughtered."

"Not all," Tate responds. "Some will survive. Listen."

We do, hearing gunfire, and when we turn the corner, we see hunters in various states of dress, taking up arms against those whom they once fought with. Bodies litter the floor, more attackers than hunters, and when they spy us, they let out a shout of determination and respect before their war cries fill the hall.

"Help them," Tate orders, and Addeus and Jarek surge into the mass of bodies. Within minutes, the fight is over.

Hunters stand before us. "We are with you."

"Get dressed and find your weapons. The armoury will be open when you approach, I promise. We will meet at the ground floor. There is safety in numbers. You know what to do," Shamus orders.

"Yes, commander!" they roar and hurry off to do his bidding.

We keep moving down the stairs to the next floor. There are no hunters here, only attackers.

One at the back of their masses turns, hearing us. He's dressed in all black with a blood-red cross through his hunting patch.

He raises a shotgun and aims at Tate.

The gun goes off, and faster than most eyes could track, she darts left then right, making the barrel swing each way as he tries to track her, all while firing wildly. She doesn't stop until she's before him, and her fist smacks into the gun so the next shot hits the ceiling. She catches it midair before knocking it from the hunter's hands and turning it on him. She fires right into his face. "If you don't know how to use a gun, don't try," she growls as she tosses it behind her and steps over his body.

The rest of the attackers turn, and she grins. "Hello! I believe you're here for me." She sprints forward, giving them no warning, and pops up behind their defensive line. One falls instantly, a dagger in his neck, and when the others turn to fire at her, she runs at the wall, kicking off it and flipping over them. Once she's behind them, she grabs a man and uses him as a shield, all while firing his gun, spraying the others. They fall with screams, their blood filling the hall, making me hungry, but I hold it back since my mistress has not released me yet.

When they are all dead, she flips the man she was using, lifts his gun, and kills him with it. Dropping it to his body, she dusts off her hands and carries on, making us follow after her.

"You know, I'm really glad she's on our side," Fang murmurs to me. "She's hot as fuck when she's fighting, but also slightly terrifying."

"She's magnificent," I murmur. "Look at how easily she took their lives. I shall keep count for her, and we can celebrate each one later."

"Sure, sure, or do something normal like take a bath," Fang scoffs as she picks up a gun and checks its chamber like Tate taught her. "Come on, lover boy, let's keep our girl safe so she can save the world."

The next floor is filled with hunters, and when we arrive, they nod at Shamus and my mistress. "This floor is clear. We will keep working down as well. We heard they are gathering in the gym. Meet us there, commander."

Shamus looks to Tate, waiting for her opinion. "Of course. We will clear a path as well." She looks at us. "To the gym. Addeus, can you confirm?"

"Large gathering in the gym. They are smart. They are disabling the cameras, suspecting we are using them against them," he replies.

"Not smart enough," she scoffs and nods at the hunters, then she continues descending the stairs. Most floors are now filled with hunters holding weapons, and when they see us pass, they join us.

The farther we travel down the building, the more hunters join us. They nod in respect to Shamus and Tate before joining our numbers. She worried she ruined this place and everything Shamus built, but seeing their faith and loyalty has her standing taller.

She's not alone, she has all of us, and no matter what will happen, she will face it with her people.

The last few floors are empty, eerily so, and when we head down to the gym, we see why. They are gathered there, waiting. She peeks through the glass door to the dark interior, where they move about and plot. Other hunters surge inside from a different entrance, attacking them from behind. Tate swears as the difference between them becomes hard to determine. Hunters versus hunters, a tangled crowd that would take forever to pick apart.

They need our help, but the threat from outside grows closer. "More vehicles are congregating outside. The hillside is now filled with enemies," Addeus offers helpfully as if reading my thoughts.

The gym is filled with assailants and hunters—friend and foe.

"Tem." She looks at me. "We do not have time to pick them off one by one. You can do this, yes? Just those who would harm us. No friends."

"Yes, mistress, I can do anything you ask," I reply.

"Then do it." She looks back at the gym with a sinister smile. "I'm ordering you to kill anyone who would harm us."

Finally, my mistress sets me free. She's using me like so many have in the past, but this time, I'm happy to obey.

Stepping inside the gym, I close the door behind me to keep my mistress from being covered in blood as I release my tight control.

There is a reason so many tried to become my master.

There is a reason I was locked away.

It was not for my safety, but theirs.

My shadows eclipse the room, obscuring everything as I turn it into my dungeon and show them the true power of a tempest. My whispers funnel into the ears of our friends, and I wrap myself around them tightly to protect them from what will happen.

I wander through the shadows, transforming as I do, growing bigger and taller. My skin turns red with the blood of my enemies and horns sprout from my skull, burning with hellfire. When I faced Tate, I held back in case she was the one I was searching for. My soul told me she was not an enemy, but these are enemies, and they would hurt my mistress if given the chance.

The first attacker I come across is blindly swinging around in the dark, his gun raised. I see the hair on his arms rise as I slide through the shadows and breathe along his neck. He gasps as he turns. "Who's there?"

"A tempest," I whisper. "And your blood smells tainted."

I carve his neck open, spraying his blood everywhere as he screams and chokes, falling to his knees. Sliding through the shadows, I slay any enemies I come across. My shadows rip into them, tearing them apart until their cries of agony fill the air. Their pleas for mercy go unheard until they scream her name.

"Tate! Please! We're sorry! Tate!"

I despise hearing her beautiful name on their lips, so I silence them.

Standing in the middle of my shadows, I send one thought out—

silence. They choke on their pleas, on her name, and my shadows flow into their mouths and down into their bodies. I stand in the midst of it all, wearing a hungry grin as I feed on their tainted blood. It fills me, making me stronger. My shadows grow, expanding inside them.

The floor is covered with their blood.

They keep feeding me, and I keep expanding, until their bodies cannot hold any more. They explode, and I feast on their flesh and bones, pulling it into me until there is nothing left of them. Where enemies once stood, only a memory remains.

I pull my shadows back into me, bigger than before due to the mass feeding, and when the lights flicker back on, the hunters are left looking around, but all that is left of the attackers are their clothes.

The door opens, and Tate looks them over before meeting my gaze. "Good job, Tem. Let's go. They are outside."

"Yes, mistress." I smile and skip over to her. I follow her out and up until we stand in the entryway of Stalkers' Rest. It's filled with hunters waiting for orders, and I see why. Grey metal shutters cover the doors and windows. The security checkpoint is empty, with weapons spread across the table.

"What now?" a hunter asks Shamus, who looks over their numbers.

"Rogue units as well as hunters who were on field work are gathered outside," Shamus calls, but I follow my mistress as she stops before the doors. Her eyes seem far away for a moment. I feel her mind then, pushing and moving.

She is using her gift.

"This doesn't end until they are gone. We make a stand here. Don't you . . . Angel?" Shamus hurries over, placing his hand on her shoulder, but when he sees she's concentrating, he silences himself.

She blinks a moment later and glances at us, her face closed down. Something in her eyes makes me narrow my own. She saw something that has made her more determined than ever. She looks at us as if she's deciding something. Does she not realise we would march into hell for her?

Some well-meaning tech no doubt hit the button to drop the shutters and activate the security measures, but now all it does is buy the others time to regroup. "Open them." She looks to Addeus, her decision made. "Open the shutters." She turns to the group behind us.

"We do not hide, not like those who wait in the shadows. We are hunters! We are warriors. We fight or die trying. Never before has a fight been more important. This time it is not just to protect our world, but it is also to protect our legacy. This is what it means to be a hunter. We will spill blood, but we do not kill innocents. Those people out there do, and they were scared we would turn on them when we found out, so they attacked first. If they had their way, we would all be dead, and the hunters would be destroyed within days, relegated to nothing but serial killers with patches. I will not let that happen. I ask you to stand with me today and face your brothers. It will haunt you, but they stopped being our brothers the moment they used their weapons against us. We'll end this tonight. We'll burn away the rotted, infected flesh tainting our name and be reborn. Tonight, we'll show them what it means to be hunters. Who is with me?"

A cheer goes up, the hunters calling their agreement, and Shamus nods at her. "I'm with you, angel, until the end. This will be over before dawn."

She turns back to the shutters and waits. There's a click before a whirring sound fills the air. The shutters slowly start to rise, exposing the night sky beyond and the filled courtyard of Stalkers' Rest.

The shutters continue to rise, and when they peel back from the rest of the building, she opens the front doors and steps out. Headlights flood the courtyard, aimed at her.

She stands at the head of our people, her chin tilted back, waiting as the horde of rogue hunters heads towards her.

They want to kill her to cover their own sins.

As she faces her own people, she smiles.

CHAPTER 54

Tate

The courtyard is silent, and my team and hunters gather behind me as we await their first move. If they expect us to hide or back down, they are wrong. My decision is made. We will see this through to the end or die trying. Shamus is right. This isn't just about him or me. This is about our people.

It's time to reclaim our legacy, starting now.

"Open the garage doors," I murmur. Addeus does not question me, opening them, and trucks peel out, heading straight for the ones in the courtyard. One of our biggest trucks, practically a tank for extreme missions, rams into the front line, flipping cars into the air.

"Jarek, control them. Bring them down on the others," I order.

He waves his hands, and those trucks change direction midair, smashing down on the others behind it. Explosions rock the courtyard as our tank carves a path through their masses. Some of the vehicles at the back notice and reverse out of Stalkers' Rest, leaving the trucks behind as they spread across the hill, just like I wanted.

More trucks pull out of the garage, following the path the tank made, and they skid to a stop before the entrance to Stalkers' Rest, creating a barrier with only a small gap for our army to get through. Hunters pour from the cars, taking aim over the hoods and open doors.

Shots fill the air as they fire into the other trucks. I see some wind-screens shatter and blood exploding within. Some tires pop, stranding them, and it creates enough of a distraction to have them climbing from their trucks and making a stand, but they are quickly picked off by the hunters hiding behind our trucks.

"Push them back!" I roar. "I want snipers up on the entrance. I want them surrounded!"

"How?" Shamus asks.

"I saw them," I tell him, "waiting for their chance. Our hunters are smart. Trust them. Trust me."

Hunters surge past me, making a run for the entrance to the wall of trucks. Some fall as they run, and I feel every death keenly, so I swing my rifle around, head to the closest car, and press the stand to the bonnet before I put my eye to the scope.

I fire and move, fire and move, picking them off like flies.

"Zeev, Jarek, trap them in here with us!" I shout, giving them no chance to escape. I glance over to see Shamus on the roof of a nearby truck, the scope to his eye as well. Fang is at his side. Shamus's shots are deadly, and hers miss, but it does the trick and keeps them suppressed. Ronan floats into their masses, turning solid behind them and snapping their necks before moving on. Addeus's eyes glow, and their cars suddenly stop working, as do their timed grenades.

Tem waits at my side as I take aim again and fire. Some flee, but Zeev and Jarek's barrier must be working because they cannot get out to join those waiting on the hill and they cannot get in to help. Sniper fire from the wall takes care of both until there is no one left in the courtyard but our own people and the hiss of smoking trucks.

Swinging my rifle around, I climb over the hood of the truck I used for cover and make my way through the wreckage and bodies to the gate where Zeev and Jarek wait. I peer outside, seeing hundreds, maybe even thousands of hunters still gathered. "They will have some people in the trees. The one good thing about Stalkers' Rest is that they can't get behind us."

"I have some traps in the forest," Shamus says as he joins me. "Just in case."

. "Fuck, I love a prepared man." I smirk. "Spring them. The less that can sneak up on us, the better. I don't want to get a bullet to the skull from the trees."

He pulls out his phone and does something, and within seconds, flames erupt within the trees and screams can be heard. He winks at me. "Just in case."

"You have been busy." I grin as I look to Jarek and Zeev. "Drop the barrier. Tem and Addeus, I want you in the trees. Surround them like they would us. Zeev and Jarek, spread out and pick off as many as you can. Fang, you're with me and Shamus. Ronan, do whatever you wish. We'll push them back, disorienting them and splitting their forces. We'll show them just what monsters are capable of. Free rein, no holding back. Use whatever you want." She looks us over. "If we do not make it until dawn, I want you to know it has been an honour to hunt and fight at your side. I never expected to be able to trust anyone again, never mind find a family, but I have. I'm grateful to every single one of you for following me, trusting me, and helping me. If tonight is all we have, then I need you to know these last few weeks have been the best of my life. I have a hard job, and you have made it easier. You made it fun, you brought back joy and hope, and I wouldn't have made it here without you." I look over each of them, hoping they take my words to heart. "I have been searching for a home for so long, and I found it here with you. If I die tonight, know that I'll die happy."

"You're not dying tonight," Shamus snarls. "You have a long life in front of you, a life shared with all of us."

I smile despite the situation we are in. "I hope you're right, but I needed you to know just in case. I don't want to die with regrets."

"You won't. There will be no dying tonight," Fang snaps. "Stop being so morbid. Let's kick some ass, and then you can tell us all in the morning over breakfast." She laughs. "As long as Tem isn't cooking again."

"Deal." I spare them all one more glance before turning away. They are right. I need to believe we will survive this or I might chicken out. I've never backed down from a fight before, but the thought of losing them has me second-guessing myself. I can't afford to. I need to be strong and confident for this to work.

"Lift the barrier," I order.

I feel the moment the magic drops. I have to trust in my team and the hunters behind me. I step out onto the field where they wait. Suddenly, something surrounds my body, and I glance down at myself, but I see nothing.

"Just in case." Zeev winks. "Go ahead. Make them pay. Their human weapons cannot hurt you now."

"But you'll need your strength—"

"I need you alive more," he counters before he kisses me quickly. "Trust us. Go."

Nodding, I watch him disappear into the dark and then turn back to the horde. "Let's do this—"

A war cry goes up behind me, and the hunters from the courtyard surge out to meet their brethren. Guns fire, bodies start to drop, and the clash of knives fills the air. Explosions rock the earth down the hill where grenades are being tossed, and sniper rifles can be heard overhead. The scents of blood and death fill my nostrils as I take a deep breath in before swinging my sword around—my father's weapon—and without hesitation, I throw myself into their masses. Shamus and Fang follow me, but I have to trust them to hold their own.

I duck under an axe and bring my sword down on the back of the hunter's knee. His scream tears through the air, and when I glance back, Shamus is driving a blade into his neck. I keep moving. We either need to make them retreat or kill them. It's the only way to win.

I keep moving forward, my sword carving through blood and skin. Screams fill the air, and when I glance over, I see flames springing up from one of our hunters' flamethrowers.

I can see Tem's shadows in the trees, making waves. Addeus has them crawling all over him as he takes on a whole horde himself. Fang swings her gun around, firing like crazy, while Shamus moves seamlessly at my side. Jarek's magic leaks across the ground, killing anyone it touches. Zeev's laughter can be heard from here as he carves a bloody path through the masses. Shaking my head, I focus in front of me, my sword slicing through more men as we wade into the centre. The trucks' lights splash over the macabre massacre, the moon high above us.

A familiar face catches my attention, and my entire focus narrows to him. Fred is a lieutenant back east. He was transferred away from here after he tried out for Black's team two years ago. Black said he was skilled but unhinged, and I've only heard bad reports about him since. He needs someone to keep him in line, but he likes death and killing. I carve my way to him, and he turns when he senses me, a mocking grin on his ugly lips.

I stop before him, my sword dripping blood. "So you're in charge."

"Looks like it since all our commanders inside are dead. I suppose I have you to thank for that?" he retorts.

"That would be me." I tilt my head. "You know you cannot win."

He glances around. "It looks like we are to me. We'll kill you and your little monsters, and then we'll take over Stalkers' Rest. By morning, we will send word to the other outposts. We will reclaim our guild and heritage without all these rules and laws, and you'll be dead."

He's right. We are losing. There are too many of them, even with my monsters. I need time. I need to make it happen.

"We'll see about that. Don't worry, I'll pike your head next to your hero—Black." I smirk.

He snarls and leaps at me, but I capture his mind midair. I managed it without touch, but for what I plan, I'll need more. It's risky. I haven't trained that hard. It could kill me, but I have no choice.

I press my hands to the ground, anchoring myself. Everybody is touching it in some way, so I use it like a conduit. My powers flow through it to them, capturing minds. Every now and then, I feel their minds slip away as they die from my hunters' hands, and I let them go as my eyes shut.

I pour everything I have into the ground, trying to widen my net. I need time. I need . . . the world to freeze.

I repeat it as my body strains under the weight. My hands seem to burn as I dig my fingers deeper into the soil, and my body heats as if

I'm running a fever but worse. It feels like the sun is trapped inside me and I'm pushing to let it out.

My agonised scream fills the air as I fall to my knees, power flowing from me. I connect to all the minds here belonging to those who would stand against us. Power burns me from the inside out, connected to my bloodline. I feel them standing behind me like ghosts, their hands slipping into mine as my body burns.

I embrace the pain and let it tear me to pieces as I capture our enemies' minds and freeze them, throwing their own worst sins back at them. I use their nightmares and darkest secrets against them.

I channel everything I have.

Every failed hunt.

My father's death.

My own betrayal.

The taste of the afterlife.

The taste of happiness.

I use it all and let it fuel me, and my ancestors offer their strength until time stands still. I open my eyes to see an army frozen in time, fighting their own nightmares in their heads.

My whole body strains, and I feel like I might pass out.

"Let go." The whispers come from inside me. *"It's enough. You have given enough. Let go."*

I do as they say. I let go. My power flows back to me as I slump before forcing myself to my feet. I refuse to kneel as Fred's eyes clear, tears racing down his face before his lips twist in a sneer. "I heard rumours you were just as much of a monster as them. I guess they were true."

"That's right. I'm a monster," I reply. "What does that make you?"

"Is that all you have?" he scoffs. "You did nothing. We are still standing."

"I wasn't trying to kill you," I mumble. Even my mouth is tired, almost too tired to talk. "I was buying time." I nod over his shoulder. "For them."

A horn fills the air, the same horn I saw in my vision tonight when I touched the future—one that shocked even me.

There is an almighty roar, and I cannot help but smile as the very monsters they hunt surge over the hill, coming to our aid, called by those I have saved and offered kindness to in the past.

When I had no hope left, my visions gifted me this. Monsters from every corner of our world are coming to help us. They race towards the hunters who would do them wrong . . . who have done them wrong.

Fae, vamps, wolves, trolls, and dragons . . .

You name it, I can see it.

Fred's eyes flare before he turns back to me. "You bitch!"

Shamus suddenly stands before me, and Fred stills, blinking as he glances down at a knife in his chest, Shamus holding the other end. "You do not touch what is mine."

Shamus pulls his blade free, and he falls to the ground as Shamus looks to me. "It looks like they were right. It was a long shot, and we didn't want to tell you in case we couldn't make it happen."

"I saw it," I whisper. "Thank you." I look around at the monsters fighting with the hunters.

"It was not me. This was your team. You saved their lives, and now they are repaying you," he murmurs as a familiar fae stops before me.

"Seer." She nods.

"Zeev's sister," I greet. "I would offer my thanks but—"

"No thanks needed for my brother's bride," she says.

"Bride? I am going to kill him." She chuckles as she slides a golden helmet down her face.

"Besides, it has been much too long since our people were allowed to seek revenge for the crimes committed against us. My brother was right. We have stayed out of this fight for far too long. If one little human can stand up for the injustice of monsters, then so can we. We can be as brave as you are." She lifts her sword. "For our people!"

Shaking my head, I watch her move into the crowd with the elegant grace of a dancer, even as her sword claims the lives of those who dare to stop her.

I jerk back as something pops into existence in front of me. It's Ronan, and he has ghosts on either side of him. "I called some friends, hope you don't mind." He winks at me. "Ghost army, attack!" I watch him go before something makes me turn. In the distance, I see familiar wolves.

Simon stands with Althea at his side. She nods to me as ancient creatures pour from the forest.

I stand in a field surrounded by the bodies of my peers, their blood covering every inch of me, and yet I have never felt so relieved.

Monsters cover the hillside and Stalkers' Rest, working alongside hunters to finish off those who would try to lay claim to this organisation. Two worlds come together, knowing that if the true hunters fall here, there will be nothing to stop them.

I scan the masses to see they are losing, being driven back into the arms of beasts in the trees and my team. None will escape. Death is plentiful, but we all know the cost if we do not eradicate them. They made their choice, and we made ours. Besides, this is about more than me and the hunters—this is for the monsters who have been hunted for generations, their families stolen and innocence tainted by evil.

This is their war, and I am simply the conduit.

Shamus and I share a look before we dive into the fight with our own war cries. My sword cuts through them as I fight alongside monsters and men alike, killing anyone who would dare harm us or our people.

Centuries of anger, oppression, and pain cover the hillside.

I slam my hilt into an enemy's face, and as he falls back, Fang cuts his throat before dancing away.

All of my men draw closer, unleashing their wrath alongside the strongest beings in this world.

I continue on until my body and blade are covered in blood and no more foes stand before me.

"You did this." Shamus pants at my side, blood splattered across his face as I kick a rogue hunter into the open jaws of a wolf. I scan the area and see barely any of our assailants remaining, and those who do are quickly dealt with. It's done. It's over. "You brought us all together."

"To end it," I say as my eyes rove across our people, checking on them and my men. My heart still hammers like a war drum, my body swaying with exhaustion.

"No, Tate. It might have begun with bloodshed, but I have a feeling when you are through, it will end with hope." He looks out at the crowd as all eyes seem to turn to me. "Your work is not done. Not yet, angel."

"He is right." We both turn as a chill goes through me at the calm words. A man picks his way through the dead, looking far too calm and perfect in the middle of so much death and pain. He's beautiful, dark, and deadly, but something about him makes terror clench my chest. A beautiful woman walks behind him, with glowing eyes and hair the colour of the sun.

"Ignore his creepy introduction. I'm working on his people skills. We have been watching. Gods can't interfere really, but we have both been rooting for you. Haven't we, Mors?" She smacks his side.

"Yes, dear." He nods obediently before looking at me. "You have caused much death today. I will be busy indeed."

"What do you mean?" I ask.

"You know what I mean. You sense it." He smiles, and I swear my heart stops for a moment. "Come on, Avea. Let's begin our work." He glances around before looking back to me. "Oh, and Tate Havelock? It is not our time to meet yet, but know when we do, I will be honoured to help you cross. You have the heart of a warrior—one I have not seen in a very long time. You have a purpose, or so I am told. Stay true to who you are and you will never go astray." His words echo that of my ancestors', and he winks like he knows it before he sighs, whirling around.

"Phrixius, I can feel your little heathen playing with my dead. Tell her to stop!" He stomps off as the woman waves at me and skips after him, beasts from the forest walking at her side. Simon waves at me from the forest and slips back into the trees with the wolves and Althea.

"Was that the god of death?" I turn to Shamus in shock.

"I think so." He shakes his head. "Far above my pay grade."

"And mine," I scoff. "I don't know about you, but I could use a fucking shower and some sleep."

"Maybe a stiff drink." He holds out his hand. "Let's leave the monsters to their duties. It's time to reclaim Stalkers' Rest. Tomorrow, we'll deal with everything else."

"Tomorrow." I nod as I look around at those we lost, those we will need to honour.

It won't be easy to clean up after this, but it's what we do as hunters.

Tonight, we made a stand, and we won.

Tomorrow, we'll set our future on the right path.

For now, though, I want my team, and I want my bed.

Everything else can wait.

CHAPTER 55

Shamus

Tate is resting. Using her powers like that drained her, and for once, she sleeps like a baby. I keep watch as I work on my iPad. There is much to do, and I am the commander, after all. I will take this burden from her. She has done more than I could have ever asked for. She righted the wrongs of our people and joined the supernatural world and ours together in a way that will echo for generations to come.

She has become the bridge between their world and ours, and all it took was a little love and a whole lot of revenge.

She turns with a sigh, and I glance over. She's pale, but other than that, she's unharmed.

She was right. No other blow landed on her bar the small cut on her lip.

When I'm sure she's still asleep, I focus on my phone and the orders. I have a cleanup on the way and families are being notified. There are too many bodies to bury, so they will be transported to a local crematorium and burnt. They don't deserve to be buried here, not on our sacred ground, but their families are innocent, and they deserve to have something to grieve. Their funerals will all be paid for, and their final wages as well as the insurance policies will be given to their families. I could invalidate them, but no one else has to suffer.

It's over.

Now, we need to rebuild and make the guild into what it should have always been—a beacon for the lost and damned, both humans and monsters alike.

Tate has only proved that the monsters need us as much as the humans do, and we will deliver. I will spend my life making sure we do with her at my side—if that is what she still wants. No one would blame her if she wanted to walk away and live a quiet life. She has given everything for this. If she wanted peace, I would move this world and the next to grant it to her.

No one deserves a long, happy life more than Tate.

She jerks away with a gasp, and her monsters sit up with her, reaching for her, but it's my eyes she seeks. I search her face. She doesn't look scared. It's something else entirely.

"I know what we have to do."

I tilt my head, and she smiles.

"In the morning at least. I saw it. I saw what we must do."

"What's that?" I murmur.

"Unite everyone. We'll make a new treaty." She turns and falls back asleep as I blink, a smile curling my lips.

I guess that answers my question. Tate will stay here, and I couldn't be more relieved about that.

"You did good, brother," Ronan murmurs as the others settle down with her. He kicks back on his chair next to me. "This is what you always wanted, right? So what now?"

"She's right. We'll unite everyone." I speak softly so I do not disturb them.

"You are going to be busy," he scoffs.

"Not me, her. They won't follow me, but they will follow her." I look at him. "That's good because if I asked you to stay with me even if she left, you would choose her, right?"

He winces, a guilty expression clouding his features. "Brother, I have followed you my entire life—"

"You don't have to explain. I'd choose her too. I get it. That is the exact reason it has to be her. She inspires loyalty." I glance at her again, feeling my expression soften as it always does when I look at her. "She makes me want to be a better man, more than just a commander, but someone she is proud to have at her side. I have loved Tate Havelock since the moment she walked into my office, and I will not stop, not in this life or the next. She is the one I have been searching for. She is the reason I have been reborn so many times. I don't know what will happen when I die this time, but I do know that I'll spend this life at her side with you, my brother. It's time I followed you."

"She won't like it." He grins, and I can't help but laugh.

"No, she won't. I have a feeling she will never be alone again. They aren't going anywhere either."

He chuckles, knowing I'm right, and we lapse into silence for a bit.

"Get some sleep, brother," Ronan says. "I'll keep watch. Sleep next to our girl and let me keep you all safe. In the morning, you can start on your never-ending to-do list. For now, just experience this. It's called peace, Shy, enjoy it."

Nodding, I put my phone down, knowing he's right. When I hesitantly step towards the puppy pile, Tem, who is next to her, rolls away with a sleepy smile, leaving me a space at her side. I slip into it and tug her into my arms, pressing my lips to her forehead. She sighs and turns to me, seeking my heat, and I hold her tighter.

Ronan is right. I need to enjoy this.

I don't know if I'll be reborn again now that I've found my purpose, but even if I'm not, I'm going to make this lifetime feel like a thousand as long as she's at my side.

I'm up before dawn, out on the hills helping move bodies. I would never ask the hunters to do something I am not willing to do myself. I left Tate and the others sleeping, knowing they need it, but I have no doubt she will be out here soon. She doesn't need to help, but I know telling her that will only piss her off and make her do it, so I don't even bother.

"Commander." One of my analysts walks over, handing me an iPad. "I stayed up taking count and talking to the other command posts. We estimate just over thirty percent of hunters defected and around twenty-eight percent died here last night."

"The other two percent?" I frown, looking over the numbers.

"Either hid or abandoned their posts," he answers. "The other command posts noticed unrest, but after last night, everything seems to be calming down."

"Good. Until then, I want restricted hunts, only necessary ones, and everyone needs to check in. We'll have a curfew and make it known that any hunters in that two percent are now rogues and must be killed on sight. Also, tell the other commanders to allow any hunters who want out the opportunity to leave with full pay and benefits. We do not need to keep them if they don't want to be here."

"Yes, sir." He types as I speak. "Repairs have been ordered on Stalkers' Rest. Other units have started to make enquiries about the elite level and inhabiting it since Black is not here," he says hesitantly.

"It's Tate's," I snap.

"Sir, out of respect, she must earn it." I narrow my eyes, and he holds out his hands, looking scared. "If you hand it to her, they won't respect your decision. Everyone feels the need to be rewarded after last night, and even though she sacrificed more than most, there are still some nervous hunters after what she did on the battlefield."

"Then we will hold a test. Whoever wins will get that level. Make no mistake, it will be hers, though, so begin preparations. I want it all torn out and changed and all bedrooms combined into one for her."

"One, sir?" He blinks.

"One, with the biggest bed you can find." I chuckle. Turning away, I pick up the next corpse and heave it into the truck closest to me. There are many out here, and as the body hits the flatbed, the birds feasting on the dead take flight. When I turn back, the fae is before me, and I blink.

"My sister has sent a message. She will meet with Tate when she is ready. She also wishes to let you know the treaty is still in place." He nods and then turns away, walking across the hill to Tate who must have come down when I wasn't looking and is now helping clear bodies.

"Commander."

I sigh and turn away as my name is called again.

Duty waits for no one.

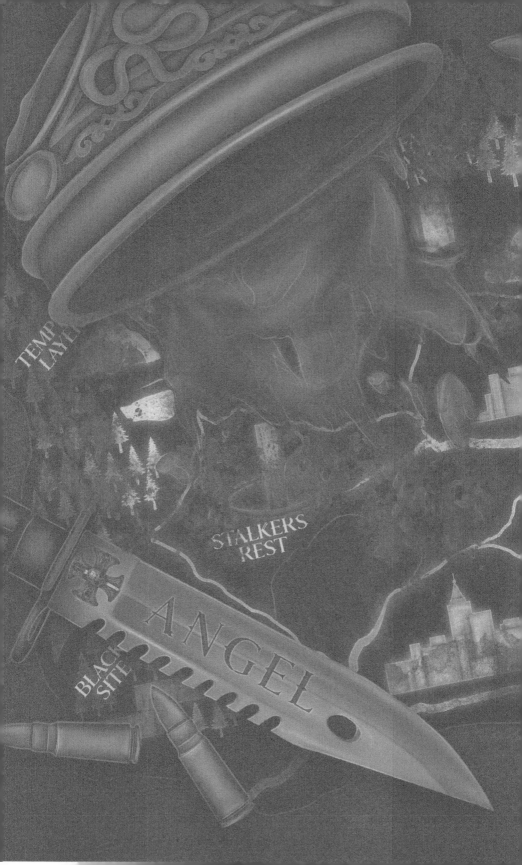

CHAPTER 56

By mid-afternoon, my muscles are strained, I'm covered in sweat, and death coats every inch of me, but all the bodies are ready to be disposed of. I leave the arrangements to Shamus. I'm not exactly one for paperwork, but I needed to be out there. This was my fight as well as theirs, and I will not rest while they work. I am a hunter, and I pull my weight.

Bowing my head under my showerhead, I let the warm water wash over my skin. I know I will never be fully clean, not after the things I have done to get here, but I can't bring myself to care, not with everyone I love still alive.

It's not been an easy journey, and I know this is just the beginning, but I'm not alone anymore. I don't have to shoulder the burden by myself.

As if my thoughts conjure them, arms wrap around me, and I lean back with a sigh. A soft kiss is dropped onto my shoulder, and from their height, I can guess who it is.

"You okay, babe?" Fang whispers.

"Just tired," I murmur as I turn and drape my arms around her shoulders. "I think I need a holiday."

She laughs. "Definitely somewhere warm. I want to see you in a bikini."

My smile grows, and she leans up to kiss me. "They are cooking, so when you're done, come out and join us, okay?"

Nodding, I catch her arm as she turns to leave and drag her back to me, kissing her deeply. When I let go, she's blinking in confusion. "What was that for?"

"Just because." I shrug as I slap her thigh. "I'll be right out."

She nods and leaves, and I wash. After I'm dried and dressed, I pad into the kitchen, only to freeze. The scene reminds me so much of the first day I stepped in here, only now the laughter is louder and the feelings of love and friendship fill the air. Fang is helping Tem set the table, Jarek is teaching Addeus to cook, and Zeev sips from a mug while watching them. Ronan floats above the stove, and Shamus is at the table, reading something on his phone.

For a moment, I just observe them, my heart so full it hurts.

No matter how hard it gets, I know I can always come back to this family. "Can I help?"

All eyes turn to me, and all that hate and pain caused by the others from this apartment fade away. "Nope, you sit, mistress." Tem pulls out a chair at the opposite end of the table, and I sink into it as they hurry around. The table overflows with food, and they sit and start to dish up. Conversation flows, as does their laughter, and I just look around, overwhelmed and so grateful that my life led me to them.

It was worth all the hurt.

It was worth all the blood I had to shed to get here.

I hold my glass up as all eyes turn to me. "I just want to thank you all once more and say . . . to family, new and old."

"To family," they repeat, even Zeev, before they dig into their food as I sip my drink, happy to watch them.

"Hey, that's mine!" Tem whines and looks to me as Jarek munches on a roll he stole. "Mistress."

Snorting, I sip my drink and watch them bicker amongst themselves, even Fang. Shamus catches my eye and grins.

He knew this was what I needed, and he gave it to me.

At this moment, I know two things for certain.

I will never leave this place, and I love him.

I love them all. I never thought I would be able to love again, but my heart has been stolen and divided amongst them for protection, and I couldn't care less. Let them have it because I know I have theirs as well.

"I love you too, mistress," Tem says, and everyone turns to look at him. "That's what she was thinking, that she loves us all."

My cheeks heat, but I can't be mad.

"Really? Well, well, well," Jarek teases.

"Knew it." Fang holds out her hand, and Ronan passes over some bills as I gawk at them.

Zeev catches my hand and kisses the back of it in a rare, tender gesture. "Love is nothing to be ashamed of. Love is the reason wars are fought and poetry is written. Love is the reason for everything. Without it, we would have nothing. Love is . . . life. I finally understand that. I think we all do. We have all been hurt and left behind in some way, but with you, we have found a second chance."

"A new beginning," Fang says.

"A family," Tem remarks.

"Safety," Jarek adds.

Shamus grins. "Brothers."

"Friends!" Ronan exclaims.

"Home," Addeus says, voicing my own thought. "We found home with each other."

"I did too," I admit. "It's something I never really had, but it's loud," I joke, making them chuckle. "I wouldn't have it any other way. Now let's eat. I'm starving."

No one dies. No one attacks. No one interrupts.

We have our very first family meal of many.

"What? No," I grumble. "I am not battling it out for his floor. Let them have it."

"Fine, then you can move onto my floor," Shamus says over break-fast the next day. "Fine by me."

"Is this all a big plan of yours to get me in your bed every night?" I mutter.

His smirk makes my thighs clench, but I keep my glare trained on him. "That's something I would love, but we both know we would end up killing each other, so no, angel. I know where I belong in your life. You can visit my bed when you wish, not the other way around. You need your space, but you'll have to fight for it. I can't just hand it to you."

I look away for a moment, and he leans in, covering my hand. "What is it?"

"I don't know if I can stay there. There are too many memories. Besides, I don't even know what I'm going to do now," I tell him.

"You'll do the same thing you did before—hunt. It's what you were born to do, only this time you'll hunt for those who would ruin our guild. They are still out there, and only you can find them. You'll travel the world with your new team, rid it of evil, and then you'll come back home to me. If you don't want that floor, take another one, but you will have a base here, a place to retreat to when you need it. Name it and I'll make it happen." He kisses the back of my hand as I stare at him. "But I wasn't planning on making you stay in the same rooms. I was going to have it all redone if you wanted it—another fuck you to Black and your old team. It's the elite floor, Tate, and it's where you belong, but it's your choice. It will always be your choice."

"I guess having a commander for a lover is a good thing," I remark. "Though I did expect more perks."

"You want perks?" He kicks the table out of the way, the screech loud, and my eyes widen as he grips my chair and drags me over, his lips meeting mine in a brutal kiss that has me gasping as he leans back, his eyes glistening. "You get me. Isn't that enough, angel?" His voice is soft and seductive as his hands slide up my arms to my neck, tilting my head back as he brushes his lips over my cheek to my ear. "Now get your sexy ass dressed and prove why you're mine. Take that elite floor back and I'll spend the night between your thighs, reminding you why you risked it all for me."

"Not for you," I mutter as I push him away with a glare. "For the cause."

"Sure, angel, whatever you say." He kisses me quickly, avoiding my slap as he dances out of reach. "They are waiting in the courtyard."

"I never agreed to it!" I yell.

"But you were going to!" He waves me away as he leaves.

Crossing my arms, I sit back in my chair, determined to ignore him and the others. I don't need this floor. Let them fight over it.

But if they win, they will think they won against me and my monsters.

I can't fucking have that, so even though I don't care that much, I get my ass dressed and head downstairs.

What's one more battle?

CHAPTER 57

Ronan

"Well, where is she?" Major Williams asks, cracking his neck as he jumps up and down on the spot. All the group leaders and majors are here, ready to fight for the elite floor and what it means—all but ours.

"Maybe she won't come. It will make it easy for me to kick all your asses," Major Isa scoffs as she stretches her muscles.

The others start arguing between themselves, but Williams steps up to us. Shamus promised she would be right down. I feel the others bristle at the hostile environment. The fae looks them over boredly, while Addeus simply stares them down with his cold, hard gaze.

"Well, you're all her little toys, so where's your master?" he spits. "Or maybe she's scared. She can end a war with our help, but she doesn't think she can win against us, does she?"

It's all battle talk, and insulting each other is what hunters do. He might be an ass, but he's not evil. It doesn't make "Tate's Toys" happy though. I feel their magic reach out, washing across the area.

Glancing at the big fucker next to me, I mimic him and cross my arms. My muscles don't bulge nearly as much, but we present a united front.

"She'll be here," Shamus calls out as he stops between us. "Impatient to bleed, major?"

"Impatient to claim my new rooms, sir." Williams bows his head in respect but throws us another glare. "The time was clear. If she isn't here soon, she'll forfeit her right to them."

"Then they'll be mine," Isa declares, making the gathered crowd laugh. Their teams wait for their new floor allocations, coming to cheer on their leaders and watch a fight.

Hunters love bloodshed.

"Three minutes and then that floor is mine. Maybe your lieutenant isn't as strong as she seems when she's all alone." Williams smirks as he steps closer, going toe to toe with me. Before now, nobody could see me, but with the help of the fae and my own powers, we let them. I don't want to be invisible in Tate's life.

"And maybe you should eat less garlic. Your breath stinks," I taunt.

"You little fucker—" His hand raises, but it stills midair, his eyes widening in fear before he abruptly steps back. I puff up in pride as I stick my tongue out at him.

"Yeah, you better step back—oh, they were scared of you," I mumble as the others part next to me for Tate. She's wearing leggings and a sports bra.

"Well, it isn't going to be you, cutie, sorry." She winks before her expression turns cold and empty, and the transformation shocks me, making me realise how much she shows us without meaning to. "Let's do this. I'm hungry, so we'll make it quick."

The mood instantly changes as she steps into the impromptu arena. Unlike the others who are warming up, she simply waits, scanning them before she nods and looks to Shamus. "The rules?"

"There are none. Last person left standing gets their pick." He smirks as he lifts a flare gun. "Ready?" He pulls the trigger, and the red lights soar into the air, but her eyes, as well as ours and the crowd's, are on the hunters circling each other, waiting for their chance to pounce. Williams hangs back, trying to play it smart and be the last one standing while the others fight it out. Isa takes the initiative and leaps on the back of an unsuspecting major, her muscular arms wrapping around his throat and dragging him down to the ground as she chokes him out.

Tate watches and waits. She kicks out when someone gets too close, but otherwise she simply observes, knowing she is the one to beat. She doesn't waste her energy or time on the smaller squabbles she could win with her eyes closed.

Isa leaves her opponent knocked out in the dust as she turns to the closest man and yanks him back, slamming her fist into his face over and over until he joins the pile of her conquests. A big bastard is taking on two—I think his name is Mo. He's pretty new, but he takes out two old-school leaders quickly before focusing on Isa.

She shakes out her arms, her buzzed head glowing in the sun as she circles him. Williams is finally in the game, fighting off two other leaders, but he seems to be winning. I glance between them as Tate sighs.

"This is taking too long," she mutters. "Can you hurry up?"

That seems to enrage them all, and Williams knocks out one of his opponents with a brutal headbutt before the other drags him to the ground, and they tumble around, exchanging blows. Mo and Isa are still facing off.

"You're big," she comments. "I'm better." She leaps at him, but he smacks her out of the air, and she hits the ground hard. She throws herself around his legs and up his back, dragging him backwards with a chokehold, and once he's more at her level, she throws some epic punches into his side before he lifts her over his head and tosses her aside. It only seems to infuriate her, and with a mighty roar, she leaps at Mo, wrapping her legs around his neck, and she takes him down, pummelling her fists into his face until Shamus has to drag her off.

"He's done," he snaps as he pushes her aside.

Williams leaps to his feet, covered in blood, but then they both turn their attention to Tate, who is inspecting her nails with a bored expression.

It's so fucking hot, I have to rearrange my hard-on, which I do before I remember people can see me now.

Whoops.

Williams, Isa, and Tate are all who are left.

"Kick their asses and then eat mine—wait." I cover my mouth as every gaze swings to me. "Oops. I mean, go Tate!"

She simply sighs as she shakes her head and faces them.

Williams smirks. "Well, I guess it's just us."

"Enough talking, you're boring," Tate says. One moment, she's standing still, and the next, she's sprinting towards them like a vengeful god.

There is something very attractive about an unhinged woman covered in blood. It just does it for me. Read into that what you will.

All I know is that I love her more than life itself.

ADDEUS

Tate wastes no time heading for her opponents, and I narrow my eyes, calculating the odds with her every move. Her chance of winning is high, ninety-nine percent, but my heart tells me a hundred percent because my girl doesn't lose.

She kicks out Williams's leg, and he goes down hard before she slams her elbow into his face, busting his nose as she spins to avoid Isa's wicked punch. Isabell reaches for her, but she weaves away, wagging her finger with a small smile.

She's enjoying this.

Turning to avoid Isa's swing, Tate grabs her arm and flips her over her back so she hits the ground, and then Tate kneels on Isa's neck, applying pressure as Isa's head turns into the dirt. Her face becomes purple as she smacks Tate uselessly. All the while, Tate looks bored as she knocks the fighter out, standing when Isa is motionless. Tate checks her pulse before turning to Williams, who is still clutching his nose. "Your turn, little boy. Looks like I'll be done in time for dinner. I heard they are serving souvlaki, my favourite."

He spits his blood on the ground and comes at her. She dances back, avoiding his punches, when he pulls a knife, holding it in one hand as he swipes out. "No weapons!" Shamus calls, ready to wade in.

"Let him. It evens the score," she replies as she ducks under a swipe and jumps back to avoid another. Isa's arms wrap around her from behind, none of us noticing her waking up, and start to lift her in the air. Tate lets her and lifts both feet, kicking Williams back before she heaves forward, flipping Isa again and smashing her boot into her face. Isa is finally out cold this time.

Tate flips over Isa and slams her hand into Williams. The blade he's holding flies into the air, and she roundhouse kicks it, hitting it perfectly so the trajectory changes. It flips over and over, heading towards him, and I see his eyes widen in fear, but our girl timed it perfectly, so the handle of the blade smacks into the middle of his head.

He drops to the ground, out cold, as she looks at the bodies that are groaning and waking up but not standing. "Guess I win. I'll take the elite floor," she announces as she wipes away some dirt on her arm and then looks to Shamus. "Now I'm going to eat."

Turning to us, she winks and heads our way. We part for her and then close ranks around her back as she heads inside. My circuits sizzle with awareness, and I turn around to see an enraged Williams reaching for his blade, his eyes on Tate's retreating back. I stomp on his hand, crushing his bones as he screams.

"It's over," I warn as I lean down, flashing my fangs. "If you ever look at her wrong, I'll drain you dry and offer your corpse to her as an apology." I grind my boot into his crushed bones until he cries out. "Say yes."

"Yes, yes, yes!" he pleads, and I lift my foot. He cradles his ruined hand to his chest, peering up at me in fear. When I'm sure he won't make a move, I give him my back and stride towards Tate, who is smirking as she stares at me. When I reach her side, I shrug. "I'll always protect you, even when you don't need it."

"Cute. Remind me of that later and I'll climb you like a tree," she says.

"Why would you climb him?" Tem asks. I had been wondering the same thing. "Do you enjoy climbing, mistress?"

Fang chuckles, and Ronan hides his laughter behind his hand as I frown.

"Oh, I enjoy climbing a lot." She grins. "I'll show you later."

"Can I come?" Tem asks. "I like climbing."

"I bet you do." Ronan coughs as my frown deepens.

"Why do I feel like we are not actually talking about climbing?" I respond.

Ronan slaps my side. "Come on, big guy, we'll talk and eat. So when a mommy and daddy love each other very much—"

I listen carefully as we head inside, Tate's laughter following us the entire way.

CHAPTER 58

Tate

When I head into Shamus's office the next day, I don't bother knocking. He looks up from behind his desk. I plop down in a chair and kick up my feet. "I want to find the pack Black was hunting, and I want to talk to the alpha who left that message."

"Hello, angel, please do come in," he deadpans.

I shrug. "Your house is my house now."

"Since when?" He smirks as he leans back, his focus entirely on me. It used to annoy me, but now I like it. How the mighty have fallen.

"Since you stuck your dick in me. I might as well get something out of it."

He blinks for a moment. "Orgasms were not enough?" he responds.

"Eh, they are a bonus," I retort as I pull out my blade. I carry the jewelled dagger I killed Black and my team with on me at all times now. I still wear its scars, and it seems to fit my hand better than any other, so I flip it idly as I talk. "The alpha, I want to find her. She's . . . important for what we have planned. I feel it."

"Erm, Commander Vilaran," a hesitant voice calls, and I tilt my head with a frown.

Smirking, Shamus turns his computer so I can see three other men on the screen watching me with wide eyes. "Commanders, this is who I was telling you about, Major Havelock."

I blink at his comment. When did I get a promotion? I mean, I deserve it, but still. The three men just continue to stare at me.

"Hey." I nod in greeting. "Nice to see you can actually get involved, you know, as long as it's not in a war for the soul of our organisation."

Shamus grins as he turns the screen back around.

"You were right. She's very straightforward," one remarks.

Another laughs. "I see why you like her."

"We can finish this later. Thanks for the update, Commander Vilaran."

Shamus hits some buttons and leans back, looking far too proud.

"You could have told me you were on a call," I mutter.

"Why would I do that?"

I purse my lips as he stands and heads my way. My blade stills as he tilts my chin back with a soft, possessive touch.

"You think I care if they know we are together, angel? I plan on telling the whole world. Let them talk, I don't care. Why would I when I get you?" He kisses me deeply, stealing my train of thought for a moment, and when he leans back, he looks far too smug. "The wolf?"

I clear my throat, trying to regain my composure, and his smirk deepens. "Yes, her name is Quinn. I've been speaking to a friend who knows her. He gave me her location. I'm going to speak to her. We will need her in the future."

"Are you asking permission or telling me?" He tilts his head.

Standing, I press the dagger under his chin and tilt it up as I lean in as if I'm going to kiss him. His lips part, his eyes blowing with desire as he watches me. "When do I ever ask for permission?" I whisper before pulling back. "See you in a few days." I saunter to the door, hearing him mutter after me, and this time, it's my turn to grin.

We step through the portal outside of the forest. We could go straight into the Red Mountain Pack's land, but that would be an act of aggression, and I'm a hunter, so appearing right in the middle of their pack would be stupid. This way, their sentries and outer warning systems will alert them that I am here.

"Wait here," I instruct the others as I hand my weapons over.

"This is really dumb," Fang scoffs.

"If I go in there armed, they will kill me on sight. If I'm unarmed, then they will let me see their alpha . . . maybe," I explain. "Out of curiosity. Quinn seems like the curious type, but she also seems like the vengeful type. I am betting on her curiosity winning out."

I shrug back into my leather trench coat after stripping off all my gear. "Besides, we need her. I will go into her land as a friend and find out what I need to know."

"And what's that?" Ronan asks.

"If she's what I think she is," I explain. "I saw this place in my vision. I need to be here, but I need you all to stay back. One sniff of you and they'll try to kill us. I'll go alone."

"Very dumb," Fang repeats.

"What if she orders her wolves to kill you for trespassing on her land?" Zeev asks, but he doesn't seem overly concerned.

"Then I'll get the fuck out of there, and I'll have my answer either way, but she won't." I shrug. "I saw her video. She's an alpha through and through, which means she's more than brawn. I have a good feeling about her." Slipping my gloves on, I grin at them. "I'll be back soon. No killing any wolves."

I nod at them and head into the forest alone. It's the first time I've been by myself in a long time. My instincts rise sharply, as if enhanced now that they aren't at my back. My heart pounds, but I ignore it and the urge to reach for a blade that isn't there.

Instead, I walk slowly and loudly. I don't sneak or hide, and my hands are held out at my sides.

I can feel their eyes on me and sense the wolves hiding in the trees. It's a good sign that they don't instantly leap out to kill me though.

I'm about two miles in when two wolves step into my path. One changes back to a man with beautiful auburn hair and bright green eyes. He's definitely attractive, but I prefer my men more . . . crazed. "You are trespassing."

"I wish to see your alpha, Quinn. I come as a friend," I reply carefully.

He frowns. "You're a hunter."

"So I am." I smile. "But I'm not her enemy."

I see him debating what to do, and I let them choose. His eyes go far away for a moment before he says, "Follow us. We will escort you. I'm not saying she won't kill you on sight though."

"Her land, her choice." I shrug as I lower my hands and follow behind them.

We stop a mile in. "We will be there soon, but I have to check for weapons."

I press my hands behind my head and let him search me. He is thorough, checking every inch of me, even the seams of my coat, and when he steps back, he shakes his head. "You really are unarmed. You're either crazy or stupid."

"A bit of both," I admit. "I'll keep my hands here, less intimidating."

"I have a feeling you wouldn't need weapons to kill us. Come on," he says, but he's smiling happily.

Strange wolf.

The other wolf who has been stalking us in the trees moves closer —a female, if I'm not mistaken. She circles me before walking at my back. I don't like it, but I have no choice. The walk is long, and when we reach the tree line, the male wolf lets out a sharp whistle. It cuts across the sprawling, luscious green grass leading up to a bustling area where there seems to be a house of sorts. I see many wolves there, but I search for the familiar face, finding her in the crowd in the distance.

I recognise her from the video. She's in a man's arms, but she pulls from his embrace when she hears the whistle, turning to see us.

"Come on," the male wolf says. I follow them across the land, seeing the other wolves in human form peeking out at me. A crowd begins to gather as I am led over before stopping in front of her.

Quinn looks exactly as she did in the video. Her eyes are sharp, intelligent, and strong, and her body is muscular, letting me know she's not afraid to get her hands dirty. She's kind, I can tell it instantly, but the way she checks on the wolves and the way they defer to her with respect tells me she has earned their loyalty. I'm even more sure now that this is where I should be.

We eye each other for a moment.

I know I'm surrounded by enemies, but I remain calm and collected. If need be, I can slip away, but I have a feeling this is exactly where I should be right now. The male wolf carefully pushes me to my knees, not unkindly but with intention. I kneel before her, but we both know I'm not helpless if need be.

"Who are you?" she asks, her voice sultry but strong. This is a woman who's used to getting her way. I can respect that, plus we both had a common enemy.

"Tate, but some people call me angel," I reply.

"Shit." The man at her side groans, and I eye him carefully. He's human, and he also seems familiar, but I can't place him. The way he moves speaks of training though.

She glances at him with a frown, clearly trusting his instincts and advice. Interesting. The look they share is filled with more than friendship though.

"I know her," he says, answering her unspoken question, and leans in with a familiar, easy movement. He lowers his voice, but I hear him as he explains. "She's a sector leader from up north. She was rising through the ranks quickly last time we heard. I think she might have even been with Black. She's brutal, but I also heard she's fair. Rumour is Black didn't like her because she wouldn't listen to him and even let some monsters go. That's how she got the scar."

"Her own people?" Quinn frowns, the idea troubling her.

"My own people." I smile, knowing it is not a very nice one. "I didn't agree with them killing a young vampyr. They didn't like that and tried to kill me."

She watches me, her brows drawn together. "What happened to them?"

"I killed them." I choose my next words wisely, knowing it will set the tone for how this will go. "I do not hurt innocents, which is why I'm here."

"My message," she says, her eyes widening in understanding.

"Message?" The man at her side frowns, looking between us.

I spare him a look, remembering where I saw him. "I guess Simon was right. I've heard of you. It's nice to meet you. I have to say, I'm surprised, but in a good way." I look back at Quinn, since she is in charge. "And you are Quinn, Alpha of the Red Mountain Pack."

"How do you know?" she asks, crossing her arms in a defensive gesture.

Truth is important here. If we are to build the friendships I need to forge a better future, then we need to start on the right foot.

"I know a lot. Besides your message, I have friends in your world. I might be a hunter, but I'm a fair one, and they know that. They come to me for help. There's a wolf not too far from here with a mate called Simon. We get together for game night sometimes, and he told me about you. He's the reason I'm here, along with your message. He said he knew you and your father and that you are a force to be reckoned with. I also think we both could use the other's help."

I see her process my words as she drops her hands to her hips. "How did you even find us?"

My smirk is vicious, but I can't help it. "Hunter, remember?"

"You have no weapons," she retorts.

I shrug leisurely, my hands aching behind my head. "I'm not here to hurt anyone."

"So you walked into a wolf pack unarmed?" Disbelief colours her tone. I get it. I would feel the same way. It could be a trap, so I don't blame her for not trusting me.

"I figured you would either kill me or listen, so weapons wouldn't matter much either way. Besides, I still have my hands," I say, offering another truth. I won't hide who I am, and they already know.

Her laughter fills the air, a soft sound that makes the man at her side smile even as he watches me carefully. "Fine, why are you here,

Tate?" she asks, and I know then she might still kill me, but her curiosity is winning out.

The fact that I haven't offered her violence is confusing her. Good.

"I have a feeling we are going to be good friends. Can I get to my feet? I fucked up one of my knees last month chasing a dragon, and it still hasn't healed right." My first lie, but I need to get up. If this is going to happen, then we need to be equals and I need my hands. She considers my request before nodding, and I stand, drop my hands, and pull off my gloves.

"I saw your message. I like your handiwork, by the way. I went and checked it out. My new team is there now, cleaning up the mess and burning the bodies." Another lie—well, kind of, because the bodies were already dealt with, but I want her to know we are helping her. She simply stares however. Time for the reason I'm here. "Hard, I like that. Anyway, you're right. The hunters are an ancient group, but we were not always bad. My father was a good man, a good hunter, and he showed me his ways, helping not just humans but your kind as well. I'd like to get back to that again, and I think you can help me. So, Quinn, let's work together. I'll clean up the hunters, and then we can stop the evil in this world together, both human and monsters alike. Sound good?" I hold out my hand, hoping she'll take it. I need to know who I am trusting with this. I need to know if she's the woman I think she is and, more so, the leader I will need.

She considers me, and I wait, not moving my hand. A warm breeze smelling of flowers and fresh grass washes over us, and her eyes seem to soften in acceptance before she places her hand in mine. The moment her skin touches mine, I am in her mind. I flip through her memories, not invading her privacy but looking for what I need.

I find it and smile.

She's trustworthy, and she's also strong enough to be what I need and has the morality to back it up. Quinn, Alpha of the Red Mountain Pack, is a true leader. She's exactly who I need at my side and has the same dreams I have.

"I'd like a truce, but between me and you. I don't trust other hunters," she murmurs, and I blink, bringing myself out of her head now that I know. This is exactly why I needed to come in person.

"You'd be stupid to, and you are not stupid, Alpha." I grin and shake her hand, noticing she doesn't test her strength against mine— another thing I like. She doesn't feel the need to show off because she's secure in her place. "Strong grip. Yes, I think we will be friends, Quinn. I'll head back now and help clean up. Once my house is clear, I'll send a message, and then I think we should get together along with some other friends I have and send out an accord."

"What other friends?" she asks, not sure how to handle me or my words.

Truth is also important to her, so I offer her another.

"Oh, some vampyrs I met along the way. They are a good bunch, but slightly crazy, especially their queen. I met her on a hunt. She was hunting them too—sorry, judging them. We worked together at the end," I admit. Althea is already on my list, and I know she will be involved in what I have planned. I do not need to ask. She actually told me. Besides, she probably saw it before I did. Another breeze washes over me then, tasting like freedom and home, and I close my eyes for a moment, letting it relax my taut muscles.

"Change is coming, and it starts with us women—queens this time, not kings." I bow out of respect because she deserves it. "I'll be seeing you again, Quinn." I glance to the men at her side, the hunters. "Always room for more hunters with us."

"Our place is here," he replies without hesitation. Good.

"I had a feeling. Oh well, but once a hunter, always a hunter. Best of luck." Turning away, I whistle as I walk over the grass to the trees, hearing her call out to her wolves.

"Escort her off the land, but let her go." Her voice carries on the wind. "I have a feeling Tate is about to become our best asset."

She has no idea.

I'm about to make her dreams a reality. I'm about to change every-thing, and she will help me do it.

CHAPTER 59

Tate

W e are walking through the forest, their questions hitting me left, right, and centre, when I feel it. "Do you feel that?" I whisper.

"Yes." Jarek suddenly stills. "Magic, dark magic. Death magic. It's not too far from here. Zombie."

Worrying my lip, I look him over. We have all read the reports on what happened recently. Could it be an escaped one wandering about? They aren't picky about who they attack or eat, so innocents could get hurt. "Take me there," I demand.

We step through a portal and out into an old graveyard where we see a zombie in better condition than I expected. It even has a shirt and pants on . . . as well as a collar like a dog, but it's still a zombie.

"Shit, I've never seen an actual zombie," Fang mutters. "Have you?"

"No, but I've read about them. They are notoriously hard to kill," I reply, but then my head tilts as I watch it. "This one is not rampaging though, just walking." I hold up my hand to stop them. "Let's wait and watch."

"Boring," Zeev mutters, but we do just that. It wanders closer, seemingly curious, and we let it, but then darkness suddenly leaks across the ground, and four figures step out of it and towards us.

I pull my blade out of instinct, and I feel the others ready themselves as I eye the new arrivals. Three men—er, two, one monster, and a woman in a lacy gown. They seem just as surprised to see us as we are to see them.

"The dark magic is coming from them," Jarek whispers helpfully.

Where there's a zombie, there's a master.

I stare at them for a moment, but they don't attack, and I know looks can be deceiving, but something about this woman makes me want to trust her. "Is this yours?" I ask as I nod at the zombie sniffing Addeus in confusion.

The monster steps in front of her, glaring at me, while the demon at her side watches me curiously, but the golden man smiles.

"Ah, sorry about that. Our zombie got loose. He likes to wander sometimes," the woman says with a wide grin. "Thanks for not killing Bobby. He's part of the family."

I simply nod as the zombie wanders over to them and sits at their side. She pets his head. "You're a necromancer." It's rare, and I've never met one, but I made it my business to know everything. While everything had been going down with us, there was a big war in another city up north, and a necromancer was there.

This must be her. The reports said she tried to save them all.

She swallows, watching me carefully. "Are you here to kill me?"

"Why would I be?" I ask.

"You're a hunter. It's what you do, isn't it?" she counters.

"You're a necromancer. Isn't evil what you do?" I retort, and she smiles.

"I guess you have a point. I'm Freya. This is Phrixius, Bobby, Sha, and my demon," she says.

"Um, Tate, and this is my team." I quickly introduce them all, following suit. "But no, I am not here to hunt or kill you. We heard reports of a zombie and came to check it out. I guess we don't need to worry."

My hands tingle as I watch her, and I know this woman is important, just like I knew Quinn was. "You're the one building the new court for the necromancers?"

Her eyes widen. "How did you know?"

"I know everything. Don't worry, I have no plans to stop you. Everyone should have a home, a safe place." I glance back at my team. "I understand that." I hold out my hand. "I mean you no harm. It's nice to meet you, Freya of the Court of Heathens."

She watches me carefully before shaking hands, and like with Quinn, I sort through her memories before a barrier comes down, her eyes narrowing. "You're in my head. How?"

Pulling back, I grin. "Clever. It's my gift. I'm the descendant of a fae. I had to be sure."

"Sure of what?" she snaps.

"Sure you are what I think you are." I smile. "You're building a better world, and so am I—one where monsters do not have to fear us or humans."

"A fairy tale," Phrixius scoffs.

"No, it's the truth. I met your friend Mors and his bride, Avea. I have met vampyrs and wolves. Look at those behind me. Not a fairy tale or a dream. I plan to make it happen."

"How?" Freya asks.

"An accord," I answer. "A treaty if you will, between the courts of your world and mine."

"I am nobody," she begins.

"You are somebody," I correct. "I don't care if others forsake you or do not accept your kind. You deserve a seat at that table. When I am sure, I will send a message, but until then, it was nice to meet you. Good luck with your court."

"Tate?" I still at her voice. "If your invitation comes, I will attend. I'd like a treaty. I'm sick of innocents dying. If we can stop that from happening, then I'll help in any way I can."

"I knew you would." I let Zeev summon a portal, and we step through, back into our floor at home.

TEM

"Mistress, help!" I rush into the room she is sleeping in and bounce on her bed. She groans but spins me, her eyes narrowed as she looks down into my grinning face. Her hair, which is growing out, frames her stunning features.

"What is it?" she asks, holding a weapon in her hand as she scans the area, ready to protect me.

"Zeev and Fang were being mean." I pout, and she relaxes, rolling her eyes. "Can I play with you instead?"

"Tem." She sighs. "What did I tell you?"

"To not let them bully me and give it back to them, but they just laughed," I mutter. "Besides, I missed you."

"I've been gone for ten minutes," she mumbles, but she sits up, watching me with a soft smile. "You want to play?"

I nod eagerly as her eyes run down my body with a hungry gleam. Desire courses through me, alongside hope. She has claimed me before, but that doesn't mean she will again. Her intentions become clear, however, when she leans down. "Then let's play. It turns out I'm tired of thinking through my plan anyway. A distraction will be good." Her teeth dig into my lip, the pain making me groan. "Do you want to distract me, my tempest?"

"Yes, mistress," I answer breathlessly, and her smirk is cruel as her hands slide down my body.

"Then let's play," she says before her lips press against mine, and she claims my body and heart once more.

CHAPTER 60

Jarek

Shamus nods as Tate runs through it one more time. "Jarek?" she asks.

"It's doable," I say. "I would need to speak with some friends on how to make it binding, probably blood, but it's doable."

Her plan is solid. Some might not like it, but when has that ever stopped her? "This will work," Shamus states. "See to it." He kisses her head as he rises. "I need to get on with the inspections, so I'll leave it to you."

I pull my phone out and shoot off some messages. "I'll let you know when they get back to me."

"What shall we do in the meantime?" She sighs, looking around. "It's so quiet. Are you sure they are all okay?"

"They are shopping for furniture," I answer. They were so excited, since most of them never have before. "But Fang and Ronan will keep them in line."

She nods again, biting her lip, and I lean over and free it. "Don't do that," I warn. "It makes me want to bite it too."

"Then why don't you?" she retorts.

My eyes narrow, and then I'm on her. Our lips crush together as we fall back into the table. I hear its contents smash, but neither of us care as I slide my magic over her and quickly rid her of her clothes so I can touch her perfect skin. Groaning into her mouth, I sweep my tongue deeper before I break the kiss and move down her body, until I can swipe my tongue through her glistening cunt.

I groan at her taste. I had her just the other day, but it never gets old. I was so sure of my life before I was captured and then so lost after, but like the others, she gave me a home, a purpose, and a family to care for and protect. I don't know how long we will have together, but it doesn't matter to me as long as I have her right now.

Okay, and forever.

"No time, fuck me." She grips my hair and drags me up her body, wrapping her thighs around me as she urges me on. Chuckling, I bite her chin, but I snarl when she palms my hard cock and presses it to her entrance. Smirking, she sucks on my lip as she lifts her hips and takes me inside her tight, hot body. Her core drips around my length as I sink deeper before pulling out and forcing myself back in. Her mouth drops open on a moan, and I kiss along her neck, biting and sucking as I fight her tight channel. Both of us want it hard and fast, and that shows as she cuts into my shoulders with her nails.

"Move faster, fuck," she orders, and I'm always happy to obey her, so I grip the edge of the table, pull out, and slam back in. I give it to her hard and fast like she wants. Her hands drag up my neck and tangle in my hair as she brings my mouth to hers, our kiss sloppy and fast like our bodies. Pleasure courses through us as I stroke her skin with my magic, curling it around her nipples and clit until she cries out, clenching around me. I feel my own pleasure crawl down my spine, my balls drawing up as her tight cunt demands my release.

I slam my magic into her ass at the same time I press it against her clit, and she comes with a scream. Her cunt grips my cock, pulsing as she locks up beneath me, and that tight grip is what sends me over the edge. I empty my balls as I come, pleasure bowing my spine as I give into it and her.

Pleasure flows between us, and we ride it until we can't take anymore. It finally releases us, leaving us slumped together on the table.

"We're back!" A voice suddenly fills the air, and we both look over, my bare ass facing them. "Well, we had fun shopping, looks like you both did too!" Ronan jokes. "And you were worried about going to that sex shop, Fang. Looks like your wife opened one here anyway."

CHAPTER 61

Fang

I don't know when she arranged it, but it shouldn't shock me.

I stare down at the grave right next to my parents' plots, his name in bold text thanks to Tate. The portal had been ready when I woke up, and I stepped through to find this.

It's a grave for my brother—a place to come to so I can pay my respects and remember him alongside my parents. I know he is buried in the field Zeev took us to, but this is a physical marker for him and my family, and I'm thankful for it.

We have been moving and fighting since his death, so I've barely had time to think of him. It still hurts all the time, though, and he's always in the back of my mind. I wonder if he would be proud of me or if he would like everything we've done.

Seeing his grave causes tears to flow down my face. He's gone. He's really gone. I know that deep down, but staring at the last reminder has my heart splintering apart and pain ricocheting through me—pain I haven't allowed myself to feel yet.

It overflows as I grieve for the brother I lost and the life I would have had.

I'm happy now, and I've found a new family, but that doesn't mean

I don't miss the one I had, and somehow Tate knew that and knew I needed to come here.

"I'll never forget you," I promise him. "No matter who else becomes my brother, you will always be my little brother, and when the time comes, I'll see you again. I promise."

I fall to my knees, brushing some leaves aside before running my fingers over his name. "I miss you so much, but I'm trying to be happy and live for you and me. I hope you know that."

Bowing my head, I let my tears fall to the ground, and where they hit, flowers seem to bloom. I don't know how long I sit like that, happy memories of our time together running through my head until I feel magic.

I knew she would come for me, and I'm grateful for it as she takes my hand and squeezes, offering me her strength.

Turning, I bury my head in her shoulder. "I miss him so much."

"I know," she whispers, rubbing my back comfortingly as she speaks. "He'd be so proud of you, babe, so very proud of who you have become. You're making the world a better place. Your brother loved you so very much. I'm sorry you had to lose him, but death is not the end. It's just another beginning, and he will be waiting for you. Until then, he'd want you to be happy."

"I know." I lift my head, and she wipes my tears away. I look back at his grave. "I'll be back soon, okay? Don't be lonely while I'm gone."

"I brought him this so he never will be." She lays teddy on his grave along with a photo, one we took the other night. It's of us after a meal, everyone smiling widely. "Now he has an entire family with him."

"Thank you," I croak as she helps me to my feet. I let her guide me away and back into our quarters, but I find them empty.

"They gave us some space," she explains as she holds my hand. "Come on."

When we get to the bathroom, there are flickering candles and a bath. She turns me and carefully strips off my clothes, kissing my skin as she goes. It sends a shiver through me. My pain is still there, but as she helps me into the water, gets in behind me, and starts to bathe me, she washes it away.

Leaning back into her, I let her take care of me before she turns me in her arms, kissing my forehead. "I am thankful for your brother, you know?"

"Why?"

"He brought me to you," she replies, and I lift my head. She strokes my cheek with a soft smile on her lips.

"I always thought eyes were made to cry and lips were only meant to tell lies, but you taught me so much more. My lips were made to form promises of love to you, and my eyes were made to reflect yours. Before you, Fang, I was a warrior, nothing else, but you made me a lover. You gave me a home and a family, and I will spend the rest of our lives repaying that so you never hurt again." She places a soft kiss on my lips. "I vow it to you and him. I'll protect you, my love, until you can meet again. Grieve and cry, and I'll be right here to wipe your tears away every time."

I glance from her eyes to her lips, and I can't resist. I kiss her, tasting my tears and her love, and when I pull back, her eyes are closed. "Thank you for coming that day, for saving me then and every day since. I think he knew on a deeper level I would need you. I like to think he knew what you would become to me."

"What's that?" Her words are soft as her stunning eyes open and lock me in place.

"My everything," I respond before I crush my lips to hers again. I need her more in this moment than I've ever needed anything. I was alone for so long, looking after my little brother, and it took its toll. I wouldn't trade those years for anything, but having her here, looking after me and loving me, is my undoing.

I love Tate, and I want to show her that. My cheeks heat when I think about the bag I have stashed in here, hoping she would use it on me.

Our kiss breaks as I turn and straddle her thigh. She leans her head back against the white tub, her heavy-lidded eyes watching me. The water laps at the tops of her incredible breasts, and her beautiful, scarred skin is on display as she watches me. I wiggle on her hard thigh, biting my lip.

"What is it?" she murmurs, running her eyes down my exposed body, and that hungry look I adore enters her eyes. I'm a being of lust, so I'm used to being wanted, but from her, it's different. I can taste how much she wants me, but under that desire is a strong emotion I have never felt before—love.

I can feel her love.

"I bought us some things the other day. Will you use them on me?" I blurt out, feeling shy for once in my life.

"Things, huh? The sex shop Ronan mentioned?" My cheeks burn hot, and I slap my hands to my face to cool them down. Laughing, she leans up and captures my wrists, tugging them away as her dark eyes meet mine. "Show me what you want me to do to you, babe."

Slipping from the bath, I hurry to pull the bag from the drawer and pick out the thing I wanted her to use on me the most. We have a long time to play with everything else, but I want Tate to fuck me. I want to be completely hers. Turning back, I step over to the bath hesitantly, and she offers me her hand as I step in and sink to my knees and offer her what I bought.

Her eyebrows rise as she takes it, but the heat in her gaze only grows as she takes in the strap-on. It's the colour of skin and pretty big, but the tilt of her lips lets me know she likes it too.

"I want you inside me," I admit. "Zeev spelled it so it will feel like you. I don't know what he did, but he said it will become an extension of you."

"Really?" That piques her interest, and she takes it from me as I sit back on my heels in the warm water and wait. "Well then, we better try it out, hadn't we?"

Sliding the strap around her body, she deftly fastens it, and the length protrudes from her obscenely. A shudder goes through me and my thighs clench as I stare at her. I drag my tongue along my lips as I wait for her to move. I can sense her desire, which adds to my own, until I feel my own cream covering my thighs in anticipation.

Sliding through the water, she kneels before me, brushing her hands up my bent thighs, across my stomach, and then my nipples until I gasp. I sway into her touch as her fingers glide across my throat to my chin, and then she pulls me closer. I fall forward, the water splashing around me, but she catches me. Her lips press to mine. "I love that look you get in your eyes," she murmurs against my skin as her hand slides down my side and teases my thigh before pulling them apart. "That look right there—a wild sort of desperation. It's addictive. I can't wait to see it while I fuck you."

"Tate—" My words cut off as her hand cups my pussy, gripping it tightly, and I rock into it, biting my lip, but she frees my teeth and kisses me. I rock into her palm, needing more, and then her fingers stroke through my folds. She rubs my clit until I moan and then slips inside me, stretching me out. She fucks me with her fingers before pulling away, and I whine as she sits back.

"You're dripping for me, babe. You want this a lot, don't you?" she taunts as she gets to her feet. My head drops back so I can meet her gaze, and her fingers tangle in the wet ends of my pink hair as she smirks. "Look at you. Fucking hell, I was going to go slow and show you I love you, but not now."

Her hand drops to the length attached to her, and her eyes widen. "That's so fucking weird. He's right. I can feel it. When I stroke it, it's like stroking my own pussy. Remind me to thank him later. I wonder how it will feel when I bury it inside your tight, needy cunt."

My cunt throbs as I beg wordlessly, my eyes big and needy.

"Please." It slips free, and I feel her desire triple at my soft plea.

"Then get me nice and wet," she orders as she stands before me with her hand on the strap-on, offering it to my mouth. "Make me drip so I can get inside your tight cunt and make you scream."

I wrap my lips around the length, and she slides deeper into my mouth before pulling out with a grunt. "Fuck, it feels like your tongue is on my cunt," she growls.

That gives me an idea. Shuffling closer, I grip the base of it and drag my tongue down the full length before going back to the tip. Her moan fills the air, and that only urges me on as I lick it. Her hips rock before she pulls back, her face flushed.

"Enough or I'll come," she says as she drops to her knees and backs me up so I sprawl in the seat of the tub. My hands fist in the water as she crawls up my body, one hand gripping and lifting my thigh until I wrap it around her hip. I feel the strap-on press to my entrance, teasing me, and I rock my hips without thinking as her lips meet mine again. I tangle my tongue with hers as I fist her short locks and drag her close, begging without words.

Her other hand slides down my body, rubbing my clit until I whimper in her mouth and try to slide myself onto her. Smirking into our kiss, she slides her hand up and pinches my nipple, and I fall back with a cry.

I'm so needy it hurts. My channel feels so empty. I need her to fuck me or I might just—

My thoughts scatter as she thrusts inside me, burying that length deep as she stretches me. It hurts for a moment, but it soon turns into a hum of pleasure as my eyes open to see her own unfocused gaze, her lip trapped between her teeth.

"Fuck, fuck." She pants as her eyes meet mine. "I don't know how to explain it, but I can feel your tight cunt around me, even while it feels like I'm being fucked, like this is inside me as well." She slowly pulls out and thrusts back in, and her groan matches my own.

Our eyes meet, and she laughs before I dive at her, silencing her with my lips as she moves. Pleasure rolls through us, but I don't know what is mine and what is hers. I feed without thinking, but my entire focus is on her and the huge length impaling me. It feels soft and real, like it's truly her inside me, and I love it. I lift my hips to meet hers as she speeds up. Her lips slide away from my mouth and down my throat, where she bites, and I cry out, clenching around her. She slides lower until her mouth wraps around my nipple, and she sucks. Pleasure zips to my throbbing clit, and I grip her hips, urging her on. The water splashes around us with our movements, but neither of us cares as she fucks me.

"Tate," I beg, and her hips ram into mine, the force of it making me cry out. It feels so good, and it's clear it does for her as well. I can taste her pleasure growing with each thrust, and she pants against my skin as she slides up until our sweaty foreheads press together. Our hands grip each other as we find a quick, deep rhythm that has us both crying out.

Pleasure flows between us so strongly, I practically glow from how full I am on it.

"Tate." Her name is a moan, and she shudders, her hips speeding up. Her length spears me faster, taking me like no one else ever has.

Her touch is possessive and loving as she drives into me. "Baby," she groans, and I know she's close. I am too, I feel it deep inside me, growing like a wave heading to shore. When her lips find mine, it crashes across us, both of us crying out as we come.

We find our release together. My powers hold us together until pleasure is all we know. I can't even feel my body anymore, but I still feel her soul, her kiss . . . my everything.

Eventually, we come down from the high, both of us weak and shocked.

She falls into my open arms, and I wrap them around her, even as I twitch and pant. I hold her close, pressing my lips to her wet hair as my eyes close, a blissful smile curling my lips. I float in the afterglow as we lie together in the cooling water, our bodies locked together.

"I love you, Tate," I say truthfully, needing her to know. "I love you so much. I was made for sex and lust, but you turned me into a being of love. I need you to know that."

She lazily lifts her head, smiling as she kisses me gently. "I love you too, Isabella, my beautiful girl, now until forever."

Eventually, we break apart, and she takes the strap-on off, washing it before bathing us both and helping me out, since I'm still weak. She dries every inch of my skin before blow-drying my hair, plaiting it back, and leading me into her room.

We tumble into her bed, exhausted and sated, our skin still pruned from the water as our eyes meet. Our smiles disappear, and we crash together once more, our lips pressing together as our bodies move so not an inch of space exists between us.

I want this for a lifetime, and I'll have it.

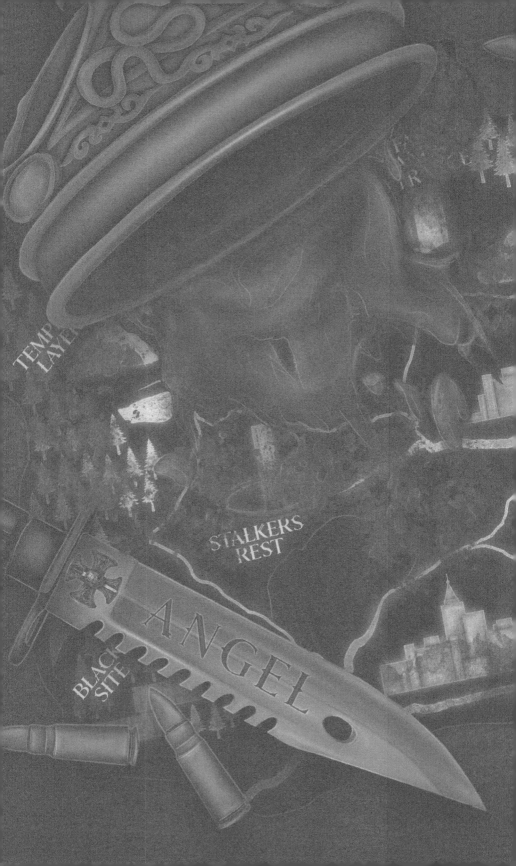

CHAPTER 62

Tate

Three weeks later . . .

I t's taken us a while to prepare, but today is the day. The invitations have been sent, the documents are ready, and my team is with me as I pace at the head of the table.

I chose this place because it turns out it's real, not just in my mind, and my ancestors guided me here. Shamus found out it used to be a meeting place of sorts between worlds, which makes sense, and I couldn't imagine a more perfect place to do this.

The walls are covered in flowers and a tree, and the moon is bright above us. Candles are placed everywhere to welcome them and guide them to us, and the huge wooden table is empty bar the cream parchment, waiting for its use.

"Stop worrying. It will be fine," Shamus promises as he joins me. "Look at me, angel." I glance at him, and he gives me the look he first gave me when we met in his office, full of awe and respect. "You're changing the world, angel. The hard bit is done. Trust in yourself and in us."

"I do," I whisper just as there's a noise, and we turn.

Althea and her men step into the table area, Simon and his mate at her side. "Hello, Tate. I told you we would be seeing each other again." She smiles at me and glances at my men then nods. "I read your invitation. I am very excited to see you and it."

"As am I. Thank you for coming. Please sit," I offer as kindly as I can despite my nerves. She takes a seat.

Moments after, Quinn appears with her wolves. She takes her seat quickly, and then Freya appears, looking hesitantly at me. "Please sit. We are all friends here." She takes a seat, her men behind her. I wait nervously as I glance at Jarek, but moments later, Avea steps inside, joining us, and holding her hand is the god of death.

"We meet again," he says.

"I'll admit I was surprised to be invited to this . . . gathering," Avea begins. "But we are here. Now play nice, Mors," she admonishes, making him sigh.

"Yes, my love," he replies as he leads her to a seat. He sits and then tugs her down onto his lap as if he cannot bear to be parted from her. He ignores us, playing with her hair, which is fine by me. It's not him I want. It's her.

Everyone is here, so it's time to begin.

I walk to the head of the table where no seat waits, and I lean into the wood. "I have gathered you all here for a reason. You are visionaries and fighters who are trying to make this world a better place. You are like me. You've been hurt." I look at Althea. "Betrayed." My eyes land on Avea. "Forgotten." My gaze settles on Quinn. "Ripped apart."

Lastly, I meet Freya's eyes. "Died for this belief in good and evil. I am one of you. We come from all walks of life, and we are different races, but we all have one common goal—to keep our family, our people, and this world safe. I offer peace between us all through shared knowledge, a place to come when in need, and a shoulder to lean on—a treaty"—I glance around, my heart beating nervously, which I'm sure they can sense—"between the courts and its queens." I grin. "You may not know much about me, but I am Tate Havelock, a hunter and a descendant of a fae who was the protector of this place. I have cleansed my own people and will continue to do so. The hunters were once a proud guild focused on protecting people, but we cannot let this happen again, so I propose a treaty between our courts and a helping hand for when it's needed."

"How?" Avea asks.

"We sign this document and seal it with our blood. It will link us. If anyone breaks it, we face death." I glance at Mors. "Er, or him, I guess. We'll come when called, but most of all, we'll become a united force for change in the fight between good and evil. With all the power we have in this room, we stand a chance. Who would dare challenge a vampyrs queen blessed by gods, an ancient magical being mated to death, a prophesied alpha wolf, and the first necromancer to survive the gods?"

"You forget yourself," Shamus offers as he comes to my side. "The hunter of the ages."

"And me," I add, smiling at him and my loves. "I am willing to fight and die for what I believe in. Are you?"

Quinn frowns. "If we sign this, we become yours?"

"No. Not at all. You lead your people, and I will lead mine. This is simply a treaty between us, a contract of friendship, if you will. It's how we'll keep our world safe for the next generation. It's how we'll assure what happened to us doesn't happen again. We'll become . . . united."

"I'm in." Freya nods. "Our people have faced enough prosecution for a lifetime. I think it would be good to have friends."

"I'm in too," Althea agrees. "We have always needed this. I knew it would happen eventually."

"I am also with you," Avea says. "Our people need protection at night."

"Quinn?" I ask as she thinks, looking around.

"Wolves are pack creatures, so what's one more pack?" She smiles.

My smile is wide as I tug the document to me, relief filling me. "Then allow me to be the first to spill my blood. It would be my honour to prove my dedication to this alliance."

Picking up the spelled chalice and dagger, I close my eyes for a moment, offering my thanks, and then I run the blade across my palm and fist my hand over the chalice. Then, I pass it on.

One by one, they cut their hands and add their blood before it's passed back to me. Jarek nods, and I dip my fingers into it then touch the agreement. Our blood mingles, binding us together.

The moment it touches the paper, I feel it wash over me and I jerk. I hear the others gasp as they feel it too, and when I lean away, I can't help but smile. Something deep within me relaxes now that this is dealt with, something I have been dreaming about for weeks. "It's done. The treaty of the courts and queens is complete. We are sisters in arms now. We are the protectors of the world. When called, we will come."

Their smiles reflect my own as Quinn leans over, eyeing the document. "There's space at the bottom. Why?" she asks curiously.

"To allow any new courts to sign," I answer, my eyes going far away. "I have a feeling we will need it."

"Freaky," she whispers as she leans back.

"No, that is her gift." Althea stands. "I look forward to fighting alongside you, my fellow queens." She winks, and then she is gone.

One by one, the others offer their gratitude, and they leave until only I and my team remain.

Jarek carefully rolls up the agreement and seals it away, and it disappears.

I look over my monsters and sigh happily. "It's done. Let's go home. We have a long future ahead of us. This fight is far from over. We have the whole world to protect now, monsters and humans alike."

"Fine, but I call shotgun," Ronan yells.

"Nah, that's mine," Fang responds.

"I would like shot of the gun," Tem responds.

I look back at this place once more, sensing the generations of my people here. I offer them my thanks before I turn away.

"We fight to the death for shotgun?" Addeus asks.

"Fucking hell," Shamus grumbles.

"I can make a shotgun," Jarek adds helpfully.

Rolling my eyes, I step through the portal Zeev creates, and they follow.

We are not alone now.

I am not alone.

EPILOGUE

Tate

"Fuck! Addeus, you giant bastard," I snap as I tug him down next to me to avoid the rocks being thrown at him by the shapeshifter. It thinks we are hunting it when that couldn't be further from the truth. We are hunting the rogue hunter who is hunting the shapeshifter.

They are spread out around the world now, and it's our task to track each and every one down, which is what we have been doing for the last six months. Our job will never be done. As long as there is good in the world, there will be evil, and it's our duty to stand in its way.

The others are only a call away if I need them. I haven't had to as of yet, but we set up quarterly meetings just to check in on how everyone is doing. They have their own lives to lead, which brings me back to mine.

"I mean it. We are not here for you!" I roar to the shapeshifter as another boulder sails over my and Addeus's heads and down the mountainside. The others are concealed behind their own rocks. Shamus will be glad he didn't come this time, that's for sure. He splits his time between hunting with us and leading. It works for him, and I'm always glad when he's at my side.

"Lies!" it shouts.

429

"Fuck this," I mutter as I watch another rock sail overhead. "A little hand, Zeev?" I call.

"Why? This is amusing." He chuckles. He's still an asshole. It just so happens I love that asshole. More fool me.

"Jarek?" I try.

"Nope." He grins. "All yours."

"Great, thanks," I mutter.

"I can help, mistress." Tem pops up behind me, grinning.

"Nuh-uh, you're banned. Remember the last time you helped?" I snap.

"I accidentally tore down the temple." He pouts. "Okay."

"Are you not offering?" I ask Ronan.

"Not a chance," he scoffs.

"Scaredy cat ghost," I mutter as I peek over then duck when another rock hits where I was. "Fuck it," I mutter again, leaping over it. I race towards the shapeshifter, ducking and rolling as boulders soar at me. I make it to him and slam a fist into his face. He goes down hard, and I pant as I stand over him. "I meant it. I'm not here for you."

"Then why are you on my land?" he yells.

"For him." I point out the hunter coming for us in the distance. "Think you can stand not throwing a rock for a minute while I deal with him?"

"Fine," he grumbles, and I nod as I climb up onto the nearest boulder and pull out my rifle. I can use magic or my men, but sometimes the old ways are the best. I put my eye to the scope and take aim. He's sneaking up on the shapeshifter. He enjoys killing too much to stop, uncaring if the monster is innocent or not—like this shapeshifter, no matter how annoying he is.

"Gotcha!" I whoop as I squeeze the trigger just as a rock hits him. I gape, turning to the shapeshifter.

"He was stepping on my flowers!" he says, and I turn back to the scope with a growl as the hunter races towards the trees, knowing he's under attack. I fire rapidly, and bark explodes around him before my last shot clips his shoulder, spinning him back into view. Blowing out a breath, I line up my next shot and squeeze the trigger, and his head explodes.

"Got him," I exclaim triumphantly as I stand, slinging my rifle back over my shoulder.

"Yay, mistress!" Tem cheers.

Ronan appears with a handheld chalkboard. "Tate, ten. Hunters, zero."

Snorting, I sling my rifle higher over my shoulder and look at the shapeshifter. "We will take care of the body. Enjoy your day, sir."

"Why did you help me?" he asks. "Hunters don't help our kind."

"They do now." I grin as I head to the portal waiting for me, showing Shamus on the other side.

I step through and into his waiting arms. He kisses me quickly as he holds me tighter with a happy sigh. "Are you home for a while, angel?"

"Two days. We have reports of a band of hunters up north moving against us."

"Then I have two days with you." He smirks as the others come through behind me. "Let's test out that new giant bed, shall we?"

I can't help but laugh as I'm tossed over his shoulder. We all know I could stop him, but I don't want to.

Shamus and this place are my home, these people are my home, and they are exactly where I want to be as we hunt and rid this world of evil.

It's why we took our name for the other supes.

For humans, we are hunters, but our elite team?

We are the Court of Evil.

THE END . . . FOR NOW.

ARE YOU READY FOR THE NEXT GENERATION?

ABOUT K.A. KNIGHT

K.A Knight is an USA Today bestselling indie author trying to get all of the stories and characters out of her head, writing the monsters that you love to hate. She loves reading and devours every book she can get her hands on, and she also has a worrying caffeine addiction.

She leads her double life in a sleepy English town, where she spends her days writing like a crazy person.

Read more at K.A Knight's website or join her Facebook Reader Group.
Sign up for exclusive content and my newsletter here
http://eepurl.com/drLLoj

OTHER BOOKS BY K.A. KNIGHT

CONTEMPORARY

LEGENDS AND LOVE *CONTEMPORARY RH*

Revolt

Rebel

Riot

PRETTY LIARS *CONTEMPORARY RH*

Unstoppable

Unbreakable

PINE VALLEY COLLEGE *CONTEMPORARY*

Racing Hearts

Crashing Hearts

DEN OF VIPERS UNIVERSE STANDALONES

Scarlett Limerence *CONTEMPORARY*

Nadia's Salvation *CONTEMPORARY*

Alena's Revenge *CONTEMPORARY*

Den of Vipers *CONTEMPORARY RH*

Gangsters and Guns (Co-Write with Loxley Savage) *CONTEMPORARY RH*

FORBIDDEN READS *(STANDALONES)*

Daddy's Angel *CONTEMPORARY*

Stepbrothers' Darling *CONTEMPORARY RH*

STANDALONES

The Standby *CONTEMPORARY*

Diver's Heart *CONTEMPORARY RH*

DYSTOPIAN

THEIR CHAMPION SERIES *Dystopian RH*

The Wasteland

The Summit

The Cities

The Nations

Their Champion Coloring Book

Their Champion - the omnibus

The Forgotten

The Lost

The Damned

Their Champion Companion - the omnibus

PARANORMAL

THE LOST COVEN SERIES *PNR RH*

Aurora's Coven

Aurora's Betrayal

Book 3 - *coming soon..*

HER MONSTERS SERIES *PNR RH*

Rage

Hate

Book 3 - *coming soon..*

COURTS AND KINGS *PNR RH*

Court of Nightmares

Court of Death

Court of Beasts

Court of Heathens

Court of Evil

THE FALLEN GODS SERIES *PNR*

Pretty Painful

Pretty Bloody

Pretty Stormy

Pretty Wild

Pretty Hot

Pretty Faces

Pretty Spelled

Fallen Gods - the omnibus 1

Fallen Gods - the omnibus 2

FORGOTTEN CITY *PNR*

Monstrous Lies

Monstrous Truths

Monstrous Ends

SCIENCE FICTION

DAWNBREAKER SERIES *SCI FI RH*

Voyage to Ayama

Dreaming of Ayama

STANDALONES

Crown of Stars *SCI FI RH*

SHARED WORLD PROJECTS

Blade of Iris - Mafia Wars *CONTEMPORARY RH*

CO-WRITES

CO-AUTHOR PROJECTS - *Erin O'Kane*

HER FREAKS SERIES *PNR Dystopian RH*

Circus Save Me

Taming The Ringmaster

Walking the Tightrope

Her Freaks Series - the omnibus

THE WILD BOYS SERIES *CONTEMPORARY RH*

The Wild Interview

The Wild Tour

The Wild Finale

The Wild Boys - the omnibus

STANDALONES

Kingdom of Crowns and Daggers *Dark Fantasy RH*

The Hero Complex *PNR RH*

Dark Temptations *Collection of Short Stories, ft. One Night Only & Circus Saves Christmas*

CO-AUTHOR PROJECTS - *Ivy Fox*

Deadly Love Series *CONTEMPORARY*

Deadly Affair

Deadly Match

Deadly Encounter

CO-AUTHOR PROJECTS - *Kendra Moreno*

STANDALONES

Stolen Trophy *CONTEMPORARY RH*

Fractured Shadows *PNR RH*

Shadowed Heart

Burn Me *PNR*

Cirque Obscurum *PNR RH*

CO-AUTHOR PROJECTS - *Loxley Savage*

THE FORSAKEN SERIES *SCI FI RH*

Capturing Carmen

Stealing Shiloh

Harboring Harlow

STANDALONES

Gangsters and Guns *CONTEMPORARY*, IN DEN OF VIPERS' UNIVERSE

OTHER CO-WRITES

Shipwreck Souls *(with Kendra Moreno & Poppy Woods)*

The Horror Emporium *(with Kendra Moreno & Poppy Woods)*

AUDIOBOOKS

The Wasteland

The Summit

The Cities

The Nations

Rage

Hate

Den of Vipers *(From Podium Audio)*

Gangsters and Guns *(From Podium Audio)*

Daddy's Angel *(From Podium Audio)*

Stepbrothers' Darling *(From Podium Audio)*

Blade of Iris *(From Podium Audio)*

Deadly Affair *(From Podium Audio)*

Deadly Match *(From Podium Audio)*

Deadly Encounter *(From Podium Audio)*

Stolen Trophy *(From Podium Audio)*

Crown of Stars *(From Podium Audio)*

Monstrous Lies *(From Podium Audio)*

Monstrous Truth *(From Podium Audio)*

Monstrous Ends *(From Podium Audio)*

Court of Nightmares *(From Podium Audio)*

Court of Death *(From Podium Audio)*

Court of Beasts *(From Podium Audio)*

Unstoppable *(From Podium Audio)*

Unbreakable *(From Podium Audio)*

Fractured Shadows *(From Podium Audio)*

Shadowed Heart *(From Podium Audio)*

Revolt *(From Podium Audio)*

Rebel *(From Podium Audio)*

Riot *(From Podium Audio)* Coming soon…

Cirque Obscurum *(From Podium Audio)* Coming soon…

Kingdom of Crowns and Daggers *(From Podium Audio)*

Diver's Heart *(From Podium Audio)*

Racing Hearts *(From Podium Audio)*

FIND AN ERROR?

Please email this information to thenuttyformatter1@gmail.com:

- *the author name*
- *title of the book*
- *screenshot of the error*
- *suggested correction*

Made in United States
Cleveland, OH
25 April 2025

16407658R20246